The Aji of Dead Stones

By Pear Makeru

© 2025 Pear Makeru

The game known as *go* in Japanese, *weichi* in Mandarin Chinese and *baduk* in Korean was invented at least two thousand five hundred years ago, almost certainly in China. Legend has it that Emperor Yao invented Go to educate his son. Go is widely thought of as being the most complex and strategic game in the world, despite having so few rules and only two types of piece, black stones and white stones. Go has been used to train military leaders in East Asia.

In Go, one player takes black and the other white, and they take turns to place their pieces on one of the three hundred and sixty-one intersections of a nineteen-by-nineteen grid. Once placed, a piece can never be moved; only removed if it is surrounded.

The goal is to use your pieces to make walls that surround more territory than your opponent. A game is over when both players choose to pass. Although pieces never move, they have influence and hold the potential to connect to other stones in the future. That potential is called *aji*.

If you play too close to your other stones and too timidly and cautiously, you only surround a small amount of territory. If you play too loosely and greedily, in an attempt to grab too much land, your opponent can cut through your walls, invade the territory you hoped to secure, and possibly even kill and remove some of your pieces.

Unlike other board games like chess, checkers, shogi and Chinese chess, a go board is big enough to have multiple battles going on all around the board. It is possible to lose a battle, sometimes deliberately, but win the overall war. Sometimes battles remain fairly separate. Sometimes they end up bleeding into each other.

Sometimes stones get cut off, deep behind enemy lines, and, although the opponent hasn't actually surrounded and taken them, it is clear to both players that they are, effectively, dead. There is no way for the player to save them. Despite this fact, there is sometimes the possibility to use the potential that they possess to create positive effects in other parts of the board.

Rather poetically, this situation is known as "the aji of dead stones".

Section 1 – Fuseki

In the game of Go, the first few moves are referred to as *fuseki* in Japanese. The Japanese language is wholly different from Chinese in grammar and pronunciation, but has borrowed Chinese characters for the main parts of its written form, starting in the fifth century. Many words are made up of two characters. The first character of *fuseki*, the *fu* (布), means cloth, or to spread or distribute. The second, *seki* (石), means stone, the word used for a Go piece. Hence, fuseki might best be translated as the spreading or distribution of stones.

The fuseki is where the players set out the general direction of the game. Players attempt to build their *moyo*, their large frameworks, to be filled out as the game goes on. Nothing is guaranteed in the opening. No territory is secured, but the players set out their general direction, their intent. This includes creating options for the future.

Beginners and amateur players often rush through the opening. Experienced players and professionals understand that the *fuseki* is where the potential is set for each player, and the game can be largely won or lost based on the beginning few moves, if the players are good enough to execute on that potential in the rest of the game.

In *The Direction of Play*, a Go book by nine dan professional Takeo Kajiwara, written for high level players, there is a chapter entitled "Move Two Lost the Game". There are typically more than one hundred and fifty moves in a game. A player can invest in a hundred moves of pain with little hope if they get the first few wrong. In that way, the game of Go can be said to be quite unforgiving.

It has been said that life is a simpler version of Go.

1. *June 1, 1984. Evanston. Chicago.*

The school had a very specific smell. A mix of industrial cleaning fluids, children's incontinence, and the scent of boiled vegetables that continually, insistently, seeped out of the school's kitchens, even when they weren't being cooked. Eleven-year-old Artie Wilson stood outside his home room classroom savoring that familiar smell while trying to control his blubbering.

He was ashamed that he was crying, but he couldn't stop it. It was rising from somewhere deep within him. Sometimes, just people's eyes cry. In this case, the whole of Artie's body was crying. He wasn't sure, but he thought that a little pee had escaped too, making him even more self-conscious.

Inside room 1A, his homeroom teacher, Miss Johnson, had just announced to the class that since it was the last day of the school year, and since they had all been such good students, she was going to give them each a candy bar. It wasn't like they didn't get candy bars regularly from their parents, but somehow this was an exciting treat for a group of 11-year-olds.

"But before I give out the candy bars, there is one student who doesn't deserve a candy bar. We all know which student that is, don't we class?"

The class all snickered. Everyone knew it was Artie. Including Artie himself. It wasn't like he had done anything terrible. He just seemed to be a constant irritant to everyone. Although Artie was classed as a bright kid at school, teachers didn't like him. His intellect and personality somehow never really fit into the container that school was. He talked at the wrong times. He often didn't finish his homework. He didn't show his work. He dressed poorly. His shirts were always untucked.

He was also uniquely unpopular with his fellow students. Again, there wasn't a very clear reason why. He was awkward and overweight. Shy, but coming off as arrogant. Big, but not tough, which meant he got beat up from time to time. And somehow, not a member of any clique. He didn't have any close friends. The best evidence of that was an incident on May the seventeenth of that same year.

At lunchtime on that day, Artie was walking down the main hallway at school, and saw a temporary board in an alcove, displaying a bunch of students' poems. He read that they were the winners of a school poetry competition. There were about twenty poems. It wasn't the sort of thing he would normally stop and look at, but he just happened to glance through them. Most of them were pretty meh. Nothing special. But then he happened upon one written by Mike Longstaff, a kid in another class. It was entitled "Artie Wilson".

Artie was pretty confused that there could be a poem about him. He read it. It started, "Wobbling down the hall / Looking pathetic / Everyone avoiding him / Glad I'm not Artie Wilson." There were four stanzas like this. Every stanza had four lines. The first three lines were different in each, but the last line was always "Glad I'm not Artie Wilson".

Reading this poem was like an assault on Artie's senses. First, he couldn't believe that guy had written a poem like this. Artie barely knew him. Second, he couldn't believe that anyone hated him that much to write it. Third, he couldn't believe that it had won a poetry competition. And fourth, most importantly, he couldn't believe the school had permitted it to win, much less to be displayed.

He ripped the poem down. He didn't tell anyone about it. He was too ashamed to tell his parents. He also couldn't face the ordeal of talking to the head teacher about it. He didn't really have any friends to tell. He was kind of scared of confronting Mike Longstaff, too. Mike was a big, tough-looking kid. And very popular.

Also, as an only child, Artie didn't have any siblings around to back him up. He often envied fellow students who had siblings at the school, even if those siblings were mean to them.

Artie got up and headed toward the door. The walk of shame. Johnson hadn't explicitly told him to do so yet, but he knew the story. It was a pretty common occurrence for him to be sent to stand outside the classroom or sent to the head teacher.

The other kids watched him trudge, head lowered in shame, towards the doorway. Even though none of them knew the word yet, and some of them never would, they were all connoisseurs of *schadenfreude*. Deriving pleasure from the suffering of others. Sometimes because they were glad it wasn't them. Sometimes to experience a shared community feeling. Sometimes indulging the need for a scapegoat. And sometimes just because humans have that meanness in them. That black spot in their hearts and souls.

Johnson walked between desks, eulogizing about the year gone and the year to come, remembering achievements, challenges, and funny and memorable moments. As the other kids smiled, laughed, chit-chatted, and gossiped, Artie stood there in the doorway of classroom 1A, Dewey Elementary School. Rocking on the balls of his feet. Shaking gently as he cried. Sad, but not surprised.

He wondered if this was what the rest of his life would be like. In truth, it was more like he knew that this was training for what the rest of his life was bound to become.

When Artie first saw the title of a book of short stories by author Irvine Welsh on the shelves of Powell's bookshop in 2008, he was somehow reminded of this time and how it had ended up being a pretty clear signal of what lay ahead. The book was called *If You Liked School, You'll Love Work*.

2. August 3, 1985. The Wisconsin Dells.

Artie suddenly grimaced. His mom, Ellen, noticed. *"Are you all right dear? Is something wrong with your sandwich? Joe, I think he's choking."* Artie gave them a half-smile and raised his hand to say everything was OK.

The family were sitting at an outdoor wooden table in the Wisconsin Dells, an area of natural beauty about four hours' drive from their Chicago home. It was their custom to come for a cheap family break here most summers. Carrying on a tradition of his mom's family, the Holtz's, when she grew up. It was even closer to Green Bay, her hometown.

Artie used to love coming here as a kid. His age of innocence. Getting to hang out with his mom and dad. Those halcyon days lasted until he was about eight or nine years old, when he finally started becoming concerned with what others thought about him.

Then he started feeling ashamed of himself. He felt inadequate that he didn't have siblings. That he didn't have close friends to holiday with. That their holiday destination wasn't exotic enough.

The truth was, today, he wasn't grimacing because of the tuna sandwich. He was grimacing, remembering a random bad memory. In this case, it was a day when the teacher discovered he had peed his pants. Or rather when a class member told the teacher he had peed his pants. It stung the most because the person who told the teacher was supposedly Artie's best friend, Jack. They were both eight years old.

Peeing, or rather Artie's dysfunctional relationship with peeing, was the defining factor behind a surprisingly large proportion of his childhood trauma. He was a bedwetter. Up until the age of eleven. His parents tried everything. One thing they tried was putting a mesh underneath his bedsheet that conducted electricity when he peed, setting off a loud alarm. Artie remembered repeatedly waking up to this loud alarm in the middle of the night, then knowing it had been deliberately placed there by his parents. Not a warm, comforting feeling. Which, rather ironically, lying in a pool of your own warm pee sort of was.

Even though he was only thirteen now, Artie realized recently that he didn't remember a lot of the details of his life so far. What Artie remembered in 3D, high-definition detail were incidents that were extremely embarrassing or shameful to him.

Like peeing his pants in public. Like not getting picked for sports or any peer-selected group activity. Like every time an adult asked him about his friends, and Artie having to admit that he had none.

At only thirteen years old Artie had hit on one of the surprising truths in life. Our brains are wired to remember extreme emotional experiences. Not the stuff we are supposed to remember, like births, marriages, deaths, graduations. Nor conjugations of verbs. Nor mathematical formulae. Our memory was wired to remember the weird. Could be good-weird or bad-weird. In Artie's case, it mostly seemed to land on the dark side.

3. July 2, 1986. Evanston. Chicago.

It was the most exciting gift he had ever received. It was probably the physical object that excited him most from the moment he laid eyes on it, and he wasn't even sure why. He wasn't sure why Uncle Phil had chosen this as his fourteenth birthday present, but from the moment he received it, he knew it was going to change his life.

Older kids in his neighborhood still had older computers, like the Timex ZX80 and 81, and the Commodore Vic 20 and 64. He had played a couple of games on them like Manic Miner and Blogger. Some had Atari game consoles too. They were all great. But this was next level.

The Commodore Amiga was launched in the last year, 1985, costing over a thousand dollars. A powerful Motorola 68000 CPU running at 7.16 Megahertz. 256K of Read Only Memory and 256k of RAM, upgradeable to 512K. Custom graphics and sound chips. Screen resolution of 640 by 400 pixels. Those stats excited him the same way car enthusiasts got all hot under the collar about the number of cylinders and brake horsepower.

State-of-the-art personal computing. And most importantly, it belonged to him. Best birthday ever.

He didn't really have any friends, but a few of his relatives and his parents' friends had come over to celebrate his birthday. He tried to make his escape as soon as he got the big box, wrapped in shiny silver wrapping paper from Uncle Phil. But his mom scolded him and made him stay downstairs, open all his presents in front of the assembled crowd, and thank them all. Then, he had to sit with a glass of lemonade, answer a bunch of boring questions, and even sit through about half an hour of adult blah blah, before his mom gave him the nod, and he headed upstairs with the Amiga box in hand.

He could see Phil thought it was kind of funny and was maybe even a little bit proud that that was what Artie wanted to do. Maybe partly because it was Phil's present that had got him so excited. And partly because that is how Phil behaved. He was able to fit in in a crowd but was basically a loner too.

During the next few months, Artie consummated his love affair with his computer. Over and over again. From playing games to learning to program in BASIC, a high-level language for beginners. Then on to the dark arts of machine coding programming. A step that most computer owners never made but was necessary to write complex programs that ran fast enough to be useful.

He wasn't doing very well at school. He found it hard to sit still and concentrate in class, even though he found studying easy. Perhaps, at least partly, *because* he found it easy. He often got detentions and occasional physical punishment from the teachers.

His home computer, on the other hand, felt like home to him. He felt like he was having a conversation with the Amiga, and it was talking back when he ran his programs on it. And although he was not doing it for that reason, he was sowing the seeds for what would become his career.

4. September 9, 1988. Evanston, Chicago.

Seventy-five dollars. Cash. Moolah. In his hand. Money that he had earned. Not a gift. Not doing chores for his parents. Artie couldn't believe it. He walked around the house with a grin as wide as his round face would accommodate. His mom and dad couldn't be happier, either. In truth, they both worried about Artie a lot. Both individually, and quietly on their own, and together, out loud. They also shared their concerns in quiet, confidential moments with their family and a few close friends.

Artie didn't seem to have the best social skills. He wasn't easy to get along with, and he seemed to spend way too much time alone in his room. One of the reasons he spent that time in the room was his computer. That little machine had transformed his alone time into something a bit more productive. Creative. Educational.

He started off by playing games on it. Then he started writing little programs in the computer language built into the computer, called BASIC. BASIC was a rather ugly acronym, standing for *Beginners' All-Purpose Symbolic Instruction Code*. Later in life, Artie would learn that the IT world was full of these ugly acronyms, and he would keep an informal list of the worst ones. His favorite was WSFN, a language from the 1970s. The acronym meant *Which Stands For Nothing*. He also enjoyed the military acronym SNAFU, *Situation Normal All Fucked Up*.

At first, his programs were really simple, like asking the user to type in two numbers, then adding them up and telling the user the answer. Artie kept a printout of his first ever program, copied from the pages of a computer magazine, on his wall, printed out using a dot matrix printer, his fifteenth birthday present. It was only five lines of code, but it filled his heart with joy:

```
10 INPUT "Enter the first number: ", A
20 INPUT "Enter the second number: ", B
30 SUM = A + B
40 PRINT "The sum of the two numbers is: "; SUM
50 GOTO 10
```

Artie quickly moved on to more complicated programs, and then, over the winter of 1987, he taught himself assembly language and machine code, the languages underlying everything. Much harder to code in, but lightning fast. In Artie's sixteen-year-old brain, people who stopped at Basic programming were tourists in the technology world. Those who took on the machine code beast and won were the real techies.

The previous Monday, September 5, Graham and Joan Howton, the Wilsons' neighbors, came over for a coffee in the evening. It was to discuss some community project. Artie didn't know what, nor did he want to know. Artie's mom served homemade chocolate chip cookies. She was known in the neighborhood for them.

As usual, Artie stayed in his room with his door closed. The subject of computers happened to come up, and Artie's dad mentioned that Artie had developed a fondness and a bit of talent with them. He excused himself and popped up to Artie's room.

"Artie. The Howton's are here."
"I know. I heard them."
"Well, how about you come down and say hi."
"Can I not, Dad? I am just in the middle of something."
"Graham mentioned computers, and I said you knew a thing or two about them."

Artie was torn. He didn't like people. He was painfully shy and awkward, and even worse he knew it. But he was so proud of his coding achievements, and he had almost no one to show them to.

In the end, he agreed to show the neighbors some of his programs. As his dad went down to get them, Artie hurriedly tidied up. Underwear off the floor, coke cans in the trash. He couldn't get rid of the smell. A hard-to-describe odor that most teenage boys' rooms smelled of. The olfactory expression of teenage hormones and existential angst.

"*Well, these are certainly impressive, young man. How did you learn?*"

Artie couldn't stop himself from beaming. "*I taught myself.*"

"*Well, well, well.*", Joan added. "*With your parents' permission, how would you feel coming to have a look at our computer? We've got a problem with the spreadsheet, and your skills might come in handy. There's some money in it for you.*"

Both Graham and Artie looked at Joe, Artie's dad. Joe nodded his approval. It was clear that he was enjoying this moment.

5. September 6, 1988. Evanston, Chicago.

Artie was in the Howtons' house. In Graham's home office. Sat at his fancy, huge, dark wood desk with leather inlay, with the green and gold glow of his banker's lamp. In front of Artie was an IBM desktop PC.

Graham and Joan had a small business selling Latin American handicrafts. During the 1970s, they had taken a few holidays in Central and South America, visiting Mexico, Chile, Peru, Costa Rica, and Uruguay. They brought back wonderful souvenirs for themselves and friends and family. Locally produced handicrafts. Pottery. Wood carvings. Leather goods. Folk Art. People seemed to love them. When Graham and Joan visited them, they often had some on display in prominent locations in their houses.

By the early 1980s, Graham had quit his job as a clerical officer in a small regional bank. Joan had been a full-time housewife and was now effectively head of sales and customer relations at Latin Wonders, the small business the couple had set up. Graham ran the back end of the business, the engine. He was responsible for import and supplier management, logistics, finance, and operations. Joan handled the front end. Sales, marketing, advertising, pricing. They made it a point to work with the indigenous people who created the objects directly and give them a really fair price.

The Howtons didn't have kids, and they were pulling in about sixty thousand per year. Enough to live a comfortable, if not lavish life. It was also quite neat that their semi-annual trips to Latin America were both holidays and genuine business expenses.

They tried to keep other expenses pretty tight and did all their own financial bookkeeping using a spreadsheet program called Visicalc. When they started their business, it was the leading-edge tool, but now Lotus 1-2-3 was beginning to dominate. The Howtons hadn't made the jump to Lotus yet.

Lotus 1-2-3 had a feature called macros, which allowed you to write little programs inside the spreadsheet to automate tasks, like calculating margins, or shipping costs. Visicalc didn't have that, so Graham had tried to program everything using formulas.

Graham had hit on a snag. The tax calculations which used to work seemed to have gone awry. He sat Artie down, explained the issue, and then showed it to him. It was the first time Artie had seen a spreadsheet, and he was a bit scared of not being able to help, but also fascinated. He asked Graham if he could be left alone to investigate. Graham agreed.

About 10 minutes later, Joan showed up with milk and cookies. Artie politely declined. He really wanted both the milk and the cookies too, but something within him made him say no. Joan looked a little crestfallen. *Why did I do that? I'm such a fucking idiot,* Artie thought, after she left.

Across that night and the next, Artie spent about six and a half hours understanding spreadsheets and the Visicalc user interface. Then, understanding Graham's spreadsheet and its logic. Then, diagnosing and fixing the problem. It came down to the wrong position of a pair of brackets in a formula. This meant that the tax calculation gave the wrong result under certain conditions, but not always.

Later in life, he would come to realize that those are the hardest computer bugs to fix. When the system works sometimes, but not all the time. It would lead Artie to a love of the art of rigorous testing, and the creation of test scripts. Something very few other people loved. Not even many computer geeks loved testing. Where programming was considered a fine art, like sculpture and painting, testing was considered the double entry accounting of IT. Everyone needed it. No one loved it. Except Artie.

At university, Artie would also learn, to his great amusement, that the use of the term bug for a computer error came from the fact that some of the earliest computers, in the 1940s, malfunctioned due to actual insects getting trapped in their electronic components. Artie loved this kind of knowledge: esoteric, amusing, and ultimately useless.

A few times during the two nights Graham and Joan had offered for Artie to give up. He strongly resisted. In fact, he would have liked to stay there all night the first night and skip school the next day, but that wasn't in the window of acceptability with either his parents or the Howtons.

When he was done, Artie enjoyed explaining how he had fixed the problem to Graham and Joan. They made lots of appreciative noises, which Artie wished he didn't enjoy as much as he did. During the explanation, Joan leaned in to see some detail on the screen, put her hand on Artie's shoulder, and one of her breasts touched his shoulder. He tried not to notice, but to the wholly sexually inexperienced and frustrated sixteen-year-old Artie, that part of the project was perhaps the peak moment, literally and metaphorically.

However, it was also pretty great when, on Friday night, Graham and Joan came over, had a drink with the Wilsons, told them how smart their son was, and gave him an envelope containing seventy-five dollars in cash. The intellectual and financial rewards made this the best week of Artie's life, so far, and sparked the passion within him that drove his university studies and his career choices.

For the next few years, the Howtons occasionally called on Artie to fix or extend their home-made business management spreadsheets, until in the summer of 2001, when they made the big decision to stump up and buy a piece of software that did everything for them. While it lasted, this period of technical support for his neighbors was a welcome addition to Artie's otherwise limited life.

6. September 1, 1990. DePaul University, Chicago.

"*See you later man*", Al said. Artie nodded.

He had chosen shared accommodation for this first semester at DePaul because he was worried about being alone. Turns out that you can be lonely, even with a roommate. Artie was reminded of a line from a Grateful Dead song "I don't know but I've been told, that in the heat of the sun, a man died of cold." Maybe it was the song "New Speedway Boogie".

It was a Saturday night. Al was heading out to a sports bar with his friends. Artie sat in his room reading Kurt Vonnegut's *God Bless You Mr. Rosewater*. The one good thing about Artie's first few months of college was that he hit on a treasure trove of really great books. From August to November, he read almost everything by Kurt Vonnegut, John Irving, Tom Robbins, and Joseph Heller. Epic. On the weekends, he would get through three or four novels. And that was on top of all the studying he was required to do for his degree.

He started with Kurt Vonnegut and thought that no other novelist could come close. But he ended up loving Tom Robbins' quirky, humorous, and supremely insightful works the best. Even the titles were amazing. *Even Cowgirls Get the Blues. Jitterbug Perfume. Still Life with Woodpecker. Half Asleep in Frog Pajamas.* And a bunch of others. Perhaps his favorite Robbins, both title and book, was *Fierce Invalids Home from Hot Climates*.

His favorite Robbins quote was from *Even Cowgirls Get the Blues*. "There are many things worth living for, a few things worth dying for, and nothing worth killing for." As a young, somewhat idealistic man, that quote really resonated with him. Although he didn't know it, Artie would come to love the first two-thirds of that quote more and more but would take a radically different stance on the third part.

He would look back on this time as kind of spoiling him in terms of future reading. He had somehow hit the jackpot with these four amazing authors. The books grabbed him so much that he found himself laughing out loud, or sometimes, crying, when he read in public places.

There is a moment in one of John Irving's novels, *The World According to Garp*, that caused Artie significant embarrassment. The main character, Garp, has quite a hard time as a child and is terrorized by a dog called Bonkers. At one point in his youth, the dog bites a piece of his ear off, and someone shouts "*Bonkie bit Garp*". Many years later in the book's chronology, and many pages later, Garp returns as a young man, a wrestler. By then the dog is old, and Garp jumps out and takes his revenge, using a wrestling move to take the dog down, then biting a piece of the dog's ear off.

Artie read this while drinking a Coke in the student café. When he read that "*Garp bit Bonkie*", he guffawed, and Coke came out of his mouth and both nostrils. He never went back to that café.

And so, it went for him at university. Physically close to other vibrant young people who were having a good time, and yet somehow a million miles away from them. Reading, studying, existing. But not much more.

7. March 3, 1991, DePaul University, Chicago.

As he wandered through the halls of DePaul, Artie felt like almost everyone was living the undergrad dream of pounding beers with their friends, hooking up with chicks and guys for fun, casual, no-strings-attached sex, and generally just living the life of the student tribe. He knew that it wasn't perfect for everyone, but it seemed pretty close for many of the people he was aware of.

He couldn't know for sure, but Artie felt that movies, music, and books meant more to him than other people. He needed them more. He related to them more. His relationship with them was deeper. More personal. Because of this, he defined himself by what he liked. If he ever had a conversation with anyone about the arts, he needed people to know what his favorites were. When he came across people who said they just kinda liked everything, Artie felt like he was a different species than them. He felt angry with them.

Because of this, Artie felt inexplicably powerful feelings when he walked past Harry's tonight. A favorite bar of DePaul students, Harry's Bar, was having a movie night. It was standing room only, as *One Flew Over the Cuckoo's Nest* was projected on a large white wall inside. Even though Artie was mega-uncomfortable entering on his own, he couldn't help himself. He was drawn in like he was caught in a tractor beam.

Artie must have watched the movie on an old VHS tape literally hundreds of times. It was his favorite movie by far. By a country mile. The explicit narrative of the movie was about a petty criminal locked up in a mental hospital. Played by Jack Nicholson, the main character Randall McMurphy thought he was being smart feigning madness in order to get transferred from prison to the asylum. It turned out that the nursing staff, in particular the head nurse, were cruel and dehumanizing to the patients/ inmates.

To Artie, the subject of the movie was really about human dignity. Something he felt very much aware of in his own life. Two scenes in the film really stood out to him. The first was when McMurphy stole a bus and snuck his fellow inmates out on a fishing trip. When the harbormaster caught him stealing a boat, McMurphy told him that they were doctors on an away day. As he introduced each of the inmates with the title Doctor, each of them puffed their chest out with pride.

The second scene that really moved Artie was playing on the wall of Harry's bar right now. This time, McMurphy had broken some girls and booze into the asylum one night. They had a wild party, and a very nervous young boy, Billy Bibbit, had got to have sex for the first time. The stuttering Billy suddenly relaxed and lost his stutter. The head nurse arrived the next morning to find the carnage from the party. She saw Billy with his romantic partner and threatened to tell his mother, who obviously had a terrible hold over Billy.

It was an incredibly poignant scene, and Artie cried pretty much every time he watched as Billy slashed his wrists with broken glass and killed himself. Tonight, for inexplicable reasons, as Artie watched this scene, surrounded by fellow students captivated by the powerful scene, just as it was revealed that Billy had killed himself, Artie started laughing uncontrollably.

Artie left the bar quickly, head hung low, as everyone stared at him. As he walked home, he felt ninety percent disgusted and ashamed of himself. Ten percent of him was strangely satisfied that he had rescued defeat from the jaws of victory. Found an incredibly rare moment that he could empathize with and be close to fellow students, but instead ruined the moment. It was a very Artie move, Artie thought.

8. November 4, 1992. DePaul University, Chicago.

"*And essentially every computer can be boiled down to a Turing Machine*". The teaching assistant taking this theoretical computation class beamed with pride at this last statement of the lecture. Some of the students present clapped. Many just packed their bags and sauntered out of the lecture theatre.

The guy sitting next to Artie turned to him. "*What the hell are they teaching us this for? No one is ever going to ask us to program a Turing Machine.*" Artie said nothing but stared him in the eyes, giving him a look a psychopath would be proud of. The *Turing Machine* was an invention of the famous British mathematician, cryptanalyst, and computer scientist Alan Turing. It was the concept of a minimal computer, consisting of an infinitely long tape and a state machine that operated on it.

Artie had read a bit about the life of Alan Turing. A hell of a genius. As well as the Turing Machine, he was known for the *Turing Test*, a way of deciding if a computer was intelligent or not. Turing proposed that if you had a conversation with a machine in another room and couldn't be sure if it was a machine or human, then it should be labeled as intelligent. Artie actually didn't like this definition of Artificial Intelligence. He thought it should be more about how well the computer could reason. How difficult the problems it could solve. Not necessarily that it solved them in a way indistinguishable from a human.

Turing also designed one of the first real computers, the Automatic Computing Engine, and during the Second World War, played a leading role in decrypting messages created by Germany's Enigma machine in the Second World War. And identified a major issue in computing with his *Halting Problem*. He was also quite a character, and created a game called *round the house* chess, combining running and that board game.

The buffoon next to Artie was pointing out that the Turing Machine was an abstract concept, not a real, or even realistic, machine, which rendered it useless, in his opinion. Artie, a lover of abstract concepts, couldn't agree less with this moron. A sound understanding of abstract concepts meant that programming any real computer became a piece of cake.

Artie remembered that he had talked to this guy once before. About a year ago in the lunchroom. His name was Max, and he had a very specific and clear ambition. To be a bank manager. Over lunch, he expounded on how he wasn't at university to learn. He was there specifically to get a good degree, to build the perfect resume to power his career.

Max aimed to manage a branch of a major bank by thirty and retire by forty. Artie remembered at that moment feeling incredible distance from and disdain for the guy, but also having the sense that Max would probably achieve his goals. When Artie watched the movie Good Will Hunting several years after graduating, he thought of Max, when a rather loathsome character in a Harvard bar says to the hero *"You'll be serving my kids fries at a drive-through on our way to a skiing trip."* Artie would not be at all surprised if that came to pass for him and Max.

Artie also felt extra angry and disgusted by this so-called student because he had read how badly Turing was treated by the British government. In his almost forty-two years of life, Turing had come up with four or five major breakthroughs in the world of math and computing. Despite all this, he was prosecuted for homosexual acts, and chemically castrated. He then died from cyanide poisoning. It remains unclear whether or not this was suicide.

Artie was studying for a degree in mathematics, but he had become particularly interested in theoretical computation, and the area of math that related to computing the most, discrete mathematics. Group theory, set theory, graph theory, number theory, logic, and Boolean algebra. He loved them all.

He also loved mathematical and logical puzzles. He tried to wrestle with one every week. Last week's was the two computer drop test problem.

"A new personal computer has just come out. You need to know how high a floor of a building you could drop them from without harming them. You have only two of these computers to test with, which you can destroy in the process of testing. You have access to a 100-floor building to perform the tests. What is the best strategy to minimize the number of tests you need to do, but still be sure to have an accurate answer at the end?"

It took him ages to solve this one. The simplest answer is to start at floor 1, then keep going until the PC you drop breaks. But that could take up to 100 tests in the worst case, and it didn't take advantage of the fact that you had two PCs.

Then he thought about a classic divide and conquer strategy. You start at floor 50. If the PC doesn't break, then you go to floor 50 + 25 = 75. If that doesn't break, you try floor 50 + 25 + 12 = 87. And so on. That stratagem works really well if the answer is high. But if the first PC breaks at floor 50, you have to revert to the brute force method and start at floor one with the second PC. So, in the worst case that could take fifty tries.

After five days of letting this problem rattle around in his head, Artie found the solution, using a technique called proof by invariant. Artie noted that if you add up the first thirteen numbers, you get 93, which is less than 100. If you add up the first fourteen, you get 107. So, the strategy is to first try floor 14. If the PC breaks, you start at floor 1 and work up, giving a maximum of 14 tests. If it doesn't break, you go to floor 14 + 13 = 27. If the PC breaks then, you start at floor 14 + 1 = 15 and work up, again giving a maximum of 14 tests. And so on. Artie felt so happy and proud when he solved the problem. But he had no one to share it with. No one to tell. No one who would care. No one who would think it was of any value. No one around him who would understand.

He had just started on this week's problem, but he hadn't solved it yet. "*You are a king. It is Friday morning. Tomorrow is your birthday, and you plan to have a big birthday party tomorrow night. You have got one hundred bottles of the best wine. But you have just found out that one of them is poisoned. The poison is so deadly that even the tiniest drop from the poisoned bottle will kill the drinker, but it may take up to twenty-four hours to kill them. You need to find and remove the poisoned bottle. You have thousands of slaves who you can use to taste the wine, but you want to minimize the number of slaves involved in tasting the wine. What is the smallest number of slaves he can involve?*" Fascinating.

Artie's intellectual life at university was proving to be everything he hoped for. But unfortunately, his social life was not. He hoped that he would get to reinvent himself at university. But he was reminded of the old saying "*Wherever you go, there you are.*" In other words, Artie had brought his essential 'Artie-ness' with him. Whatever made him socially annoying, unpopular, and invisible at school followed him to DePaul.

Books were his friends. Lectures were his friends. Computers were his friends. Puzzles were his friends.

The humans? Not so much.

9. January 18, 1993. DePaul University, Chicago.

Artie woke up confused. He looked at his bedside clock. 11:37 am. He had missed his first two classes of the day already. What the hell was going on? Although he was a fuckup in almost every other way, he always set his alarm, didn't sleep in, and never skipped classes.

As his brain emerged from the fog of sleep, he started to remember. He had, in fact, received a call just after 6 am, from the police. It turned out that his parents had been involved in a car accident. On vacation in Florida. A fatal car accident.

He couldn't believe that his reaction had been to fall back to sleep straight after hearing that news. It was almost like his brain couldn't handle it and shut down.

The truth was that he wasn't close to his parents anymore. He only saw them two or three times a year. He wasn't quite sure why, but their relationship had become more and more distant over the last few years, despite him being their only child. There hadn't been any specific incident. Any argument. Any reason.

He kind of got it. He didn't think much of himself, so he couldn't imagine them thinking much of him either. Or being proud of him. Or even wanting to spend time with him. Despite them being his parents, he felt awkward in their presence. He felt awkward in everyone's presence, but it felt worse with his parents. He felt pressure to be closer to them. Comfortable. Happy. Like in the movies and TV shows.

His dad had retired early with a modest pension, and they seemed to spend most of their time vacationing around the country, particularly visiting friends and relatives.

And now, very suddenly, they were gone. Artie felt kind of guilty that he didn't feel what he thought he was supposed to. How a son would feel in a movie, learning that his parents were killed in a car crash. In fact, he felt... well... nothing. He wasn't sure if he was numb, and the grief would come later. Or whether he really didn't feel anything about his mom's and dad's death.

He felt guilty when he realized his brain had already jumped to selfish practicalities. What did he have to do? How long would he have to be away from his studies? How much inheritance would he get?

The next couple of weeks, he did what he had to do. A small, perfunctory funeral. Official registrations. Managing bank accounts, bills, and other administrivia. He quickly sold the house. The house he grew up in.

By early February, it was all done and dusted. $473,182 added to Artie's net worth. Two fewer things that tied him to reality. To this earth. Two fewer anchors to prevent him from floating off into permanent isolation.

And he still felt nothing.

10. September 1, 1994. Chicago.

7:34 am. Sitting on a packed commuter train. Wearing a dark blue business suit, crisp white shirt, and red silk necktie. Artie was sweating profusely. He had the strangest sensation. A kind of dizziness that he had never experienced before. He closed his eyes for a second and had a really weird vision. A kind of hallucination. He saw himself as a little kid inside his own adult body, operating his limbs using sticks, from the inside. A kind of internal puppetry.

He opened his eyes. Pretty much everyone around him was wearing serious business attire, like him. But they all seemed to be adults, fully inhabiting the role of businesspeople. Artie was definitely still like a kid, just pretending to be an adult. Pretending to know what he was doing. But he had no idea.

It was a stupid little thing, but when he got to the station this morning, he couldn't work out how to open the train door. A woman pushed him out of the way and opened it, muttering something that he couldn't quite catch.

Artie had heard of the phrase *impostor syndrome* before. It seemed to be one of those terms that people who weren't very smart loved to use in order to sound smart. To sound like they were wise. Like they were expert psychologists.

The truth was that there were such a wide variety of conditions, of feelings that could be described as impostor syndrome that it was almost useless. Artie felt sure that someone highly successful going into a meeting only ninety-five percent prepared might be described as, or describe themselves as, having impostor syndrome.

At the other end of the scale was Artie, today, September 1, 1994, his first day of work. His issue went way beyond not knowing a particular piece of knowledge or having specific work experience.

His version of impostor syndrome was not feeling like part of the human race.

He already knew he was going to be awkward to the max all day. He didn't know what to say or what facial expression to hold. Where to put his hands. How to be a working guy. How to be an adult. How to be a human being.

He was suddenly transported back to his most embarrassing incident at university. There were many to choose from, but this one was a real peach. It was early into his first semester at DePaul. He had developed an unusual rash on his dick. He was mortally embarrassed, but fear led him to book a doctor's appointment.

"So, what brings you here son?"
"It's. It's. It's down there."

Artie pointed vaguely towards his midriff.

"Alright son. Nothing to be embarrassed about. Tell me what's going on?"

Artie managed to bumble out a few works stating that he had a rash.

"Take your pants down and lie on that table."

It was murder for Artie, but he did as he was told. He took his pants and briefs down and lay on the bed. The doctor came up, slipped on some surgical gloves, and started examining Artie. Artie's arms seemed to be in the doctor's way, and he wasn't sure what to do. So, Artie put his hands behind his head.

In retrospect, it was obvious that this was an insane move. It looked like he was getting ready for a sexual service in a medical fetish gay porn movie. But Artie didn't realize that until way too late. The doctor had seen him do it, eyes wide with shock.

The whole incident ended soon after. It turned out that Artie had a fairly standard jock itch, and a few days of applying an anti-fungal cream cleared the rash right up.

But the embarrassment stayed with him a lot longer than the rash. In fact, he still felt it acutely today, on the train, as he headed to his first day at Roberts Services. Still not quite sure what to do with his hands.

11.   *April 15, 2002. Elk Grove Village, Chicago.*

Artie was proud to have recently finished installing the newest version of Microsoft Windows, XP, on all forty-three of the PCs at Roberts Services, the company he had been working at since he graduated in 1994. He had started as an assistant technician and had now, eight years later, achieved the heady height of senior technician. His salary had risen in those eight years from $27,000 to $38,000 per year. That wasn't a fortune, but given Artie's fairly modest lifestyle, and the fact that he was single, that meant he could live comfortably in a small apartment and save some money for trips, and his future.

An imagined future with a wife, two or three kids, a black-and-white border collie, a house in the suburbs, a holiday home in Florida. It had to be a border collie. He wasn't sure why.

He had done the installation over the weekend. He always used music to power him when he did these long sessions. His music of choice this weekend was the album *Silver Side Up*, released the previous year by Canadian rockers Nickelback. He was really into the single *How You Remind Me*, but the rest of the album wasn't bad either. He knew that, for some mysterious reason, people had started hating Nickelback. Which drew him toward them even more.

He had cleverly pre-prepared as much as possible by writing and running scripts remotely on the company's PCs the week before, to make sure they were all backed up and ready. If worst came to worst, he could have rolled the PCs back to their pre-upgrade state.

He had done it all himself, on a very tight budget, and without great fanfare. The only major cost was the burger, fries, and strawberry milkshake he had ordered for both lunch and dinner, both Saturday and Sunday. Four identical meals. $13 each, including tip. He wouldn't even be shocked if Jim, the head of finance, challenged him on those expenses. Especially since Keith, the Mac guy, popped in and pretended to help for a few minutes, just so he could charge a few overtime hours, and get a free lunch.

Like most things Artie did at Roberts, no one really noticed. Almost no one ever thanked him. No one ever celebrated the things he did, even though IT was rapidly becoming the most mission-critical part of Roberts's business, and indeed most others. Being the PC guy at a mid-sized warehousing company was a bit like being an insurance salesman. You just seemed like an unnecessary cost unless and until things went wrong. And even worse than the insurance gig, in the case of the PC guy, when things did go wrong, it kind of looked like the bad things were your fault.

Today, the PCs were working well, except for the one on Jim Arnold's deck. Jim was the head of finance at Roberts. A physically small, wiry, and wired man in his mid-fifties, Jim seemed a remarkably ungenerous man. He was confident and self-assured in the most unattractive way. Not charismatic, and also not the slightest bit interested in the social lubrication that many of us think is compulsory in business, and in life. It wasn't so much that he didn't mind what others thought of him. It was more that he never even considered that as a thing to think about. Or even that such a thing existed.

There are many ways to think of a company. As a brand. As a maker of products. As a community of people with shared goals. As a money machine. It was always clear what Jim's perspective was.

Artie was in Jim's office, ministering to his broken PC. Jim's accounting software was complaining that it couldn't find the D: drive, an extra hard disk installed on Jim's PC to keep all his data. As Artie worked to diagnose the problem, a string of people flowed in and out of Jim's office, variously reporting, offering, and requesting things from Jim.

Although everyone in the 200-person, $25 million revenue business knew Artie (and indeed everyone else in the company), there was no reason for any of them to engage with him. Still, he might have expected one or two of them to say "*Hi Artie*". But that just wasn't his life. He dressed invisibly, in a grey cardigan, a plain white t-shirt that bore the faded stains of more than a few messy lunches, light green khakis with a profusion of unnecessary pockets, and black sneakers.

Artie often felt invisible to his colleagues, and indeed in his private life. He was used to it, but when he thought about it, it made him sad. 260 pounds, but somehow invisible. Ironically, in the next phase of his life, he would love and strive for invisibility. The more transparent the better. But right now, it was a real drag.

"*How long?*" Jim asked. He had been saying that to Artie every thirty minutes or so since Artie arrived to attend to Jim's machine. "*Not sure, hopefully less than an hour,*" Artie had replied each time. Followed by a series of tutting noises and rolling eyeballs from Jim.

Diagnosing a fault in an IT system was both an art and a science. There was such a profusion of things that could go wrong that some inspiration and creativity were needed, as well as Sherlock Holmes-like deductive skills. After one hour and forty-seven uncomfortable minutes in Jim's office, Artie finally tracked the error down to the IDE cable at the back of the disk drive having come loose. He performed a controlled shutdown, reattached the cable, and then restarted. Having confirmed everything was working, Artie insisted, to Jim's chagrin, that he would do a quick backup of Jim's data before releasing the PC back to him. More tutting. More eyeball rolling.

Artie left Jim's office about 2 hours and 20 minutes after he started. He felt Jim treating him to a withering look of disappointment as he left the room. Diagnosing and fixing an issue with a PC could be a very satisfying and rewarding task. Like solving a puzzle. It was like that when Artie could do it at his own desk, in his own time.

But it was a whole different ball of wax when he was out in the office.

12.   September 11, 2002. Old Town, Chicago.

Artie woke up around 7 am and made himself a pot of beef-flavored Cup Noodles for breakfast. Introduced to the US by the Japanese company Nissin in 1971, Cup Noodles were a very simple food to prepare, a nutritionist's worst nightmare, and a poignant reminder of how sad and lonely one's life is. Especially if eaten for breakfast. Artie occasionally sliced up some vegetables he had in the fridge, like a carrot or an onion, and dropped them in the noodle pot, along with the requisite amount of boiling water. In his head, he thought it was funny to consider whether that act could be considered cooking.

He sat down in his chocolate brown La-Z-Boy chair. He had treated himself to the top-end La-Z-Boy, with the fridge in the armrest, so he could keep a few cold beers with him while he vegged out watching porn and bad martial arts movies. He turned up the volume on the TV. The news was on. It was dominated by the anniversary of the suicide bombing attacks one year earlier. Al-Qaeda terrorists had hijacked four planes. Two had been flown into the twin towers of the World Trade Center. A third was flown into the Pentagon. The fourth crashed in rural Pennsylvania after the passengers fought back.

The attacks cost almost three thousand people their lives and sent Americans into a state of shock. Although all decent people condemned the attacks as atrocities, from an amoral perspective, one had to recognize that they were quite an amazing accomplishment.

Years later, Artie heard a joke from the controversial comedian Louis CK about the attacks that got Louis into a bit of trouble. He claimed that you could tell how good a person you were by how long you waited before masturbating after the twin towers had fallen. Louis then followed up by telling the audience that for him, it was between the two towers falling. (Which was, in reality, a twenty-nine-minute window.) Louis then added "*I had to do it. Otherwise, they win.*"

Artie immediately changed the channel. He specifically enjoyed watching inappropriate TV in the morning. Like horror movies. Or standup comedy. Stuff that no wholesome person with a decent lifestyle would consider watching in the morning. This morning, he found an episode of *Hong Kong Phooey*, one of his favorite cartoons.

He had come to enjoy, even to be a little proud of, being a bit broken and twisted. He was reminded of a great poem he read at school that stuck with him. It was by the 18th-century English poet William Blake. The title of the poem was *My Pretty Rose Tree*, and the last two lines were "*But my Rose turn'd away with jealousy/ And her thorns were my only delight.*" Thorns were my only delight. Somehow, that deeply resonated with Artie.

Although he felt guilty about it, he wasn't that interested in the attacks. The truth was that he wasn't interested in world problems. He was far too consumed by his own problems. It was like when you take a close-up picture of a person with something huge and dramatic in the background, like the pyramids or the Taj Mahal. Because the lens is so close to the person, it appears much bigger than the monument. So it was with his issues, compared to 9/11.

13. October 23, 2002. Elk Grove Village, Chicago.

"That sure looks better than my lunch," Artie ventured.
"Would you like to share it with me?" Harjit responded.

They were sitting in the lunchroom at the office. Harjit was not strictly an employee of Roberts, but he worked for a small IT company and was deployed by them as a contractor to Roberts for a few months to help with a supply chain project.

Today Artie had brought a hastily put-together tuna sandwich with tomatoes, crushed potato chips, and mayo. Although he was being self-deprecating with Harjit, and Harjit's Indian lunch looked and smelled a hell of a lot more interesting than a sandwich, Artie was quite proud of having his shit together enough to shop for the ingredients, make the sandwich, remember to bring it with him, and not scoff it down before lunchbreak.

"No. It's fine thanks. I was just admiring it from afar. Enjoy."
"Thank you, sir. I will. My wife made it for me."
"Please. Call me Artie. You are a lucky man, Harjit. Did your wife come with you from India?"
"Yes, she is here with me thankfully, Artie."
"Which part of India are you from? I know it's a big place."
"That it is. That it is. We are Sikhs. From a region of India called Punjab. My wife and I live very close to Amritsar, the city with the Sikh's most holy temple, the Golden Temple. If you ever have a chance, you should come visit."
"What a lovely idea. I hope to one day. So, you here in Chicago because the opportunities are better? Career-wise? Financially?"
"Yes. That's right. We plan to go back in a few years, but for now, we are very happy and grateful to be here in Chicago. We can save more money here."
"Nice. For a nice place back home, and getting ready to start a family, I guess."

"Yes, sir. Sorry – Artie. Sort of. But we also have another mission. Another use for money."
"Oh, tell me more."
"Well, India is quite an unusual country. More than a billion people. Some very, very rich people. But also, some abject poverty. A few years ago, my wife and I got involved in a charitable project to create a school for poor children.
"As part of this project, I built the project plan and financial model. I realized that we could repeat this and build lots of schools for the poor. To give them a good education. And more chance to be lifted from a life of poverty.
"Do you know, Artie, that in rural India, it only takes twenty-five thousand dollars to set up a school and employ teachers to teach fifty students?"

"Wow, Harjit. That's amazing. You make me feel so pathetic. All my money goes on pizza and video games."
"Not at all, Artie. You are a good man. It is just that our religion, Sikhism, calls us to be charitable. One of our core principles, seva, requires selfless service. At our temples, called Gurdwara, you will see everyone eating communally and freely. And you will see Sikhs all over the world feeding the poor.
"I have to say I am super impressed, Harj. But I guess setting those schools up is one thing. Keeping them running a whole other ball of wax."
"Well, yes and no. All organizations go through their struggles. But the twenty-five thousand dollars I mentioned is to support those schools in perpetuity. Fifteen thousand goes to setting each school up. Then ten thousand is invested in an annuity that supports them year on year. Paying the teachers and other staff salaries, materials for the students, and maintenance of the building.
"Unbelievable. So, you have set a school like this up, Harjit?"

Artie somehow felt like shortening his colleague's name to Harj, and he suspected others did, but he knew he didn't have the right to.

"Actually, we have set up four such schools so far. We are saving for the fifth. We have decided that when we have funded ten of these, we

will begin saving for our own family, and eventually go back home."

"That is awesome, Harjit. One question though. Did you think of just giving to a charity, rather than getting so involved? It would be easier, wouldn't it?"

"Well, Artie. I am not sure if it is the right decision. Or even an honorable one. But we couldn't help feeling that we could be sure we would do a good job, whereas there are all kinds of uncertainties about giving to a charity. The possibilities of incompetence and corruption, for example.

"I feel terrible saying that. I know lots of great people who dedicate themselves to working for charity missions. But, nevertheless, that was our decision. I also suspect that my wife and I chose this path because it gives us such personal fulfillment."

They finished their conversation, and their lunch, and both went back to their respective offices and tasks. But Artie was left with a lasting sense of awe. He loved the idea of direct action and the modular architecture of Harjit and his wife's charity strategy.

Unbeknownst to him, Artie would be inspired later in his life by the seeds sown by this conversation.

Artie was also a bit ashamed of himself. In his mind, he had previously thought of Harjit in a very one-dimensional, stereotypical, rather negative way. As an Indian techie who had come to America to make a quick buck, before exfiltrating his 'American treasure' back to his homeland.

Artie also felt even more inadequate than usual about his random, purposeless walk through life. He felt bad when he saw millionaire CEOs wearing Raybans and Rolexes, driving Porsches and Ferraris, with hot wives who had their shit together. At least he had an internal narrative that said he didn't want to be like them anyway. But he had no such defense when he heard Harjit's story.

"Shame on me. Stupid me." thought Artie.

14. December 31, 2002. New Year's Eve. Old Town, Chicago.

Artie sat at his computer, playing with a website he was trying to build, mainly to learn more about Javascript. Websites were first built using HTML. HTML wasn't really a programming language. It was more of a way to describe how a page looked. Write this piece of text in twenty-point Arial font. Create a table here with two columns. That sort of thing.

Javascript was an actual programming language that could be embedded in websites to make them more dynamic. For example, to take action when a user clicks a button. Artie was finding it fascinating to add one more language to his collection. Just like human languages, every computer language has its own personality, and its own way of looking at things. Its own focus areas. The programming ideology it was based on, like procedural, functional, or object-oriented. And also, the particular eccentricities of its designers.

Rather confusingly, there was another programming language called Java, which Artie hadn't learned yet, which had almost nothing in common with Javascript. He would get to that one later.

He was drinking cranberry juice, which tasted way too sweet tonight. Actually, it was more like a cranberry-flavored drink, with juice as one of its ingredients. He had the album "Rattlesnakes" by Lloyd Cole and the Commotions playing in the background. It was released in 1984, back when he was too young and uninterested in music. Artie normally preferred harder, punkier, more alternative music these days. But some things were so well-crafted that they were undeniable. He felt that way about Rattlesnakes, Cole's debut album.

If he had tried hard, Artie probably could have found somewhere to go, someone to be with. A party, or something like that. It seemed almost a duty for people to attend New Year's Eve gatherings. But he just didn't feel like fighting anymore. He could feel that he was accepting this fate more and more. Being sad and lonely. Losing connection with the world and losing purpose.

It always struck him as a strange dilemma. Accepting his sadness and loneliness felt authentic, but ultimately an unrelenting road to perma-pain. Not accepting it, fighting for connection, meaning, and purpose felt useful, even somewhat noble, but it also felt inauthentic. Allowing himself to be cloaked in the dark grey, velvet, comforting cloak of failure felt real and comfortable. He was ready to accept his fate.

He had realized recently that one of his only hopes left, one of his fantasies, was that some people he knew would attend his funeral when he died, by his own hand or otherwise, and feel at least some measure of sadness. Maybe even remember him for a while.

From time to time, Artie found himself daydreaming about his epitaph. What he'd like written on his gravestone. This reminded him of the quirky English/Irish/Australian comedian Spike Milligan, whose gravestone read "*I told you I was ill*".

Sometimes he thought about what he would write in a final letter to the world, even though he wasn't sure anyone would read it. He came up with the rather offbeat little two-liner: "I just can't stay at the sanity party any longer. I tried to get a ghost shirt but couldn't find one in my size." A ghost shirt was a shirt thought to have protective spiritual powers by some native American tribes. Artie first came across ghost shirts in a Kurt Vonnegut novel, from which he borrowed the term for a modern group he called the Ghost Shirt Society.

Somehow, for Artie, wearing a ghost shirt was a powerful metaphor for having a purpose. Not being able to find a ghost shirt that fit him was a coded message that he could never find a purpose, or a community to fit into. And also, the pun that he couldn't find one his size linked to his lifelong struggle with obesity. Artie was really satisfied with this pun.

Later in his life, he would reflect that it felt like the universe, or maybe God, or maybe Sigmund Freud was laughing at him, placing this bookmark for him to look back on and laugh, as he found a purpose and also escaped obesity. But he certainly couldn't have consciously known that at the time. At the time he was cynical, fatalistic, and nihilistic, not prescient or hopeful.

When he read about the Samurai, the Japanese warrior class, he read that under certain circumstances, such as them betraying their code of honor, they would be expected to commit suicide. The way they were supposed to do that was by slicing their insides open with a knife. A ritual called *hara kiri*. This was an excruciating way to die, and samurais would typically have a close friend act as a *kaishaku*. The *kaishaku* would stand by them, and when the *kaishaku* felt that the samurai couldn't take the pain anymore, they would whip out their ultra-sharp katana and chop their buddy's head off to end their pain. Artie felt that that was a very beautiful, almost romantic ideal.

He sometimes fantasized about writing his own life story. Not that there would be very much to tell. But he thought that he would like to name that book *"Looking for a Kaishaku"*.

At 1 am, unable to sleep, he walked a couple of blocks to the local all-night pool hall. There was almost nobody there. Most people were out partying, celebrating the new year, or tucked up in bed. But a few people like him, who in his head he referred to as 'the broken and the lost' hung around the pool hall, knocking a few balls around the table, nursing a drink or two.

He took a sip from the bottle of Heineken he had ordered. He was no connoisseur of beer and not a particular lover of Heineken, but he just couldn't take the standard-issue American beers like Budweiser, Miller, and Coors. He set up the fifteen numbered, colored balls in a triangle, and began a game of eight-ball, playing against himself. Player one was Artie playing left-handed. Player two was Artie playing right-handed. Left-handed Artie almost always won. Artie was right-handed in everything else in life, but somehow, when he first picked up a cue, he held the back of the cue with his left hand and made the bridge at the front with his right.

After nine frames, left-handed, Artie was winning 6-3. Artie went to the bar to grab another Heineken. He glanced at the clock. 3:40 am. At $10 per hour, he'd racked up about a $27 bill so far. He thanked Al, the late-night barman, gave him a couple of dollars tip, then ambled back to his table for a few more frames.

Was this the way he was going to live the rest of his life? Detached, purposeless, wandering without moving?

15. Feb 2, 2003. Lakeview, Chicago.

Artie wasn't quite sure where to put himself. Where to sit. Where to stand. Who to talk to. He had shown up at the Chicago Go Club this evening for the first time. And no one seemed to be offering to help.

He had enjoyed playing Go since he picked it up at university, but he mostly played it on his computer, and occasionally with his old university roommate Al. Al and he didn't see each other much these days, so it was mainly playing programs like CrazyStone and GnuGo. Artie also owned quite a number of books on Go. He particularly liked the ones that consisted of Go problems.

Despite playing mainly on the computer, Artie had splashed out a couple of years ago and bought a high-end Go board. All full-sized Go boards have nineteen rows by nineteen columns. The columns tend to be slightly longer than the rows to counteract the optical illusion that they are not square when viewed from the normal player's perspective.

Some boards are only a couple of inches thick and are put on a table, like most other board games. A high-end Go board is a table itself, with its own legs. These require you to sit on the floor to play on them, either cross-legged or kneeling.

The best boards are made of a wood called *kaya*. There is a hole cut in the underside of the board, so it makes a more satisfying clicking sound when a stone is placed on it. The best white stones are made of clamshell. The best black stones are made of slate. Artie also had some lovely dark wood bowls to keep the Go stones in.

Artie had paid over seven thousand dollars for his Go setup. Sad to say, he hadn't had anyone to play on it with in person since he bought it.

Despite his reservations, he forced himself to show up at this Go club tonight. He wasn't sure how to get picked to have a game with anyone, so he just sat and watched others playing for a while.

"I'm Dan. Want a game?"
"Sure. I'm not very experienced."
"What level are you?"
"Not sure. Maybe about five kyu. I mainly play on the computer."
"OK. I am 1 dan. I will give you a nine-stone handicap. Sound fair?"
"Sure."

That was actually more than fair. Go ratings were measured in *kyu* and *dan* grades. An absolute beginner started off at about thirty kyu, then as he or she improved, their kyu number went down, until they were one *kyu*. The next step after that was to one *dan*. After that, the numbers went up. Two *dan*. Three *dan*, etc.

The term *dan* was actually the same as black belt ratings in Japanese martial arts like Judo and Karate. One dan was the first black belt level, then the numbers went up from there. In Go, there was one extra wrinkle. All these gradings were amateur. But there were a few hundred professional Go players, and they had their own *dan* grades. A one-dan professional was equivalent to about a four- or five-*dan* amateur.

One level of difference in Go, say from five *kyu* to four *kyu*, is thought of as about ten points of difference in score. All things being equal, a four-kyu player should beat a five-kyu player by approximately ten points in a straight game.

One level of difference is also equivalent to having one extra stone on the board at the start of the game. A so-called handicap stone. There were nine special points on the board, called star points, (*hoshi* in Japanese) where handicap stones are placed before the board begins.

Dan really should have given Artie more like a six-stone handicap. He was being generous. Or maybe showing off.

Dan set up a board with nine stones on the nine 'star' points, set the clock to 15 minutes each, then played his first move. A stone on the (3,6) point, threatening one of Artie's corners. Artie nervously sat down. He wasn't sure what to play, but played on the (3,5) point, touching Dan's stone. Dan made a noise. Could have been a grunt. A smirk. A giggle.

Artie forgot to press the clock. Dan had to remind him.

About forty minutes later, Artie resigned. Dan was not at all gentlemanly or kind about it.

"Jeez. I think you are more like 7 or 8 kyu. You need to go back to some of the basics. Read a book on joseki."

Joseki were set sequences of moves, usually played in the corners of the Go board, that had been tried and tested over centuries. A half-decent Go player knew a wide variety of joseki. Artie couldn't seem to remember any in that moment.

"Look. I'll show you some of your biggest mistakes. OK?"

Artie nodded his acquiescence, despite feeling that Dan's motive was less to help him learn and more to self-aggrandize. Artie remembered having the idea that in war, it was important to learn from your enemies as well as your friends. It was a stratagem that would serve him well later in life.

Dan unceremoniously wiped the 150 or so black and white stones off the board, then, incredibly, played back their game in the correct sequence, stopping every now and then to show Artie what he should have played.

In the end, Artie thanked Dan. He stayed a while longer, watched a couple of other games, then left. He didn't talk to anyone else while he was there. He didn't mind losing, but he hadn't really enjoyed the whole experience either. It reminded him a lot of school. And work. He realized the common denominator was him. Wherever he went, there he was. He had heard others saying they reinvented themselves when they started university. Or their first job. Or even when they joined a gym.

That had never been the case for Artie.

Artie had always had a kind of fantasy that the best Go players were really wise, cool, smart people who were enlightened, or at least on the path to enlightenment. But Dan was just an asshole. A great Go player, but an asshole. And when Artie watched two three-*dan* players go at it, one of them had a kind of meltdown and started throwing stones around the room when he made a mistake. The other didn't seem surprised, or even fazed, by his opponent's behavior.

The evening's experience had shattered Artie's illusions. It also reminded him of a great book called "The Master of Go" written by one of Japan's most famous authors, Yasunari Kawabata, published in 1954. Loosely based on a real match between master Honinbo Shusai and challenger Minoru Kitani, it was a book about the last more traditional, kimono-wearing Go master playing, and ultimately getting beaten by, a modern Japanese Go player, who dressed in a western suit. It was both a literal and a metaphorical example of Japan's modernization and westernization.

Artie never went back to the Chicago Go Club. Or any other. He didn't even play Go on the computer for a few months after that night.

16. March 17, 2003. The West Loop. Chicago.

The West Loop's transformation over the last few years had been amazing. The area had been packed with only warehouses and manufacturing plants until recently. Now it had lots of up-and-coming bars, restaurants, and galleries. Artie looked out the window of Mulligans, marveling at the layers of history you could see by simply checking out the architecture of the buildings here on Randolph Street. Historical, industrial, and now more modern buildings all stood side by side, like generations of relatives at a family gathering.

Despite its traditional Irish pub-sounding name, Mulligans was a brightly-lit modern bar, covered with neon signs, TVs, pinball machines, and other distractions. It kept the clientele from thinking about the futility of their lives, Artie thought.

Roberts Services, the company where he had worked for the last nine years, had chosen this place for a social. It wasn't quite clear what the reason was, but they hadn't had a get together since Christmas. Artie had noticed that companies often had a cadence not dissimilar from religions. A common pattern in many religions is for people to pray individually every day, get together for a meeting every week (the sabbath), and have a big festival every three months or so. So it was with companies.

Artie dreaded these events, but felt he had to come. Ironically, he felt that being the socially awkward scapegoat was actually the useful function he played at these events. It made everyone else feel better about themselves.

Tonight was no different than normal. He had a few unsuccessful and embarrassing social interactions, and now, at 8:15 p.m., was sitting on his own, at a table on the periphery of the group, hoping no one would notice him until about 9, when he could acceptably slink off home.

This time, the embarrassments started about 6:30 p.m.. He was sitting at a table where Jerry Frantz was holding court. Jerry was the slightly larger-than-life head of operations at Roberts. Everyone knew he had a bit of a drinking problem, but he was a senior guy, and no one had called him on it. Yet. Artie suspected that his alcoholism was getting to a point that he would become less functional at work soon and get kicked out. But that hadn't happened yet.

Jerry seemed to have started drinking early tonight. He was already buzzing. He was telling jokes to a table of about a dozen younger Roberts staff, including a few girls who Artie guessed were in their very early twenties. Jerry's jokes were getting more and more obscene and biological.

"*Hey, hey. What do you call a lesbian dinosaur? A Lickalotopus.*"
"*Who can tell me what tofu and dildos have in common? They are both meat substitutes.*"
"Anyone know *what's the difference between oral sex and anal sex? Oral sex makes your day. Anal sex makes your hole weak.*"
"*How about this one? What's the difference between a homosexual and a microwave? You can't brown your meat in a microwave.*"

At least two of the girls looked very uncomfortable.

Artie saw his chance to be a hero. In his mind's eye, he would save the day, all the girls would love him, and one of them would come home with him, perhaps make sweet, sweet love with him all night long. That didn't happen.

Artie said "*Hey, I have got a joke for you.*" He was sitting at the opposite end of the table from Jerry, and everyone swiveled around with a look of collective surprise on their faces. This nobody, wearing the least cool cardigan in the world, wanted their attention.

Artie proceeded.

"*So, this kid, Billy, is talking to his dad after dinner, and asks him what economics is, right?*"

Artie already felt that he was losing them, but he couldn't back down now.

"So, the dad says 'Let me give you an example son. In this family, I represent the capital. Your mother is management. Our maid, Maria, represents the labor. You, young Billy, represent technology. And your baby sister, Jasmine, represents the future. Makes sense?' Billy says, 'I am not sure, Dad'. The dad says just sleep on it, and we will discuss tomorrow at breakfast'.

Only about half the dozen or so people round the table were still listening to Artie. And those that were clearly didn't want to be. Awkwardness levels were off the chart. Artie was locked into this death spiral. He had heard of comedians bombing on stage. He could relate. But he continued.

"While Billy lies awake that night thinking about economics, he needs to pee. As he gets up and goes to the bathroom. He walked past his parents' bedroom, and sees his mom flat out on the bed, snoring. Then he walks past Maria's room, and hears his dad inside, grunting and groaning. When he goes back to bed, his baby sister has done a number two in her diaper, and he changes her.

Only two people are listening.

"The next morning his dad says. 'So, did you think about the economics stuff, Billy? Do you get it?' Billy says 'I think so, Dad, let me check. I think what you are saying is capital screws labor while management sleeps. The future is in the shit, and we are all relying on technology to clean it up."

Artie looked up with pride. When he first heard this joke, he thought it was genius. He was really proud to have remembered it. Turns out no one was really listening by the end. It seemed like they all realized Jerry's line of biological humor wasn't the worst option after all.

Later on, he got caught at a table with all the young studs. All the party animals. He didn't even know most of their names. He wasn't part of their world, and they weren't part of his. They were all talking about their favorite pastimes. Surfing, snowboarding, bodybuilding. And so on.

Then Artie heard "*Hey tech nerd. What do you like? What do you get off on, on the weekend? Upgrading PCs?*" Everyone snickered.

"*Yeah, a bit of that.*" Artie said. "*But I also like reading. And just thinking. Thinking about stuff. Philosophy. You know.*"

He could feel a gulf opening up between his admission of how he used his time and what this group of dudes thought was acceptable.

"*Philosophy? What the fuck do you mean?*"

"*Well. For example. Have you ever thought about the nature of time? That it both must have and can't have a beginning.*" Artie looked around as he dropped his favorite paradox on them.

"*Dude. Get a life. Drink your beer. And maybe go on a date or two.*"

They all laughed, turned away from him, and continued partying. Artie had done one more thing to guarantee his isolation and ostracization at Roberts, and indeed in life as a whole. He remembered a concept from politics – the Overton Window. It is the window of acceptable things to say. He had just stepped outside that window. He also remembered the medieval method of killing someone by throwing them out of a window, known as defenestration.

As he sat there in the wake of his failed joke, it amused him to think that he had just defenestrated himself through the social Overton window. The metaphor didn't quite work, but it made him happy to think of it. He certainly wouldn't try sharing that idea with anyone. That would go down even worse than his economics joke.

He scored a couple more minor social failures, then slunk off home about 9-ish. The awfulness of his experience was no surprise to him, and certainly not the first time, but just added a layer of polish and lacquer to his already advanced sense of self-disgust.

17. *May 3, 2003. Marriott Chicago Downtown Convention Centre.*

Saturday. 8:53 am. Artie counted eleven rows of eleven seats on the left side of the room, the same on the right. All positioned in perfect lines. Artie had always quite liked the number eleven. The first five powers of eleven were palindromes. Eleven to the power zero was 1. To the power one was 11. Squared was 121. Then came 1331 and 14641. They were palindromic, in that they read the same forwards and backward. Just like words that were palindromes. Like *"Nun," "Noon,"* and *"Level."* Palindromic phrases and sentences were even cooler to Artie. Like *"Was it a car or a cat I saw."* Or *"A man, a plan, a canal, Panama."*

About two hundred and thirty of the two hundred and forty-two chairs were occupied. Artie strategically chose an aisle seat on the left side, three rows from the back. He always chose an aisle seat – he wanted a quick escape route if he felt the need to get out quickly. A particular kind of claustrophobia. He also didn't want to be near the front here. Didn't want to be called upon. And finally, he didn't want to be conspicuous by choosing a seat at the very back. He wanted to be the grey man. Invisible. One of the very few characteristics that would continue for the rest of his life.

The woman he sat next to looked at him briefly, seeming kind of disgusted that he sat next to her. He wasn't sure what to do. He wanted to run for the hills but he was here now. It was also comforting to remind himself that she was probably a fuckup like him. Why else was she here?

He had heard of things like 'The Life Training' before. Group self-help weekends where participants were led through exercises to help with their self-development. Often based on the branch of psychology called Transactional Analysis (TA), developed in the 1950s by a guy called Eric Berne. Working in pairs, threes, or larger groups to unearth your deepest fears, self-perceptions, and aspirations, and work out how to address them. Group-guided meditations.

This one was quite intense. It started last night, Friday, 9 p.m. to midnight. Then today 9 am to midnight. Same tomorrow. Then, Monday evening, 9 p.m. to midnight, too. It sounded like a cult induction, but Artie quickly sensed that the intentions of the leaders seemed genuine. The only slight issue was the price tag of one thousand dollars for the weekend. And lots more courses to come if you wanted them.

Still, Artie couldn't believe he was here. The whole self-help industry seemed pretty cheesy, insincere, and ineffective to him. Also, he couldn't bear the thought of baring his soul, his deepest fears, that he normally worked so hard to hide, to strangers. He had the fleeting realization that sometimes we do things not because we want to, but because we fear the alternative even more. In his case, the perceived alternative to attending this course was an ever-shrinking life with ever-shrinking hope.

He was surprised by really enjoying the first night. He got through the exercises with limited pain. Even his fear of not getting chosen as a partner for exercises, stemming from schoolyard isolation and humiliation, didn't come to pass. And the guided meditation was quite a special experience. For one hour, the facilitator dimmed the lights, asked the participants to close their eyes, and then took them through a story of walking through a beautiful forest, finding a secret clearing where all their friends, families, and enemies were, and making peace with them. Even the cynical, perma-disappointed Artie had to admit that it was special.

In the first session, last night, they had emphasized that being on time for all the sessions was critical, and a part of the learning. Latecomers would not be allowed in until the next break. Artie was often late and hated being pushed around and told what to do, but somehow, he was enjoying the discipline on this weekend course.

Just before nine o'clock arrived he turned and smiled at the woman next to him. She seemed to scowl back. Before arriving, he had somehow imagined that people who go on self-help weekends would all be really cool, self-aware, open, high-integrity people who were willing to be vulnerable with others. Turned out it was the opposite. It was people who knew they didn't have any of those things. But wanted them. Fuckups. Like him. Artie smiled to himself. Self-deprecating humor for an audience of himself. And not that funny, either.

There was one particularly uncomfortable moment on Sunday afternoon. Throughout the whole course, the participants were asked to do exercises in groups of two or three. On this occasion, he had been teamed up with a very attractive blond woman who seemed to be Scandinavian. The exercise they were asked to do was to ask each other a series of questions to uncover their deepest fears about themselves.

The idea was that the questioner would get their partner to realize and articulate their deepest fear, then ask them a series of questions to make them realize that that was all in their heads, and they didn't know if their fears were real or not. So far so good.

Artie asked Maja first. She revealed that her deepest fear was that she wasn't good enough to be an actress, specifically, she was concerned that her looks would let her down. A specific instance of impostor syndrome. Artie duly went through the series of questions to make her realize that those fears didn't hold any water and were all in her head. He also thought it was amazing that this woman, who was one of the most attractive women he had ever talked to, felt inadequate in that way.

When they reversed roles, something altogether different happened. The series of pre-designed questions, when addressed to him by Maja, ended up with him saying something he had never consciously thought about. He said that his deepest fear was that he was a monster. A monster! He also said it in a voice that he didn't recognize, that seemed to come from deep within him.

This freaked Maja out completely and she didn't finish the exercise with Artie. In fact, she got up and left the course. Not exactly achieving the desired outcome of the exercise. But Artie got it. He got it. He actually felt like it was a good experience, even though it had ended in this way. He had reached some internal belief that he had never managed to be conscious of before.

At the end of the course, on Monday night, he felt some excitement and hope for the future. Within a few days that had dissipated. In two weeks, it was barely a distant memory. Making him sink even lower than before.

He had read somewhere about the term *cherophobia*, which psychiatrists use to describe a fear of happiness. There were two reasons for fuckups like Artie to fear happiness. First was impostor syndrome – feeling that he didn't deserve it. Second was the fear of the happiness being fleeting, going away soon. Like standing on the edge of a cliff with a beautiful view, overwhelmed by a fear of falling.

These days Artie seemed to live life in a cherophobic daze.

18. *July 2, 2003. Old Town, Chicago.*

Sweet and sour pork balls. Egg fried rice. Hot and sour soup. Artie unpacked his birthday dinner and ate it while watching a Steven Seagal movie. His favorite one, *Above the Law*. He had a version from Europe, where it was titled *Nico*, the main character's name, for some reason. It was Seagal's first movie and, in Artie's view, his third best. A not-too-terrible storyline, and some other decent actors in the cast, including an early appearance by Sharon Stone who became famous a few years later for her role in *Basic Instinct*.

Henry Silva also appeared as a very convincing bad guy, and Pam Grier played Seagal's police partner. Grier had been acting since the 1970s, often in what were referred to as *blaxploitation* movies, and the truth was Artie had a bit of a thing for her. He had also recently seen her in Quentin Tarantino's *Jackie Brown*.

Under Siege was a higher production value Seagal movie with a better story and better cast. *Marked For Death*, a story about bad guy Jamaican Yardie drug dealers, was somehow more exciting. But Artie loved the way *Nico* highlighted Seagal's Aikido skills.

Artie's plan was to watch four or five Seagal films as a kind of treat for his special day. But somehow, he got bored after three. So, at about ten thirty, he headed over to the local pool hall. He was a bit tired and didn't really fancy it, but he wanted to do something on his birthday.

He ordered a Jack Daniels and Coke and bought one for Al, the barman. He thought about telling Al it was his birthday, but somehow that seemed a bit too pathetic, even for him.

Instead of playing games of pool this time, he decided to practice his skills at sinking balls. He lined up all fifteen colored balls down the center of the table and tried to put all of them in the pockets without missing one. He managed twelve the first time before missing one.

Then eleven the next time. Then nine the next. Things weren't going in the right direction.

Then he went rogue and started playing trick shots. Bending the ball round object balls with extreme sidespin. Jump shots. He played a game where he had to make every shot banking off at least one cushion.

He then went even more crazy and started playing with only one hand. Not using a bridge hand at the front, simply swinging the cue from the back. He had seen a couple of guys do this for fun, so he thought he would have a go. He had to be careful that he didn't slip and tear the felt of the table. Little did he know that in countries like Thailand, there were pool players who practiced this one-handed skill quite seriously.

At just after four am he settled his bill, then made the short walk home. There were a few unsavory characters on the street, but he was hoping that in his old army jacket, ripped jeans, and dirty white sneakers, he didn't look worth mugging.

When he arrived home, he was too tired to go to bed properly. He flung his tired body and brain into his La-Z-Boy chair, turned on the TV, and let the awfulness of some of Steven Seagal's more recent movies, like *Half Past Dead* and *The Foreigner,* wash over him as he slept like a log, forgetting the sadness of another lonely birthday.

19.   September 4, 2003. Elk Grove Village, Chicago.

Artie still bought physical newspapers most days. Normally the Chicago Tribune, occasionally the Sun-Times. He was ashamed to say that he never really read the newspapers – he just bought them for their puzzles. He remembered years ago, having an idea for a newspaper with no news. Just stuff you could learn that wasn't connected to current affairs, like history or math. And games. He thought of calling it a *knowspaper*. He was particularly satisfied with that name – a pun on news, knows, and the word no. Of course, he failed to have the courage, the commitment, or the *cojones* to actually do anything about his idea.

He liked the general knowledge crosswords (not the cryptic ones) and *sudoku*. Sudoku was a relatively recent game from Japan that was surprisingly addictive. The goal was to fill a nine-by-nine grid with the numbers one through nine such that every row, column, and three-by-three grid contained the numbers one through nine, once each. In every puzzle, a few numbers were given as a starting point.

More recently he had fallen for *killer sudoku*, a variant that added an extra layer of complexity, by not revealing any numbers at the start, but instead encircling parts of the puzzle and stating what all the numbers inside added up to.

He also loved video games, although he was a little stuck in the past. He didn't much care for the 3D immersive shooting games that were becoming the norm, like Resident Evil and Splinter Cell. He liked old-fashioned 2D games. Particularly the genre called platform games, where the player's icon had to run and jump around an artificial terrain, picking up treasures and avoiding obstacles. Although they looked nowhere near as fancy as the 3D games, he felt like the core gameplay elements were often better thought out and more fun.

His earliest memories were playing games on Commodore 64 and Amiga personal computers, as well as in amusement arcades. He enjoyed a platformer on the C64 called Lode Runner and arcade games called Elevator Action and Donkey Kong. But in his view, the greatest game ever made was Robotron. Running around an incredibly busy screen, looking top down at a room full of enemies, and a few humans to save. Using one joystick to move and one to shoot, Robotron was so immersive that it almost required the player to enter a trance or a meditative state to have any chance of succeeding.

Today, Artie had spent his whole lunch break playing various games, finishing with a round of Robotron in a local amusement arcade. It occurred to him that these games were a bit cruel and perverse in that the reward for doing well and completing a round successfully was entry into the next round, which was even harder work. The only thing absolutely guaranteed was that you would die in the end, as the levels of difficulty rose relentlessly.

This realization made Artie feel kind of stupid wasting his time playing these games. Then he went back to work, and it briefly struck him that work, and indeed life itself, were not too dissimilar from video games. At least in that way.

A couple of years ago, he had acquired a T-shirt that contained an image of a Space Invaders game, with the text "*Game Over*" written largely in blocky digital font. Indeed. Indeed.

20. *June 5, 2004. Andersonville, Chicago.*

Artie was meeting Keith Hannerty, one of his colleagues, for lunch at a place called Bill's Diner, near Keith's apartment. They always seemed to meet near Keith's place. Although it wasn't a Mexican place, Bill's offered a fully loaded Nachos dish that Artie just adored. He normally abided by the 'never order burgers in a pizza joint' rule, but in this case, he couldn't resist.

He loved almost every taste in Tex-Mex food, except for refried beans. Melted cheese: to die for. Guacamole: delightful. Spicy ground beef: delicious. The salty, crispy nachos themselves: awesome. But refried beans. Not only did Artie not enjoy them. He just couldn't understand how anyone else could like them.

He had once been to a 'pre-Spanish' Mexican restaurant in San Francisco when he was taking a break there. He learned there that a lot of the food many Americans associated with Mexico, including all those variants of a pancake wrapped around spicy ground beef, did not exist before the Spanish *conquistadores* arrived. Apparently, before then, dishes like *mole* and *ceviche* were more central to Mexican cuisine. He wasn't 100% sure that was true, but that was what the restaurant was saying. Artie loved *ceviche*, but despite having several serious runs at it, he had never been able to really enjoy *mole*.

Artie was the PC guy at work. Keith looked after the Macintoshes. Like in so many companies, Macs were used for the front-office creative disciplines, like marketing and product design, and PCs were used for back-office tasks like finance and accounting.

To be honest, Artie wasn't very keen on Keith, but it was a Saturday, and sometimes the weekends felt interminably long for him. He had to punctuate them with activities, including some human contact. Just to stay sane. This was hard because Keith was quite pushy and arrogant, especially in his relationship with Artie.

And, like a lot of Mac guys, Keith couldn't stop going on and on about how the Mac was a superior computer to the PC. Not only did Artie think Keith was wrong. He also thought comparing the two was the most boring and fruitless conversation on earth. Macs were a step up in physical design, had a nice user interface, and had some great software in areas like art and desktop publishing. But PCs had a much broader range of software available and were much more open coding platforms.

"How's the omelet, Keith?"

"Yeah, not bad. Can't believe you ordered the nachos. Epic fail man. This isn't a Mexican joint, you know?"

"Yeah, I was just hungry, and they are just comfort food and quite filling. You know?"

"I used to behave like that too... until I realized it was the quality of the food that really matters. May as well eat well."

That last line of Keith's was what Artie had heard a psychology professor call a *crapdrop*. It was starting a sentence positively, then finishing critically. Very similar to the Greek concept of *bathos*, switching from the sublime to the ridiculous or trivial. Bathos is used in theater to undermine the seriousness of a subject. Keith used crapdrops to show his disdain for Artie.

And so the conversation went through lunch. Talking about trivialities. Artie asking Keith questions. Keith answering, but never asking Artie anything. Keith in tell mode. Keith taking the opportunity to put down and disrespect Artie from time to time.

Although he had lunched with Keith many times before and would again, just like always, Artie left lunch feeling a bit worse than when he arrived. He didn't like how Keith talked to him, and he really didn't like how he just sat back and took it from Keith. And it reminded Artie how limited his options were for weekend lunch partners.

One time at work, a nice older lady from accounts called Janice heard Keith treating Artie poorly. She could see it upset him. Later, she found Artie alone in the coffee room. She said to him "*You know, dear, they say that living well is the best revenge.*" Artie smiled at her, and genuinely appreciated her intent. But a voice deep inside him spoke to him, saying "*Maybe living well is actually the second-best revenge.*" Even though Artie never intended to do anything about Keith's behavior toward him, and suspected he couldn't, even if he tried, he was somehow amused by this 'second best revenge' quip, that he made silently to himself.

When he attended the Life Training, part of the transactional analysis approach was the framing of people's roles as Parent, Adult, or Child. So, in a relationship, there were nine possibilities: I play an Adult – you play a Child, or I play a Parent – you play an Adult. And so on.

Artie always seemed to end up playing the child role, even when he was talking to actual children. Certainly, with Keith. When he was with Keith, Keith was always telling Artie what was what. Correcting him. Advising him. Artie couldn't remember Keith ever asking for his opinion, or even asking him an open question.

Charlie, a guy Artie had known in his undergrad days, once told him a story about his dog. Charlie's dad was a very affluent, successful stockbroker. Charlie's family lived in a beautiful, spacious house in Stamford, Connecticut. His dad commuted to Wall Street every day to ply his trade.

Their house was filled with the trappings and signals of a well-to-do family. It seemed more like an art gallery or museum than a home to Charlie, the one time he visited. He distinctly remembered when he visited the bathroom, there was a hook for a towel, but instead of a towel being on there, there was a wooden sculpture of a denim jacket. It was so cleverly crafted that from a distance it looked exactly like a real denim jacket, folded and creased naturally, as if it had just been taken off and hung, without any attempt to straighten it out.

Charlie's family had a dog called Chief, a pedigree Weimaraner. A beautiful breed of dog with a steel gray coat and blue eyes whose appearance was wholly compatible with the family's tasteful yet opulent lifestyle. But his behaviors weren't. Chief suffered from a condition called submissive urination. Whenever any human or other animal approached him, Chief peed on the floor as a sign of submission, letting the other animal know that he was the boss.

Artie felt a lot like Chief in his daily life.

21. *August 20, 2004. Old Town, Chicago.*

It was 3:15 in the morning and Artie was nowhere near done. He'd cleaned the worst excesses of the kitchen and bathroom and tidied up his bedroom and the living room. But all the rooms needed a deep clean before tomorrow night. Artie debated whether to give up and go to bed.

"*Screw it. Let's power through.*" Artie decided. "There's nothing that important to do in work today. And I really want to have it presentable for when they arrive tomorrow." He went to his fridge and cracked a can of Red Bull and took a big gulp. Then he went over to the record player and put on *Appetite for Destruction* by Guns'N'Roses. He wouldn't say he really liked them as a band. They felt like empty calories to him. But they served a purpose. The first track "Welcome to the Jungle" began, and Artie's adrenalin kicked in.

At just after 5:30, before the sun had risen, Artie called it a day. He wasn't sure but he thought it was habitable.

He struggled through Friday at work. Fridays were always pretty quiet at Roberts Services, for reasons Artie didn't really understand. But he was very grateful for that fact today. He was tired but he could power through. He always slept pretty terribly anyway, so he was used to this feeling. He had joked with a friend once a long time ago that his awful sleeping habits were kind of a competitive advantage because he could handle periods of limited sleep, and jet lag, better than others. They were business as usual for Artie.

He got home at six and began cooking. They were arriving at seven, and he wanted to have the food ready. He had made the green curry paste from scratch last weekend. He went and bought all the necessary ingredients in Chinatown early Saturday morning, then spent the whole day making it.

Almost nobody makes curry paste from scratch, even working-class Thais buy it in the market. But it felt like a fun challenge for Artie.

And he had bought a book years ago, simply called *Thai Food* by an Australian chef called David Thompson. Published in 2002, it was a great big hardback book, with a bright pink cover. It was almost seven hundred pages long.

Artie had been dying to use it. And he almost never had visitors.

The book was very thorough. The curry section alone was sixty pages long, starting at page 273. It started off by introducing foreigners to the ingredients needed to make Thai curries like galangal (*ka*), wild ginger (*grachai*), and fermented fish (*pla ra*). It then went on to talk about ways to make curry paste. Then finally, on page 281, it listed recipes for specific curries.

The author seemed to list exotic, unusual curries first like "young jackfruit curry with pork ribs", "minced rabbit curry" and "sour orange curry of salted fish, watermelon rind and egg". It wasn't till page 311, nearly forty pages into the curry section that the red and green curries Artie was familiar with started to appear. That section also had *panaeng* and *massaman* curries which Artie loved. He finally found Green Curry Chicken at the bottom of page 318. Pages 318 to 320 became Artie's manual for the weekend, both for shopping and paste preparation.

His shopping list was long and included coconut cream, coconut milk, bird's eye chilis, coriander root, kaffir lime, cumin seeds, white peppercorns, baby corn, shallots, and about twenty other ingredients. As Artie walked around the grocery store, simply and appropriately named *Thai Grocery*, he found that most of the ingredients he wanted to buy were sold in quantities way too big for his needs. But what could he do? He bought them, knowing that he could cook Thai food every day for about a week, but also knowing that he would probably throw the excess away after Friday night.

On Friday it was a relatively simple task of cooking the chicken fillets with the paste, some coconut milk, and a few other ingredients. He tasted it and it was awesome. Spicy but not crazy hot. The pea aubergines were perfectly cooked, but still with some crunch. The curry was thicker than Thais traditionally have it, but he thought it was tastier that way.

He cooked the rice in a pan – he didn't have a fancy rice cooker. He had bought Thai jasmine rice (*khao hom mali*), and he just threw it in the pan with some boiling water and simmered it for a while. He didn't time it.

Allie and Pete showed up at around 7:30.

"Sorry, we're a bit late buddy. Terrible traffic."
"No problem, Pete. Just nice to see you both."

Allie gave him a hug.

"Artie. You look so great."
"Thanks, Allie. You do too."

Allie was Artie's first cousin, on his father's side. Artie's father was the older brother of Allie's mom. Pete had been married to her for about five or six years, and he and Artie knew each other well.

They never had much to say to each other, but they got on fine. Every year or so, they would meet up, either at their place, Artie's, or outside.

Artie suspected they viewed him as a bit of a charity case and made the effort to meet him out of a kind of familial duty. He didn't mind. It broke up his year.

Pete looked at the digital clock on the wall.

"Hey. Your clock is flashing zeroes, man. You forgot to set it!"

Artie looked at him and grinned sheepishly. At work, Artie was known as *flashing zeroes dude*. Despite being highly technical, Artie was awful at reading manuals and setting stuff up. He just couldn't force his brain to go there. All the electronic devices in his house were flashing zeroes. The phone stand. The video player. The clocks around the house. It was part of his identity now.

Artie brought Pete a beer and Allie a Diet Coke. He had a beer himself. He had put Doritos and dips on the table before they arrived. He knew it was a bit like an undergrad frat house appetizer, but hey, he was a bachelor.

"Don't eat too many chips, I am really excited for you to taste what I cooked for you."

"You cooked?" said Allie, trying not to sound too surprised, and failing.

"Yeah, I just felt the urge. I learned how to make Thai curries from scratch, and I made us a green chicken curry. I hope that's OK."

"Sure. Sounds awesome." Pete sounded sincere. Artie suspected that Allie's tastes were quite boring and healthy. Like green salads, green veggies, and steamed white fish. Things like that.

Artie went to the kitchen to serve a plate of curry and rice each. He was so proud for them to try his curry. But then he saw that his rice had turned into a pile of sludge. It was like some bastard lovechild of rice, grits, and soggy mashed potatoes. Artie paused for a moment, then decided he had no option. He served it anyway.

"Really sorry guys. I screwed up the rice, it's more like porridge."
"We don't mind. I am sure it will be lovely. And we're here to see you, not a plate of food."

But the rice was so awful. Inedible, in fact. So bad neither of them could actually eat it. They both made some attempt to eat some of the curry, but in reality, they just pushed the rice sludge around their plates. Artie forced himself to eat it, but he couldn't say that he enjoyed his creation.

Allie and Pete made an excuse to leave early. Artie disremembered what their reason was. He knew it was just an excuse. And they kind of knew he knew.

Over the next few hours, he ate what was on all three of their plates, green curry rice sludge, while watching a strongman competition that happened to be showing on TV.

Artie had a sense that Allie and Pete's visits would get shorter and shorter over the next few years, more spaced out. When they had kids, he wouldn't be surprised if their visits stopped. And that would be fine.

And so it goes, and so it goes.

22.   March 3, 2005. In the air between Chicago and Los Angeles.

He sat in seat 38C. Left aisle at the back of the plane. A bad joke went through his head about his boobs being much bigger than a size 38C. But it didn't quite make sense, so he shut that thought stream down.

He hated, hated, hated traveling on planes. But when he had to do it, he always tried to choose the left-side aisle seat right at the back of the plane. He chose it for three reasons. Firstly, he chose the back so that he was visible to the least number of people. Secondly, he chose the back because he felt that the back was sometimes less full, so the middle seat next to him might be empty.

Third, he chose the aisle seat so he could 'overflow' a little into the aisle. If he chose the window, or even worse the middle, seat, there was no wiggle room. He was gonna encroach on his neighbor without a doubt. If he was in the aisle seat, he could lean that way a bit, although there were often issues with the crew bringing trolleys down the aisle, or even other passengers with their luggage hitting him. He wasn't quite sure why he favored the left side aisle, so his right side did the overflowing. But he knew that he did.

In his own head, Artie often joked that a flight was typically a one-cheek experience for him. And trying to use an airline toilet was like playing Tetris with his body parts.

He also typically had to suffer the indignity of needing an extension seatbelt. And, for reasons he never understood, many airlines had the standard seatbelts in a subdued color like black or dark blue but had extension seatbelts in a garish red or orange color.

Then there was the indignity of watching people fearful of him as he walked down the aisle, hoping against hope that he wouldn't be sitting next to them.

There was surely a really rich comedy sketch to be written about being a fat man on a plane. It would almost certainly involve farting. But as is often the case, great sadness was an inseparable bedfellow of great comedy. Artie had reached the point that he hated flying. Was ashamed of himself when he flew. And he did all sorts of logistical gymnastics and excuse-making to avoid having to fly.

But here he was, going to LA for a training course in database architecture. Not quite the most fun reason for traveling to LA. But a change in the monotony of Artie's life. And paid for by the company. And at least for the next three days, he had a purpose. His friendless, purposeless, meaningless life back in Chicago was put on hold for seventy-two hours.

Artie remembered hearing that life during wartime was far worse than life during peacetime in almost every way. Except one. That was that war gave you a purpose. Perhaps it was overdramatic to compare a three-day database course with a war, but at least Artie could dial down his existential angst for a few days and immerse himself in the training. Maybe even some pleasant socializing with fellow attendees.

Maybe. Maybe.

23.   2006. Temptation

Artie discovered Bangkok in 2006. At that time, he was thirty-four years old, and his life was closing in on him. By day, he was a technical service representative in a small warehousing business in Chicago. Which meant he was the guy that showed up when anyone's PC stopped working. He lived in a third-floor apartment that was exactly what you would expect a single guy's apartment to look like. Not quite tidy. Only the basics in the kitchen. Plenty of electronics and computers. And a complex, slightly unpleasant odor that seemed to include week-old sweat, day-old farts, and the olfactory equivalent of disappointment.

Artie's life at that point had settled into a rather uneventful routine that included working eight a.m. to six p.m. five days a week, with the occasional late-night or weekend session. Overtime is unpaid, of course. Shopping for ready meals every few days - to punctuate the fast-food deliveries. TV, video games, reading, and adult websites every night. He occasionally met a friend or ex-colleague at night or on the weekend, maybe a dozen times a year.

It was not unusual for Artie to sleep in his La-Z-Boy armchair with the TV on all night. In fact, it was unusual for him not to. He would often wake up at four or five in the morning, covered in the shame glaze of an overactive session on the adult websites, infomercials for steam mops and knife sets playing over and over on the TV. Perhaps the saddest part was that he didn't turn off the infomercials – they provided a strange kind of company for him.

He used his holidays to visit friends and family but had an increasing sense that they weren't so keen to see him anymore, and he tried to make himself busy while he was with them, so as not to be too much of a burden. So that he wouldn't use up his welcome.

Then one day, a particularly chatty cab driver told Artie about his friend, who had taken to saving up all his time off and going to

Thailand, Cambodia, or the Philippines once a year, 'renting a wife' for two weeks and having a whale of a time.

Artie was a fairly normal guy in terms of morals and was both vaguely disgusted and somewhat titillated by this concept. The idea wouldn't leave his head, and within 3 months of that fateful cab ride, Artie was on a plane to Bangkok, full of excitement and trepidation.

Looking at how Artie conducted that first holiday in Bangkok was both funny and pathetic. He continued to lie to himself about why he was there. He busied himself going to temples and museums during the day, bought local souvenirs for no one in particular, and then went to bars every evening. In the bars, he pretended to the girls and himself that he was just there for a drink, and that made everyone uncomfortable.

Then the night before he was due to go home, he submitted to the persuasive skills of one of the more experienced bargirls, *Neung*. Sitting in the bar, nursing a Chang beer, listening to *Hotel California* in the background, Artie was dreading returning home. Neung had a practiced, easy manner, and struck up a conversation with him. He bought her a couple of drinks and they played a game of pool together. Artie had never played pool with a woman before, and although he hated to admit it, he harbored discriminatory assumptions that women couldn't be good at pool. Neung wasn't half bad, and he sensed that she wasn't trying very hard either. In fact, he sensed that she would deliberately avoid winning, based on her experience with fragile male egos.

They went back to his hotel room together, and things got kinda weird. He still was putting up some kind of front that he wasn't interested in anything sexual. She went to the bathroom and came back naked. He resisted her attention as she sat next to him, trying to understand what he wanted. Eventually, she fell asleep, and he sat up all night, stressing out and listening to her surprisingly loud snoring.

The next morning, he gave her a rather generous tip as she left. He liked to think it was because he was being kind. In reality, he knew it was only a bit of that, but mainly his attempt to create a less sad, less pathetic narrative of the events of the last night in his head. As he sat on the flight home, he sarcastically congratulated himself on continually finding novel and creative ways and contexts in which to be a fuck-up.

24. March 3, 2007. Pattaya.

Artie played a combination shot, knocking the orange number five ball into the green number six, sending the green into the corner pocket. He had also predicted the trajectory of the number five ball and the white ball, the cue ball, so he was set up to sink that one next with a fairly easy shot, where the white ball should then drift into position to take on the number seven next. Nine-ball wasn't really Artie's favorite game, but he still enjoyed it. The table was set up for nine-ball, but he would have preferred eight-ball. And back home in the US, he also liked to play straight pool too.

Tip, the bar girl he was playing against, didn't even notice his shot. She was playing with her phone. This made him a bit sad because he was really proud of that combination. It wasn't so much that he wanted to show off to her, or to anyone else, really. It was more that he craved the human connection that a competitive game can engender.

This was his first time in Pattaya, and he hadn't explored it all yet, but so far Artie felt like he didn't enjoy Pattaya quite as much as Bangkok. Half of Pattaya was a bit more civilized and family-friendly, with nice beaches like Jomtien and some water parks, zoos, and gardens. But the half of it he was in was wall-to-wall bars, especially the area called Walking Street. And each bar was basically the same. A couple of pool tables and a dozen or so girls. No real personality to any bar. And, other than the beach, nothing else was really notable about the place that appealed to Artie.

The ugly truth that Artie hated to admit, that he was primarily there to hook up with bar girls, meant that he couldn't really complain. But the bar scene was a bit distasteful to him. It was too obviously like a meat market. It was like a continual slap in the face, reminding him that he was a pathetic pervert who was so broken that he couldn't get his kicks any other way. He thought he would probably not come back here. But he knew he couldn't be sure of that.

Nearly everything Artie did or liked was intellectual, brain-not-body-focused. (Which always reminded him of Woody Allen's infamous statement that he loved his brain, as it was his second favorite organ.) Reading, working with computers, watching movies. He never really was a sports guy. But he happened upon the game of pool at a kids' camp when he was twelve, and he really loved it. He had developed his skills over the years and now was really quite good, if he did say so himself.

One of the wonderful surprises Artie found as he began visiting Southeast Asia was that nearly every bar had at least one pool table. And also played pretty decent rock music. In Chicago, he was continually reminded of what a loser he was because he didn't even have anyone to play pool with. Here in Pattaya, just like most other resorts in Southeast Asia, there was always either a fellow customer or a bar girl willing to play with him. With fellow customers, it tended to be winner-stays-on. You write your name on a chalkboard, and when it is your turn, you pay to play. As long as you win, you don't pay, and other players keep coming. When you lose, you are off the table and can add your name back on the chalkboard if you still fancy playing more.

Unfortunately, many of the bar girls weren't very good at or interested in playing pool. They had needed to play it too much as part of their job and were often never really interested anyway. But Artie found that there was often at least one girl in each bar who was very good at pool and reasonably interested in it. He would buy them drinks and tip them heavily when they played with him and sometimes offer them extra if they could beat him. He always gave them that extra at the end, whether they beat him or not. Some of them appreciated both the fun of the game and the tip. Some appreciated one or the other. Some accepted the scenario Artie created but appreciated neither.

The way most people played pool was fairly mindless. They just looked for the easiest way to sink a ball in a pocket, then considered their next shot if they were successful. Artie tried to plan the whole game in advance, spending at least as much time thinking about where to position the cue ball for his next shot as he did on sinking the object ball.

Over the years, he had learned how to apply backspin, topspin, and sidespin, how to swerve the ball around others, jump the cue ball over balls that are in the way, and even how to factor the weave of the cloth into his plans, particularly when he played long slow shots.

But in bars like this, the table was often very uneven, more like curvy golf terrain than a flat table. He would often come into bars and observe other people's games to learn the lay of the land before playing.

He really loved the fact that he could do well at pool even though he wasn't particularly good at the main skill people noticed – sinking balls. Every time Artie hit the ball, he was thinking of three things – sinking the object ball, leaving as easy a follow-on shot as possible if successful, and leaving the opponent in a poor position if he was unsuccessful. Artie wouldn't go as far as saying pool was a strategic game, but it was highly tactical, whereas most players played it as a pure game of skill and luck.

Artie never really knew his Uncle Phil well, but he got to learn as he grew up that, although Phil's official job was a market trader, his real money came from being a pool and poker hustler. When Uncle Phil came over, he brought an air of the glamorous lifestyle with him. He always smoked big, fancy cigars, drank huge glasses of cognac with ice, and drove exciting-looking sports cars.

Artie never had quite the right type of relationship to get taught by Uncle Phil, but Phil's visits definitely left him with a feeling that being good at pool was cool as all hell. One thing Artie did remember Phil talking about was winning the best possible way as a hustler. That was winning by seeming to be lucky so that your mark never knew they had been hustled, or that you were a much, much better player than them. Uncle Phil once remarked in passing that his right hand could beat his left hand eight games out of ten.

Artie's skill of calculating how to leave the next shot easy for himself or hard for his opponent often went unnoticed. He almost always avoided playing fast, loud, or otherwise flamboyant shorts. And he occasionally deliberately played bad or badly thought-out shots, to throw any observant opponent off the trail.

After downing the eight ball and winning the game with Stairway to Heaven by Led Zeppelin playing in the background, Artie gave Tip a healthy five hundred Baht tip and retired from play for the night. Tip came and sat with him, and they enjoyed a drink and a laugh together. At some point, Tip made it clear that she would be happy to continue the evening back at Artie's room. He agreed and felt some excitement about what was about to come, even though it wasn't the first time this had happened. If he listened closely, he could also hear something dying a little inside him.

25. Whiskey/ Whisky

Until Artie discovered Bangkok, and later Southeast Asia in general, Artie hadn't really been a regular drinker. His only addictions were unhealthy food, terrible sleep patterns, video games, and sadness.

But somehow his recent holiday lifestyle in girlie bars had led him to start drinking regularly, and that habit came back home with him. He had always felt like his food addiction was the least glamorous of all addictions. Even though drug and alcohol addictions were terrible, they did have a certain chic. A certain cachet. At least until the addict descended into the depths of despair.

Artie had felt inadequate all his adult life because he didn't even know what his favorite drink was. A lot of the men and women he knew seemed to know exactly what their drink was. Whether it was Bourbon, Margaritas, or Budweiser. At a company event, he once marveled at a colleague instructing the bartender quite carefully about how dirty he wanted his Martini to be. Not only did Artie have no idea what was in a Martini, or what 'dirty' meant in that context, but he was also sure that even if he knew all those things, he would never be as sure of what he wanted as his colleague or be willing to ask for it so stridently.

Artie quite liked everything he drank but didn't really have a drink identity. (Or any other kind of identity, really.) In this context, he often thought about a Woody Allen movie called *Zelig*. It was a strange little mockumentary where Allen plays the title character. Zelig has a very severe confidence problem and tries to fit in with whoever he is with. The movie shows clips of him becoming all rabbinical when he is with a group of rabbis, then fitting in with a group of black blues musicians.

In the movie, Diane Keaton's therapist character takes him away for a while and builds his confidence. But she builds it too far, and when a group of psychiatrists comes to visit, they disagree about something minor, like the weather, and Zelig attempts to attack them with a garden tool.

Artie only shared the lack of confidence with Zelig, not the desire to fit in. He was quietly addicted to not fitting in. He was sort of an anti-Zelig. He didn't know what he wanted, but he was pretty sure it wasn't what most people had or talked about. He wanted to both fit in and not fit in. Which meant the only thing he was guaranteed was feeling like he had failed.

As Artie found himself drinking in Southeast Asia, he genuinely developed a taste for whiskey. Initially, bourbons like Jack Daniels, which were often available in all his favorite sex tourist hangouts. But he later settled on Scotch Whisky. It seemed more sophisticated and exotic to Artie. Seemed to make him seem international and interesting.

Back home in Chicago, he began exploring the world of whiskey. Buying and drinking bottles of bourbon, Irish whiskey, and Scotch whisky. He soon learned that blended scotches like Grants, Teachers, and Johnnie Walker were often a bit harsh for him. Single malts became his favorite.

He flirted with smoky and peaty ones, like Laphroaig, Lagavulin, Talisker, and Jura. But Artie fairly quickly realized that he actually preferred more smooth, rounded whiskies that were neither smoky nor peaty. Like Glenmorangie, Glenlivet and Macallan.

His favorite ended up being Dalmore, a lesser known, rather expensive whisky. Artie read about the history of the Dalmore distillery, dating back to 1839. Many of Dalmore's whiskies are aged in sherry casks and other similar vessels. Artie's absolute favorite, King Alexander III, was a mix of six cask finishes: bourbon, sherry, madeira, marsala, port, and cabernet sauvignon.

Of course, most of the fancier whiskies were not available in the kind of places Artie frequented on his travels. In Thailand, for example, the local Mekhong was the most common option. It was labeled a whisky but was really more of a rum. However, given why he was really there, and given that he normally started with two or three beers to loosen his tongue and his palate, by the time Artie got to whisky, almost anything would do.

Whisky became the center of a dark fantasy Artie developed at that time. He fantasized about giving up everything, buying a nice pool cue, moving to Bangkok, hustling pool, hanging out in bars, sleeping with bargirls, and slowly drinking himself to death.

He felt pathetic for having that fantasy, yet somehow even more pathetic for not executing it.

26. February 7, 2008. Bangkok.

"*No farang in here. Don't worry. I protect you.*" *Oy* squeezed Artie's hand and giggled.

Artie had met Oy a couple of nights ago in a bar in Nana Plaza. They spent that night together, and the next day and night too. She was very easy company and had made Artie feel much less awkward than normal about this latest in his catalog of 'love for sale' experiences.

She was also much closer in age to him than normal. He was thirty-six and she was thirty-one. "*Almost normal*", Artie thought.

As well as their adventures in the bedroom, Oy had proved good company at breakfast, lunch, dinner, and every time in between. They wandered around hand in hand. A true GFE (Girlfriend Experience). Artie had bought her a few bits and pieces. Cosmetics in Robinson department store, a knock-off Louis Vuitton purse in the MBK mall. And a nice gold bracelet.

Artie had learned that Thais really value gold. Particularly working-class Thais. It appeals to them to wear as a way of showing and feeling things are going well. And, also, as a store of value. Something to be sold if times get tough.

The measure for gold in Thailand has confusingly got the same name as the currency, Baht. One Baht weighs just over fifteen grams. And Thais tend to prefer very pure gold. Twenty-three karats, equivalent to 96.5% pure gold, is common in Thailand, compared to twenty-two or eighteen karats in many other countries.

Because of how much Thais value gold, there were a bunch of gold jewelry chain stores in all the shopping malls, especially those that foreigners and their temporary girlfriends frequent. *Prima Gold* was

Oy's store of choice this time, and Artie bought her a one Baht bracelet with hearts for fifteen thousand Baht. It slightly dampened Artie's girlfriend experience when it became obvious that Oy knew the sales assistant at Prima Gold. Not her first rodeo.

At that moment, Oy was taking Artie to an internet café. Not just any internet café. You might call it Boyfriend Central. All the working women from the Sukhumvit area came in here to get help reading and writing emails to their foreign boyfriends.

On the way here, Artie had realized something. In the back of his mind, he had always had the idea of what a successful life would look like. How he should be living. Probably fueled a great deal by advertisers and the creators of TV shows. But quietly, in the background, without him realizing it, Artie's dream had shifted. From living in a beautiful house in Chicago with a wife, two kids, and a border collie to living with a beautiful Thai partner in a reasonably priced bungalow with a swimming pool, having breakfast outside on the patio, and a dip in the pool every morning. It was too early to say whether that partner could be Oy, but it was a nice fantasy.

Most of the women working in bars in Bangkok didn't have very strong English skills. (Or German, or French, or whatever the language of their customers was.) They spoke enough to seal the deal on the night they met and to keep their customer/ boyfriend happy while they were together. Which often didn't need to be very much since conversation wasn't the main attraction. For either party.

These women and their customers/ boyfriends often liked to keep in touch while they weren't in Thailand. Because of their limited language and cost reasons, email had become the communication channel of choice in the last few years. This was kind of a blessing in disguise, since voice calls were much harder to handle with the bargirls limited foreign language skills, and their boyfriends' typically non-existent Thai.

Sometimes the boyfriends were interested in pursuing marriage or a long-term relationship. Some sent money to support their girlfriends. For many, the implication was that their girlfriend would stop working in the bars. Some of the women did this, either because they were serious about the relationship, or just to take a break from the action while they could.

Some had one 'boyfriend'. Some had many. Some were honest about this, some weren't. Some even kept working the bars, with a few boyfriends sending several tens of thousands of Baht per month, believing their 'girlfriends' were faithful to them alone, and 'off-the-market'.

Artie drew looks from everyone as he wandered around the café. From the working women getting help and the staff helping them with their electronic love letters. There was no real reason for him to be there.

He heard and read lots of stock phrases being re-used around the place.

"I love you so much my darling."

"My mom is sick in hospital. Can you send extra twenty thousand this month?"

"Can't wait to see you tii-rak." ("tii-rak" is Thai for darling.*)*

"Our buffalo died. Need new buffalo."

"Don't come in April. I go home Isaan. You come May."

The staff helping the girls were mostly women. There were a couple of men and one ladyboy. They seemed to take their jobs seriously, trying hard to understand what their clients wanted out of the relationship. Not judging whether they were being genuine or manipulative with their foreign boyfriends. Remaining neutral and impassive. Receiving one or two hundred Baht for each of their communications.

Oy later told Artie that some of the staff were ex-bargirls themselves who had developed superior language skills, either from time in the business or occasionally from having lived abroad with their own boyfriends for a while.

It was interesting to Artie that Oy had taken him to that place. He couldn't work out whether Oy just thought he wasn't boyfriend material, so why not show him, or as a kind of sophisticated stratagem to make him feel that she couldn't be conning him because she 'opened the kimono'. Or maybe because she was actually very genuine with him and interested in a real relationship.

It also occurred to Artie that Oy might not exactly know the reason herself. People don't have to have clear, logical reasons for things that they do. Even if observers want them to.

27. January 4, 2009. Koh Samui.

"*Check,*" Alistair stated confidently. Artie didn't rush. Despite being a bit thick-headed from too many bottles of Singha and Chang beer, and despite Alistair being a bit of an asshole, Artie was quite enjoying himself. Alistair was a proud Scot and former backpacker who had opened and owned "The Last Stand", a makeshift bar on the outskirts of Chaweng, Koh Samui since 1988.

Alistair's Glaswegian accent must have softened at least a little over the years, but it was still pretty tough for Artie to catch every word. Artie was constantly amazed at how little the UK was, but how rich and varied the accents were. Scottish ones were tough for Artie, and the Scouse accent from Liverpool threw him sometimes. But this year was the first time he had met people from Newcastle. Their accent, called Geordie, was pretty much impossible to understand. Other Brits told him they often couldn't understand Geordies either. And all of this playing out in a country just over a third the size of the State of Texas.

Australia was almost the opposite. It was a country two-thirds the size of the US, but everyone basically sounded the same. Perhaps it was because it was still a relatively new country. Brits loved reminding Aussies that they were all basically convicts. The UK shipped over 100,000 convicts out to Oz from the late 1780s to the late 1860s. A Brit once told Artie a rather cruel joke about Oz, which one could argue was a reason for the mono-accent.

Q: "*What's the difference between Australia and a bucket of yogurt?*"

A: "*If you leave a bucket of yogurt long enough, it will grow a culture.*"

Alistair told Artie that when he went to the local produce markets in the mornings to get food, he had learned to use some of the local Koh Samui dialect and accent. It amused Artie to think of what Glaswegian-accented southern Thai sounded like.

It was rare for Alistair to find someone to play chess with these days. When he opened The Last Stand, Koh Samui was more of an outpost for intrepid travelers. Now it was a booze and neon-filled holiday spot for groups of late teenage boys and girls to sunbathe and play water sports in the day, and drink, snort coke, and fuck at night.

Artie wasn't a great chess player, but he felt like he had the measure of Alistair. He had always loved sacrifice plays in chess and other games. In chess, a sacrifice play involves letting your opponent get a material advantage, usually by taking one of your pieces, for a better position. The subtle beauty of sacrifice plays had always entranced Artie.

Years ago, he read about a game dubbed 'The Immortal Game' played in 1851. The players were Adolf Anderssen and Lionel Kieseritzky. It was notable because Anderssen sacrificed most of his major pieces, including a bishop, both rooks, and his queen, in order to checkmate Kieseritzky, who in turn had only lost three pawns. Artie couldn't imagine anything more romantic.

Tonight, Artie had allowed Alistair to take his most valuable piece, his queen, but achieved a rather unusual position, where all of his major pieces, his rooks, bishops, and knights, were in the center of the board. As Alistair tried to attack him from the outside with his queen, Artie just rotated these pieces around in the center. Artie had to admit he was particularly enjoying this because Alistair's girlfriend, a breathtaking beauty, was sitting next to Alistair watching on. Artie was pretty sure that she wasn't a chess player, but she could see Alistair squirm as Artie slowly broke him down on the board.

For reasons that weren't wholly clear to Artie, he decided at one point that he was going to throw the game. He pretended to accidentally make a weak move, and Alistair pounced. Four moves later, Artie was forced to resign. He wasn't sure whether he threw the game out of some kind of cowardice, a feeling that he didn't deserve to win, some kind of gift to Tan, Alistair's girlfriend, or another, unknown reason.

Two hours later, at 1am, the crowd had thinned out, and Artie continued to sit there. Not playing chess now, but just hanging out with Alistair and Tan. Alistair went off to serve customers, and Artie and Tan kept chatting. Although he didn't want to, the semi-inebriated Artie felt like he was getting lost in Tan's beautiful, almond-shaped eyes. He knew that she knew it too, and he could see that it amused her.

At one point in the conversation, she let Artie know that she wasn't born female. She was a *katoey*, commonly referred to in English as a ladyboy. Artie had heard of ladyboys and had even seen a cabaret show in Pattaya where the cast was all of the third gender. But he had never had a chance to get to know a ladyboy up close.

Because it was clear that Artie was neither trying to proposition her, nor treat her like a circus freak, and because they were in Alistair's bar, they were able to have a really relaxed conversation. Tan gave Artie tacit permission to ask anything he wanted. And he did. At one point, he became really quite embarrassed, even in his drunken state, when Tan talked about state-of-the-art transgender surgery. She argued that you couldn't be sure whether someone was a ladyboy or not by the absence of an Adam's apple, the size of their hands, or the tone of their voice.

Tan waded fearlessly into very graphic territory by describing how Thailand's cosmetic surgeons were the best in the world at transgender surgery and could shape perfect vaginas in place of male genitalia. But, she said, the one giveaway was the responsiveness of the clitoris. As well as being insanely embarrassing to hear, Artie couldn't really understand what she meant. Although at this point, he had had quite a bit of sex (most of it paid, unfortunately), and he hadn't really got too intimately acquainted with the lady parts of most of his nighttime partners. He was a rather unimaginative, unconfident missionary position kinda guy.

It wasn't until the next morning, actually, the next afternoon, when he woke up with a banging hangover at one, that it crossed his mind that, given the conversation last night, there was every chance that at least one of his partners in Thailand, and maybe even other Southeast Asian countries, had been a *katoey*. Possibly quite a few of them.

He wasn't exactly sure about how he felt about that. He felt that he should feel horrified, and sort of did on principle. But if he listened to his true, inner voice, he thought *what does it matter?* If he hadn't noticed at the time, it didn't seem to make sense to be not OK with a tryst in retrospect.

28. August 3, 2009. Bangkok.

The evening started well. Artie had visited three or four bars on the side street connected to Sukhumvit Road called Nana. He had had a good time in each, drinking a few beers, playing a few games of pool, chatting to the bargirls, and giving them generous tips.

At 10 p.m., he settled into Big Dog 4, a place he had been to a couple of times before. Basically, all the bars in Nana were the same. A couple of pool tables, old-school rock music, and hot, available women. The vibe was slightly different each night in each place, depending on which girls were working, and how many and what type of customers were in there.

He had been trying to learn a little Thai. He had a Thai language course on cassette that he had just started studying. Also, he had bought a book called "Making Out in Thai", that focused on dating Thai women, and contained some rather colorful language.

Artie had a bit of a facility with languages. He picked up decent Spanish in high school and had tried to learn some German too. But he was awful at tones. Thai was a language that had tones. Five of them in fact. Mid, low, falling, high, and rising. Mandarin had four tones. Cantonese was probably the language where tones were most important. It was more of an informal, spoken language than a written language, and scholars couldn't even agree on how many tones Cantonese had. Maybe seven.

Artie couldn't quite hear the differences between the tones or deliberately choose one of them. He always hoped that the context would make his poorly pronounced Thai intelligible, especially to the bar girls, who heard lots of foreigners try to speak Thai.

But the truth is that tones in Thai are as important as, say, vowels in English. Artie found this out to his cost this evening, by announcing to the girls in Big Dog 4 that he had been sunbathing today. Now the word for sunbathing was pronounced *ap daed*. When he announced this, the whole staff of the bar doubled over laughing for what felt like hours but was probably a minute or so.

When things all calmed down, Artie was told that what he had actually said was a differently toned *ap daed*, which, it turned out, meant bathing in clitorises. Biologically hard to imagine, and brutally embarrassing for Artie. Still, he managed to have a laugh about it with the girls, and then move on.

At about 1:20 a.m., Artie paid his bill and left a generous tip for both the girl he had been playing pool and chatting with and the mama-san. Although he always tried to eat local, Artie kind of craved some McDonalds before bed, and he knew there was a 24-hour one about ten minutes down the road, attached to Robinsons department store, at the corner of Soi 19.

As Artie stepped out of the bar, he felt a massive thump on the back of his neck. He went down like a sack of potatoes. He remembered getting kicked. Repeatedly. All over his body. He remembered the bar staff screaming. Then it all went black.

Artie woke up two days later, on August 5, in Bumrungrad Hospital, the most famous hospital in Bangkok for foreigners. A popular place for medical tourism, Bumrungrad offers comprehensive health check packages as well as cosmetic surgery. It was only a couple of streets over from Nana, so that's probably why they brought him here.

He was bruised and bandaged up all over. He had two black eyes. And the cracked ribs meant that he experienced a sharp pain every time he breathed.

Later that day, the police came and talked to him. There was no video footage, but the bar staff had reported that four Italian guys jumped Artie the moment he left Big Dog 4. Artie told them that he had played pool with a bunch of Italian guys that night. He had been winning, and they were playing winner-stays-on, loser-pays. Essentially these four Italian guys kept paying 50 baht to play Artie. And Artie was on fire that night. Couldn't miss a ball. Started calling each shot before he played it. Playing trick shots. Jump shots.

Swerves. A few times he broke off, then sank all the balls and won the game without his opponent even getting a shot.

Each of them had a bargirl sitting with them, who they were buying drinks for throughout the evening. It was doubly embarrassing for them to all be continually losing to this fat, Yankee nothing of a man. But on the face of it, everyone seemed to be having a good time. Laughing and joking. Enjoying a bit of banter.

Artie remembered telling his favorite Italian Second World War joke: "*Question: How can you tell if a tank is Italian? Answer: Because it has one forward gear and five reverse.*" A reference to Italy's changing of allegiance during the war, and an indirect implication that the Italians were cowards. Thinking about that in the cold light of day, maybe that was a step too far.

Artie ended up staying in Bumrungrad for four more days then being flown back to Chicago in business class, paid for by his travel insurance. The travel insurance covered his stay and treatments in Bumrungrad too, apart from a $100 excess fee.

Although it pained Artie to admit it, those four days in Bumrungrad may have been the best part of his trip. His pain wasn't too, too bad. The nurses and doctors were really friendly and helpful. And he didn't feel lonely.

The truth was that his trips to Thailand and other Southeast Asia countries over the last few years had all been solo. And he really didn't have anything to do except at night. Other than the standard conversations with his paid company, he had no one to talk to. He was quite introverted, so he tended not to get into chats with other tourists, or locals.

Also, the conversations with the bar girls got pretty old pretty quickly. There were only about ten things that were said in these conversations. "*Handsome man, where you from?*" "*What you name?*" "*What your country?*" "*What your job?*" "*How long you stay Thailand?*" "*You want a drink?*" "*Buy me a drink?*" "*You like me?*" That was about it. Except when it came time to pay their bar fine and take them home. They usually had quite sophisticated bargaining skills for that transaction.

And some of them had some pretty outrageous dirty talk in the bedroom. Artie guessed that some guys liked that. He also heard that some people came to Southeast Asia looking to indulge in some fairly exotic fetishes and fantasies. But that wasn't for him.

Artie was looking for what was popularly known as the *girlfriend experience (GFE)*. Where, just for the night, he and his partner could pretend that they were lovers and be sweet and thoughtful to each other. He could suspend disbelief for the night and feel loved, and even more importantly not alone.

A bit like drinking alcohol, the temporary warmth of this girlfriend experience made you feel even colder when it was gone.

The few days in the hospital were a breath of fresh air. Some transactional conversations with doctors and nurses, and also some fun chats with nurses. Many of them were fun, young, and well-educated. Wanting to learn English. Considering a move overseas.

As Artie luxuriated in business class on the way back to Chicago, he felt an even greater sadness than normal returning home. Back to the loneliness of his regular life. And the shame that his sojourn in hospital was possibly the best week of his adult life. Even though he was unconscious for the first couple of days of it.

Also, the pain, the feeling of vulnerability, and the failure to defend himself, even a tiny bit, didn't sit too well with his fragile ego either.

29. January 12, 2010. Old Town, Chicago.

Artie's life had sunk to an all-time low. He had been to Thailand, the Philippines, and Cambodia eleven times between 2006 and 2010. He had used up a significant chunk of his savings and failed to heed his own moral compass on multiple occasions.

Years ago, he had read the writings of a Chinese neo-Confucian scholar called Wang Yang-Ming. Master Wang proposed that humans had an internal moral compass, *liangzhi*. The more they acted in accordance with their own innate morality, the clearer their intuition about the world became. This was very reminiscent of William Blake's idea that 'if the doors of perception were cleansed, man would see everything as it is. Infinite.' Artie's intuition was not clear, but very cloudy these days. His view was very finite and closing in fast.

Sat now in the same old apartment in Chicago, he was opening the mail. He didn't get much physical mail, so he let it build up for a while before opening it. The one he opened was from a hospital he had visited a couple of months earlier for a routine checkup. Had he forgotten to pay the bill? Or given his health insurance details properly? He opened it, and it turned out that samples had gotten mixed up at the time of his checkup. The blood samples that were actually his contained some worrying markers. He was going to need to return for some further tests.

Fast forward to February 23, 2010. Several rounds of tests had been done, and the news wasn't good. It seemed that there was some pretty serious stuff going on with him. An incurable, inoperable brain tumor.

He ducked into a bar not far from the hospital and ordered a beer and a bourbon chaser. He didn't go to bars in the US, certainly not on his own. And he didn't drink much normally, certainly not beer and bourbon together. But somehow it felt like the thing to do as he tried to digest the news. Like so many others in modern society, his actions were pre-designed by TV, movie, and marketing executives. He remembered thinking that the uber-popular TV show Friends functioned not only as entertainment but also a sort of user guide for how to live as a twenty-something in a modern urban city. (He saw himself as a much sadder, lonelier version of the Chandler character, with possibly a touch of Ross.)

It was at times like these that he really noticed how few friends he had. He had a few people he called friends here and there, even a couple in Chicago. But no one you would call a close friend. Certainly not a best friend.

One of his fantasies in life was having a friend that he met with on a regular basis. Once a week. Once a month. Or even once a year. Come rain or shine. No matter what. Seemed like a modest goal, but Artie never even came close. He always felt at best a second-class friend. Someone to see if there was nothing better to do. Nothing on at the movies. No one else to hang out with.

Since his parents had died, he wasn't close to any family members either. No one to talk about his news to. He imagined a movie character might get talking to the barman about their diagnosis, but he just wasn't that kind of guy. And as the barman whisked around behind the bar busying himself cleaning glasses and moving bottles around, he wasn't exactly giving off talk-to-me vibes either.

So, Artie drank his beer and bourbon, paid the bill, slunk out the door, and quietly made his way home. He certainly hadn't been very good at living, and now he could see that he would be equally inept at dying, too.

30. February 27, 2010. Old Town, Chicago.

Of the sciences, biology was definitely Artie's weakest. Math was his strongest. Then came physics. Third was chemistry. Biology came a solid fourth on the list. It is almost always true that you get good at things you are interested in. Things you are passionate about. Things you can relate to.

Having said that, Artie knew the quality of teachers, and your relationship with them could make a big difference too. Even though he was genuinely quite gifted at math, he developed a bit of an adversarial relationship with his high school math teacher, who he just remembered now by his surname, Kelly. The opposite was true of his chemistry teacher, Doctor Wilson. Although he felt like math was the essence of things, and chemistry was essentially just colors, smells, and noises, he ended up outperforming in chemistry and significantly underperforming in math in high school.

Looking at his order of science topic preferences, it was obvious to Artie that the more abstract a subject is, the more divorced it is from the reality of life, particularly his own life, and the more Artie could relate to it. The closer it was to his life, his body, his daily experience, the more Artie hated it, the more he couldn't relate to it.

He was never exactly sure what the difference between a psychopath and a sociopath was, but as Artie understood it, they were both descriptors of people who didn't care about others. Were numb and indifferent to the feelings of others. Saw others as objects in their world. To be ignored, eliminated, or manipulated if it pleased them or furthered their goals. He thought that maybe psychopathy was caused more by nature, and sociopathy more by nurture. Psychopaths were born. Sociopaths were bred.

Artie wasn't a psychopath or a sociopath, but he thought that maybe he was an auto-psychopath. A term that he just made up in his head. Someone who can't relate to themselves. Their own body. Their own mind. Their own life.

Anyway, his lack of biological knowledge and understanding meant that he had to study brain tumors now. Specifically, benign thalamic tumors. He learned that tumors are essentially lumps in your body that grow. They can happen anywhere. Tumors can be benign or malignant. Malignant tumors are commonly referred to as cancerous.

Malignant tumors are generally more dangerous. They grow rapidly, can infiltrate surrounding tissue, and metastasize, breaking off and traveling around the body to form tumors in other areas. Benign tumors grow slowly and in a well-defined way, and don't spread to other parts of the body. Many types of benign tumors are removable and are less likely to recur.

Another distinction was between high-grade and low-grade tumors. A high-grade tumor grows very aggressively and is more likely to recur.

Now, brain tumors are obviously tumors that sit within the brain, which is a pretty complex, delicate organ. Brain tumors can be pretty tricky to remove or treat. Another characteristic of brain tumors is whether they are deep-seated or not. Deep-seated brain tumors are stuck in the middle of the brain, in hard-to-get-to places, making them pretty impossible to operate on.

With all this background information, Artie was beginning to understand. He had a benign, low-grade thalamic tumor. Turns out the thalamus is a small, egg-shaped structure deep within the brain that has a few really important functions, including regulating consciousness and relaying sensory and motor signals. He wasn't sure why it was important to know that the thalamus was egg-shaped, but every reference he read about it included that fact.

Because it was so deep-seated, the tumor was inoperable. It couldn't be removed. Because it was benign, the doctors could be fairly sure how it would grow and how long it would take to impact Artie's brain functions. Their prognosis was that Artie was likely to die in five to seven years. He was thirty-seven now. Medical statistics told the doctors that Artie only had a three percent chance of making it to his fiftieth birthday.

Doctors had discussed all the treatment options with Artie. Surgery, even the most sophisticated micro-neurosurgery and stereotactic radiosurgery, were not an option. As Artie understood it, they had a very high chance of scrambling his brains if they tried to root out the tumor. Like, a more than ninety-percent chance.

For reasons he didn't fully understand, his particular condition wasn't susceptible to radiation therapy or chemotherapy either. The doctors explained that this was related to hypoxia and drug efflux pumps. Most medical texts on these topics were either super-simplistic, for lay people, or required several years of medical training to understand. But from what Artie could understand, hypoxia meant that limited oxygen supply to the tumor meant that radiation wouldn't be very effective. And drug efflux pumps were a feature of some tumor cells that actively removed chemotherapeutic drugs.

The best that the doctors could offer was to provide Artie with medicines to handle the symptoms that arose when the tumor did start to kick in, like pain, seizures, and hormonal imbalances.

The only good news was that the exact positioning and growth vectors of his tumor meant that Artie was unlikely to experience any symptoms, any loss of physical or mental performance, or any pain, until a few months before the end.

His end.

31. March 1, 2010. Chicago.

"Cast your mind back to the moment you heard the news. That confirmed your diagnosis and the likely outcome. Are you there?"

"Yes ma'am."

"How were you feeling at that exact moment?"

Artie was still processing the news he got. He had the idea that he would do a week of different therapies, tasting each one, to see if they could help him in the process of digesting the news about his health, and deciding what to do next.

He had taken this week off work and lined up a truly diverse array of therapies. Flotation tanks. Indian head massage. Primal scream therapy. Rolfing. Hypnosis. A psychic. And what was happening right now? Straightforward talking therapy. He was pretty sure anyone in their right mind would have told him that taking all these therapies in rapid succession was a terrible idea. Which was the main reason he liked it.

Jen, the therapist, looked to be in her mid-40s and had a kind but serious energy. She prompted Artie again.

"So, how did you feel the moment you heard?"

"I think my dominant feeling was actually a lack of feeling. A numbness. Shock."

"Makes perfect sense. Overload. Your systems shut down. How about the next few days."

"Probably best described as a cocktail. Of fear, sadness, disappointment. I had always thought the crap of my life was gonna resolve itself, and things would turn good. But now I knew that was not how this story ends."

"I got you. Anything else?" Artie noted that Jen was firmly in receiving mode. Not judging. Not commenting. At least for now. He could tell she was smart and practiced at this stuff.

He paused, then responded. *"Yeah. I guess. Rage. A deep down, dark grey, rumbling train of rage. A wave of anger that this is what had happened to me. This news had stolen my life. My hopes. My dreams. A feeling of unfairness."*

Jen could see sweat glistening on Artie's forehead. She could feel like he was immersing himself in his emotions. Being vulnerable. Not running away from the pain.

"That's really great work, Artie. I think that's probably enough for this first session. Next time let's start digging in to how you deal with that rage. How you get that monkey off your back. OK?"

Artie agreed, thanked her, and said he was looking forward to their next session. He smiled, got up, then left her office. He knew he wouldn't come back. The therapies he had tried this week had all been very different, but they had one thing in common. They were intensely personal to him, but they were business to the therapists who he had met.

He wasn't saying that they didn't care. But the way things were set up, they had to maintain a certain sense of detachment, and there were very strict boundaries in terms of how they could and would interact with their clients. Even though Artie completely understood the necessity of this, it didn't sit well with him, the opening up the Pandora's Box of your soul to someone who would politely close the session out after thirty, forty-five, or sixty minutes.

He remembered meeting a German programmer, Alex, a few years ago. Alex lived in Chicago now but went back home to Munich every year to spend time with a therapist. Alex told him that this therapist's technique was to spend forty-eight hours together with his patients in a small apartment, with no breaks. The patient and therapist talked together, ate, and drank together, and even slept in the same room. Alex felt like this unbroken period meant that his inhibitions broke down, the therapist and he formed a tight, real bond, and then the insights flowed.

Artie remembered feeling tremendously jealous when he heard that story. He lost touch with Alex and later wished that he had asked for his therapist's details, in case they could speak English, and would be willing to work with Artie. Epic fail.

As Artie left Jen's office, he had a powerful realization. An epiphany that was going to drive the purpose for the rest of his life. Somehow, he had tapped into a powerful, primordial knowledge that sprang from deep within himself. When he had identified his rage, and Jen talked about how to deal with it, Artie realized he didn't want to make it go away. He wanted to nurture it. To let it breathe. To give in to it and let it have its way. To become its servant.

Artie remembered the famous line from Thoreau: "*Most men lead lives of quiet desperation.*" He felt that, in fact, most people spent most of their lives suppressing their anger. Denying it. Trying to forget and eliminate it. But all the while it lurked in the deeper, darker recesses of our souls, like an alligator, almost fully submerged, with just its eyes visible, constantly looking for, longing for, a chance to strike.

He wasn't sure of the details yet, but he was going to unleash this beast. Let his anger out. Hopefully by doing good things with it. But definitely by letting it free.

32. April 4, 2010. Old Town, Chicago

Artie set his pen down and went for a pee. Although his apartment was full of computer equipment, he was doing all his planning and writing using pen and paper, on a hard board that he later planned to throw away. Anything written on a computer could often be retrieved, even if you overwrote the disk drive it was stored on multiple times.

It was just over a month since Artie had had his epiphany. He had been shaping his plans since then. He had changed his mind multiple times about the details, but now was closing in on a plan that worked. Once he was done, he would execute the plan with more discipline, commitment, and determination than he had ever done anything before in his life. That much he knew.

He couldn't guarantee he would be successful, but he could guarantee that he would give it his all. No holding back. No self-doubt. No self-sabotage. No self-damage.

One of the many weird phases in his life till now was a deep dive into cults and conspiracy theories. Not modern stuff about JFK's assassination or the moon landings. More stuff from the Middle Ages and earlier. The Templar Knights and their sudden disappearance. The potential that Jesus had a family, that the term 'Holy Grail' was actually a mistranslation of holy blood. The Rosicrucians. More recently, the Order of the Golden Dawn. Madame Blavatsky. Gurdjieff and Ouspensky. And the infamous Aleister Crowley.

It was not clear who was a truth-seeker and truth-teller, and who was a charlatan. Maybe some were both, some were neither, and some were confused about which they were. Crowley definitely seemed to be a narcissist and showman, but he also seemed to be quite an achiever, in fields as diverse as chess-playing and mountaineering.

Crowley was and is known for his famous phrase, *"Do what thou wilt shall be the whole of the law."*

Fans of Crowley state that this statement was not one encouraging hedonism or debauchery, but instead encouraging us all to focus on our true calling, our true purpose. Not to let that get diluted, or get distracted, or to try to fit in with society's expectations and norms.

Although Artie had been left with slightly ambivalent feelings about the man, he felt that his unusual circumstances and the decisions he had now made meant that he could finally follow Crowley's advice.

And so, his preparations began.

33. July 11, 2010. Old Town, Chicago. Day - 991.

Two hundred and forty pounds. Artie moved slowly and purposefully around the gym. He was still refining his plans, but building core fitness and strength were what a strategist would call 'no regrets moves'. However he refined his plan, he could be sure that fitness and strength would be prerequisites.

He had just finished the aerobic segment of today's training. He had decided to use the elliptical cross-trainer as his fitness exercise for at least the first fifty days. It was low impact on his joints and massively reduced the likelihood of him sustaining an injury while he was so heavy. Time out to recover from a joint, tendon or muscle strain, or broken bone was time Artie could ill afford. So, he was stepping up the time, speed, and intensity gradually, day by day, from fifteen minutes at minimum intensity to start. Using a wrist-based heart rate monitor, Artie tried to keep his heart rate below one hundred and twenty for now, recognizing his low level of fitness, and also keeping himself in the zone recommended for weight loss. As his weight came down and his fitness level rose, Artie planned to step his target rate up to more like one hundred and sixty for forty-five minutes.

As he wandered into the free weights section, he realized that he was sweating a lot and probably smelling pretty ropey. Just eleven days ago, he would have been too embarrassed to continue walking around the gym. In fact, imagining scenarios like this was exactly why Artie never joined a gym. Until now.

The last time he was in a gym was during his undergrad years. He went to a gym close to the DePaul campus but filled with serious bodybuilders. They were quite nice to him considering. He had a tryout with a personal trainer who kept shouting slogans at him while he lifted weights. "*Big arms, big arms.*" "*No pain, no gain.*" Even while he was struggling with the weight, he remembered smirking a little as he transmuted that second one into "*No brain, no pain*" in his head. The whole experience wasn't for him. He never went back.

Now, Artie favored free weights over modern gym equipment for almost every exercise. Even though those multigym stations were nice and clean and easy, they allowed you to lift heavier weights because you were only using the main muscle groups you were training, like the chest, triceps, or biceps.

He only used the multigym to exercise muscles that were hard to target with free weights. Like the leg adductors and abductors, the inner and outer thigh muscles.

Artie knew that he wasn't training to look good or to compete with Alpha Male buddies. In fact, Artie had never really either associated with or aspired to be an alpha male. A term first popularized in the 1960s about wolves, it has come to be used for men who are confident, dominant, and in positions of power.

Artie heard the term Sigma Male more recently on social media. It referred to a man who was introverted, self-reliant, and independent, preferring to operate outside traditional social hierarchies. A man who didn't seek leadership positions. It was close to what was more traditionally known as a *lone wolf*. Much more Artie's speed. Not what he was, but what he aspired to.

Artie was training for real action, where the small muscles that controlled twisting and balance were as important as the heavy-duty muscles doing the big, obvious work. And, although he was never really a macho man kind of guy, the old-school, down-and-dirty image of bars with weights on either end kind of appealed to him. So, free weights it was.

After about an hour of lifting, he finished with four sets of ten repetitions of an exercise he liked very much. He rested his shoulder blades back on a bench, so his torso and upper legs were horizontal, his lower legs still vertical. He held a twenty-pound dumbbell in his hands. Not in the normal way but holding one of the weights on the side of the dumbbell in his two hands. Then he slowly swung the weight over his head and behind him, with his elbows bent. When his forearms were vertical behind his head, he reversed the motion.

It was a great exercise, strengthening multiple muscle groups, extending their range of motion, and providing an overall body stretch. But definitely not one to use a big weight for.

Throughout the hour, he kept in his mind the saying that muscle is built by tension, not momentum, and executed his lifts at a deliberate, smooth, almost excruciatingly slow pace. So slow that multiple people were drawn to look at him quizzically. Most of the gym bunnies thought that made him a weirdo, but he could see that the more knowledgeable ones were impressed. Not that he was doing it to impress anyone or cared much about anyone's opinion of him anymore.

He started and finished each session with a very thorough stretching sequence. First rotating his neck in 3 different ways – up and down, leaning left and right, looking left and right. Then shoulder rolls, side stretches, body rotations, and hip rotations. Then on to upper and lower leg stretches and ankle rolls. Finally, he finished with a series of wrist and forearm stretches that he had learned from Aikido.

He knew that the slow, boring details, repeated hundreds of times now would be the keys to achieving his mission's goals later. The fact that he was repeating the same things over and over also allowed him to achieve a kind of meditative state.

34. Dec 1, 2010. Skokie, Chicago. Day -848.

7 p.m. on a cold Wednesday evening. Artie lined up with the other students at the Delta Krav Maga studio in Skokie, a diverse suburb of Chicago. Wednesday nights were Krav Maga in Artie's tight, disciplined weekly schedule. He managed to also fit in Brazilian Jiu Jutsu, Wing Chun, Chi Kung, Kundalini yoga, weight training sessions, running, and language study. As well as these regular classes, he also took short courses in a number of areas that he thought might come in handy, such as first aid, memorization techniques, computer hacking, toxicology, lip reading, and lock picking. He joined a gun club and learned to fire various weapons too. He marveled at what you could achieve when you had a clear purpose, and when you were committed, not wrestling with any internal angst. When you were out of your own way.

Artie believed Brazilian Jiu Jutsu (BJJ) to be the most technical martial art he was studying. In BJJ, you never allow the opponent to dominate, even if they are on top of you on the ground. Wing Chun was the martial art that Bruce Lee famously started with, before he developed his own art, Jeet Kune Do. Wing Chun was particularly helpful for small, fast striking techniques that worked in small, confined spaces, like, for example, a public toilet cubicle.

But Artie felt like Krav Maga's philosophy of brutal pragmatism was perfectly aligned with his mission. It was developed for the Israeli military. Whatever one felt about Israel from a political or religious standpoint, it was clear that it was surrounded by enemies on all sides from day one, and brutal practicality was the only way Israel was going to survive.

Artie had spent a couple of weeks at the start of this process carefully weighing up what he would study. In terms of martial arts, others that made the shortlist included Aikido, Capoeira, Judo, Sambo, Savate, Arnis, Pentjak Silat, Kalarippayattu and various forms of Karate and Kung Fu. As did Thai boxing, and its more brutal cousin, Burmese boxing. All had their merits, but when Artie factored in the fit with his mission, the availability of good schools nearby, and the synergies with other arts, Krav Maga, BJJ, and Wing Chun were the winners.

Artie had also read a wonderful novel called "Shibumi" by Trevanian many years earlier. In that book, the hero, Nicholai Hel, learns the art of killing using everyday objects, which Trevanian calls *hoda korosu*, or naked kill. Artie believed that the term was made up by Trevanian, but he felt sure that ninjas would have trained in this concept, and Artie paid some attention to it in his preparations. It also reminded Artie of one of the principles of improv acting. Improv teaches us to treat everything that happens and everything we encounter as a gift and work out how to accept those gifts and use them.

The dojo was a hell of a lot warmer than outside tonight, but you could still just about see everyone's warm breath as they breathed out during the initial stretching, training, then sparring exercises. Artie always gave as much as he could in the sessions. Completely immersed himself. Tried to learn and be a good fellow student. Stay fully present in the moment.

He remembered reading in a book called "Zen in the Martial Arts" years earlier that the word *dōjōs*, a Japanese word commonly used for martial arts training facilities, had a beautiful origin. *Dōjō* literally means "place of the way" in Japanese, but the book said it was derived from the Sanskrit word *bodhimaṇḍa*, meaning "place of the transformation from ego self to egoless self". He didn't remember the details of the book or the author, but he remembered that he loved this idea, and also, he kind of doubted that this etymological story was true. But the truth of its derivation didn't matter to him. It was still a beautiful sentiment.

The only complication for Artie in this class, and in all his other classes, was that he never wanted to reveal even the slightest clue about his mission; why he was doing all this stuff. He sometimes made efforts to seem a bit weak, cowardly, or distracted. He wanted to appear a bit pathetic. Like a lost, middle-aged, middle-class guy having a mid-life crisis.

Ironically, before he got his diagnosis, that was exactly what he was, and at that time he wanted to appear anything but that. Now that he had a razor-sharp purpose and a continuously focused mind, he needed to portray that old self to keep everyone in the dark. His meticulous planning included not shaving very well, wearing slightly grubby, torn workout clothes, and occasionally pretending to flinch out of fear.

Tonight, they had learned some very useful moves related to escaping when someone held you from behind. Artie bowed to the teacher and all his fellow students at the end when he left at around nine thirty that night. He didn't shower with the others after class, feigning self-consciousness about his body.

35.   March 6, 2011. Old Town, Chicago. Day -753.

Thai: "Mâi dtông kangwon. Chăn yùu tîi nîi pêua chûay kun."

Lao: "Yuen yan, khoy ma phoeu suay than."

Vietnamese: "Đừng lo lắng. Tôi ở đây để giúp bạn."

Khmer: "Kom tien sambot te, khnhom nov ti nis deumbi chuoy anak."

Tagalog: "Huwag mag-alala. Narito ako upang tulungan ka."

Bahasa Indonesia: "Jangan khawatir. Saya di sini untuk membantu Anda."

Bahasa Malaysia: "Jangan risau. Saya di sini untuk membantu awak."

Mandarin Chinese: "Bùyòng dānxīn. Wǒ shì lái bāngzhù nǐ de."

Cantonese: "M'sai daam sam. Ngo hai lei bong nei ge."

Burmese: "hcatemapuuparnae . ngarmainnko kuunyehphoet demhar."

English: "Don't worry. I am here to help you."

Artie was learning to say twenty things relevant to his mission in the ten languages he was likely to need most. Twenty statements in ten languages. Already very challenging. But he knew that there were hundreds, maybe even thousands of local languages in East and Southeast Asia. For example, along with Tagalog, it is estimated that there are one hundred and twenty languages spoken in the Philippines, some of the more well-known ones being Cebuano, Ilocano, and Ilonggo. Many of the people he would encounter would likely have little or no formal education and speak local languages only. Fortunately, he was only learning a small number of set phrases in each language, only learning to speak (not read, write, or even listen), and he didn't have to pronounce them perfectly, or try to pass himself off as a local. He just needed to be understood to help fulfill his mission.

His phrases included, *"Don't worry I am here to help you,"* *"Do exactly as I say or I will kill you,"* *"Drive faster,"* and more mundanely, *"Hello,"* *"Thank you,"* and *"How much?"* Not exactly your classic introduction to a language. But these were the things that Artie thought he would need to say most in local languages, and that were not too difficult to remember.

In his previous life, Artie had taken a little Spanish at school, and a night class in the same to fill some of the emptiness of his evenings. He still wasn't very good, mainly because he wasn't committed. He didn't really have a purpose for learning Spanish. Nevertheless, he had always had a respect for languages and people who could speak more than one. He thought he remembered some kind of biblical story about Solomon going to meet a king, where you could ascend one step for every language you could speak. The wise Solomon was the only one who could climb all the steps to meet the king.

Artie knew quite a few people in his previous life who were good at languages. There seemed to be three types of people.

First were the ones from countries that just rolled that way. The Netherlands and the Nordics were ridiculous. They were the opposite of the USA. In the Netherlands, for example, pretty much everyone seemed to speak, Dutch, English, German, and French. Then the linguists amongst them would speak Spanish, Italian, or some more exotic language as well.

Second, Artie also knew people who just had a knack for picking up languages by talking to people in a bar. Without studying any kind of grammar or anything. Kind of like people who can somehow play music by ear, without even knowing how to read or write a music score.

And third, some people were really good and learning and remembering languages formally, through classes. They tended to learn grammar, vocabulary, reading, and writing. The whole schmeer.

Artie didn't fit in any of those three categories and hadn't been good at languages till now. But needs must. He was following the third path, as well as he could.

Before learning his two hundred statements, Artie spent some time learning memorization techniques. The one he found most useful was the idea of memory palaces. You created a place in your head, like a house or a garden, or whatever in your head, with a number of locations within that place, and a path through them. Artie had used his parents' house, the one he grew up in, and a path he would naturally walk around the house. He had focused on five rooms: his bedroom, the upstairs bathroom, the kitchen, the living room then the back garden. He had identified five locations in each room. For example, in his bedroom, it started with his bed, then the right windowsill, the left windowsill, his desk, and his wardrobe. All in all, this gave him a memory palace with twenty-five locations.

The idea was that whenever he needed to remember something, he could 'put' it into those twenty-five locations, and it would then be easier to remember the components and the order they came in.

The extra trick was to make each of the things he had to remember really memorable – e.g. bright colors, an associate smell and noise, and maybe something grotesque, rude, or otherwise shocking. He would then practice walking through his memory palace looking at all the things.

He used this technique to learn the full name of Bangkok, just to practice. Literally meaning village of wild plums, Bangkok is a name only used by foreigners. It referred to the original location of the city on the west side of the Chao Phraya River. The capital was moved across to the east side of the river in 1782 during the reign of King Rama I. It is known by locals by the name *Krung Thep*. Its full name is: *Krungthepmahanakhon Amonrattanakosin Mahintharayutthaya Mahadilokphop Noppharatratchathaniburirom*

Udomratchaniwetmahasathan Amonphimanawatansathit Sakkathattiyawitsanukamprasit.

It is officially the longest place name in the world, and is a description of Bangkok: "Great city of angels," "Immutable city of God Indra," "Great city of the world endowed with nine precious gems," "Happy city, abounding in an enormous royal palace that resembles the heavenly abode where reigns the reincarnated god," "A place that is the grand royal dwelling and grand royal palace established and flourishing," "In the magnificent abode of gods incarnate, full of perfect splendor," "And executed according to a grand architectural design; the construction being complete in every respect and renowned so exceedingly for its elegance as to be worthy of praise by hosts of tiny sprites."

When Artie remembered that name, the first place on his route was his old bed. The first piece of the word is Krungtep. Although it is written with a K, it is pronounced as a G. In his mind it sounded a bit like "grungy step," so he put an image of a really dirty, grungy, stinky staircase on the bed in his memory palace.

Artie used his memory palace to remember all of these phrases, which he would no doubt find useful as he executed his mission.

36. November 14, 2011. Lincoln Park, Chicago. Day -500.

Artie stepped up to the checkout of a local organic food store. He tried to shop around, sometimes traveling for up to one hour to keep his routine irregular. His basket mostly contained stuff that might be described as superfoods. A mix of fish, like mackerel and trout. Broccoli. Kale. Avocado. A variety of berries. Greek yogurt.

He briefly reflected on how far his eating habits were now from only a year ago. After receiving his health news in April last year, Artie had taken a couple of months digesting the news along with an even more substantial array of kebabs, burgers, and pizzas than normal. There had been the whole range of emotions, bouts of crying, a little occasional screaming, quiet disappointment, and resignation.

In fact, as well as fully experiencing these feelings, Artie seemed to exist detached on a meta-level, looking down on himself. And as was Artie's wont, he over-intellectualized it. He was reminded of a model he had read about called the Five Stages of Grief by Elisabeth Kubler-Ross. Working with terminally ill patients, she said that people went through five stages – denial, anger, bargaining, depression then acceptance. Artie recognized himself in that process.

But Artie's particular journey took an unexpected left turn off that grief curve a couple of months in. Around the end of June, a plan started to form in Artie's head, and the more he thought about it, the more it felt right. Righter than anything he had ever thought about in his life.

On July 2, his birthday, which also happened to be the exact middle day of the year, Artie began implementing his plan. Today was day 500, exactly halfway through the thousand-day preparation phase. He celebrated by doing exactly what he had done the previous 499 days. Following his newfound routine of diet, exercise, sleeping, meditation, and training in a variety of disciplines.

His dietary regime was quite strict, and could be described as follows:

- Intermittent fasting, with no food before 12 noon or after 6 p.m.
- Very low carbohydrate meals and snacks.
- No sugar, potatoes, bread, rice or pasta.
- No fruit or juice.
- No starchy vegetables.
- Typically, two eggs for brunch, with spinach or other green veggies for bulk.
- Meat or fish with either hot vegetables or salad for dinner.
- Beef jerky as a snack.
- Hot water with lemon and room-temperature water as his main drinks.
- A mix of supplements containing magnesium, potassium, calcium, vitamin D, omega-3 fatty acids, fiber, B vitamins, iron, zinc, and vitamin C. Chia seeds provided a significant part of this.

Artie was aware that his life now contained a number of ironies. Perhaps the most obvious was that now that his life was definitely over, it had finally begun. Whilst he spent many years poisoning his body when he could have prolonged his life, he was now following the ancient dictum, "Make food your medicine," despite the fact that he knew it could not cure him. And while he had arguably nothing to live for, he had suddenly found a more intense sense of purpose than he could ever have imagined.

He was often reminded of Friedrich Nietzsche's quote: "He who has a why to live for can bear almost any how." And of Viktor Frankl, the Jewish psychiatrist and holocaust survivor who had created logotherapy, building directly on Nietschze's quote. Logotherapy took the position that whatever a patient's symptoms, the key was to help them find their purpose in life, rather than curing the symptoms. Artie liked to think that Frankl, and maybe even Nietzsche, would enjoy watching his journey, which would be a perfect case study in logotherapeutic success.

Every now and then, he wondered whether giving himself one thousand days to prepare before taking action was too slow. However, Artie felt that it was critical to prepare well so that he was able to handle more challenging interventions and make no mistakes in execution. He thought of the opening stages in games like chess and go. Amateurs often rush through them, but professionals know that the opening is where the potential is set for the whole game. He was also somehow inspired by the Einstein quote, "If I had an hour to solve a problem, I'd spend fifty-five minutes thinking about the problem and five minutes thinking about solutions."

Not quite the same thing, but it inspired him to be deliberate and thorough in his preparations.

37. March 12, 2012. Old Town, Chicago. Day -381.

Artie had always been into theory and abstraction. Even in his previous life. He used to consider it a bit of a weakness and an indulgence, because he knew a lot and thought a lot, but couldn't do much. He could tell you the names of almost every martial art from every country in his previous life, but he couldn't defend himself on the street. He had an advanced understanding of computer algorithms, but almost every device with a digital clock he had ever bought was still flashing zeros on the display because he hadn't worked out how to set them.

But he had always known in his heart of hearts that theory and abstraction are useful, particularly when combined with practical knowledge and practice. He had heard once that one of the Greek Philosophers, maybe Plato, talked about a triangle of knowledge. Practical things like building a wall or cooking chicken schnitzel were at the bottom of the triangle. Super useful in a narrow set of circumstances, but not generalizable. Patterns like general construction and cooking techniques were a little higher in the triangle. Much higher were general knowledge about problem-solving, listening to feedback, learning, and thinking. The higher up you go, the more widely applicable something is, but it requires work to be immediately and practically useful. When he first heard about this triangle, Artie spent some time contemplating what might be at the very top, the point. He never really got to an answer, but it was a fun ride.

Now that he was fully immersed in his thousand-day preparations, he intentionally balanced his time across the levels of the triangle. There was a very heavy emphasis on practical stuff like fighting and first aid, but he also made time for some abstract learning about how to succeed in his mission. One area he went after here was tactics. Stratagems to win. He read a bunch of books on the subject and distilled out his thoughts on when to use each tactic, and how to do it well.

He drew his main ideas from seven books: "The Book of Five Rings" by Miyamoto Musashi. "Finite and Infinite Games" by James P. Carse. "The Art of War" by Sun Tzu. "On War" by Carl von Clausewitz. "The 48 Laws of Power" by Robert Greene. "The Unfettered Mind," an anthology of three letters from Zen master Takuan Soho to Swordsman Yagyu Munenori. "The Art of Strategy" by Dixit and Nalebuff. "The Direction of Play", a book of advanced tactics for winning at the board game Go.

He knew there were many other sources of tactical thought. Machiavelli's "The Prince", for example. But these seven seemed enough. And, in fact, Green's book referenced Machiavelli and many others. He realized that "The Art of War" was perhaps the most famous, but in his eyes, it was also the weakest and most obvious. Towards the bottom of the triangle. "The Unfettered Mind" was probably top for him.

In order to remember the more than one hundred distinct tactics that he learned and thought of himself, he categorized them into three types. Attacks on the spirit of the opponent. Attacks on their mind. And attacks on their body/resources.

An example of the first is deliberately giving the opponent a way out, as a way of weakening their will to fight. (The opposite of burning bridges behind you so there is no return without winning.)

An example of the second is a feinting strategy, where you send false signals to the enemy to confuse them. Like pretending to strike in one area/ way, so they defend against the feint, leaving them open to attack in other areas.

An example of a body-based stratagem is to strike at an opponent's weak point, their Achilles heel.

Some of them had fancy names, like *"Beat the grass to reveal the snakes,"* or *"Rat's head, Ox's neck."* But some were much more plain, like *"Brute force"* or *"Divide and conquer."*

At this point, Artie had gathered and thought of more than one hundred stratagems, that fell satisfyingly and usefully fairly equally into the three categories of spirit, mind, and body. He was now spending time trying to make decision trees to help decide which stratagems to pick under what circumstances.

He knew that he would have to adapt his plans in real-time based on unexpected events. He was reminded of the boxer Mike Tyson's famous statement that everyone has a plan until they get punched in the face. But he liked the idea of starting off before an intervention with a prioritized set of three or four stratagems to use. To tilt the balance in his favor.

This compendium of tactics with advice on when to use them would make a very attractive book for many different types of readers. He imagined the title *"The Essence of Stratagems."* In his previous life, he fantasized about writing such books and them becoming bestsellers. Those kinds of motivation were gone now. He was writing this book for his own use, and a very small, select audience who would emerge later. Which somehow made it much, much easier for him to write. He had gotten out of his own way.

38. May 2, 2012. Old Town, Chicago. Day - 330.

As well as Artie's meticulous and demanding exercise regime and more serious studies of martial arts, he was forcing himself to read what one might describe as Southeast Asian pulp fiction and non-fiction books. They are often written by world foreign journalist and author wannabes who end up living in those countries. They usually don't make it out of local bookshops and airports. They are often rather poorly written and sensationalist. They usually deal with dark and dirty subjects. Crime. Corruption. Prostitution. Drug Use. Trafficking of humans and contraband. The knowledge revealed in these books often makes you question the activities and morality of the author.

Perfect fodder for Artie's learning. These books often contained details of the darker side of life that would come in very handy. Last night, Artie finished "*Off the Rails in Phnom Penh*" by Amit Gilboa. Hardly Shakespeare. Artie didn't feel he could trust all the details. But, nevertheless, it provided some great ideas and insight into how the dark economy and its various perpetrators, and victims, in the Khmer kingdom operated.

Artie also read four novels by John Burdett. "*Bangkok 8*," "*Bangkok Tattoo*," "*Bangkok Haunts*," and "*Bangkok Dangerous*." The first was enjoyable, the rest not so much. But the main protagonist was a Thai policeman, and Artie found the books helped him think about law enforcement in the region. Particularly from the perspective of the rank-and-file police officer.

He consumed Jake Needham's books about crime in various Asian cities. Colin Cotterill's mystery series set in Laos. He read "*Sacred Skin*," a book about Thai tattoo artists. The novel "*The Cambodian Book of the Dead*," by Tom Vater, who was also a co-author of "*Sacred Skin*." And "*Bangkok Days*" by Lawrence Osborne.

Perhaps Artie's favorite book in this genre was "*The Chinaman*" by Stephen Leather. Despite the title, it was about an older Vietnamese man with guerilla fighting skills whose daughter gets blown up by Northern Irish terrorists in the UK. The rest of his family had already lost their lives in tragic circumstances, so he had nothing to lose. Quan single-handedly goes after dangerous members of the Irish Republic Army (IRA). Some of his tactics are very smart, and the book explores the life of a vigilante.

Artie didn't take any of these books to be one hundred percent factually accurate. But especially reading them all in a short space of time, Artie was building up what you might call tacit-knowledge-by-proxy.

39. Jan 15, 2013. Old Town, Chicago. Day -72.

Artie practiced wearing one of the prosthetic bellies. He had bought a range of different-sized bellies, designed for actors, each between $80 and $120. Most were made out of silicone, and a few out of foam. Combining that with just the right t-shirt, he felt like he looked very convincingly out-of-shape. The only concern was if someone chose to touch his belly. He had to be hyper-aware of those coming close to him when he wore one of these fake bellies.

The bellies had two purposes. The first was to make him look out-of-shape. Overweight. Weak. Incapable of moving fast or fighting. The second, along with a range of wigs, colored contact lenses, different types of glasses, oils to change the hue of his skin, and a wide variety of clothing, were to help him continually change appearance in small ways, to make himself harder to track.

A friend once insulted Artie by describing him as emotionally labile. He had to look up what the word labile meant. It turns out it meant that his mood was liable to change quickly and easily. His friend meant that he couldn't control his emotions. That stung at the time. It just occurred to Artie that in this next phase of his life, his appearance would be visually labile. In a mathematical sense, Artie's appearance would be a variable, whereas most people's were a constant, at least in the short term.

The irony of the fake bellies was not lost on Artie. For so many years, he had a genuine paunch and dreamed of having a six-pack. Now that his rigorous exercise regime had delivered him that six-pack (in fact, it was more like an eight-pack these days), he hid it behind a prosthetic belly.

He was even doing this at home in Chicago, both to get used to wearing the bellies and to make himself just a little harder to track as he prepared here, even though he couldn't imagine a specific circumstance where that would be an issue.

40. February 3, 2013. Gold Coast, Chicago. Day – 53.

Artie wandered around the large Jewel-Osco's supermarket at the corner of Clark Street and Division Street, with a trolley in hand. Ostensibly, he was doing a weekly shop. And he gathered a fairly predictable set of items in his trolley to perpetuate that image: orange juice, milk, sausages, eggs, potatoes, cheese. But his actual reason for being there was different.

As Artie had read about warriors, after being diagnosed and making his decision, he read a bunch of books about warrior training and warrior mindset. He was surprised to read, in a text about the Samurai, that estimation was an important skill identified for a successful warrior.

Estimating the weight of an object, the distance and time taken to reach a given destination, and the cost of products. These were all very useful skills. Along with the more general skills of logical and critical thinking.

In 1994, as he was graduating, Artie had interviewed with a bunch of companies, because he wasn't sure what he wanted to, or could, do as a career. He interviewed for junior trader and researcher jobs with a few banks. For the management training program with a couple of manufacturing companies. For entry-level positions at management consultancies too.

The management consultancies, especially the elite ones like McKinsey, Boston Consulting Group, and Bain, were famous for their interviewing techniques. Along with other types of interviews, each candidate would typically get either a case study interview, an estimation question, or both.

Artie got through a couple of rounds of interview with McKinsey. One interview included a case study about a Brazilian mayonnaise manufacturer. The manufacturer in question had suddenly become uncompetitive, and the interviewee (Artie) had to ask questions to work out the reason why. (The answer turned out to be because the competitor had a relationship with the manufacturer of glass jars, hence was able to get them at a significant discount.) He also got asked a couple of estimation questions.

He remembered one of the estimation questions was a request to estimate the market for skis in the US. These estimation tests weren't about getting the right answer. They were an opportunity to see how the candidate would approach the problem.

They really liked it if you could use multiple approaches and triangulate them, as a reasonableness test. They also liked it if you 'thought out loud', showing them how you came up with your answer. They quite liked it if you asked how the estimate you came up with would be used, so you could work out how accurate your answer needed to be.

Artie remembered when he faced the market for skis question, he nearly answered with an estimate of how many pairs of skis the US population owns. But that on its own would be an epic fail. There was a need to factor in how many people bought versus rented skis, and also how often people replace/ renew their skis. Artie remembered just in time and, hence, was able to add these considerations to his calculations.

Despite his love of puzzles, the interview process left him with a bad taste in his mouth. The management consultancies let him know that they didn't want him, despite him acing their tests. He also realized that he didn't want them. The work they did seemed interesting, but they reeked of arrogance and self-importance.

Every cloud has a silver lining, though. The skills he learned back then, like triangulation, were really helpful now as he tried to improve his observation, calculation, and estimation skills as much as possible.

As he wandered around the supermarket aisles, he surreptitiously looked into people's shopping carts and tried to infer as much as possible about their lives. Were they single or married? Straight or gay? Own or rent? House or apartment? What kind of work did they do? What kind of car did they drive? How much did they earn? What was their ethnicity?

It was a somewhat unsatisfying game to play since he never got to find out the real answers. But nevertheless, it was a very real way of practicing his deduction skills. He was practicing what he had heard an ex-FBI officer describe as de-anonymization. Taking data that doesn't include identifying information, but using that to build a rich picture of a person.

Artie fervently hoped to bring his 'A Game' in terms of critical thinking, analyzing, and predicting to his mission. Which was looming ever larger as he approached March 28. D-day.

41. *Mar 27, 2013.* Old Town, *Chicago. Day - 1.*

Artie sat at the Ikea desk he had bought and rather clumsily assembled about eight years ago. It had wobbled from the first day he had put it together. Not sure if it was his fault or Ikea's, but he used to use it as evidence that he was a failure. A loser. He never even tried to fix it. Of course, now his head was in a very different place. He wasn't thinking about it much. It was just a reminder of a world he inhabited before. A world without purpose. A world without commitment. A world without direction.

It was 8:42 p.m., and he was flying out in the morning. As with everything these days, he was right on schedule. He had written twenty-three letters already and had three more to complete before 9:30. He started the twenty-fourth letter: "Dear Anna,". He had identified twenty-six people he wanted to write to before he slipped away to his new life. His mission.

Seventeen of the twenty-six letters were written to people who were alive, nine to people who had already died, including both his parents, but he had decided he needed to write letters to them anyway. One of the seventeen letters was to someone he hadn't met yet. In each letter, he communicated directly from the heart to these twenty-six people who had played significant roles in his life. Some of the letters centered around apologies to people he felt he had wronged. In some he allowed himself angry outbursts, berating those who had wronged him. To some others were messages of thanks. To all of them, he included a short explanation of exactly what he planned to do with the rest of his life and why.

He was reminded of a leadership course he once attended at a local night school. The lecturer had asked the students, in the last session of the course, to write a letter to themselves that they would open six months later, telling themselves what they were planning to achieve in those six months.

Finishing the last of the twenty-six letters just before 9:30, he popped it into its envelope and sealed it. He then took the metal tray he had placed at the side of his desk earlier that day and placed it on top of his desk. He put twenty-four of the letters in the tray, and neatly arranged them in a spiral.

He then took the small bottle of methylated spirits on his desk and doused the letters thoroughly, using the whole bottle. Finally, he picked up the box of matches he bought across the street earlier, struck one match, and lit the trayful of letters. He watched them all slowly burn.

Then, at about 9:40, he put the remaining two letters in his already packed hand luggage, went into his bedroom, meditated for fifteen minutes, set his alarm, and then entered a deep, dreamless sleep.

42. *Mar 28, 2013.* Old Town, *Chicago.* Day 0.

Artie got up at 5am and headed straight for the shower. He had left a disposable toothbrush, one of those tiny tubes of toothpaste for travelling, and a disposable razor, on the counter by the sink, all single-use, to be thrown away after he used them this morning.

Considering his life was about to change forever, he was preternaturally calm. One of the many gifts that a sense of purpose gives people. He had finalized his affairs yesterday. The apartment was spotless. The trash had all been taken out and disposed of in various places around the neighborhood. He had been careful not to leave any evidence in his own apartment block's trash, or any two significant items of trash in the same place.

His bags were fully packed. One large suitcase and a backpack for hand luggage. Both were chosen to be very unremarkable colors and designs. A black Samsonite backpack he chose because it looked plain, was a common brand, and was quite functional. It had lots of compartments, including watertight ones to seal wet stuff in.

The suitcase was from American Tourister, one of their lower-end offerings. A hard-cased, dark blue, mid-size suitcase. Less than a hundred dollars. Artie spent some time scuffing them up, so they didn't look brand new. He wasn't 100% sure why he was doing that, but his rule was whenever he had the time, money, and opportunity he would make things seem different from what they actually were.

He would ditch the suitcase soon after he arrived in Bangkok, but for now, he wanted to ensure he seemed like a stereotypical tourist in every way. No anomalies. No red flags.

He left just after 6am and hopped in a cab to O'Hare airport. As he left his apartment for the last time, he put his keys in an envelope and posted them through the door, as agreed with the landlord. No turning back now.

In the cab, he greeted the driver, told him the destination, then slipped his iPod's headphones into his ears and listened to the playlist he had prepared over the last few days. He didn't need music to focus and motivate him, but he thought it might help. It also meant that the driver wouldn't try to converse with him or ask him any questions about himself or his plans.

He had chosen the songs on his playlist mainly for their rhythm, not so much for the theme or topic. He had honed his tastes in music for this next phase of his life during his regular gym visits. It had amazed Artie how much of a difference the right music had made to his performance. It wasn't the loudest, fastest, or most aggressive songs that got Artie going. It was those with a driving, insistent rhythm.

They seemed to give him a quiet determination to fulfill his mission. For the next half hour or so he expected it to take to cover the fifteen-to-twenty-mile journey at this time of day (depending on which route the driver took), he had prepared ten songs.

- "Vengeance" by Zack Hemsey (6m 34s)
- "The Man Who Sold The World" by David Bowie. (4m 3s)
- "Perfect Strangers" by Deep Purple. (5m 21s)
- "Ode to Billie Joe" by Bobby Gentry (4m 15s)
- "Born to Run" by Bruce Springsteen (4m 30s)
- "Seven Nation Army" by The White Stripes (3m 52s)
- "Enter Sandman" by Metallica (5m 32s)
- "Barracuda" by Heart (4m 23s)
- "Sunday Bloody Sunday" by U2 (4m 40s)
- "Because the Night" by Patti Smith (3m 23s)

The total was forty-six minutes and thirty-three seconds. Artie expected that would be more than enough for the ride unless there was some kind of traffic or other problem, in which case he could restart the playlist, or listen to something else.

As they pulled into the airport, he was still enjoying Nancy Wilson's distinctive guitar riffs on Barracuda. He paid the driver and left a decent, but not memorable, tip. At the airport, he went to the bathroom and tweaked his appearance, before he checked in. A habit he had forced himself to get used to in the last few months, and which would be his constant companion for the next few years.

"Good morning Mr Wilson. I see you will be flying to Bangkok via Incheon Airport in Seoul. How many bags do you have to check in?"

Artie went through the check-in conversation with the minimum of fuss. In his previous life, he might have hoped for a particular seat or hoped for a check-in staff member who would have a nice conversation with him. That was not his goal today.

He passed through security with no problems, then found himself airside by 8:30am, in plenty of time for his 10:40 flight. So far, so good. Everything smooth. Everything safe and conservative. Every step unmemorable.

And every step irreversible. Although he had bought a return ticket, Artie would never use the homebound leg. Unless something very wrong and very out of Artie's control happened, this was the last time he would be here on American soil.

He popped into the airside bathrooms to do another small appearance change, involving a baseball cap, glasses, and colored contact lenses. He bought a bottle of water and then sat in an area of the airport that seemed the least densely populated. He nibbled on a protein bar he had brought with him and spent the time calmly going through his plans.

Then he heard the call for his flight. He was traveling on a Delta Airlines ticket, operated by Korean Airways, via Seoul, so he had to listen for flight KE38. As soon as he heard the announcement, he got up and walked in a medium-paced, measured way to gate M7.

As he walked, he thought of some lyrics from the Dire Straits song "Private Investigations," from their wonderfully atmospheric album "Love Over Gold": "...*the game commences// for the usual fee // plus expenses...*"

Section 2 – Chuban

The middle game in Go is called chuban. This is where all the action takes place. The strategic potential set out in the opening is either realized or it is not. On rare occasions, players could overturn their weak opening, and turn the tables on their opponents. Success in the middle game requires discipline, focus and the ability to adapt as the nature of the game and one's opponent's plans reveal themselves.

On the vast 19 x 19 Go board, the middle game consists of many battles, both important in themselves, and also in terms of the ripple effects they have on the rest of the board. A great Go player has to both commit to and concentrate on each battle, but at the same time be aware of the bigger picture, the overall war for territory.

Artie read a book during his undergraduate years called *"Finite and Infinite Games."* It was a very unusual little book. Written by a New York University professor of history and religion called James P. Carse. It was probably Artie's favorite book of all. One of the beautiful notions in the book was the distinction the author made between education and training.

Carse argued that training was an attempt to get you to bring things to a previously studied, known conclusion. To close down surprises and possibilities. Education, on the other hand, was the opposite. Allowing you to open up to play and possibility. Artie never forgot the language Carse used about this. He argued that training could be viewed as the triumph of the past over the future, whereas education was a triumph of the future over the past. Education could allow you to reinterpret things you had already experienced, things you thought you already knew, in the light of new things happening.

In the middle game of Go, as fights from all over the board began to influence each other, Artie viscerally felt this concept of the future making you reinterpret the past. Making you reexamine situations you thought were already decided. Already dead. This was one of the main reasons Artie loved Go, and considered it a whole other level of game to chess and other strategy games.

As well as playing strongly to make and secure territory in Go's middle game, sometimes there is a need to play very lightly and adaptively in the enemy's strongholds, in order to survive and destroy or massively reduce the enemy's territory.

This light, flexible spirit is known as Sabaki.

43. May 7, 2013. Near Luang Prabang, Laos.

As he was installing the door reinforcement bars, he decided that that was enough for now. Known as "London bars" in the UK, these bars made it much harder to force the front door open. The ones Artie had installed would withstand a substantial battering ram. He could continue adding safety features and making the house more and more comfortable. But he was on a clock. And to some extent on a budget. And this felt sufficient to him. More than sufficient for the house's purpose.

The four-bedroom, slightly run-down house itself had cost 160 million Lao *kip*, equivalent to twenty thousand dollars at current exchange rates. But, with the various additions and extensions Artie had had added, and those that he installed himself, the total came to about seventy thousand dollars.

The main cost was an extensive security system. It included a home alarm, multiple internal and external cameras with night vision, and heat and pressure sensors all over the house and the grounds. Artie had also installed an internet server with redundant connections to the wired internet and satellites, that allowed him to monitor the cameras, even when he wasn't there.

He had also created a basement with a panic room. Popular with the rich and famous back in the US, a panic room was a room that residents could get into and lock in the case of home invasion, with very hard-to-penetrate fire-proof doors and walls, a hard-to-disrupt supply of air, water, and power, and multiple phone lines and satellite connections.

Artie first heard of these when he watched the 2002 movie called "Panic Room", starring Jodie Foster and Forest Whitaker. Not either of those great actors' finest hours in Artie's opinion. But the relatively simple home invasion plot hadn't detracted from Artie's enjoyment. One of his great skills was to be able to suspend disbelief, forgive a movie for its failings, immerse himself in it, and enjoy the best things about it. In the case of "Panic Room", the room itself was the real star. Or at least the concept of it was.

Artie had also provided his panic room with a supply of long-life foods and a variety of weaponry. The foods included a bunch of canned goods, peanut butter, energy, and protein bars, and some vacuum-packed jerky. He had procured a whole bunch of bottled water and some powdered milk for it too.

He was hoping hard that he or anyone else would never have to use this room, but if they did, up to ten people could probably spend a good six months down here. When Artie was preparing for this phase of his life, he researched the people in the US known as *preppers*, people who were ready for outcomes like a zombie apocalypse. He thought their fears were a bit crazy, but they had very rationally prepared a wide range of accommodations for such an event. There was much for him to learn.

When Artie was preparing back home, he read a philosophical idea that the winners learned from everywhere, including their enemies. You don't have to approve of someone, their ideology, or their motives to learn from them. Learning should be amoral. The famous martial artist Bruce Lee put it so well: "Absorb what is useful. Discard what is useless."

Artie tried to learn from those who had similar challenges to him, but not similar morals. Terrorists, organized criminals, pornographers, and human traffickers. If you stripped away the moral depravity of their goals, they were operating under difficult conditions, outside the law, under the radar, trying not to get caught. Artie's enemies were his teachers. Teaching him how to succeed and remain anonymous. And as a bonus, they were also teaching him how to beat them when they were his targets.

Artie had purchased all the more 'exotic' additions to this place himself in Thailand and Vietnam. Partly because they weren't available in Laos, and partly just to throw any interested parties off the scent. He had driven them over the border and installed them himself. As well as the security system, Artie's extensions included two emergency power generators, three really excellent bathrooms, with Japanese-style deep but not long baths, and powerful showers. They would help him and the temporary residents that Artie expected to live here from time to time to recover, relax, and feel better about themselves.

His final addition was a match-quality pool table. Set up in the basement, alongside the panic room. Partly for him to relax. Partly to practice, since hustling pool would be one of his main ways of making money in this next phase of his life. This table was a nine-foot regulation-size table. The playing surface was 100 inches long by 50 inches wide. The felt was a kind of cyan color. Artie had ensured that there was more than five feet of clearance on all sides of the table, so players could make shots from all positions unimpeded, even with a generous backswing.

Artie had chosen a table from Brunswick Billiards. Not the cheapest, but worth the investment. He had spent just over $4000 on one of Brunswick's mid-range tables. It would have been possible to spend more than $10,000 on the very best ones but Artie had felt that unnecessary. He had spent another thousand dollars on five cues and accessories.

Wooden racks for both eight-ball and nine-ball. Table lighting, a scoreboard, rests, a table brush, tools to repair the tip of the cues, chalk, talcum powder, and a powder dispenser. Talc was particularly important in hot, humid countries to stop your hands from getting sticky while playing. Not handling that issue was a rookie error in this part of the world, because the cue no longer ran smoothly over your bridge hand.

The one facet of the house that Artie did not renovate was the outside. He ensured that the foundations of the house were secure and that it was free from mold. But he wanted the outside to look a bit run down. Nothing special. Matching its surroundings. Not worthy of anyone's attention. Even the entrance area inside the front door was left a bit tired looking, just in case unexpected visitors, such as delivery staff, got a quick peek.

Artie had named the house Oasis in his head shortly after he bought it. He had always liked the image of an Oasis, both literally and as a metaphor. He once looked up the origins of the word. It had come to English via French, before that Latin, from Greek, and probably originally from a language called Hamitic.

Its origins were in the word for "dwelling place". But it had come to mean any fertile place in the midst of a wasteland. Artie thought this was a perfect name for this place. It worked on a number of levels. No one else got to know the name. There was no sign on the door. No need to draw unwanted attention.

It was 6 p.m. and getting dark. Having grown up far from the equator, it always amazed Artie that here it got light at 6 a.m. and dark at 6 p.m. pretty much every day of the year. In Chicago, in the summer, it got light at about 5:15 a.m. and didn't get dark until about eight thirty at night. In the winter, the sun didn't rise until more like 7:15 in the morning and got dark by 4:20 p.m.

He remembered telling a bar girl about that, and she wouldn't believe him. He realized that if you spent your whole life in a country where sunrise and sunset never varied, you would probably find that really hard to take in. He remembered when he first heard of some places, like Barrow in northern Alaska, which were basically dark all winter and light all summer, it was hard for him to imagine too.

Artie sat on a wooden box in the living room and ate some canned food and protein bars that he had brought with him. He had consciously tried to limit his presence in the local community for now. He was the only white guy around, and as such very noticeable.

It did briefly occur to him that his fantasy house, his ideal living environment had changed three times in his life. When he was young, he fantasized about the standard American dream. A lovely house in a suburb of Chicago, with a wife, two kids, and a dog. When he discovered the pleasures of Southeast Asia, carnal and otherwise, he fantasized about a pool villa somewhere like Hua Hin in Thailand. And now, in this final chapter, his fantasy was an extremely secure, comfortable place for him to base himself, and those he helped to recuperate.

He was reminded of something an old Japanese colleague, Hiro, said to him once.

"Artie. You should think of your life in three phases. Whether you are studying, working, or whatever. In the first phase, you are fundamentally absorbing from the world. Learning. Receiving. In the second phase you are a workhorse, part of the engine of the world. And in the third, you are giving back. Advising others on their way up. You are an elder of the tribe."

Hiro's words struck him as wise back when he first heard them. Now he could see them clearly. He was in the third phase now. Even though it was much faster than he expected. He had taken on the mantle of an elder. Making decisions to help the tribe, for better or for worse. Hopefully for the better. And that was why Oasis was his fantasy base. Not his first dream of a cookie-cutter American family life. Or his second dream of a babe-filled perma-resort.

He played some pool to relax before going to bed. He mainly practiced a particular kind of bank shot, where the object ball bounced off three cushions before landing in the center pocket. It didn't have a specific name in pool but having once played a Scottish guy in a pool hall in Chicago, he learned that in the UK it was called a *cocked-hat-double*. What Artie particularly liked about that shot is that it could easily be interpreted by the untrained eye as a fluke. When high-level players play pool, they may insist that you name the pocket you intend to sink a ball in, and if it ends up in another pocket, it doesn't count as a successful shot. This style of pool is sometimes known as "no slops". But the kind of pool Artie would be required to play over the next few years, hustling tourists who were casual players, would not require any such constraints. So, the cocked-hat-double would be a particularly useful tool to have in Artie's kit bag.

At 7 p.m., Artie called it a night. He did some stretching, fifteen minutes of meditation, and then lay down and fell asleep almost instantly. "*A good day's work*" was Artie's last conscious thought of the day.

44. June 2, 2013. Bangkok.

"*Singha?*" the waitress asked. "*Yes, please,*" Artie replied. When he drank beer for pleasure in his previous life, Artie preferred Chang, or at least Singha Gold. In his eyes, Singha was the second worst Thai beer, after Leo. Amongst foreigners, Singha was known to bestow upon its consumers a mighty hangover the next day. Artie had heard rumors that was due to the chemicals used in the brewing process, but he didn't know for sure. It could also be because those foreigners drinking it were drinking maybe a dozen of them in a night, not drinking water, and getting badly dehydrated.

When he saw working-class Thais sitting around having a drink, they were often drinking a strong colorless alcohol known as *lao khao* (เหล้าขาว), which literally meant white spirit. Often containing more than 40% alcohol, most regular drinkers of *lao khao* ended up as alcoholics with liver problems.

Artie was spending these first few days in the field learning the ropes. Sitting in bars, restaurants, and adult-oriented clubs. Riding the bus, the Skytrain, the underground. Taxis, motorbikes, and tuk-tuks. Looking around temples, shopping malls, food courts, outside markets. Even the infamously hot and oppressive Jatujak market.

He had once read about the famous black cab drivers in London. In order to pass the very rigorous tests required to get a black cab license, trainees would buy a cheap moped and drive around London for two or three years, learning every road, famous building, and landmark. They would then be tested by inspectors who were ex-policemen, asking questions like "what's the quickest route from Camden Town to Heathrow Airport on a Sunday afternoon." The ones who made it through that grilling really knew London. Artie was trying to do the same with Bangkok.

Famous and popular with Thais and tourists alike, Bangkok's Jatujak market seemed to go on forever and contained every type of shop, from tourist tat to expensive paintings. From noodle restaurants to pet stores. It was so big that it was almost impossible to avoid getting lost at some point.

The only bigger, more overfacing market Artie knew of was the Qingping market in Guangzhou in mainland China. He went there briefly in his previous life as a tourist. Like Japan, he found it much less 'user-friendly' than Southeast Asia, but fascinating, nonetheless. Qingping market was absolutely huge, and seemed to have everything you could possibly imagine. One famous aspect of that market was that there was an area full of animals to be bought as pets. Another area was full of animals to take home, kill, and eat. Some species of animal were unlucky enough to feature in both areas.

Artie remembered eating a scorpion on a stick bought from a street stall in Qingping market. He experienced an intense burning sensation around the outside of his mouth for a few hours that day. Later that night, his hotel concierge explained that that happened when the scorpion's poison had not been completely cleaned out.

Artie knew that Thailand was not the only place where his mission would take place, but he figured that it would host at least 60% of his interventions. And he estimated that Bangkok would provide the backdrop for more than half of those.

So, he was spending a few days getting acclimatized and observing as much as he could. He had been in all these types of places and used all the modes of transport before, back when he was a sex tourist. When he was both perpetrator and victim. When he was the sucker in the room.

He needed to see these places through new eyes now. He remembered years ago studying the notion of the drama triangle. The drama triangle was a theory that suggested in any difficult situation, people tend to place one of three roles: the perpetrator, the victim, and the savior. People who aren't very good at coaching, mentoring, or helping tend to jump immediately to the role of savior, assuming the perpetrator is wholly evil, the victim is wholly right, and leaping to the victim's defense.

In fact, as we all know, things are often more complicated than that. And even if they are exactly like that, it often benefits the advisor to remain a bit neutral, at least for a while, to try to understand the context, the history, and everyone's perspective.

So here he sat, in a bar rather oddly named "Happy Happy III", sipping a beer for show, trying to understand the movements, tactics, and perspectives of all the stakeholders. The mama-san. The barman. The waitresses who brought you drinks. The 'ladies' who sat with the customers encouraged them to drink more, tip more, and maybe take them home. The guy in the toilet who offered you a hot towel and a mint after you peed. (He even massaged Artie's shoulders while he peed, which Artie found highly surprising, and not very welcome.) And the customers.

Artie tried to observe everything going on. Unobviously, of course. He had seen it all before. Been in a bar like this many times. But never with this motive. Like a hawk studying its prey before diving.

When the waitresses brought drinks, they took the customers' money and brought back the change on a tray. If the foreigners left the money on the tray as a tip, the waitresses had to give the tip to the mama-san, who noted it down and gave them half of it as a kickback at the end of the night. If the customers gave the tip to them in their hands, they got to keep all of it, although he noticed that some of them still gave some of that money to the mama-san to keep her sweet. Most of the customers seemed blissfully unaware of these two forms of tipping.

When a customer paid the bar fine to the mama-san to release their lady for the night, they sometimes stayed drinking for a while, and sometimes they left the bar immediately. Just before they left the bar, the lady went into the back room to change clothes. They sometimes continued their skimpily-clad, highly made-up look. Other times they dressed much more conservatively, so their profession would not be so obvious on the walk back to the customer's hotel. Sometimes this choice seemed to be made based on an explicit decision with their customer. Sometimes through their intuition about what the customer wanted. Which was nearly always right.

Occasionally he felt that they deliberately dressed provocatively to leave the bar with their customer, to kind of torture the customer as they walked past everyone on the way to their hotel and through the lobby of the hotel. Artie remembered one particular night in his previous life. He was fairly new to the experience of bringing a bar girl home, and he ended up in the elevator of his hotel with two very attractive, very provocatively dressed companions.

Their clothes were what Japanese people would call *bodycon*, standing for body conscious, meaning figure hugging. That night, the other occupants of the elevator were a family of five. Mom, dad, three kids, two of whom were very young, one who was a teenage boy. Artie and his two friends had gotten into the elevator first, and he was desperately hoping for the doors to shut before anyone else got in. But just as they shut, the dad ran to the doors, pried them open, then signaled for his family to jump in. Before he had realized who the other occupants were.

There was not one word spoken in that elevator. The short time they were all together in that confined space felt to Artie like it was going on forever. There was all sorts of eye contact and eye contact avoidance.

The family was very well dressed. Much smarter than your average Bangkok tourist. The two young kids were blissfully unaware of what was going on but felt the tension. The parents clearly just wanted this shared experience to be over as soon as possible. The teenage boy felt the need to show his disgust at what was going on. He was young and idealistic. Ironically, although Artie was the target of his disgust, Artie admired him.

He also registered that the boy's mom had a very complicated look on her face. On the one hand, Artie believed she was very proud of her son for understanding what was going on with Artie and his companions, and not approving. On the other hand, he thought she was hoping and praying that her son didn't say or do anything and cause an incident.

Artie was mortified throughout the whole time they were together. The two girls, on the other hand, had developed a very thick skin and thought it was hilarious. I think they liked the fact that their customer had to suffer a bit. They probably thought he deserved it. They were, of course, right.

Back at the bar, it was amazing how the customers fit national stereotypes. The Japanese were often very drunk and matter-of-fact about picking up girls. The Russians and Israelis were a bit aggressive. The Brits fell into two camps, either timid and nervous, or overly loud, boisterous hooligans. The Arabs were quietish. And Artie's fellow Americans were fairly relaxed, like they were at a simple sports bar or a Hooters. A simple bar where they were guaranteed to get lucky at the end of the night.

Very occasionally there were Thai customers there, but usually only to accompany visiting foreigners. Occasionally there were foreign female customers present, either in hen groups or accompanying their men. Artie hadn't ever seen a lone, female customer yet.

Tonight, the only guy who looked out of place was an older Asian man. Short with longish, unkempt white hair and a beard. He was smoking a cigar, chatting to the mama-san a little, and laughing a lot. Artie couldn't quite fit him into any category, and he only stayed a short while.

At around 11 p.m., Artie made his way out, handing the waitress who served him and the mama-san a few hundred baht each, enough to be a generous tip, but not enough for them to single him out and identify him as a 'hot prospect'.

He picked up a bunch of bottled water at one of the many 7-11s near his hotel. The density of 7-11 stores in Bangkok was unbelievable to Artie. And he knew that working-class Thais loved them. Partly for the snacks and drinks they offered. But also because they all had the air conditioning cranked up high. A welcome break from the never-ending sweltering heat and humidity in the Land of Smiles, as Thailand was sometimes called.

He sat drinking a bunch of water while making some notes to remind himself of everything he'd seen tonight. He then did a few minutes of stretching. Then meditated. He lay his head down to sleep at nearly midnight, happy and confident that he had done a good day's (and night's) work. One step further in fulfilling his mission.

45.   Aug 28, 2013. Bangkok.

Artie left his fairly basic, spartan room in the Honey Hotel on Sukhumvit Soi 19, and strolled casually towards the main road. One of the motorcycle taxi gang members, hanging around on the street corner, shouted out to Artie as he saw him coming: *"Hey pumpui, you late today."* Pumpui meant 'fatty' in Thai, but wasn't considered quite as rude as it would be in English.

Many major roads in Thailand have side roads, called sois. They sometimes have names, but generally go by numbers, and are a good way to navigate. Public transport tends to run along the major roads, but not down the sois, which are often narrow and in poor repair. But some of the sois are really long, taking more than half an hour to walk down.

As a solution to this, many of the larger sois have motorcycle taxi gangs at the junction of the Soi with the main road. They operate a bit like gangs, tend to have fluorescent vests with their gang's logo on, and are fiercely territorial. It is also very common for them to take drugs to keep themselves going.

Artie had been staying in the same hotel, and walking to Soi Cowboy, one of the famous Bangkok 'adult entertainment' areas every night for the last two weeks. It was like that a lot around here. *Farangs* (foreigners) showed up, stayed a couple of weeks, then left again. While they were here, they often developed their own little routines, having breakfast at the same place, going to the same bars, and finishing their nights in the same restaurants in the early hours of the morning, sometimes alone, sometimes accompanied. The local Thais got to recognize them from their daily routines, sometimes even when they came back months later. Hotel workers. The staff at the local 7/11. Restaurant waiters. Taxi drivers. And, of course, the women who worked in the bars. For them, carefully noting these farangs, assessing their behaviors, and influencing their choices was a core competence and source of competitive advantage.

Artie looked very standard for this kind of tourist. A little overweight. Poor posture. Some very questionable fashion choices. (Are shorts with full-length socks and sandals ever okay?) He smiled back at the motorbike guy, pretending not to understand, and pretending to be a little afraid of him, like he used to be a few years ago.

As Artie entered Princess Queen bar, all the staff chorused "*Welcome*" in Thai-accented English. Maybe Artie would transliterate it something like "*Wew-caam.*" In the half-second they looked at him, each performed their own sophisticated estimate of where he was from, what his job and his salary were, what he liked and was looking for, what he might be worth to them, whether he was dangerous and/or gullible, and the best attack vectors to influence him.

Artie's strategy was well-honed these days. He would buy a beer (which he wouldn't normally drink), tip the mama-san five hundred baht, and two or three of the girls two or three hundred baht each, explaining to them quietly, in English, that he just wanted to sit and drink, and wasn't looking for company.

He got them to secure him a seat in an unobtrusive part of the bar. He did all this in a way that was a careful balance between on the one hand making it clear that he knew how things worked and he wasn't looking for anything more than a beer and a quiet place to sit, and on the other hand, appearing to be a relatively ignorant foreigner. Most of all, he didn't want to be very memorable to anyone. Which was a tough trick to pull off with the observational skills of everyone who worked there.

46. Aug 29, 2013. Bangkok.

"They love it they do. Dirty bitches. I took two of them home last night. Promised them two thousand Baht each but kicked them out with one thousand between them because they wouldn't let me give it to them up the ass. That will teach them who's boss. I could easily have forced them to, but I am not that kind of guy. You know what I mean?" So said Veteran Bill, sitting in his camouflage gear and baseball cap.

Artie listened, nodded, and laughed, not quite in Bill's group, but close enough for it to make sense for him to be listening and making appreciative signals. Artie doubted at least three aspects of Bill's story: that he could '*easily have forced them to*', that he was not '*that kind of guy*', and that he was actually a decorated war veteran, a fact that everyone learned about Bill within approximately five minutes of meeting him.

Artie had watched Bill for a few days now, seeing how he treated the bar girls, staff in his guest house, street sellers, and others. Tonight, Artie had reached his conclusions and had no more doubts. Over the last few days, he had been getting closer and closer to Bill. Starting off as the invisible grey man in the corner of the bar, and the surer he was that Bill was a target, the closer he got.

As the other customers of the bar slowly peeled away, Artie started buying Bill drinks, and stroking his ego, letting the creep opine about this, that, and the other.

"These girls fucking love sex. And they love it with foreigners. If I didn't pay them, they'd still come looking for it."

Inside, Artie couldn't believe that pretty much everything coming out of this prick's mouth was a self-aggrandizing lie. Was he so stupid to believe his own garbage rhetoric? Or did he need to make it up to protect himself from accepting what a pathetic, evil fuckwit he was?

Although he knew he couldn't break character, Artie felt sorely tempted to lay some truth bombs on this buffoon. He might do that later, as he was meting out the punishment that he had designed for him, but he couldn't do that now. He also consoled himself with the fact that he didn't need to correct this guy. He wouldn't be a danger to anyone anymore after tonight.

Artie had also held a personal value for a long time that you reserved the truth, however hard it was, for those that you loved and cared about. You could let others run around the world thinking whatever dumb thoughts they had, as long as it didn't harm anyone except themselves.

He also felt like trying to explain how things really were to a guy like Bill would be what Thais call "playing violin for a buffalo". (*"See sor hai kwai fang."*) Not too dissimilar from the English "casting pearls before swine". A waste of time.

At about 1am, he told Bill that he knew a great late-night bar with "young chicks that'll let you do whatever you want." Bill liked the sound of that. They left the bar together and strolled down the dark alley that Artie had scouted out when he was here about a month ago, and again, earlier tonight, just to make sure things were as he planned. All the time, Artie stayed alert to who was around, who seemed to be watching, and tried to make the scene look as typical and unmemorable as possible to any observers.

Two-thirds of the way down the alley, Artie quietly reached into his right pants pocket. He had made sure Bill was on his left, to minimize the risk of Bill noticing anything. He probably didn't need to be so cautious, but there was no downside to it, so he did. He pulled out a piece of strong adhesive tape, ripped the back off it, positioned it in his cupped right hand, then in one quick movement, grabbed the back of Bill's head with his left hand, and slammed his cupped right hand over Bill's mouth, sealing it with tape.

To say Bill was shocked would be the understatement of the year. Despite his considerable alcoholic lubrication, Bill's eyes opened wider than they ever had before. The combination of thinking Artie was a bit of a weak non-entity, thinking Artie was a fellow seedy pleasure seeker, and generally just thinking he himself was a king of the world, made this a considerable left turn in Bill's expected evening.

While Bill was still stunned, making bubbling noises through his nose, Artie twisted to his left and brought his right knee up fast into Bill's solar plexus, making him double over in pain. Artie then pushed Bill into the small clearing that he had prepared in advance. Bill was pretty helpless, and Artie positioned him, like a mannequin, into a seated position with his back resting against a small tree. Artie sat opposite him, made sure he had Bill's full attention, then he began:

"You behaved monstrously towards the bar girls you took home, and arrogantly and unkindly to all the service staff you encountered here. As such, I am going to visit monstrous cruelty on you. Partly because you deserve it, and partly so that you will never be able to repeat those behaviors. You will be dead in about fifteen minutes. They are going to feel like a very long fifteen minutes for you."

Artie then went to work on Bill exactly as he had planned. When he was planning his mission, he debated whether he should cause his targets pain or not. On the one hand, it seemed unnecessary since he was taking them out of the gene pool. But something deep within him insisted that it was their karmic destiny to be paid back for the pain they inflicted on others.

He was reminded of a Thai phrase he had heard bargirls say a few times. *"sŏm nám-nâa"*. Literally meaning 'serve your face', it was used to mean you got what you deserved.

Artie did a few things to make the body harder to identify, then buried it shallowly. He didn't expect it would take too long before it was found or identified. His actions were just calculated moves to continually tilt things in his favor. Making it just a bit harder and slower to reveal the facts about Bill. Wearing different colored contact lenses for this 'Bill episode'. Using a different-sized prosthetic belly. Nothing foolproof. Just the combination of everything that makes it statistically very unlikely he would get caught and prevented from completing his mission.

As he had planned, Artie hadn't got any blood on his body or clothes, so he could just walk away quietly, into the night.

Before sleeping that night, Artie got out a small notebook, opened it to the middle, and then added one stroke to a partially written Chinese character. There was one character already written, consisting of five pen strokes. 正. A total of seven strokes were on the page now.

47. October 4, 2013. Bangrak, Bangkok.

Artie leaned back unobtrusively against the warm, rough texture of the street wall; his gaze fixed across the bustling Soi. Bangkok's relentless energy buzzed around him, a symphony of honking tuk-tuks and vibrant street vendors. But his attention was drawn elsewhere, to a grand house that stood like a quiet, dark fortress amidst the chaos.

He'd been observing the house for a few days, its inhabitants a wealthy Thai family known for their big business deals and a rumored streak of cruelty. Artie's interest, however, was piqued not by the family's wealth but by their young maid, Kwang. She was from the northeast, her darker skin and modest demeanor a sharp contrast to the opulent world she served.

Artie had first heard of Kwang's predicament from her sister, Kim, who worked in a small bar in the middle of Patpong.

Each day, Kwang would emerge just as the sun began its descent, her small frame swallowed by the oversized apron she wore. She moved with a practiced efficiency, sweeping the front porch or tending to the ornate garden that bordered the house. Her movements were graceful, yet there was a weariness in her eyes that spoke of long hours and little rest. And almost no remuneration. Yet there was something about Kwang's quiet dignity that struck a chord in him.

Artie noted the way the family treated her, their voices sharp and demeaning. The matriarch, a tall woman with a permanent scowl, seemed particularly harsh. She would stand, arms folded, issuing a barrage of commands. Kwang would nod, her voice barely above a whisper, and continue her work without complaint. Artie also witnessed her slapping Kwang across the face once. He was sure it was not the first time.

One evening, as the sky painted itself in shades of orange and purple, Artie watched a particularly cruel exchange. The youngest son, a boy of about fifteen, had carelessly knocked over an expensive-looking plant pot in the garden. The crash had drawn the family out, and the matriarch's wrath was immediate.

"*Why do we pay for such incompetence?*" she hissed in Thai, her eyes fixed on Kwang. "*You should have been watching him! I'm docking you one week's pay.*"

Kwang bowed her head, murmuring an apology, even though the fault was clearly not hers. The family berated her for several more minutes before retreating back into their house, leaving her alone to clean up the mess. Artie felt a surge of anger. He'd seen this kind of injustice many times before, the strong preying on the weak. Artie knew from Kim that Kwang could not easily leave her job for several reasons, including a large gambling debt that her father had incurred before passing away from cirrhosis of the liver. That debt had been sold to this family.

Tonight was moonless, which was perfect for Artie. The darkness formed a cloak for his intentions. He slipped through the shadows, his years of training making him a ghost in the urban landscape. He reached the house, its walls looming high but not insurmountable.

Using a grappling hook, he scaled the wall, landing silently in the lush garden. He moved with purpose, carefully avoiding the gaze of multiple security cameras. His destination was the small back room where Kwang slept.

Artie found Kwang's door quickly and briefly noted that it only locked from the outside. He gently pushed it open. The room was small, sparsely furnished with a thin mattress on the floor and a small table. Kwang was asleep, her face peaceful in the moonlight that filtered through the window.

Artie took a deep breath and gently shook Kwang awake. Her eyes flew open, fear evident in their depths. Artie quickly hushed her, speaking softly in Thai. "*Mâi dtông kangwon. Chăn yùu tîi nîi pêua chûay kun.*" The phrase Artie had learned in ten languages back in Chicago. Meaning "*Don't worry. I am here to help you.*"

He called Kim on the phone, and she explained to Kwang that Artie was going to help her escape from this employment and ensure there were no negative consequences for her or her family.

Kwang instinctively hugged Artie. He signaled for her to wait quietly in her room for a few minutes. Sadly, Kwang was used to taking orders and was very good at it. Fortunately, this time they were being given to her for the right reasons.

Artie walked down the hall to Mr. and Mrs. Lee's bedroom, while placing a black balaclava over his head. He entered the beautifully decorated master bedroom. One wall was almost covered with a huge, flat grey slab of stone, and had water constantly trickling down it. Artie saw the elegantly appointed bathroom, with two showers, a free-standing bath, and two sinks. There was a high-tech Japanese toilet next to it. One of the high-end ones, with its buttons on the wall, rather than on the side of the toilet, which Artie often found quite hard to reach.

The room was not quite dark. There was a nightlight coming from the bathroom, and the light had been left on in the walk-in closet that clearly belonged to Mrs. Lee. There was a second walk-in closet with men's clothes in it, but that one was dark.

Artie pulled out a roll of black tape from his pocket. He used his knife to cut off two pieces, each about 15 centimeters long. He quickly and expertly slapped the tape over the man's and the woman's mouth simultaneously. As they woke up with a start, Artie held a knife to Mr. Lee's throat. They both made unusual high-pitched gurgling noises.

"Listen to me very carefully, Mr. and Mrs. Lee. I will not repeat myself. Nod if you understand me."

Both nodded. Artie already knew that they both spoke fluent English.

"I am removing Kwang from your employment tonight. You will never see her again. If you look for her or contact her, or any of her family, I will come back here and slowly torture and kill your

children in front of you. And then torture you. Nod if you understand."

Both nodded again.

"You will not breathe a word of tonight's activities to anyone. If anyone asks about Kwang, you will tell them that her mother got sick, and she chose to go home to Isaan. If you choose to employ someone to replace her, you will give them a decent salary, say 30,000 Baht per month. Two days off per week. And four weeks holiday per year. If I hear any differently, I will come back to visit you. Understand?"

Both nodded yet again.

"I am a serious man, Mr. and Mrs. Lee. And I have many equally serious, loyal, capable friends. To show that I am a man of my word, I will now stab you very shallowly in the leg, Mr. Lee. Take this as a demonstration that my words are not idle threats."

Artie pulled a stiletto flick-knife out of his pants pocket and stabbed Mr. Lee lightly just above the right knee. Lee's taped mouth made a groaning noise. Bubbles of spittle escaped through the edges of the tape.

"I considered killing you both because of the way you have treated Kwang. I decided not to, at least for now. Don't make me come back and change my mind. Stay in this bed, without removing the tape from your mouths for at least 60 minutes."

Artie did a brief scan of the room and relieved the Lees of about 100,000 Baht.

In the car, driving Kwang to Hualamphong coach station, Artie gave Kwang an envelope containing the 100,000 Baht. They had established that they didn't share a language, so Kwang just looked Artie in the eye and nodded.

At the station, they met Kim, who Artie had previously given a larger sum of money, meaning that the sisters could return together to their hometown. Artie deeply hoped that they, and those around them, would make good choices with the rest of their lives.

The sisters hugged and cried together for what seemed like a very long time to Artie. He stood quietly with no expression, his heart full of happiness and a feeling of purpose.

They then turned to him and gave him a very sincere form of the *wai*, the Thai traditional greeting. He bowed to them and left.

9.

48. Nov 13, 2013. Angeles City, Philippines.

1. Hold the hands to the heavens.
2. Draw the bow.
3. Separate heaven and earth.
4. Wise owl gazes backwards.
5. Sway the head and shake the tail.
6. Two hands hold the feet.
7. Clench the fists to glare fiercely.
8. Bouncing on the toes.

Artie completed these eight movements that comprised the Eight Section Brocade (*bā duàn jǐn*), a centuries-old Chinese exercise practice that was considered part of the discipline called *qi gong*. He believed that he could feel his internal energy, his *qi*, flow better after completing the routine.

Then he sat down quietly next to his tent, in the middle of some woods just outside Angeles City. Its full name, El Pueblo de Los Ángeles translated as "The Town of the Angels" which was somewhat sad and ironic, Artie had always thought. He was aware of a concept called nominative determinism, which was usually applied to people. That concept suggested that the job you chose, the path you chose in life, was in some way influenced by your name. A John Baker might become a cook, for example.

In the case of Angeles City, it was more a case of nominative anti-determinism. A sarcastic joke by the gods. Influenced by the long presence of the US Clark Air Force base, the city had become famous as a den of iniquity, a place of nighttime entertainment for drunken servicemen. Fields Avenue in Balibago closely resembled Walking Street in Pattaya and Soi Cowboy and Patpong in Bangkok.

The closing of the base in 1991 didn't change the red-light persona that this city of angels had adopted. It was still plentifully populated with bars filled with *kalapating mababa ang lipad*. This term in Tagalog literally translates to 'low flying doves' and was the rather elegant term for the rather inelegant profession of the ladies (and men) of the night.

Earlier that day, Artie had bought a few items in Angeles's hardware shops. A short, stubby screwdriver, a small bag of cross-headed screws, a file for sharpening metal, a pair of strong bolt cutters, and some small steel brackets, designed to hold shelves up. Even looking at them together, it would be hard for anyone to guess why he had bought them, but he separated the purchases across 4 shops to make his trail just a little harder to follow.

He was pleased to be able to say thank you to each shopkeeper in the local language, *Kapampangan*. *"Maraming Salamat"*. Even though that was the only thing he could say (he could say a little more in Tagalog, the national language), he hoped that it might give them the impression that he lived there, or at least had spent a lot of time there, maybe as a military man. Constant small untruths, distractions, and diversions to remain as invisible as possible.

One of the shopkeepers was an oldish man with unkempt white hair and a beard, who giggled a lot while he was serving Artie. His laugh was somehow infectious, and Artie ended up laughing along with him for a bit. He looked a little like a guy he had once noticed in a bar in Bangkok, but this guy was a Filipino shopkeeper, and he spoke *Kapampangan*.

Sitting cross-legged by his tent, Artie methodically worked with the tools he had bought. He patiently sharpened the edges of the brackets with the file. He used the bolt cutters to trim the brackets to just the right size. Then he screwed them slowly and methodically into the holes in the corners of the tablet that he had prepared before the trip.

When he took his iPad through customs, no one was going to notice the holes in the corners. Even if they did, he had the story about using those holes to mount it on a wall. When he took his iPad into a bar and sat in the corner with it ostensibly playing a video game, no one was going to notice the thin, sharpened steel pieces attached to the corners. They were just going to think he was a sad geek playing games in a bar when he should have been socializing. He drew on his previous life to be able to play that part to perfection. He used to play board games like Go, chess, and shogi on his iPad, as well as word puzzles and arcade-style games. Not anymore. Unless he was using it as a cover. No time to waste, nowadays.

No one would ever think it a threat when he held the iPad in his hand, getting ready to strike. And he could quickly and easily remove and dispose of the sharp corners immediately after using them. The iPads he bought were a significant cost, but he didn't use them every trip. Many technologists dreamed of iPads getting lighter and lighter. He knew that was inevitable over the next few years. That wasn't what he wanted. But his mission would be over before that presented an issue for him.

49. Nov 18, 2013. Manila, Philippines.

It was like there was a pump in the back of his head pumping out tears. These weren't the hot tears accompanied by an intense feeling in the top and front of the head that he had experienced as a child, and from time to time as an adult. These were more cold, mechanical tears that were being pumped out continuously, while Artie's brain remained calm. They were as different from conventional crying as projectile vomiting was from a conventional bout of throwing up.

It was lucky that it was so early. It was 5:38 local time here in Manila. No one else was around. Artie was sat in a non-descript 24-hour American-style diner. He had ordered a 'full American breakfast', which consisted of sausage, egg, bacon, a stack of waffles with maple syrup, a glass of orange juice, and refillable coffee. He only planned to eat about half of it but ordered it as a small subterfuge. A guy ordering five portions of scrambled egg and two glasses of warm water with lemon would have drawn some attention, even if only a little.

Even as he was experiencing this tearful episode, he was analyzing why it was happening. What Artie believed was that he was having a visceral reaction to the killings. He had executed thirteen so far. Although you can plan for things as much as you want, when they actually start happening things are different. Especially things as unusual as a series of violent interventions resulting in deaths, sometimes in very brutal ways.

Artie felt like his subconscious was purging tears in response to two separate elements of his mission. The first was the enormity of taking someone's life. Probably a combination of nature and nurture, we humans are deeply programmed to respect the enormity of unaliving a person. Even unaliving an animal.

Second, the gritty, grimy, down-and-dirty reality of killing someone close up was hard to take. The sensory experience of cutting through muscle, sinew, and bone. The feeling of causing someone to draw their last breath while desperately fighting for more.

Even though Artie was very firmly committed to his mission, his subconscious couldn't be stilled. Nor, in fact, would he want it to be. He needed to let these emotions, these raw, uncontrollable feelings, pass through him and out the other side.

Along with the tears, he felt a kind of trembling. A rumbling throughout his body that wouldn't be denied its moment. He sat there, quietly in the pre-morning hours, sobbing and shaking as quietly as possible, until it was over.

When his body seemed satisfied, seemed over, he finished his breakfast. He took stock of himself. He was pleased to be left with a feeling of renewed purpose. Not of regret. Not of doubt. Not of questioning. He was even more committed to his mission.

He knew episodes like this would probably hit him a number of times in this next phase of his life. In fact, he would be a psychopath if he didn't feel them. He would acknowledge them, let them play out, let them pass through him. Then dust himself off and move forward.

50. Jan 2, 2014. Kamphaeng Phet, Thailand.

Artie made it his business to read the English-language newspapers in whichever country he was in. A few weeks ago, he read about Anuwat Pongsakorn and Nattaya Jirapong. They were a husband and wife in their mid-30s. They had jumped bail and were on the run after being found guilty of kidnapping, enslaving, and routinely torturing a young girl from the Karen ethnic group.

Apparently, the couple had acquired this girl at age seven and had been using her as their slave for five years, until she managed to escape a couple of months ago. The twelve-year-old told the authorities that she was kept in a dog cage, routinely scalded with oil and hot water, and slashed with sharp objects. Nattaya liked to put cigarettes out on her skin too.

The Thai authorities had offered one hundred thousand Baht for anyone who could catch the couple. But it was rumored that Anuwat's cousin, a reasonably senior police officer, was secretly helping them evade capture.

In Thailand, people almost always had nicknames. In this case, Anuwat was known as Noi, and Nattaya as Aom. In fact, nickname is not really a good term for this phenomenon. Most Thais are known only by their nickname to almost everyone they know. Their real names are typically only used for formal purposes, like getting a passport. They are usually much longer than the nicknames too.

Artie had used every strategy he could think of to track Noi and Aom down. In the end, he had to isolate Noi's cousin the policeman, and extract the information from him. Artie couldn't be sure he deserved the fate Artie meted out to him. But, given the fact that he was protecting two child slave owners and torturers, he probably wasn't the best example of an upstanding citizen. And, unfortunately, it was unavoidable that Artie had to take him off the game board. Because he was police, Artie was extra diligent in destroying evidence and covering his tracks.

Now here he was, sitting in the woods, observing the couple going about their daily life in the cabin just a hundred meters away from his position. He was using a powerful set of military binoculars to observe them. He had his usual camping setup, but also had two dog cages stashed nearby, just like the one their slave was held in, to help him exact karmic revenge. The pots and pans to boil the oil and water, and the sharp objects to slash with, would all be easily found inside the cabin. Artie had also brought some cigarettes and a lighter.

He supposed that Noi's cousin the policeman would be missed fairly soon, so he didn't have too much time. Given that they had made Bee, as the Karen girl was known, suffer for five long years, he would have liked to extend this intervention as long as possible, but he had given himself twelve hours with them in the cabin, once they were secured.

He chose five o'clock the next morning to enter. He didn't believe they would be sleeping well and would be most afraid and alert at night. He judged that they would be exhausted, and probably asleep, from four am to at least six or seven. From what he could see, they didn't have any animals or a house alarm. He would have with him a variety of useful implements, including a set of skeleton keys, a glass cutter, some chloroform, and a sturdy metal torch that doubled as a blunt instrument. He would leave the dog cages outside until he had secured the couple.

He left the house at just past five thirty p.m., around twelve hours after he entered, as he planned. Things had gone almost exactly as he had expected. He was a little disappointed that Noi had expired a couple of hours before the end, but at least Aom had lasted the full twelve. He wished he could somehow communicate to Bee that justice had been done, but it was probably a little too risky, too visible, to make contact with her directly. Maybe she would get to hear to hear about karma coming to her torturers. Maybe she wouldn't. But it was done now.

51.   July 2, 2014. Bangkok, Thailand.

"Fartie Artie. Fuck me. It's Fartie Artie."

Artie couldn't believe it. Today was a day of resting and replenishing supplies. He was in the food court on the sixth floor of the Mahbunkhrong Center, known to foreigners by the acronym MBK. He was staying in the Pathumwan Princess Hotel for the night, which was connected directly to MBK and super convenient.

Artie had liked staying here in his previous life, and it worked well in this phase of life too. There were enough staff and customers, and enough staff churn, that no one noticed or remembered him.

He got up at 8am, which was a very leisurely start for him. He went down to the 8th floor, where the gym, swimming pool, and one of the breakfast restaurants were. He did some stretching, some gym work, and then fifty lengths of the twenty-five-meter pool. He showered off and then had some eggs, steamed green vegetables, and a chamomile tea for breakfast.

Next, Artie got the elevator down to the first floor, called the ground floor in Thailand, like in the UK. He strolled through the connecting corridor to MBK and began shopping for the various items he needed to complete his rather unusual inventory. Artie went to different shops and stalls for each item, just to avoid giving too much away to any deliberate or accidental observers.

At about 11:45 he took the escalator to the sixth floor, then walked right to the end where the food court was located. He exchanged two hundred baht for credit on a special card. Many of the food courts in Bangkok operated on this card system. You exchanged your money for credit on this card. Then each of the food stalls had machines to take credit off your card. When you left, you exchanged any remaining credit for money.

Artie had heard various reasons for this system, including reducing the need for handling cash, hygiene, speed and efficiency, and the ability to collect customer behavior data. He also heard a rather paranoid British long-term resident tell him that it was to prevent the stall owners from ripping foreigners off. He was pretty sure that the last one wasn't the reason. Especially since the vast majority of customers were Thais.

MBK's food court was nothing much to look at but had a good reputation with locals for decent food at not-too-terrible prices. For foreigners, it seemed like an absolute bargain. As well as the general crowd, you see quite a few *farangs* (foreigners) with their Thai temporary girlfriends wandering around MBK. The guys buy the girls gifts, and they often eat lunch here too. The great thing about the food court setup was that the Thai girls could eat their favorite local food. Their boyfriends could eat Western food or accessible Thai food, and they could sit at the same table.

In his previous life, Artie had done this a few times. Even buying some girls gold jewelry from chain gold stores, like Prima Gold. For some reason, Artie's female companions often seemed to like to eat *khao ka moo* in the food court here. A dish made from slow-cooked pork leg served over rice with stewed vegetables. Not one of Artie's favorites. Very fatty.

When he heard that unwelcome voice, Artie was checking out a beef salad stall. *Yam neua*, a spicy beef salad, was delicious and fit very well with Artie's dietary regime. Everything was going well. Smooth sailing. Until he heard that voice.

"*Oh, Fartie. Fartie Artie.*" The voice still gave him the shivers. It was the voice of Chad Newton, a kid Artie went to school with, and, thankfully, hadn't had any contact with since high school. Until now. Chad was a jock. A great, big, blond, good-looking, arrogant football player. He had been one of the kids who made fun of Artie mercilessly and gave him a beating every now and then.

Artie wasn't sure if Chad had first coined his unwanted nickname "Fartie", but he used it far more than anyone else. It wasn't the rudest or the most creative nickname used for him. A nasty piece of work called Halford called him *fatburger*, which later became *whaleburger.* Pete Allen, a guy who he took Spanish with, once called him "Artie the Pig". That drew a laugh from the class at the time, and a warning to Pete from Mrs. Ramirez, the Spanish teacher. But thankfully that moniker never stuck.

One of his friends once called him 16k RAM, as a reference to a common size of memory cartridge, when he aced a math test. The bullies jumped on it and began calling him 16k RAM or RAMburger. Then they started increasing the amount to imply he was getting fatter. 32k RAM, 64k RAM. And so on. Because of its positive beginnings, and association with computers, he didn't mind that one.

But he really hated being called Fartie Artie. The bullies must have sensed it because that was the one that they used most.

Artie remembered once reading something by Henry David Thoreau, which made the point that you don't own your own name. Your name is what people choose to call you. The tribe owns your name.

Artie had no choice but to turn and acknowledge this dickhead, which was a shame for both of them.

"Wow. Chad. What are you doing here in Bangkok?"

"Fartie. Fartie. Fartie. On a Southeast Asia tour with the guys. You know. Jed, Pete, Bear, Conklin. Beer. Pussy. Golf. Then more beer. Know what I mean?"

Artie felt able to grasp Chad's sophisticated concept. *"Yeah. I get it. Cool."*

"We had a monster night drinking in Soi Cowboy last night. That Thai beer don't mix too well with Jack Daniels, I can tell you. Took a couple of hookers each back to the hotel. The rest of them are still sleeping. I came out to get breakfast and a few souvenirs. What the fuck are you doing here, Fartiepants?"

Even though they were now grown men in their forties, it didn't seem to occur to Chad that it wasn't appropriate to use such a cruel, derisive, childish nickname to refer to Artie. Dickhead.

Artie reeled off some rather weak story about being on a business trip, as he was calculating what to do about this unexpected meeting. It was crucial for Artie to remain anonymous, to remain underground, in order to complete his mission. He wasn't sure he could accept Chad going back to his hotel and telling all the other guys he had just seen Fartie Artie Wilson.

But, although he hated Chad with a passion, Chad's bad behavior towards Artie wasn't anywhere near enough for Artie to consider him a legitimate target. He persuaded Chad to go have lunch with him. He told him he knew this awesome steak and eggs place just outside MBK. Artie said he was buying. Chad gladly agreed. Artie was playing to Chad's ego and palate. That gave him time to think about how to handle things.

Artie was glad he had done so much research around central Bangkok, in his previous life and this one, so he knew of places like this. "*Kaew Steak*" was just off the main drag, and a relatively quiet place to recover from a hangover. It was connected to a guesthouse, but Artie had only ever been in the restaurant. Unlike MBK, this place didn't have any security cameras.

As they had breakfast, Artie came to the increasingly certain realization that he was going to have to take Chad out of the equation. It was very unfortunate. Even though Chad had been horrible to him at school, the guy didn't deserve to die for it. Had he not been on his mission, Artie might have enjoyed using his newfound martial skills to give Chad a bloody lip and a dented ego, but nothing more than that. As it was, Artie had to make a really tough call.

They finished their very average steak and eggs, and Artie had to say, surprisingly quite passable coffee. Although he was no coffee connoisseur. Artie paid, as promised. He left a decent, but not memorable, tip.

"*Wait till I get back and tell the guys. Fartie Wilson bought me breakfast. Hah.*"

"*Yeah.*" Said Artie. "*Have a great rest of the trip, Chad. Say hi to the guys.*"

But Artie knew that he wouldn't. Wouldn't have a great rest of the trip. Or tell the guys about Artie. Artie had studied toxins as part of his thousand-day preparation and carried a few types of poison with him at all times, for just such an occasion. By Artie's calculation, it would take about fifteen minutes for this one to take effect. And he reckoned Chad was about forty minutes away from his hotel.

Artie said his goodbyes and jumped on the Skytrain at National Stadium Station in the opposite direction from Chad, to get some distance before the inevitable occurred. He would look for the incident in the papers for the next week or so, just to make sure.

He decided that he wouldn't count this as one of his hundred. In fact, he was going to count this as a negative one. So, he had to do one extra intervention to make up for it.

As Artie sat on the Skytrain, with no destination except distance from Chad for the moment, the memory of a school trip to Moscow suddenly entered his head. His whole class had spent a week in Moscow. Visited Russia's space program and met a cosmonaut. Ate borscht, the wonderful beetroot soup with smetana, and sour cream in it. And went to the famous Red Square which had the Kremlin along one side of it, and the beautiful and iconic Cathedral of Vasily the Blessed, more commonly known as Saint Basil's Cathedral, on another side. Saint Basil's was constructed in the 1550s and is well known for its extremely colorful 'onion domes'.

Artie suddenly realized why his subconscious had put this memory in his head right now. It was rumored that Russia's ruler (Tsar) at the time, known as Ivan the Terrible, had the architect who designed Saint Basil's blinded after he finished the cathedral, so he couldn't recreate anything similar elsewhere.

Russia and Russian culture definitely had their beauty. But it always seemed to be intertwined with tragedy too.

Artie's decision wasn't quite in the same ballpark as Ivan's, but somehow it didn't feel too far off. Arthur the Terrible.

It was only late that evening that he realized it was his birthday today. He used to dread birthdays. They used to make him feel inadequate because he didn't really have anyone to celebrate them with. Now he didn't even notice them. They held absolutely no importance or significance for him.

32-1 = 31.

52. August 10, 2014. Wat Pong, Burma.

In the far North of Thailand, Chiang Rai was a city lesser known to tourists. Although it had a number of striking sights to see, like the White Temple, a beautifully sculpted building made by Thai artist Chalermchai Kositpipat, and the Black House, the eclectic home of another famous Thai artist, Thawan Duchanee, so far it never really attracted high volumes of tourists compared to places like Bangkok, Phuket, Koh Samui, Pattaya, and Chiang Rai's near neighbor Chiang Mai.

Artie didn't know much about the cuisine of Chiang Rai. He had once been given a local noodle dish that had a lot of raw blood in it and didn't enjoy it too much. He still held a tiny bit of Western squeamishness for such ingredients, but mainly it just didn't taste very nice.

Article remembered thinking years ago that more than any other country he'd visited, visiting Thailand revealed who you were. If you wanted a Theravada Buddhist, spiritual holiday, that was available. A beautiful beach break, that too. A meditation retreat. A fasting cleanse in a spa. A chemically-enhanced backpacker rave full-moon party. Scuba. Or of course, sex tourism. In that way, Thailand was a personal mirror and amplifier. If you were happy with who you were and the choices you made, Thailand could be heaven. If not, it could prove to be your hell. Artie never forgot which side of that divide he fell on in his previous life.

He was currently in Wat Pong in Burma, a country more recently renamed Myanmar. Artie was less than fifty miles northeast of Chiang Rai, in an area known as The Golden Triangle. Where Thailand, Burma, and Laos all meet. Close to Yunnan province in China too. Often portrayed as a lawless territory, which may not be quite the best way to understand it. It is more that the laws enforced there are not governed by any country recognized by the UN, or that you would find on a world map.

Many of the Chinese Kuomintang moved into the region after the defeat of the communists in the Chinese Civil War in 1949. Now there was a continually shifting landscape of groups with various motivations. The United Wa State Army in eastern Myanmar. The Shan State Army in northern Myanmar. The Golden Triangle Drug Alliance. Other powerful groups whose names are unknown to outsiders. They enforce their rules, often brutally. The region is famous for all forms of illicit activity, notably the trafficking of humans and narcotics like opium and heroin through the porous borders of all countries in the region.

Soon after Artie began planning his mission, he knew he was going to have to operate here. It was extremely dangerous, but this was also the head of the snake. Bars and massage parlors in tourist resorts were the retail end of the operation. Here was the wholesale segment of the supply chain of misery and indignity. Upstream, as they say in the oil and gas industry. Successful interventions here could change the fate of large numbers of perpetrators and victims.

So, here he was, buried in a hole, covered by leaves, using powerful military-grade night vision binoculars to watch the unloading of a truck full of human cargo that had come from Southern China. Cantonese was a notoriously harsh Chinese language even at the best of times. But hearing how these Shan soldiers screamed at their cargo somehow took Artie to a place of deep sadness. And anger.

He had watched this routine for three days running now. They would chain their cargo up, send the truck they came in on back to China, then eat and sleep in their comparatively comfortable tents before sending their victims on the next leg of the journey, typically through northern Thailand.

Sometimes, some of the soldiers would provide themselves with a little recreation with one or more of their human cargo. Sad to say that recreation could take the form of sex, violence, or both.

Providing Artie's plans came to fruition, that wasn't what was going to happen this time. Or by this crew anytime again. Ever. Of course.

Others would replace them, but that wouldn't stop Artie from making his contribution.

53. Early hours of August 11, 2014. Wat Pong, Burma.

Artie watched as the guards taking the night watch slowly lost consciousness and slumped to the ground. Then he slowly, cautiously visited each tent, making sure all the soldiers inside were in the same condition. During his reconnaissance phase, he had learned that the soldiers provided their cargo with the most basic fuel – some cold, old, moldy sticky rice. They reserved the tastier food for themselves.

This revelation provided Artie with the perfect stratagem to deal with such a large group of enemies. Poisoning was less dramatic. Less personal. Less satisfying. He would have hoped to look each of these guilty men in the eyes as they felt the pain and fear they deserved to feel. But needs must, and dispatching seventeen evildoers silently without even having to get near them was magical. No risk to his mission, no risk to the victims.

He knew that these young Shan State soldiers were themselves in many ways, victims. In, fact many of these situations could be what social scientists describe as *wicked problems*. Authors Rittel and Webber coined this term in 1973 to refer to the kinds of problems they were encountering in social science. Like obesity, bullying, and climate change.

Unlike conventional problems, wicked problems exhibited a number of conditions meaning that a different approach to solving them was needed. With wicked problems, it was hard to agree who was at fault, every situation is different and requires a nuanced approach, there is no safe way to test the solution there is no fixed set of solutions to pick from. Also, every wicked problem can be considered a symptom of other wicked problems. And beyond wicked problems, a category called super-wicked problems has been defined, where time is tight and those seeking to solve the problem are also seen as its cause.

But Artie could not always let this 'endlessly deferred' thinking slow him down. He had a window to make his impact, and his decisions were made.

He had considered doing scary things to the dead bodies, in order to strike fear of the hearts of those considering replacing them. But he wasn't sure that would work since those replacing them might not really be doing so by choice. Also, the benefit of this form of death made it hard to be sure how it happened, whether it was an accident or deliberate. So, he chose to let the bodies be.

Now he had a four-hour window to lead the victims to safety before the morning transport showed up. An operation like this wasn't over till it was over. Artie took a deep oxygenating, calming breath, then kicked into phase two. Although he had limited time, he brought to mind an old special forces motto he had heard. "*Slow is smooth. And smooth is fast.*"

54. August 19, 2014, Loyola Heights, Manila, Philippines.

Artie had spent a while studying the security systems of Miguel Santos's luxurious house in Loyola Heights, Manila. Santos hadn't opted for human security guards, but he had really gone to town on the latest and greatest technologies. High-resolution cameras, sensors, biometric access controls, and advanced alarm systems. Money was no object for a guy like Santos, and, like other wealthy Filipinos, security was paramount. Kidnapping was a routine occurrence, and the police were often complicit.

Then Artie remembered a trick he had read in a novel called *"The Evil That Men Do"*. In that book, an assassin was targeting a similarly rich, powerful man who lived on his own and had very advanced security. By sensing the water pressure, he came to know when his target took a shower. It was the same time every day. The assassin realized that when his target was taking a shower, he wasn't aware of the alerts and alarms that his security system was generating, so the assassin was able to just stroll into his target's house at that time and kill him.

Artie realized that this situation was almost identical to the one in the book. He didn't feel the need to find the water pipes and monitor their pressure. He simply monitored movements and lights through the windows of Santos's house and then worked out his daily routine.

So, at 8:32 a.m., after confirming that the shower room light had come on, Artie utilized his lock-picking skills to enter the house through the front door, dressed in workmen's clothing. After surprising and securing Santos, Artie let Santos watch him nail all the doors and windows shut in the living room, except one.

He looked the tied and bound Santos in the eye and said nothing for quite some time. He could see the unusual cocktail of the condescending anger of the privileged and the fear of the vulnerable mix in the whites of Santos's eyes. *"With the doors and windows nailed shut, it will be hard for you to escape. Just like the thirty-five workers who burned to death in your jewelry factory in Quezon City last month. You nailed those doors and windows shut to reduce the risk of break-ins and thefts. Just like you did in a plastics factory two years ago. You are 'balat kalabaw.' Now it is time for you to share the experience that your poor workers had. Perhaps that will give you some empathy in the last moments of your life. Or perhaps not."*

The Tagalog term Artie used literally translated as 'water buffalo skin', used to refer to someone insensitive or shameless.

Santos's mouth was taped shut, but he made noises indicating that he wanted to speak. Artie briefly wondered. Would Santos say:

A – *"You've got the wrong man. I didn't do it."*

B – *"How dare you. You'll never get away with this."*

C – *"I will give you a million dollars to let me go."*

Or something else that Artie wasn't expecting.

Artie decided not to find out. He left Santos's mouth taped. Opened the canister of poisoned gas. Then swiftly left by the one remaining open door, nailing that one shut after he exited. Then he calmly left the building and hopped on the small motorbike he had left concealed nearby. Motorbikes could be risky in Manila, but they were the only way to get around at speed in the near-continual gridlock.

49.

55. September 17, 2014, 10 p.m. Phnom Penh, Cambodia.

Artie sat on a bench by the Tonle Sap, a river that joined the mighty Mekong. He sat quietly, head in his hands. It was one thing planning for things, but another when they actually happened.

Artie remembered listening to a talk years ago by an adventurer, a British sailor called Pete Goss, who had famously turned around in extreme weather conditions in the Southern Ocean on his first single-handed round-the-world race and fought against the waves to go back a hundred miles to save a fellow sailor whose boat had been torn apart by the weather.

Artie was so inspired by the talk that he later read Goss's book "Close to the Wind" which discussed the incident. He read that Goss was awarded the *Legion d'Honneur* by the French President for saving Raphael Dinelli, the sailor in question.

Artie remembered that another audience member had asked Goss about the potentially life-threatening decision to go back and save his fellow sailor, a virtual stranger. Pete had answered that the decision had been made a long time before that incident. Even a long time before he was born. It was a principle of being a sailor. And when the shit hits the fan, you either stick to your principles or you don't.

Artie remembered that when Goss said that a lot of the audience, including Artie, looked like they had just got punched in the gut. So many of us are so far from having principles and sticking to them. And, in a way, the capitalist machine keeps us moving away from that state too. "Whatever get results. Whatever makes money" was the incessant drone, the backbeat of this capitalist world. Thankfully Artie had finished listening to that tune back in Chicago.

Before Artie had left Chicago, he had written his principles for this next phase. He had made his decisions. Here were Artie's principles for his mission.

1. Once I have identified a target, there will be no going back. I will unalive them. No doubt or sympathy before or during. No remorse after.

2. I will approach every challenge with a Buddha's mind, and a demon's hand. I will choose actions to take based on my integrity and values, but then execute ruthlessly.

3. Given the opportunity, I will make the target suffer in a way I feel is commensurate with the suffering they have meted out, or allowed to happen.

4. I accept that there will be mistakes along the way. That will not stop me in my mission.

5. I will always act in a way that is incredibly hard to trace. I will be patient until that opportunity arises.

6. Whenever there is an opportunity to make things look different from what they are. To lie, mislead, misdirect or obfuscate. I will take it.

7. Details matter. I will win through the little things at least as much as the big things.

He had borrowed number two from an old Chinese saying: *gui shou fo xin*, pronounced *kishu busshin* in Japanese, meaning demon's hand, buddha's heart.

Number 5 reminded him of a rather beautiful Thai idiom that an old Thai street food seller once taught him when he stopped for fried chicken at the old man's stall on the way home. They were talking about charity, and the old man taught him the phrase "*bpìt thaawng lăng phrá.*" Its literal meaning is 'putting gold sheets at the back of monk statues'. It derives from the Thai practice of buying sheets of gold leaf at temples and putting them on Buddha statues. It means performing good deeds without announcing them publicly. In other words, being truly charitable.

In his previous life, Artie had come across the twelfth-century Jewish philosopher Maimonides. He seemed like a really wise dude, and Artie loved the fact that he learned from, and was appreciated by, both the Jewish world and Islam, where he was known as Musa Ibn Maymun. He identified eight levels of charitable giving:

A. Giving reluctantly, with regret. Maybe making the recipient feel ashamed.
B. Giving willingly, but less than one should.
C. Giving enough, but only after being asked.
D. Giving before being asked.
E. Giving without knowing who the recipient is, but the recipient knows the donor.
F. Giving when the donor knows the recipient, but the recipient does not know the donor.
G. Giving when the donor and recipient are both unaware of each other's identity.
H. Giving one's money, time, and whatever else it takes to get the receiver to the point of self-reliance.

In Artie's case, doing good deeds secretively had a dual, perfectly synergistic pair of purposes. One was being truly charitable without the need to be witnessed or thanked, the other was to remain invisible, so he could keep on going.

Artie's seventh principle was more important than it sounded. It was inspired by a number of stories he had read from sports and other disciplines where the winners were often not differentiated by the big things, but by the little things. One example was Dave Brailsford, a British cycling coach. When Brailsford took the role in 2002, the Brits had never really won much in cycling. At the 2008 Beijing Olympics, they won seven out of 10 golds in track cycling. They repeated that feat at the London Olympics four years later.

Brailsford's rather unique perspective involved improving every single aspect of performance by 1%. Including tuning for aerodynamics in a wind tunnel. Getting a surgeon to teach the team how to wash their hands properly to reduce sickness. Painting the floors of the trucks that carried the team's bikes to reduce dust, hence reduced bike maintenance issues. Other improvements included using specific pillows and mattresses.

Also, hidden in Artie's principles was some inevitable pain, some suffering, some loss. And number 4 contained a host of suffering. He would occasionally inevitably misidentify targets. Victims would occasionally be injured or die. The bad guys would occasionally escape his grasp. He would try his hardest to avoid these issues, but he knew there would almost certainly be a few.

He remembered in his undergraduate degree learning about statistics. It sounded like a really dry subject, but he found it super interesting. The terms 'false positive' and 'false negative' came up. In his case a false positive was him unaliving someone who turned out not to be an appropriate target. A false negative was letting the bad guys escape. In his mission, there would inevitably be some of both.

And to conform with principle number 5, Artie knew he would sometimes have to witness the things he was there to stop: abuse, bullying, violence, rape, trafficking.

So, he got this all, in principle. But when it actually happened it was hard to take. Tonight, Artie saw a particularly mean mama-san beat a young Khmer boy to death because he didn't comply with a customer's particularly perverse wishes. The mama-san hadn't intended to kill him, just to teach him a lesson in the worst way possible. But she had wielded her choice of weapon, a stone ornament that happened to be at hand when he came to her, a little too hard, and a little too close to the boy's temples.

When Artie removed her from the gene pool later that night, he made sure she felt the fear and suffering that he saw in that boy's face, similarly encoded in the boy's body from many punishments. But that did nothing to expunge the deep pain in Artie's heart at seeing what a terrible life the boy had. How unnaturally short, too.

Artie had always hated that term – collateral damage. He liked to think of his mission as a kind of collateral repair.

51.

56.   November 3, 2014. Kabuki-cho. Shinjuku. Japan.

Japan was somewhat unfamiliar territory for Artie. He had come on holiday out of curiosity once, but it had been very expensive, and not knowing the language had proved a major barrier. Also, unlike Southeast Asia, it seemed like the water trade (*mizu shobai*), what Japanese people called the night-time entertainment business, was designed pretty much exclusively for domestic customers.

Artie found this out very directly one time in the early 2000s when he tried to follow a group of Japanese businessmen into a Soapland, the name for an establishment that offered bathing, massage, and sexual services. Interestingly, until a Turkish scholar led a campaign to address the issue, these establishments used to be called *Toruko Buro*, meaning Turkish baths.

The Japanese language had rather beautiful terms for some less-than-beautiful activities. Within the water trade, one name for a prostitute was *baishun*, which rather poetically meant 'selling springtime'.

Anyway, when Artie tried to enter on his one and only holiday here, a burly-looking Japanese man covered in tattoos stood in his path and crossed his forearms in an X, indicating that his custom wasn't welcome. (The same had happened once when Artie tried to enter a convenience store on a day trip in rural Japan.) He had heard on the grapevine that this xenophobic adult industry was changing now, probably based on the economic stagnation and demographic time bomb facing Japan. But that didn't affect him. Artie wasn't in the market for sexual services anymore.

Here was here in Japan to engage Morisawa Ichiro, a mid-level Yakuza, a Japanese mafioso. A couple of weeks ago, Artie was sitting quietly in a bar in Patpong, a famous pair of streets full of Go-Go bars just off Silom Road in Bangkok. The name came from the Patpongpanit's, a family originally from Hainan Island in China, who owned much of the property in the area. Each of the sex districts in

Bangkok had a slightly different feel. Patpong was famous for its Go-Go bars with dancing girls, ping pong shows, and exorbitant drink prices. Even at the height of his moral depravity, Artie had never really liked the Patpong scene.

While Artie was sitting in the Princess bar on Patpong I (the first of the streets), he witnessed Morisawa choose a girl who was rolling around naked on the bar and take her to the back room. When a customer chooses a girl in a Go-Go bar, there are normally three options. First, and most common, he can take her back to his hotel room.

Second, there are normally short-time hotels within a couple of minutes' walk of the bars that can be rented by the hour. Sometimes there is a third option available, where the bar itself has private rooms at the back or upstairs that can be used. Needless to say, neither the short-time hotels nor the private rooms tend to be very clean, nice, or good value for money. Artie also often wondered if they had hidden cameras.

The second and third options are often chosen by customers who, for some reason, can't take a bargirl back to their residence. Could be because they are not alone there. Could be because they are concerned about being drugged or robbed back at their room. Could simply be because they are concerned about being seen with a 'lady of the night'. Or it could be because they don't want their bargirl to know where they live. This last was often the reason for those who lived locally.

Drugging and robbing do occasionally happen, but a lot more rarely than you might expect. Considering the acts that are taking place, it is actually remarkable how decently most sex workers treat their customers, Artie thought.

Morisawa left the Princess bar about forty minutes later. The girl emerged about fifteen minutes after that, trembling, and trying to hide a variety of cuts and bruises. She spoke briefly to the mama-san, who nodded her acceptance, then left for the night.

The next night Apple, which was the nickname she went by, was back at work in the bar. Artie noticed she was wearing very heavy makeup in the areas that seemed to get injured the night before. Early in the evening he paid for her bar fine but asked her to sit with him and have a drink. This was not wholly unusual behavior. Sometimes, customers wanted to take their chosen girl 'off the market' but stay at the bar drinking for a while before taking her home. Sometimes they were a bit nervous or morally vacillating, not ready to seal the deal. Or sometimes, like in Artie's case, all they wanted was conversation.

Back in his days as a customer, Artie had occasionally paid for a few bargirls' bar fines, just so they could go home for the night and take a rest. Even though he felt morally compromised back then, he didn't behave badly in all ways, or all the time.

Apple introduced herself to Artie in her heavily accented English as '*Appn*', which Artie found endearing. Rather randomly, it also reminded him of an old story from the satirical publication The Onion about President Clinton authorizing the deployment of an emergency shipment of vowels to Bosnia. And an old comedy routine from Louis CK about being able to call your kid anything, including a name with no vowels.

He made small talk for a while, then asked her if they could go out for dinner together. He bought Apple a very nice dinner at a Japanese teppanyaki restaurant not too far from the bar. He ignored the stares of fellow diners who noticed Apple's somewhat sensual dress code and their age difference. Apple herself had developed an incredibly thick skin. She neither noticed nor cared.

Over dinner, Artie kept the conversation light. Whenever Apple took the conversation down a seductive line, Artie politely steered it back to asking about her family, her hobbies, and other such things. After dinner, he took her for dessert and coffee at Starbucks. By then Apple was pretty clear that Artie wasn't after more than conversation.

Artie then told her that he wanted to know about her Japanese customer the night before. He told her that he was sorry to bring up such a sensitive subject, and he couldn't tell her why he wanted to know. But he gave her 25,000 Baht, which was at least ten times what she might expect from a more conventional customer, and asked her to spare no details. By the time they parted at around 10 p.m. with a light hug, Artie had everything he needed to identify Morisawa and be sure that he deserved what was coming to him.

Kabuki-cho was itself a kind of adult entertainment district. It was originally developed after World War Two, to be a theatre district. Kabuki (歌舞伎) was the name of one of the famous styles of theatrical performance in Japan, its name literally meaning the art of song and dance. Japan has several unique theatrical forms, including the more serious *noh*, the more comic *rakugo* and *kyogen*, and the *bunraku* puppet theatre. Most of these forms of theatre are dominated by male performers, including playing female roles. The more recent *takarazuka* has an all-female cast.

Anyway, the *kabuki* theatre in *kabuki-cho* was never built, and the area turned into a neon-lit adult entertainment district, popular with locals and tourists alike. It was also rumored to have links to the *yakuza*, the Japanese mafia.

Like so much else about Japan, Artie found Kabuki-cho quite hard to understand. There were all sorts of unusual variants not found in the adult sectors in the rest of the world. Just for example, there was a profusion of places called *terekura*; the *tere-* standing for telephone, the *-kura* standing for club. It seemed like men would pay to enter a booth inside one of these clubs, and the phone would then ring with calls from girls willing to go on a date with the customer. The unspoken rule was that these women would ultimately be prepared to sleep with the customer for money. Artie never fancied going in on, and they were only designed for Japanese clients.

Artie felt like Japan was the most alien place on earth. Behind the bamboo curtain, China was often painted to be the most mysterious country where the rules of the Western world no longer apply. Artie hadn't been there much, but his sense was that actually, China was a fairly normal, market-based, entrepreneurial country that was temporarily being inhabited by an authoritarian, Maoist government.

Japan, however, was different in its bones. It revealed its difference everywhere you looked: sushi, bullet trains, cruelty during wartime, physical distancing, politeness, odd and perverse pornography, the unwillingness to accept tips. Thanks to its hundreds of years of isolation, Japan had imported the principles of Confucianism and taken them to the extreme.

Morisawa was inside a bar, for now, drinking with his fellow mid-level *yakuza* friends. Artie found himself a spot in a Mosburger. Mosburger was one of a handful of Japanese burger chain stores, much like McDonalds or Burger King, but with menu items catering to domestic tastes. He remembered being surprised and amused when he first came to Japan seeing burgers served in rice cakes rather than bread buns, teriyaki burgers, salmon burgers, and other such fast-food fusion cuisine. Artie sat at the window, waiting patiently for Morisawa to come out.

Morisawa stumbled out of his bar at 3:20am. Fortunately, the Mosburger was 24 hours, so Artie had been able to wait. If an opportunity didn't present itself tonight, Artie was prepared to wait for another chance. But luckily, Morisawa's buddies all got their cabs home first, and he was left on his own, senses significantly impaired by alcohol, looking for a cab.

Artie wandered down the street and accidentally on purpose bumped into Morisawa-san. He played the nervous foreign tourist and apologized profusely. Morisawa let out a string of expletives in Japanese. "*Bakayaro! Usure na! Doke yo!*" Artie had no idea exactly what Morisawa said, but he could easily guess the flavor. It turns out that what Morisawa said, in street Japanese, was something like: "You bloody idiot. You're annoying. Get the hell out of my way."

What was more important to Artie was that Morisawa didn't notice the small pin prick in his arm as the syringe-like object that Artie held delivered its liquid payload. It was only about 20 milliliters but should have taken hold of Morisawa about an hour later, treating him to a painful death due to lack of oxygen getting into his lungs.

Artie felt slightly sad that he didn't get to witness Morisawa's suffering and demise, but he recognized that he was out of his comfort zone here in Japan, and all manner of things could go wrong if he indulged his desires to watch his subject suffer, scream, and wail close up. He remembered reading a Japanese word *shouganai* once in a novel. It translated roughly as "It can't be helped."

56.

57. *January 4, 2015. 2am. Phuket, Thailand.*

Somchai barked his orders at the last few women left at the bar. His rudeness and rough treatment of the women had come as no surprise to Artie, who had been quietly observing the man for several days now. In the bars, he managed. In his transactions with other shady nightlife characters. And in the makeshift dormitory rooms where the girls slept when they had not been bought for the night by customers. Rooms which, sadly, Artie had observed, locked from the outside.

Somchai reminded Artie very much of the Thai idiom *kop nai kala*. It translates literally to frog inside a coconut shell and refers to someone who has little knowledge or experience of the world but thinks they do. A king or queen of a tiny fiefdom who is used to being the big boss of that fiefdom. Somchai was about to get yanked out of his coconut shell. He was about to get a rude awakening. Sadly, his newfound knowledge and perspective would not be useful to him for very long.

Artie reflected that perhaps the hardest aspect of what he did now was not acting to throw everyone off the scent. Not even the interventions. The hardest thing was having patience. After identifying his targets, watching them conduct their evil. Their ugliness. Always for hours. Sometimes for days. Occasionally for weeks. To make sure his assessment was right. And waiting until the right opportunity opened up for him to act.

Artie needed to act at a time and in a way that never revealed who he was, what he was capable of, or what his goals were. Sometimes that saddened him deeply, forcing him to observe cruel and terrible acts without intervening. But he was clear in his goals. If he could perform an intervention without any trail of evidence, that would leave him free to do many, many more. If he intervened prematurely, and even the slightest bit of evidence was left, that was the beginning of the end for him, and more importantly the end for his mission.

This aspect of his mission reminded him of a story he had once heard about the Israeli military. Surrounded by enemies since its declaration of independence in 1948, Israel had had to be pretty tricky in its strategies and stratagems. One such stratagem was a way of disrupting enemy communications.

If Israel had cut the communications lines of enemies, they would know it had happened and repair them, or make new ones, and maybe also work out how Israel had done that and stop them from doing it again. Instead, the Israelis fired white noise down the communication lines, making it seem to their enemies that the communication links were just noisy and performing poorly. Which made it both more effective and more repeatable. Artie knew that the story might be apocryphal, but still, he learned something from it.

He was also reminded of the Taoist concept of *wu wei*. In Chinese, *wu wei* means 'not doing'. In contemplative Taoism, it is used to remind us to sense and go with the flow. Not to try to push things unnaturally. If we go with the flow, everything takes a fraction of the effort it would otherwise, and causes minimum ripples in the environment. *Wu wei.*

Artie concealed himself in the back seat of Somchai's car, which was parked near the bar he ran. By now he knew the route of Somchai's drive home, and he waited until Somchai was in the most unpopulated area of his journey before springing out and knocking him unconscious. He then quickly took hold of the wheel and brought the car to a controlled stop.

He then took his time securing and gagging Somchai, then waking him up. He administered about an hour of the cruelty that he had seen the man administer to the girls who worked for him, then let him leave. Not leave the car but leave the world. Leave his pathetic, evil life.

59.

58.   January 4, 2015. 3:30am. Phuket, Thailand.

Artie walked back to a small side street near the bar and slipped one hundred baht into the hand of the street kid who had been watching his motorbike. He had given the kid another hundred baht earlier. They nodded to each other. Artie slipped the cover off the cheap, deliberately dirty, and broken moped and did a few cursory checks, then hopped on and drove away.

After about twenty minutes, he got off the vehicle in a place so nondescript that it didn't even have a name. Or cellphone coverage. Like almost every aspect of his life these days, the bike looked exactly like it couldn't and shouldn't be used for the forty-kilometer journey, over relatively rough terrain. That was no accident.

After checking that his three planned exit routes all still looked fine, and lighting some coils that kept the mosquitos at bay, Artie went to work on what looked like a bunch of random trash someone had dumped by the roadside. Within about ten minutes he had put up his tent and changed into a comfortable sleepsuit. He then stretched his tired body out for a few minutes, then meditated for about fifteen minutes. After that, he fell into a deep, guilt-free sleep.

59. January 4, 2015. 7am. Near Phuket, Thailand.

Artie woke, and as he had trained himself to do, immediately jumped out of bed. He learned this from studying Soyen Shaku, the first Zen master to go to America. This Zen master had a brief set of rules for living, which really appealed to Artie, and he tried to abide by them:

"My heart burns like fire but my eyes are as cold as dead ashes. In the morning before dressing, light incense and meditate. Retire at a regular hour. Partake of food at regular intervals. Eat with moderation and never to the point of satisfaction. Receive a guest with the same attitude you have when alone. When alone, maintain the same attitude you have in receiving guests. Watch what you say, and whatever you say, practice it. When an opportunity comes do not let it pass by, yet always think twice before acting. Do not regret the past. Look to the future. Have the fearless attitude of a hero and the loving heart of a child. Upon retiring, sleep as if you had entered your last sleep. Upon awakening, leave your bed behind you instantly as if you had cast away a pair of old shoes."

Given Artie's rather specific life pattern and goals these days, he couldn't always follow all the rules, especially about what he said, but it always struck him as a great way of living.

As always, Artie went to the local stream and washed, then began a series of stretching and exercise routines that lasted about an hour. He had honed this routine in his one thousand days of preparation. It was strongly influenced by kundalini yoga, chi kung, and an exercise called the eight-section brocade. Following this, Artie performed a short meditation, drank some water, ate a breakfast of nuts and berries, and then began the work of the day.

Today was focused on tidying up this camp, then leaving for Sihanoukville, Cambodia – the next stop on his journey. Named after King Norodom Sihanouk, it was a lovely beach resort, and jumping-off point for visiting many Cambodian islands. Unfortunately,

Sihanoukville also had a reputation as a paradise for foreign sexual predators. The English musician Paul Gadd, whose stage name was Gary Glitter, was one of the infamous foreign inhabitants of Sihanoukville until his arrest in 2002.

As part of Artie's camp cleanup, he spent time immersing himself in the perceptual position of people who may want to find him, including police, and friends and families of those he had dispatched. The whole process took less than an hour, then he headed to Hua Hin, a more sedate Thai city, where he could board a bus to take him to the border with Cambodia. Actually, he could get a bus that took him all the way to Sihanoukville, but preferred to cross the border alone, across a river, where there were no officials, and often no people at all.

60. January 11, 2015. Evening. Sihanoukville, Cambodia.

Artie cursed himself under his breath. He loved the martial arts dictum that the best way to win a fight was by not being there when the fight happened. A similar fighting philosophy was the idea that the fight was often won and lost before it started. In less colorful language, all of this meant that you should try to avoid situations where your opponent even has a chance of winning. You should tilt the playing field so heavily in your favor before the start that your opponent doesn't stand a chance.

You might choose a fair fight when you are training. You might even choose to give an opponent some advantages to challenge yourself to get better. But when you are on an operational mission, a fair fight is the last thing you want.

Master tacticians like Sun Tzu and Miyamoto Musashi give us an array of stratagems to help us achieve this. Such as letting the opponent tire themselves out before the fight, poisoning their food, taking the high ground, choosing a battleground that is more familiar or otherwise advantageous to you, splitting the enemy forces up, and beating each subgroup one by one. And many others.

This time, somehow, Artie had failed to employ any of those great stratagems. Despite his discipline, he couldn't wait any longer as he saw the two Danes making their moves on underage hookers. It would be hard to argue that Artie had made the wrong decision. He had just taken a slightly riskier decision in order to stop the abusive behavior earlier.

Artie found himself in the backyard parking lot of a bar facing off against these two Danish guys, both reminiscent of the martial artist and actor Dolph Lundgren. Unlike these men, Artie greatly admired Lundgren. He was a genuine martial artist, holding a fourth dan black belt in Kyokushin karate, one of the most brutal, full-contact forms. He had had a prolific, if not always top-level movie career, becoming most famous as Ivan Drago, the Russian bad guy in Rocky V. He had also received a Fulbright scholarship to MIT, although he never completed that degree.

Each of these two goons were a good six inches taller than Artie, maybe eighty pounds heavier than him, too. And neither had much fat on them. The weight difference was all muscle.

Artie felt like his potential advantages were his level of commitment to his mission, the various martial arts techniques he had learned, and that he was already experienced with, and emotionally accepting of, lethal interventions. Maybe he had a mental advantage too, but it was hard to say for sure. His disadvantages were that there were two of them, they were each bigger than him, and they looked super fit. They looked like they might be boxers or martial artists too.

He decided that surprise could be an advantage for him too. He didn't feel that these two were sufficiently mentally agile. So, the first thing he did, very quickly, was launch himself at the bigger one of the two. (Let's call him Sven. Artie never did find out his name.) Artie launched himself headfirst, aiming to headbutt Sven in the throat or upper chest. It was a calculated risk, because it made him very vulnerable to a kick, knee, elbow, or punch to his head if Sven reacted fast enough.

But his bet paid off, and he managed a really solid thud into Sven's thorax. It amazed Artie how often people try to use their fists and feet to strike, when the head, elbows, and knees could generate much more force with much less skill required. Although they did require being a little closer to the target.

The flying butt on Sven was certainly meant to injure him, but also to shock him long enough for Artie to follow up. A third aim was to shock the second Dane, let's call him Morten. Sven was a strong guy, and the butt had hurt him, and he had bent over in pain, but he didn't fall down. Artie followed up with a flying knee to the face. Sven we pretty much done before Morten engaged Artie.

Artie turned to Morten and let out an animal roar, to further put Morten on the back foot. In Japanese martial arts, the *kiai* is the short, sharp shout made as part of an attacking move. It is thought to both focus one's energies and scare the opponent. Artie's research of Japanese esoterica had also revealed a more general, but lesser-known concept from Shintoism, Japan's indigenous animist religion, called *kotodama*. Kotodama was a belief that words had mystical power.

Even so, Morten came at Artie swinging. Artie used his lower center of gravity as an advantage. He executed a low kick to Morten's left knee, just as it had all Morten's weight on it. Artie heard Morten squeal with pain, and then he gave Morten a 'dead leg' in the same leg, jamming his knee into the outside of Morten's left thigh. As Morten fell, Artie was able to use his right elbow to smash into Morten's falling face.

Within ten minutes both men had been dispatched, and within one hour, their bodies were buried in somewhat shallow holes in the ground. Artie walked away unscathed, with two more monsters having received their karmic payoff. But he couldn't feel satisfied, as he usually did. It was a bit like when a veteran poker player knew that they made the wrong move but lucked out and won the hand anyway. It was great to win, but that was somewhat tempered by the knowledge that you could have lost, even, maybe in some sense, that you deserved to lose.

61.

61. January 20, 2015. Klong Toey, Bangkok.

Artie was fairly devoid of fear these days. Not because he thought it was impossible for harm to come to him. More because he was focused on his mission and accepted that death or injury could come to him at any time as part of that mission. He had read a little about the philosophy of Japan's Samurai warriors, and their notion of deeply accepting death before battle. He had also read about the Sufi, the mystical Muslim sect, who held the tenet 'die before ye die'. Both of these resonated with this phase of Artie's life. As he understood it, this was about dying in terms of losing fear and desire, so that you could live truly and freely.

But he still felt a tinge of fear as he walked into an area of Bangkok called Klong Toey. Like someone feels pain in a limb that no longer exists after an amputation.

Klong Toey came right up to one of the famous tourist areas, Sukhumvit Road, but just a couple of hundred yards away from the tourist hustle and bustle lay a warren of ramshackle, corrugated iron-topped semi-finished little houses that were largely populated with street-level drug dealers.

As he walked down the tiny alleyways inside this hidden ghetto, Artie felt everyone's eyes following him. But they could tell he wasn't trouble. He wasn't police. He wasn't trying to buy drugs. Or out for revenge, or anything like that. They all knew that he was going to see Father John. Some of them may have seen Artie visit Father John before, but most knew it was the only real explanation for him being here.

Father John Carroll was an Irish Catholic priest who had moved to Klong Toey as a young man in the mid-1970s. He had devoted his life to helping the poor and downtrodden of Bangkok in any way he could. He had used donations to build and outfit a small hostel where the needy could stay for free. He organized donations, provided food, and even connected people to lawyers who could do pro bono work if needed.

Over the years, and then the decades, Father John felt increasingly a part of this place. It wasn't so much that he lost his faith in God and the Church, it was more that those things became secondary. His primal motive force was humanitarian these days. This meant that sometimes he would do things the church would not approve of, like giving women money for abortions. The Church, in turn, kept its distance from him more and more over the years, because it felt the same. It felt that Father John had 'gone native'.

Artie had heard that this kind of problem existed with expat staff who left the US to work in an overseas branch office to enforce global policies. They also often 'went native', identifying with the local business more than corporate headquarters. Kinda natural, Artie thought. And more so for Father John. Given what he must have seen over the decades, he would have had to be inhuman not to identify more with the local people and their issues.

Everyone loved and respected Father John. Including normal working-class people, sex workers, drug dealers, and petty criminals. Even the police. That was at least partly because John's approach was never to judge, always to help where he could, with no strings attached. He didn't judge the members of his community if they turned tricks on the street, took or sold drugs, or got into fights. He wasn't usually a snitch for the police. He just tried to help.

Artie came to see Father John for two reasons. One was to provide donations for his charity, called 'Eternal Mercy'. The other was to learn. He posed as a journalist wanting to understand more about Bangkok and its recent history, but he suspected Father John knew that he had different motives.

"*Fancy a drop of the hard stuff, fella?*" were the first words out of Father John's mouth as he saw Artie approach. This reminded Artie of the traditional Chinese greeting "*Nǐ chī fàn le ma?*", literally meaning "*Have you eaten yet?*" but actually simply meaning "*How are you?*"

"Don't mind if I do? How are you, Father?"

"Oh, fine, fine thanks Kevin," Father John replied while extracting a fancy-looking whisky box from behind his makeshift desk. *"My cousin Alfie sent me this recently. It's a lovely drop."*

It was a brand of Irish whiskey that Artie had never heard of. Midleton Very Rare. Over the next fifteen minutes Artie learned from Father John that this particular whiskey was introduced in 1984, had hints of vanilla and oak in its 'nose', and a smooth, balanced, vanilla and caramel taste palate, with mild warmth provided by nutmeg and ginger notes.

Artie was no longer a whisky connoisseur and didn't drink these days, except when his mission and role required it, but he had to admit that this was, as Father John had stated "a lovely drop". A much more rounded finish than a more traditional whisky.

Father John had spent decades seeing endless examples of the worst depravities of humanity. Victims of torture and rape. Children being born with HIV and dying of AIDS soon after. Victims of pedophiles. Victims sometimes growing up to be perpetrators of these terrible crimes themselves.

It warmed Artie's heart to see that Father John could still have a twinkle in his eye, and a smile on his face, as he shared a drop of the hard stuff with Artie.

As the afternoon went by, the two of them sat and chatted about this and that. Thai politics, soccer, religion, and health. Local residents came and went. Some came to ask Father John for money, medicine, or advice. A few asked him to give donations, of money, food, or other commodities. Some to share gossip and rumors with him – also a very helpful commodity for Father John. Artie had given his donation, a rather sizeable five million Baht, to Father John in an envelope just after he arrived.

Towards the end of the afternoon, a little well-lubricated, Father John began telling Artie stories of what he was seeing around the place.

Everything, from the flow of drugs to the behaviors of local wife beaters, cruel parents, and abusive employers in the black economy.

One particular story held Artie's attention the most. A group of Canadians holed up in an apartment complex near Asok junction. Posing as humanitarian aid workers, they took groups of deprived kids on trips to local attractions like Dream World, Safari World, and Dusit Zoo. They took them to kid-friendly restaurants, like MK. They brought the kids back to their apartment to play Xbox and eat order-in fast food. They gave them new, clean clothes.

And they abused them.

Father John recounted, in a calm, measured tone, how many people thought these foreigners were kind heroes. He also told Artie that when the kids came back to Klong Toey, they told Father John that they loved these men, and they wished they could live with them. They were much kinder than their own parents. Father John tried to intervene, tried to get the help of the police, but many of the local cops got sizeable donations from the pedophiles.

Father John said that he felt the most important skill in his role was to just keep going. Whether he saw success or failure. Horrendous abuse or people being sublimely lifted into better lives. His job was to just keep helping.

Artie, who Father John knew as Kevin, felt the most immense respect towards the man and reached out in his slightly inebriated state, and gave Father John a massive, heartfelt hug.

While he respected Father John's infinitely patient, tolerant, kind path, that was not the one Artie was on. Although Father John was careful to tell all his stories without naming names, Artie's sharp ear for details, powered by his strong motivation, allowed him to deanonymize the Canadians within 24 hours of leaving Father John's place.

It turned out that Canadians were all quite old. 63, 66, and 67. All balding old men. Went for coffee together inside Watson's department store on the corner of Soi 19 at 10 a.m. every day and chatted happily about this and that. If you didn't know what Artie knew, you might find that touching.

As he sat close to them listening to their twitter, it somehow reminded Artie of a very heartwarming Simon and Garfunkel song, "Old Friends." One line of that song always somehow brought a tear to his eye. "*Old Friends. Sat on a park bench like bookends.*" Even though he was not an old man when he listened to it, and now knew that he never would be, he still enjoyed listening to it from time to time.

The next day Artie found his way into Newman, Burns, and Rafferty's place while they enjoyed their daily coffee. The security was quite basic, and he was able to piggyback in as someone else held the main door to the complex open for him.

Although he wasn't a computer security expert, he did study the topic a little, and one fact that stood out was that by far the most important and successful way to gain access to anything was not any sophisticated technology play. It was what was called social engineering. Using human foibles to gain access or information.

The first recognized hacker, Kevin Mitnick, wrote about this extensively in his book "The Art of Deception." Piggybacking is a social engineering technique that involves simply waiting for an authorized person to open a door, and then waltzing in behind them. What kind of asshole would someone have to be to stop you coming in after them? Most people would hold the door for you, right?

Artie got inside their apartment at 10:13, while they were just getting into their cappuccinos over at Watson. It was an absolutely beautiful twentieth-floor duplex. Four bedrooms, three had walk-in wardrobes. Three well-appointed bathrooms, each with a power shower and full-size bathtub. Well-equipped kitchen with huge double-doored fridge, crushed ice maker in the door. Stocked with lots of kid-friendly snacks and drinks, of course.

It saddened Artie deeply that some charity, funded by ignorant but well-intentioned donors, was paying for these guys to live in the lap of luxury, calmly pursuing their perverse path well away from the prying eyes of headquarters.

He figured he would have at least forty minutes to get ready for them, maybe longer. But he was listening all the time, and ready to deal with one or more of them earlier if necessary.

The first thing he did was scan the apartment for weapons. Nothing much. The most dangerous thing he found was a Swiss Army knife. Next, he did a bit of hunting for evidence. He was pretty sure of the evil they enjoyed, but it would be great to find some concrete evidence. He found a desktop PC that wasn't password protected. The internet history revealed exactly what he needed. And he found a folder full of photos and videos that put the nails in these three amigos' coffins.

It was a messy and unpleasant few hours after the three came back home. Newman came in first, and Artie quickly incapacitated, gagged, and tied him. About twenty minutes later, the other two came in. They each received the same fate.

Artie couldn't let them go without them suffering. Not after what he had seen on the computer. Next, he extracted the passwords for the other computers, their social media accounts, and their bank account details. Newman and Burns put up no resistance. Rafferty was a stubborn old so-and-so, but Artie had lots of space, time, and equipment to persuade him. It turned out that a heated knife on the testicles was just the ticket.

Artie then sat the three naked in a circle. He took his time punishing them physically until each of them expired. He operated on a kind of round-robin basis, so that each of them saw the others suffer, and knew what was coming to them.

That took just over an hour. He then spent another hour diligently emailing the most lurid and clear of the photos and videos to their social media accounts, and the email addresses of loved ones, friends, family, and charity contacts of all three of them.

He now regretted allowing them to die before witnessing the social media posts and emails. It would have been wonderfully karmic. Letting them punish themselves, in a way. He wouldn't miss this opportunity in the future.

He also did a little online banking on behalf of each of them. In life, they were the recipients of charitable donations. Turns out in death they were very generous in their giving. Just over $270,000 was now winging it to Artie's coffers. Or rather the mission's coffers. Via a highly obfuscated route, of course.

Seventy-two hours after his last visit, Artie stopped by Father John's briefly and delivered a bunch of brand-new designer kids' clothes, Xboxes, and a couple of boxes full of candies that he had liberated from the Canadians' den of luxury and depravity.

Artie didn't make a big deal of it, and Father John got donations like this multiple times per day. But when Father John shook Artie's hand as he was leaving, he held on to it just a little too long, causing Artie to look Father John in the eye. Father John held Artie's gaze just a little longer than was normal and nodded almost imperceptibly.

As Artie left Klong Toey, a thought passed through his head. *"Sometimes words get in the way of real communication."*

65.

62. *February 3, 2015. Oasis.*

Artie got out of the beaten-up Volkswagen campervan at a nondescript house in a rural setting, about eighty kilometers from Luang Prabang in Laos. They had been driving for at least twelve hours along some very rough roads from the border of Laos with Thailand, not far from Udon Thani. The borderlands where Thailand met Laos and Cambodia were strewn with illegal casinos and brothels. The brothels in this area made Bangkok's nightlife look as wholesome as a church garden party. The corrupt policemen and politicians whose roles were to shut down these establishments turned a blind eye to them and were usually also some of their biggest investors and most enthusiastic customers.

After Artie executed his intervention at one of these places, he deemed it best to spirit the three girls who were present away. They saw what Artie did to their captors, so while they were afraid of him, they also suspected he had their best interests at heart. They silently walked together for two kilometers to the border, then over it, and got in the van that Artie had hidden in the bushes.

When they arrived at the house, Ploy came out to greet them. Ploy was one of the first people Artie had helped. They got to know each other afterward, and it turned out that she was perfect for this role and keen to do it. You could call Ploy the manager of Oasis. 45 years old, her life had included traumas so significant that Artie was in awe of the fact that she was still standing. Neither her husband nor her two children had been alive for the last decade, and they perished in unspeakable ways as the result of a debt the family couldn't pay off. Ploy was forced to watch her loved ones' suffering and death, then left alive as a particularly cruel form of punishment. She was also given a very significant scar on the left side of her face as a physical *aide memoire* by her tormentors.

Ploy and Artie now shared the same mission. She was the only person who really understood the entirety of what he was doing. The depth and breadth of his commitment. Ploy was kind to the people that Artie brought but also tough. Ensuring that their recovery included feeling respected and being safe, but also fulfilling duties to the community in Oasis as soon as possible. These people could stay as long as they wanted, and when they chose to leave, agreed to a code of silence. A promise that both Ploy and Artie believed they would stick to. Partly out of thankfulness and belief in Artie's mission, and maybe also a little bit because they had seen what Artie was capable of.

Ploy was tough and smart. She spoke fluent Thai and Isaan, the dialect of Thai that is very close to Lao, as well as quite good Khmer (Cambodian), and a little English. Artie had arranged for her to have a variety of weapons and safety mechanisms scattered around Oasis, but hopefully, she would never need to use them. Artie regularly 'greased the palms' of a couple of local mid-level Lao policemen to preserve the anonymity, solitude, and safety of Oasis.

Artie and Ploy had slept together a couple of times, but they both kind of realized that wasn't the place in life either of them were at. They were both mainly motivated to make Artie's mission a success. In fact, although Artie initiated everything and had the lead role, it would now be better to describe it as their shared mission.

This time Artie spent the night before leaving for his next episode. He didn't enjoy many physical pleasures these days. Everything was about his mission. Food was his fuel and his medicine. He only drank alcohol or took drugs when the role he was playing absolutely demanded it. He allowed himself to enjoy his daily stretching and exercising routine a little, as extra insurance that he would keep doing it. His one pure pleasure left was a nice, hot shower.

He had installed a couple of high-end showers in Oasis, for himself, Ploy, and whoever else was there. Wet rooms with walk-in multiple-nozzle, high-pressure showers, and very accurate temperature controls with LED display. The kitchen was nice too. And there were all sorts of water tanks and electricity generators to try to ensure things kept working, even if the Lao supplies were a bit unreliable from time to time. All of this luxury, safety, and functionality was belied by the distressed façade of Oasis, making it look a little old. Uncared for. Nothing special. Just as Artie strived to look, too.

63. May 3, 2015. Wanchai, Hong Kong.

Artie strolled around some of the green spaces in Hong Kong in the afternoon. Whenever anyone thought of Hong Kong, they imagined the noisy, busy, built-up streets of Hong Kong Island and Kowloon. But Hong Kong did have some lovely parks and green spaces too. Especially up in the New Territories.

Because today was a Sunday, the parks were filled with Filipinas. There were a large number of people from the Philippines, especially women, who worked in Hong Kong. Especially in domestic roles like nannies and cleaners. They often worked round the clock six days a week, then had Sundays off.

In the south of the Philippines, there were a significant number of Muslims, but around 80% of the country as a whole were Catholics, largely due to the Spanish occupation for nearly 400 years, until the end of the 19th century. Like in many poorer countries, Filipinos' religious beliefs tended to be quite a strong force in their lives. As such Filipina maids really appreciated the opportunity to attend church on Sundays.

They were typically paid a small wage but were able to eat and live where they worked, hence they could send most of their money home to support their families. Overseas Filipino workers were one of the Philippines' economy's most important exports and sources of income. He noted that at Manila airport, there was a separate line for them to come in. On Sunday, after church, the Filipinas tended to congregate in public parks in Hong Kong and enjoy picnics together.

As the afternoon turned to dusk, Artie walked past a street food vendor and involuntarily gagged. In his previous life, he had learned to enjoy almost all Asian foods, including ones that Westerners traditionally find difficult, such as japanese fermented beans (*natto*), cod sperm sacs (*shirako*), the sticky topping made from grated yam (*tororo*) and sea urchin (*uni*). He had also come to genuinely enjoy the so-called 'king of fruit' in Southeast Asia, the pungent durian.

Once you conquer the smell, the taste and the texture were sublime. Especially if you ate it as a dessert with sticky rice and coconut cream. He had even learned to eat fertilized eggs (balut) in the Philippines and conquered a variety of deep-fried insects in Thailand.

But Artie had never been able to eat *tsao daufu*, the Cantonese rotten tofu dish that smelled like vomit to him. Of course, things had changed now he was on his mission. Firstly, he did not eat for pleasure. He ate for fuel, and to avoid health issues. Second, he would eat or drink anything that was required to play the roles he adopted for each of his interventions. To fit in.

He started the evening in a bar called the Wanch. It was a laid-back pub with a small stage for live music. It wasn't his final destination tonight, but he was a little early, and it was his standard practice to make several unnecessary stops on every journey just to check if anyone was following him. No one was tonight.

There were only a few people in the bar, mostly hunkered down in booths in pairs, drinking and quietly chatting. A sign by the door said, "Open mic night", but no one seemed to be taking advantage of that opportunity. The dimly lit stage had remained bare for the forty-five minutes Artie had been here. Then he noticed a middle-aged Filipina enter the bar, with a soft acoustic guitar case on her back.

The woman dropped her guitar case off at a table, then went to the bar and bought a Coke. She had a brief word with the barman, and he pointed to the stage. She returned to her table, opened her guitar case, and began fiddling with her guitar. Tuning it, Artie guessed.

The song playing in the background was "*Don't Go Changing*" by Billy Joel. As the song drew to a close, the Filipina lady ambled toward the stage, guitar in hand. She looked a little tired, but nonetheless, she emanated a kind of grace as she walked on stage.

For the next few minutes, she and the bar were both transformed. The familiar acoustic guitar chords began, and then she began singing. "*25 years and my life is still// trying to get up that great big hill of hope// for a destination.*" Even though most people in the bar still couldn't name the song, they immediately remembered it. And she was singing, and strumming, it perfectly. By the time she got to the familiar line *"And I say hey ey ey, hey ey ey, what's going on?"* everyone in the bar was drawn into the beautiful rendition of such a poignant song. It seemed like the song had been written by The Four Non-Blondes just for her.

When the song was finished, she just quietly walked off stage. She took a sip of her coke, wrapped her guitar back up, and ever so gently sauntered out of the door. She was not aggressively ignoring the audience, but at the same time, it was very obvious that she was simply expressing herself. She was not performing for anyone. Artie thought it was the most sublime artistic performance he had ever seen.

At about 9:30 p.m., he left the Wanch, and wandered a few doors down to his next venue. He settled in at the back of the Devil's Due bar and ordered a lime and soda. He adopted a persona not too far from his previous life, a pathetic expat IT support guy in his forties who worked in a bank and was lost in life. He had met a lot of guys in Hong Kong who behaved like old colonial masters and thought of themselves as masters of industry. A rather cynical Brit he once met in a bar, described the more accurate truth of these idiots' stories to Artie in a rather cruel acronym: F.I.L.T.H. Failed In London, Try Hong Kong.

Then he saw Jed come in. Jed Andrews, Artie had learned, was a 25-year-old Canadian, who studied philosophy at McGill University, held a first-*dan* black belt in Shotokan Karate, and was currently working as a barman at Churchill's, a bar not too far from here. (Artie would have preferred that Jed had studied a full contact style, like Kyokushin, but that was a minor issue.) Jed was a surfer and had been bopping around the world for a couple of years after Uni, working easy, cash-paid jobs to fund his passion. He had ended up in Hong Kong, at least for now.

Jed lived on a small island called Peng Chau because it was so cheap. He commuted to work each day using a combination of ferries and trains. Most of the other residents of Peng Chau were older Cantonese people. In the quiet afternoons, all you could hear was the incessant clicking of their Mah Jong tiles.

Artie had been watching Jed for a while. He seemed like a good candidate.

Jed had a habit of popping into bars other than his own, on his way home after work, just to decompress. He liked to drink a Molson's beer, perhaps to maintain a connection with home. Or just out of habit.

Tonight, three drunk Brits approached him. Jed humored them for a few minutes, making banter as all bar staff learn to, giving as good as he got. Then he tried to close the conversation down. The well-lubricated banker-wankers didn't take the hint. Jed then asked them politely to leave. One of them took offense. Artie settled in for the show.

Despite there being three of them, and their bluff and bravado, this wasn't really a challenge for Jed. His only regret was that he was going to make a mess in the bar, and he may have some explaining to do to the police. (Jed was happy to remember that despite Hong Kong having been returned to China by the British in 1997, the Hong Kong police still shared some of the sensibilities of their British counterparts. He wouldn't fancy it if this incident kicked off in, say, Shanghai.) His opponents' reactions were slowed by alcohol. Jed had a surfer's lithe body, fitness and balance, and a preternatural calm. His Shotokan background didn't hurt either.

He knocked the most aggressive guy out with a short, firm hook punch as the guy lurched towards him. The second guy grabbed Jed's collar. Not smart. Jed used hammer fists from above to break number two's grip, then opened those hands, used them to grab number two's head, and smashed it down on the tabletop where Jed remained sitting. A bit excessive, Artie thought, but effective.

Then the third guy, unsurprisingly scared, held his hands up in a sign of submission and started making conciliatory noises. Jed ignored those, got up, and delivered a flurry of blows to number three's head until he fell down. Then Jed gave him a kick in the ribs for good measure. Jed then went up to the bar, apologized, and left a healthy tip for the barman.

So many great things about Jed, but his decision and behavior around the third banker ruled him out as a candidate. Artie closed his tab, used the bathroom, and quietly left.

Artie had learned the basics about Jed's background. What he didn't know was that Jed was beaten by his stepfather and older stepbrothers, fairly badly and fairly regularly after his mother divorced his father and remarried when he was four. That lasted until he was fifteen. He was bullied in school for a similar period. The two weren't directly connected, but Jed felt like the bullies at school could almost smell his victim status at home.

That led to Jed signing up for Karate secretly when he was thirteen. Turns out his local dojo was the Shotokan style. By the time he was fifteen, Jed was a blue belt. He was a reasonably talented fighter, and he had put on a lot of muscle mass. After a couple of fairly tasty incidents at school and at home, he didn't get bullied anymore.

He left home pretty soon after that. And school. He worked on construction sites for a couple of years, where they weren't too hot on checking your ID. After that, he worked in a burger joint in a mall. All the time, saving money to pursue his dream of becoming a globe-trotting surfer dude. A dream that, amazingly, had come true.

But his early life had left him with some psychological scars. One of the manifestations was a tremendous rage. He kept it below the surface most of the time. He seemed very chilled out and peaceful most of the time. Very Canadian. But every now and then, when provoked, the beast was unleashed.

Had Artie known that backstory, he definitely would have felt for the guy. Liked to buy him a beer or two. But that still wouldn't have changed his decision. Jed's emotions would get the better of him from time to time. That could lead him to either doing something that didn't fit with the mission's goals and values. Or getting caught. Or both.

Still, Artie didn't regret the time he spent following and researching Jed. He knew he might have to kiss a few frogs.

On his way out, Artie thought that he saw an older man with white, unkempt hair and a beard turning into a side street, giggling. A man walked up to Artie. Maybe in his late 40s. A Hong Kong Chinese businessman in a suit. He smiled at Artie. Like an uncle might smile at his nephew. In singsong, Cantonese-accented English, he said. "*5am tomorrow. KCR Shatin station. Wear white clothes. Bring an envelope with some money in it.*"

He turned away from Artie, walked to the edge of the pavement, and a taxi immediately turned up. The man got in, and the taxi pulled gently away from the curb. Artie stood still and observed everything.

64. May 4, 2015. 4:55am. Shatin Station, Hong Kong.

Shatin was in the New Territories, a part of Hong Kong very different from the stereotypical image of Hong Kong Island or Kowloon. Unlike those super-busy, built-up streets, Shatin was still relatively unoccupied, with lots of greenery and hills. The Chinese University of Hong Kong was up here, but not much else. Although, as Artie knew, capitalism and entrepreneurship hated a vacuum, so these hills would probably not remain green and unoccupied for too long.

At 5a.m. precisely, he saw the Chinese businessman approach, again with a generous smile. "Walk with me", he said. Artie hadn't questioned him last night and had decided to come here. Luckily, he had found some white clothes to wear. He bought an envelope from an all-night store and put some money in it. And again, Artie hadn't questioned the man just now. He simply fell into lockstep with him, running on intuition.

After about fifteen minutes, they arrived at a grassy clearing. There were maybe fifteen to twenty people milling around in white clothes. Artie thought that some of their faces looked familiar like they were maybe Chinese and other East Asian celebrities. Maybe one was Andy Lau, a Cantopop singer and actor. Artie remembered hearing a song of his in the 1990s called "*ben xiao hai*" (Stupid Boy). Artie didn't understand the lyrics, but he liked it. Maybe another was Michelle Yeoh, a Malaysian Chinese actress who starred alongside Piers Brosnan in "Tomorrow Never Dies", a James Bond film. Artie wasn't sure of either.

It was a bit like a scene from a movie about heaven. Everyone in white, loose-fitting cotton garments, quietly smiling and chatting to each other.

They were all gradually walking up to a kind of verandah. Artie changed position so he could see inside the verandah. The old man he had seen a few times was sitting cross-legged on the floor, smoking a cigar and laughing. The man who brought Artie here was now sitting next to him.

Each person took their turn to slip their envelope inside the small wooden box next to the old man, then the old man talked to them for a few minutes, laughing all the time. Then, each person got up and left. They all looked quietly happy and contented.

Artie tried to listen, but the guests were speaking various different languages. The old man seemed to be speaking Cantonese and Artie's chaperone was translating.

Finally, when it was Artie's turn, he walked up and duly dropped his envelope in the slot. He then kneeled down in front of the old man. The old man's face seemed dedicated to laughing. His eyes laughed, his lips laughed, and his skin was permanently wrinkled in a laughing pose.

His face reminded him of a painting Artie had read about in a popular book "The Tao of Pooh" by Benjamin Hoff. The book was an explanation of Taoism through the medium of the famous children's character Winnie the Pooh. In it, Hoff mentioned that there was a painting that summarized the three major Chinese religious traditions through depictions of vinegar tasters.

Apparently in ancient China, people tasted vinegar in the same way that the French might taste wine, to test its quality and taste. Hoff stated that the first vinegar taster in the picture was the Buddha, and he held a bitter expression, representing the belief that life was a bitter experience, which we must escape by achieving enlightenment, nirvana.

The second vinegar taster was Confucius, and he had a sour face, symbolizing his belief that the world used to be purer, with people behaving well and respecting their parents and their elders, but things had turned sour.

The third taster was Lao Tzu, the founder of Taoism, and he displayed a smile, symbolizing sweetness. This was a reference to the beauty of the natural state of things.

The businessman talked first. He explained that he used to work for Ernst and Young, an accounting firm, but then discovered the old man, and had been following and assisting him since. He spoke several languages, including Cantonese, Mandarin, Japanese, English, and Thai, and acted as a translator for the old man.

He told Artie that the old man was a reincarnation of a Taoist immortal known as The White Dragon King. He asked Artie if he had any questions for the King. Artie couldn't quite think of anything.

Then the old man let out a lovely little cackle and began talking. The businessman translated: *"Your choice is an unusual one, young man. You can succeed in your mission, but you must stay strong and focused."* He then added, *"Can you imagine if Keith could see you now. He might be paying for your lunch, instead of the other way round!"*

Both the businessman and the old man stopped talking but kept eye contact with Artie. The old man kept laughing and smoking his cigar. His eyes twinkled. He almost seemed to wink at Artie, though his eyes never moved. The old man leaned forward and slipped a red, elasticated bracelet around Artie's right wrist. It had a very small, circular jade tablet in the middle of it. The front of the jade had a small, subtle, but clearly distinguishable image of a dragon carved into it.

Artie raised his hand a little in acknowledgment and thanks and walked off the verandah smiling, even laughing a little.

He went back to his place to digest what just happened. Although he didn't know it, he would never get to see the old man again. Any questions he had about the whole experience would remain unanswered.

65. *May 15, 2015. Boeung Keng Kang district, Phnom Penh, Cambodia.*

The room Artie had rented cost forty dollars for a week. He paid for a whole week, although he would only be using it for two nights. A little subterfuge. He arrived the day before yesterday and would be leaving in a few hours, in the early hours of the morning of May 16.

The room was pretty grubby and sparsely furnished, but it was perfect for his purposes. In a relatively quiet corner of *Boeung Keng Kang*, a district where foreign backpackers sometimes chose to stay. Slightly quieter than *Daun Penh*, the more vibrant backpacker choice.

Artie had spent the afternoon and early evening in *Svay Pak*, a village thirty minutes' drive from Phnom Penh. *Svay Pak* was a very small place, known mainly for its Vietnamese immigrant community, and, sadly, its brothels. The girls and boys who worked in those brothels were usually Vietnamese too.

By now, in his previous and current lives, Artie had seen a lot. A lot of cruelty, violence, perversion, and depravity. But he was saddened by what he saw in *Svay Pak*. In general, the sex workers were young here. Maybe fifteen to sixteen on average. But there were brothels at the back that specialized in providing much younger girls and boys.

As well as the sheer depravity of the place, Artie was shocked by the brazenness of it. It was clear what was going on. Everything was out in the open. The customers of the brothels, local and foreign, shopped around like families in a shopping mall, inspecting products and comparing prices till they were happy to strike a deal.

Artie had heard a great deal about Svay Pak from the scuzzier expats he met at bars in Phnom Penh on his intelligence-gathering evenings. He had decided a while ago to visit, find a customer most deserving of his intentions, and then perform an intervention.

He arrived in *Svay Pak* at around four in the afternoon and sat in a bar watching the world go by for a couple of hours. He had started to get the very basic lay of the land. The least depraved places were on the main street, the worst down the side alleys.

He settled for a place with no name deep in a side street. He sat in the entrance area where an array of children was paraded in front of him. It took all of his resolve, and all of his acting skills, to stay in his role as a foreign sex tourist looking for this type of action. But he did it.

A voice in the back of his mind was also reminding him, that if he got caught by police at the wrong moment, he would appear as a pedophile, and wouldn't be able to convince the courts otherwise.

He selected a girl who was maybe eight or nine. Paid the mama-san, and walked with his girl, hand in hand, to one of the curtained-off areas for guests to have their fun. He chose a spot that allowed him to peep out of the curtain back at the reception. The mama-san accompanied them. "*One hour. No violence. If you want more time, you pay me more.*", she said matter-of-factly. Artie could hear the thousands of times she had said that before, and how little interest she held in the transaction about to go down.

He knew that the 'no violence' instruction was certainly not for the girl's benefit. It was just to ensure she remained in good enough condition to be resold repeatedly and would be good to go with the next customer straight after he had finished. He was also pretty sure that the 'no violence' rule could be broken if he was willing to pay more.

He paid for an extra hour right there and then. "*OK. Two hours.*" She said something in Vietnamese to the girl. Artie assumed it was something like "*Do a good job. Make the customer happy. Or else...*"

Once inside, he looked at the girl who was starting to undress. He stopped her and made the universal sign that involved bringing one's index finger up to one's closed lips. The 'shush' sign, symbolizing both quiet and secrecy. He handed the girl fifty dollars. It saddened Artie that this little girl, who was almost certainly less than ten years old, completely understood his request in a second. In other circumstances, he would have been happy and amazed at her preternatural calm and her street smarts. But he realized how she had got them.

Artie also knew that the money, even though huge for *Svay Pak*, would be meaningless and useless to the girl. She would hand everything over to the mama-san straight afterward. But Artie used the language of money to show her he was a 'big man', so that the girl would know to obey him for the time that they were together. Artie hated to think like that, but it was critical that she didn't break his cover.

After a while a prospective customer came in. A big, jovial guy with blond hair and a mustache. Artie guessed he was in his early fifties. From his accented English, Artie guessed that he was maybe German or Dutch. The fact that he was so comfortable here, and threw in a couple of words of Vietnamese, suggested this wasn't his first visit to Svay Pak. Perfect.

About an hour later, the guy, who Artie was calling Hans in his head, emerged. Artie let him tip the mama-san, and leave, then followed a couple of minutes later. After retrieving the camera from the booth Hans had been in. Artie was pleased with his timing. It was just after 6 p.m. now, and the sun was already down, which was perfect.

A scuffle, a conversation, and a thirty-minute car ride later, here they were in Artie's temporary abode in Phnom Penh. Hans, who Artie now knew was in fact called Pieter von Donckhurst, sat in the armchair Artie had put him in. Although he had become compliant once Artie showed him the video of his romantic interlude in Svay Pak, Artie had chosen to bind his arms and legs to the chair anyway. To make him feel powerless. Part of the punishment. Artie also gagged Pieter for a while too, to prevent him screaming, but then took the gag off, Pieter knowing it could be put back at any time.

Artie used the video as *kompromat* (*компромат*), a wonderful Russian portmanteau word combining the words for compromising and materials. Within an hour, Artie had gained access to all of

Pieter's liquid funds. Artie would carefully transfer them to his mission fund through a hard-to-follow trail. After his time with Pieter was over.

Artie then used Pieter's email password to gain access to all his messages. Artie's deductive skills allowed him fairly quickly to understand who Pieter's boss, colleagues, closest family members, and friends were. He was pleased when he understood that Pieter's mother was digitally savvy, and a frequent email contact of Pieter's too.

He slipped the memory stick from the video camera into a USB stick that allowed it to connect to his computer. Pieter watched as Artie slowly and methodically emailed the video material to all of them, with the title "Pieter at Play".

Artie had missed a similar kind of opportunity with some Canadians in Bangkok a while back. He was pleased that he had been able to learn and improve.

It occurred to Artie as he was doing this that although Pieter had thought this was kompromat, it was now clear to him that it was in fact *unkompromat*. A word Artie had just made up because, unlike *kompromat*, he was actually showing it to people rather than threatening to show it in order to control Pieter. Although he did do a bit of that at the start of the evening. Artie's neologism also suggested the word 'uncompromising' to him. He laughed to himself quietly, which seemed to freak Pieter out even more.

"Think of your friends. Your family. Your mom. Watching the video and knowing what you've done, Pieter."

Pieter had a look in his eyes that Artie had not quite seen before. It was like he wanted to be angry, but he was completely defeated, broken. Probably from what had just happened, being pretty sure what was about to come, and being powerless to prevent it.

Pieter was like a spring that had been overstretched and could no longer return to its original shape. Artie remembered back in high school physics, learning Hooke's law. As he remembered it, Hooke's law states that the amount a spring can stretch is proportional to the load put on it. After the load was removed, the spring would return to its original shape. Unless the load was greater than the spring's elastic limit. Loads greater than that would cause the spring to deform permanently. Artie believed that he had loaded Pieter beyond his elastic limit already tonight. And the night, and the loading, were by no means over yet.

Artie left Pieter like that, with the video from the brothel playing on a loop while he went and had a cup of tea. He came back and ended Pieter's life with what started as a headlock.

Although he was glad to have removed Pieter from this earth and felt zero remorse or regret about that, Artie felt so terribly sad. Sad for the girl Artie had allowed Pieter to violate. For the money the mama-san received from both him and Pieter for her flesh-peddling. But more importantly, for all the sex workers in Svay Pak and those like them around the world.

He knew he couldn't save everyone in the world. But being in that village. In that brothel. Seeing the faces of some of those young boys and girls. And knowing he was walking away in order to complete his mission almost broke him. Almost.

The five thousand dollars of Pieter's funds that he gave to a Cambodian charity for sex workers didn't really help how Artie felt, but nevertheless, he hoped it would do a lot of good.

71.

66.   May 28, 2015. Bangkok.

Today was a day off. Despite Artie's tight schedule and single-mindedness dedication to his mission, he knew that he needed a break from time to time, to remain effective. He had chosen to stay at the Landmark Hotel on Sukhumvit Road for this break. Only a stone's throw from Soi 4, known as Nana, one of the three infamous red-light districts for foreigners in central Bangkok. Because of that proximity, the Landmark was a perfect place for Artie to fit in and be invisible, by occupying his persona of a slightly sleazy, burned-out, middle-aged American.

This morning was massage time. He chose 11 a.m. to get his massage when many people weren't yet up from last night's debauchery. It took twenty minutes to walk to his favorite massage place, Asia Herb Association, on Soi 24. There was another branch of Asia Herb much nearer his hotel, on Soi 4, but he preferred the larger, more anonymous one, and also preferred to use a place further from his hotel.

Bangkok wasn't a great city to walk in. It was, of course, hot. And as a tourist, lots of people bothered you as you walked. Also, the sidewalks tended to be in a terrible state of repair. Lots of holes. Unevenness. There were a lot of changes in levels. Artie didn't recall ever seeing anyone in a wheelchair on the street in Bangkok, either local or tourist. He couldn't imagine it being very easy for them to get around.

Massage was a huge thing in Asia. Foreigners in Thailand often thought about the naughty massages that were available in the red-light districts. But legitimate, therapeutic massage was a huge business, and many people regularly had one. In fact, one of the main schools of massage in Thailand was connected to Wat Pho, a Buddhist temple famous for its huge, reclining Buddha figure.

Artie enjoyed the twenty-minute stroll from his hotel to the spa, despite the heat and the sidewalks. One benefit of Artie choosing an

11am massage was that most of the naughty massage places along his route weren't open yet. At peak times there would often be a handful of masseuses waiting outside these places trying to coax customers, particularly single, middle-aged foreign male customers, in.

"*Mister. Mister.*"

"*Come in. Your size. Can do.*"

"*Just three hundred Baht per hour.*"

As he knew from prior experience, most of them would get you inside, begin giving you a massage, then ask you if you wanted 'special'. If you said yes, there was often a menu of sexual services on offer, ranging from a handjob to full sex. Most didn't mention any of the illicit services before they got you inside, but it was pretty obvious that these places weren't legitimate massage studios.

A few were brazen enough to tell you upfront that was what they were offering before you went in.

He couldn't blame any of them for plying their trade, but it wasn't fun fending them off, especially after the first ten or twenty shops.

In his previous life, Artie might have stopped in at one of these places, but he was on a different program right now. He wanted a serious, therapeutic massage by a well-trained masseur. Male or female. He wanted it to be administered in a comfortable, quiet environment. In Asia Herb, he got to sit in a La-Z-Boy-like chair, in a dark booth, with a quiet, skilled therapist and the sound of running water from an artificial stream that the owners of Asia Herb had cleverly installed. In cheaper tourist-friendly massage parlors, the customers were often packed in like sardines, the therapists chatted with each other, and even sometimes watched Thai soap operas on wall-mounted TVs.

The naughty, happy-ending joints tended to be unhygienic, the masseuses weren't trained, were often not keen on doing actual massage, and were often quite aggressive in marketing the special services they offered.

Artie arrived at the refreshingly cool Asia Herb spa and was greeted by a polite receptionist. One of the novel aspects of the Asia Herb experience was that the reception staff were often from countries other than Thailand, as they were massage students from overseas.

He filled out a form specifying exactly what he wanted. In his case it was a two-hour seated massage, focusing on head, neck, shoulders for the first hour, and feet and lower legs for the remainder. He chose 'hard' as the strength he required. He indicated that he had no allergies or health conditions (even though that was far from true.) He completely fabricated all the identifying information: name, age, etc. He chose a different set of details every time. This meant that he didn't earn loyalty points, and get free massages, but he could certainly live with that.

He was led to a small waiting area. His shoes were taken from him, and he was given a pair of slippers. He was served a small green ceramic mug of a rather fragrant tea. Artie remembered that traditional Thai massage taught that it was very important for both therapist and customer to drink plenty of liquid before and after the treatment.

After a few minutes, his masseuse showed up. She looked to be in her mid-forties. She walked slowly but with a reassuringly assured manner, like she had done this hundreds of times before. She walked him to an area with stools, with an artificial stream flowing in front of them. She asked him to sit, then proceeded to scrub his feet clean. She then dried them off and led him to a dark room with individual booths, each containing a big, comfortable cream-colored chair. He sat down, and then the therapist pulled a lever to make the chair recline.

Artie smelled the familiar smell, a mixture of tiger balm, jasmine tea, and a few other notes he couldn't identify but recognized from his many previous visits. This scent made him relax, just like Pavlov's bells had made dogs salivate decades earlier in Russia. Artie had read that the sense of smell was the most powerful in evoking memories, and this particular smell served to automatically relax him. He had also read that airlines and hotel chains had started using this olfactory memory as a way to try to addict customers to their brands. Capitalism never sleeps or misses a trick, he thought.

Two hours later, Artie emerged refreshed from the darkened booth and was led back to the waiting area and served some more tea. He thanked his masseuse, gave her a sizeable but not too memorable tip, used the bathroom, and then walked out. He walked back to the top of Soi 24 to the large department store called Emporium. Unfortunately, it was past 1 p.m. now, and lots of the naughty massage parlors were fully staffed, so Artie received the attention that a man of his appearance got in Bangkok.

He slipped into the wonderfully air-conditioned Emporium, then got the escalator up to the food court on the top floor. He never really liked elevators, and always avoided them now, even if that meant climbing many flights of stairs. In this case, he just had to endure five floors of escalators.

Artie enjoyed eating in food courts because they were so anonymous, and he could mix and match dishes and cuisines. For today's lunch, Artie chose a bowl of soup noodles and a side dish of *tod man pla*, a kind of fishcake.

After lunch, Artie took a stroll to Kinokuniya, a fantastic Japanese bookshop that had branches in Bangkok. It typically had a great selection of books in Thai, English, Japanese, and Chinese. As Artie browsed the English language section on religion and spirituality, he could feel his day off starting to work just the way he hoped. His body and mind were relaxing. His chosen mission meant that he was living on his nerves constantly. Enervated. But not today.

He bought a couple of books in Kinokuniya, including one on the Buddha's life. He sat in the coffee shop connected to the bookshop, sipping a pleasantly fragrant cup of *sencha* green tea, thumbing through the book. He had read a bunch about Buddhism in his previous life, factual and fictional, including the well-known "Siddhartha" by Herman Hesse.

He had had two very distinct reactions to Buddhism. On the one hand, he didn't think he believed some of the core tenets of Buddhism, like the notion of reincarnation. He could see it as just another way of keeping people happy and, to some extent, under control.

But he also found the idea of seeking *nirvana*, the snuffing out of the candle of fear and desire, very alluring. And he found a great sense of peace when in Buddhist temples, especially those of the original Theravada Buddhism in Southeast Asia. Many modern Mahayana Buddhist temples in Japan, China, Hong Kong, and Taiwan seemed a little bit less special, less spiritual to him. A little more yang. A little less yin.

Artie also noted that in his lifetime, people the world over were attracted by Buddhist art and symbolism. Which he both understood and found curious. Buddha tattoos. Buddha bars. He knew that true Buddhists found this quite offensive. He had always wondered why there were Buddha bars around the world, but not Jesus, Moses, or Mohammad bars.

One of his regrets was that he had never made it to Tibet, to see the temples influenced by Vajrayana. A more esoteric Buddhism that was influenced by *Bon*, the older animist religion of Tibet. Artie giggled at the thought that if he believed in reincarnation, he would have hoped that he could visit Tibet in his next life. But he might need to get to Tibet to understand reincarnation better, so he could believe in it. The computer scientist polymath Douglas Hofstadter would call this predicament a strange loop. Joseph Heller would call it Catch-22.

Artie caught himself having these weird thoughts. Creative thoughts. Thoughts not related to his mission. Or his health condition. Non-transactional thoughts. He liked it. It meant his day off was working as it should.

Mid-afternoon he wandered back to his hotel for a nap. He saw the cleaning lady, a small, wiry Thai woman who appeared to be in her fifties. He gave her a 200 Baht tip. She thanked him, performing a wai, the common Thai gesture that involves putting the palms of one's hands together and bowing slightly. She seemed very happy.

Artie had always felt that the places people chose to tip and not tip, and the amounts of those tips, were very unfair. Doormen at hotels in the US made a small fortune for doing almost nothing. Waiters and waitresses at high-end restaurants typically got very generous tips, because they were a percentage of the price of the meal. Waiting staff at diners, much less often and much smaller tips. Workers at fast food chains typically got nothing. Also, cleaning staff in hotels, who have to put a hard shift in, doing work that is not much fun, typically got zilch. These days, if he didn't see the cleaning staff, he would leave a tip on the bed before he left the hotel. Not enough to be memorable, of course.

Waking up from his nap, Artie used the hotel gym. He stretched, then used the elliptical cross trainer for half an hour. Then he did four sets of repetitions using relatively light weights on a wide variety of multi-gym stations and free weights. Finally, he did a bit of work with the heavy boxing bag in the gym, making sure not to look too skillful to anyone in the gym. Finally, he did a closing set of stretches.

The whole routine took just over an hour. He stopped every few minutes to have a glass of water to remain hydrated. The whole routine was designed to keep him sharp and in shape, but to avoid the chance of injury as much as possible. He couldn't afford any prolonged time out to recover.

In the evening, he dressed as his persona, with a pair of sports shorts and a wife beater sleeveless t-shirt. He walked over to the strangely named Cabbages and Condoms restaurant. It was run as a charity, generating money to help Thais in Bangkok with sexual health. It also provided advice on sexual health issues and gave out free condoms, hence the name. But what Artie found out to his surprise was that the authentic Thai dishes were really quite good, if slightly overpriced. Tonight, he had chicken with ginger and a side dish of stir-fried vegetables. He also treated himself to a Diet Coke, a drink that he didn't normally allow himself to order these days.

When he was young, he thought of ginger as a rather innocuous spice, to be used sparingly in sweet foods like ginger cake. Over his years visiting Asia, he had learned of its medicinal properties, and that it could be equally well used in savory dishes. The amounts used in Western cuisine made it a subtle taste, whereas a Thai dish made with ginger could knock your socks off.

He wandered slowly home from his needed day of rest.

He sat down in the rather comfortable armchair in his hotel room and read from the second book he bought earlier. It was called "Three Cups of Tea." The lead author, Greg Mortenson, was a climber who had a fall and was nurtured back to health by the people of the Hunza Valley in Pakistan.

Following his recovery, Mortensen formed the Central Asia Institute, a charity dedicated to building schools in Pakistan and Afghanistan, especially to educate girls. His institute had built over a hundred schools.

The name "Three cups of tea" comes from a saying Mortensen's host family shared with him. "The first time you share a cup of tea with me, you are a stranger. The second time you are an honored guest. The third time you become family". A lot to admire about Mortensen, and about the people of the Hunza valley.

Artie liked to read books like this to keep up his inspiration levels. He knew that he didn't need them: he was fully committed to his mission. But a little inspiration every now and then couldn't hurt.

He showered, lay down, and was asleep within a minute. He managed a long, deep, and dreamless sleep in the unusually comfortable hotel environment.

67. May 29, 2015. Sukhumvit area, Bangkok.

The BTS Bangkok's Skytrain, began in 1999, before Artie first came to Bangkok, but it was continually expanding its scope. Artie was always struck by how clean and cool the Skytrain was compared to the steamy, somewhat grimy streets of Bangkok. He knew that the prices were several times the bus prices, and too expensive for some Thais at the lower end of the economic spectrum. But he still felt that the ever-expanding Skytrain network was a major positive for life in Bangkok.

Bangkok's MRT, its underground train system, started in 2004. Which was also a positive. But still, these moves didn't seem to really solve Bangkok's terrible traffic problems. Artie never got to the bottom of the reason, but it seemed like the combination of city planning and burgeoning car ownership meant that even a short journey might take several hours on the streets of the city. Artie had met several well-to-do Thais who told him that their cars always contained food and drink and equipment that allowed them to go to the bathroom inside their car if necessary.

Artie got off the Skytrain at Nana station. It was a short, seven- or eight-minute walk to Gulliver's Bar on Sukhumvit Soi 5.

He walked past the outside tables and entered the comfortably air-conditioned interior of the bar. Gulliver's was quite an unusual bar for central Bangkok. It was targeted mainly at foreigners, and like most such bars, had attractive young, female waiting staff. But unlike other places, there was no sense that the waitresses were interested in, or available for, hooking up with the customers. Gulliver's was more like an American sports bar, with lots of large TVs showing all the major games from the US and Europe.

The other unique feature of Gulliver's was the sheer number of pool tables. They had about twenty tables, all of which were in pretty decent condition, had good rests and extended rests, plenty of chalk, and a rack of straight, solid cues. The waiting staff didn't play pool, and each table had a small chalkboard for customers to sign their names on if they wanted to play.

Gulliver's was a pool player's bar. They regularly held tournaments. And it was not uncommon for players to play each other for money, even substantial amounts of money. Artie tried not to come here too often, but he felt that he could come every few months, to top up his funds, without being noticeable. Especially since he tweaked his appearance a little each time he came.

Gulliver's had one incredibly curious little feature that he had never seen anywhere else in the world. It sounded gross, but Artie thought it was a kind of genius innovation. In the men's bathroom, as well as the usual urinals, stalls, and sinks, there was a sink just as you came in the entrance, on the left. Where the normal sinks were high, round, and shallow, this one was a deep cuboidal sink installed at about knee height. Artie was confused when he first noticed it, but then he saw the sign above it, explaining its purpose.

It was a 'vomiting sink', for those who had indulged in a few too many Singhas, Tigers, or Heinekens. Designed to be comfortable to bend over and spew. No splashback. Powerful taps and a wide plughole to allow quick and easy elimination of the evidence. And of course, if the vomiter of the moment used that sink, the other sinks remained vomit, and most importantly scent-of-vomit, free. Even the positioning of the sink close to the entrance but out of sight of the outside meant that a poor over-drinker with an urgent need was more likely to make it. Less likely to hurl all over the floor or themselves.

In his previous life, Artie had liked to play the best pool players, both Thai and foreign, to challenge himself. Now his purpose was purely financial, and he tried to choose the players he could make the most money from in the most invisible way. He was looking for targets who seemed to have a decent amount of cash that they were willing to splash, weren't too observant, and overrated their own pool-playing abilities. That last trait was, fortunately for Artie, all too common.

It was an art working out how many games each of his opponents might be willing to play, letting them win a few, and slowly stepping up the stake so that Artie could walk away at the end with a good few hundred dollars in his pocket, his target having had a good time, feeling Artie was just a little luckier than them, and not remembering too much about him.

In his previous life, Artie used to like watching the top professionals on TV. Some of his favorites were. Efren "The Magician" Reyes, Earl "The Pearl" Strickland, Johnny "The Scorpion" Archer, Mika "The Iceman" Immonen and Ralf "The Kaiser" Souquet. Their nicknames were not quite as colorful as pro wrestlers, but not far off.

They all had their own styles, but one thing Artie noted about all of them. In tournaments, they played many fewer fancy shots and trick shots than he initially expected. Every shot looked ordinary. They all played percentage pool. He did the same now. Both for the same reason they did and for another. Not to reveal his capabilities. His Uncle Phil, the hustler, who hid his light under a bushel for other reasons, would be proud of him.

Today, Artie played games with four different people at different, non-adjacent tables over a few hours, and walked away with winnings of 27,000 Baht. At the current exchange rate of around 33, that would translate to $818. Although he had no plans to go back to the US, dollars were a very helpful currency in Cambodia, his next stop.

Artie reckoned he would get just under $800 at SuperRich, his favored currency exchange in the Sukhumvit area. He used other currency shops sometimes, including ones that offered very poor rates. All as part of his continued regime to stay invisible. To stay grey.

As he made his way down a dark Soi, a young woman came out of a hotel entrance and walked past him. Artie noticed that her short minidress was torn, her make-up was smeared across her face a little, and there were several red marks on her cheeks and tears in her eyes.

It was pretty clear to Artie what had happened. Artie turned round and jogged back to catch up with her. She went from a kind of thousand-yard stare to flinching nervously as she became aware of Artie. He signaled as best he could that he meant no harm to her. He quickly beckoned her to the side of the street. She followed nervously.

Artie made a snap decision, got the twenty-seven thousand Baht he had just won out of his pocket, counted out seven thousand, and kept it. He handed the remaining twenty thousand to her. She looked confused. It was clear from the words they had exchanged so far that this woman was Khmer and only spoke a few words of English, so they were unlikely to be able to have much of a conversation. Artie took her head slowly and gently in his hands and kissed her forehead. It was a spontaneous gesture, and he wasn't sure it would work, but he wanted to show this woman that there was not only evil and misfortune in her world.

She dissolved into tears, and they sat together against a wall for a while. He held her hand as she slowly recovered her composure. Through a combination of words and hand gestures, Artie learned the room number of her assailant at the hotel she had just left.

After that, Artie got in a taxi with her and accompanied her to her apartment building on the outskirts of Bangkok. He was tired, but he knew that sometimes Bangkok taxi drivers were not so honorable with vulnerable female customers.

He asked the driver to wait, giving him a hundred Baht tip. He and this poor woman, whose name and story he would never know, looked each other in the eye. She kissed him on the cheek. They hugged. Then Artie got back in the cab and instructed the driver to return to the place where he picked them up.

Artie feigned a little drunkenness as he entered the hotel grounds, and slipped the security guard a fifty Baht tip, pretending to try to give him a good-natured kiss on the cheek. The guard laughed.

About an hour later, Artie re-emerged and gave him another 50 Baht tip. The security guard probably didn't notice that Artie's eyes had changed color in the interim. The security guard offered to call Artie a taxi, but Artie did the universal scissoring motion with his fingers, showing that he wanted to walk. They waved goodnight to each other with smiles on their faces.

73.

68. June 1, 2015. Oasis.

Artie had to pop back to Oasis for some maintenance. Ploy was waiting at the door to greet him. It wasn't hard for her to know when he, or anyone, was coming. They had installed an array of security devices, including night vision cameras, microphones, infrared, heat, and pressure sensors.

As Artie arrived at the door, he saw something he had never seen before. Artie and Ploy had the most trusted relationship, a powerful shared mission and vision, and the utmost mutual respect. But their behavior towards each other was very functional. Even transactional. Even when they had sex together a couple of times there wasn't much showing of emotion or playfulness. The things that inhabited a more normal life, a more normal relationship.

But for the first time ever, Artie saw a real smile on Ploy's face. Her eyes danced with happiness. He looked at her quizzically.

Ploy took his hand and wordlessly led him into the living room. And there they were. Sat together, staring at him, with their tongues hanging out. He later learned that Ploy had already named them. Ding and Dong. Together their name meant crazy in Thai. Dingdong. Crazy in a kind of cute way. Which befitted their bouncy, overenthusiastic behavior.

Ding and Dong were brother and sister. They were what was called in Lao "village dogs" (*"ma bān"*). Artie later learned from Ploy that they had shown up a couple of weeks ago, looking dirty, hungry, and emaciated. Their ribcages were visible, in a way that they really shouldn't have been. Ploy had given them some food on the porch, then waited till the next day.

The next day they came back, so she decided to take them in. She showered them, which they seemed to enjoy. Since then, they had been glued to Ploy's side whenever they could be.

As Artie was petting them, they pushed their hard heads into Artie's legs. He hadn't grown up with animals, but he loved them. In his previous life, whenever someone had an animal, he asked permission to pet them, then wouldn't leave them alone for far too long. And although he had always dreamed of a border collie as part of his idealized, fantasy family, somehow, he often preferred the strays. The mongrels.

He had read a very touching book written by the Thai King, Rama 9, about a stray dog he adopted in 1998, called Tongdaeng (ทองแดง). Rama 9, also known as Bhumibol, loved animals, including dogs. But he developed a special relationship with Tongdaeng, and the dog seemed to have a special relationship with him too, always behaving politely in front of him. Artie had, over the years, heard more and more about the Thai royal family which meant he couldn't be sure what was and wasn't true about them. But he hoped that the Tongdaeng story was.

He hadn't thought of it before now, but of course, having a couple of dogs around the place was perfect. An extra bit of security, and also therapy for the residents of Oasis. And he reckoned that it couldn't be better for the dogs too. They would get spoiled rotten.

He felt like Ploy was showing him the dogs for two reasons. One was just pure joy. The other was implicitly asking his permission, even though she kind of knew she didn't have to.

Artie couldn't help smiling a bit also as the dogs showed him their brand of love. He turned to Ploy and said, *"Let's take them to the vet as soon as possible to make sure they are healthy."*

So, it was done. Two new members of the family. An extra level of security. More companionship for Ploy, and for the more temporary residents of Oasis. A little more continuity. And a little more charity. Artie liked to think that over time there may be a few more animals around the place. Not enough to draw attention. Just a few.

69. June 3, 2015. Bangkok, Thailand.

Derek Archer sat in the food court of the Siam Paragon shopping center, eating a bowl of boat noodles, *kuay teow rua*. He loved that you both could and were expected to tailor the taste of the dish to your own liking. Wherever you get boat noodles in Thailand, you also get a set of condiments to add to your dish. These included dried chili powder, sugar, fish sauce, and pickled chilis in vinegar. This stood in stark contrast to posh European restaurants, where it was an insult to adulterate what the chef had prepared.

At 10:07, Artie arrived. He was deliberately a few minutes late, to see how the punctuality-obsessed Archer would handle it. He passed the test, with a humorous *"Too early for you squire?"*

"Sorry buddy. A couple of unexpected complications before I left this morning," said Artie.

"Roger that. Shit happens."

Archer was, Artie learned, ex-military. Born in Newcastle in the UK. Bit of a wild child. Drinker. Football hooligan. (Soccer, that is.) Enlisted in the British Army at eighteen. After twelve years as a regular soldier, Archer had spent five years in the Special Air Services, one of the UK's largest and most respected special forces.

He had seen action in Iraq. Left at thirty-five. Did a bunch of private contracts in countries like Egypt, the UAE, and Angola. The nature of them was not that clear to Artie from his research, but he thought he could hazard a pretty good guess. Some of them protect important visitors and dignitaries. Some may have been more offensive missions. Private sector versions of what Archer had done for queen and country. None of them for the faint-hearted, for sure.

Married briefly when in the SAS. His ex-wife and two children lived in Hereford, near SAS headquarters. Provided financial support for the kids but didn't visit much.

This was the first time they were meeting in person. The seven minutes that Artie was supposedly late also gave Artie a chance to observe Archer from a distance. Artie noticed that Archer had chosen a table and seat with his back to the wall, and a really good overview of the large vista that was the food court. Archer's eyes kept flicking to the various entrances and exits. All of these behaviors and choices were consistent with Archer's special forces background.

He was forty-two now, but still looked to be in great shape to Artie, with just a few visible scars on his face and arms. Artie wondered why these special forces guys always had mustaches and beards. If he didn't know better, he could imagine that they were trying to make up for their insecurities and feelings of vulnerability by sporting very manly facial hair. But he knew that that wasn't true. Artie concluded that it was just a kind of uniform.

Artie had met Archer on a dark web website. It was, in a way, not that dissimilar to one of those dating websites where you put in some details about yourself, and the website helps you find potential dates. After a while poking around, Artie, whose id was X113 on the site was matched with Archer, who was B2416. They communicated in codes for a while, checking whether there was potential for a match and whether each felt safe with the other, finally agreeing to meet up today in person to discuss a business opportunity.

"*So, you've got some work to be done.*"

"*Yes, we have Mr. Archer. I have to tell you though, that it might get a bit messy. If you know what I mean.*"

Archer knew exactly what Artie meant. Archer thought that Artie would be terrified if Artie knew just how he knew so exactly. He was mistaken about that, but that wasn't important.

"*Well, Mr. Barker, I am not afraid of dirty or dangerous work, as long as the pay is right.*" Archer used the alias that Artie had given him.

Artie got straight to it: "*I am sure you will find our offer generous, Mr. Archer. My client owns a bar in Pattaya. He uses the back room of the bar to conduct some other business. One of the bargirls ended up seeing a little too much of his business dealings, and he needs her disappeared.*"

"*She still work at the bar?*"

"*I believe so.*"

"*She doesn't suspect he wants to off her?*"

"*I don't believe so.*"

"*Well, that shouldn't be too hard then. Might even get myself some alone time with her before I do the deed. Might be fun to be her last. If you know what I mean.*"

Artie knew exactly what Archer meant. They discussed a few of the details, including the price, and agreed to meet once more to finalize. Artie had no intention of honoring that plan. Of course, there was no contract to be fulfilled. And Archer had just disqualified himself as a candidate for Artie, in multiple ways.

Artie left the food court first, thinking he was glad that he had gone hard on the physical tweaks today. Really dark skin color, green eyes, large paunch. He hoped that would make it hard for Archer to spot him if they were ever in the same geography again.

When Artie never reached back out to him, Archer would just think that Artie was a timewaster, unable or unwilling to go through with the things they discussed. This wasn't the first time Archer would have a conversation with a potential client that didn't pan out. He would think nothing of it, and just move on to the next thing.

"*Yankee wanker,*" Archer thought to himself as he sat and finished his noodles.

70. June 5, 2015. Siem Reap, Cambodia.

Siem Reap was the town closest to Angkor Wat, the amazing temple complex built by King Suryavarman II starting in the 12th century, lost for centuries, rediscovered by French explorer Henri Mouhot in the 1840s. In Artie's previous life, his most interesting and adventurous holiday was visiting this temple complex.

Angkor Wat itself was an amazing temple in itself, the center of a city of a million people in the year 1100, when it was the capital of the Khmer empire. But the one that entranced Artie the most was the Bayon. Around every corner of that temple, there was a large stone face, thought to be modeled on the face of King Jayavarman VII. He also loved Ta Prohm, the temple that had fig, banyan, and kapok trees growing through it. That was the one that featured heavily in the first "Lara Croft: Tomb Raider" film with Angelina Jolie.

As well as being blown away by Angkor the first time he visited, a couple of things amused Artie. The first is that many of the statues have a thin line at their neck. When he asked his tour guide why, he learned that successive Khmer Kings had different allegiances to Hinduism and Buddhism. In the name of efficiency, the new King would just remove the heads of the statues and replace them with ones of their chosen religion.

The other thing that amused him was the name of the town "*Siem Reap*" itself. Artie found out the name meant 'Siam defeated', a reference to the continual conflict between Siam (Thailand) and the Khmer kingdom (Cambodia.)

Artie had seen her already a couple of times around Siem Reap. She looked like she was in her mid-30s. A quiet but very confident solo traveler. Physically fit. Naturally quite attractive, but not wearing make-up or clothes that emphasized her feminine features. She tended to wear loose-fitting khaki cargo pants with lots of pockets and an elasticated waist. And loose-fitting t-shirts in unremarkable colors. She dressed for functionality, and perhaps to actively signal that she wasn't in the market for a guy.

He'd seen a few guys try to hit on her, And one woman too. Tourists and locals. He liked the way she handled them. Starting off being friendly and polite, gently stepping up the way she rejected their approach only if necessary. And only just enough to achieve the goal of making them walk away.

Artie always felt that people were like holograms. Because you can look at a hologram from any angle, every piece of it actually contains a representation of the whole thing. People and incidents are like that. If you look at them carefully, and from every angle, you can see almost everything about them from any one interaction, any one moment.

Tonight, Artie found her in a small bar on the edge of town. A bar without a name. Black walls and floor. Dark and dirty, but the seats and tables were surprisingly comfortable. A bar and two pool tables. Artie didn't imagine he would play on them tonight.

When he arrived, the song "Interzone" by Joy Division was playing. A post-punk outfit from Manchester, England, Joy Division was one of his favorite bands. Satisfyingly twisted and tormented. And "Interzone" was probably his favorite Joy Division song, even though "Love Will Tear Us Apart" and "Transmission" were by far their most famous songs. It struck him as strange that such an obscure song would be playing here. Southeast Asia's bars all tended to play popular rock classics from the 1970s and 1980s. All those who hung out in bars here got repeated overdoses of "Hotel California", "Born in the USA", "Sweet Child O' Mine" and the like.

But "Interzone" here tonight? Maybe it was a special request by a customer. Strange, but very welcome.

Artie loved, loved, loved Joy Division. Somehow their twisted sound and the lyrics of their troubled genius of a lead singer, Ian Curtis, really spoke to him. After Curtis took his own life, the band became New Order, whose single "Blue Monday" seemed to own the year

1983. Artie had met lots of people who loved both Joy Division and New Order. For him, Joy Division was connected to the source, but New Order was a poppy electronic nothing of a band.

She was sitting reading a dog-eared paperback book. He caught a glimpse of the cover and saw that it was a copy of "The Sailor Who Fell From Grace With the Sea", by Yukio Mishima. He couldn't help smiling a little, remembering how good he found Mishima's work, and that book in particular, to be. Back when reading books for pleasure was a thing for him. He even loved the title.

He also remembered reading a couple of other books by Mishima, including a spectacular book of short stories called Acts of Worship, and then looking into Mishima's life a little. Mishima was full of opposites and ironies. Mishima was fiercely patriotic and a lover of Japan's traditions yet viewed by most Japanese as narcissistic and an embarrassment. Also, he was and is one of the most famous and popular Japanese authors for foreigners to read, yet not thought of by most Japanese people as one of their famous or important authors.

A bit like most countries exporting what they judge to be their worst beers, keeping the good stuff for the locals, thought Artie. Although he liked them too. In his previous life, he was a big fan of a Corona with a wedge of lime shoved into it, especially in the summer, although he knew beer aficionados thought of it as one of the weaker Mexican beers. Dos Equis was much better thought of by those connoisseurs, especially Dos Equis Dark.

Artie reckoned she was in her early thirties, and the two guys approaching her to be in their mid-twenties. He had heard her talk before, and she was clearly Australian. He guessed the guys were Israelis. Maybe doing the almost obligatory travel after the end of their military service. *"Hey baby, what's your name?"*, the taller one of the two said. She waited a fraction of a second and let her book dip a little bit, so she made direct eye contact with him, paused, and then brought her book back up.

Artie admired the conciseness of her behavior. In that tiny act, she made it clear she had heard the guy, was not afraid or intimidated by him, and non-verbally declined any offer or request he was about to make. That should have been enough, but he was a bold, young gun, a bit drunk and a lot cocky, and not up for being dissed by this bitch. (His thoughts, not Arties.) And his wingman snickered, egging him on.

"What the fuck's wrong with you. Why you do me like that?" Artie could see Jess calculating the minimal path to getting through this incident quickly and painlessly so she could return to her book and her lime and soda. *"Look. I'm not interested. Move on."* Artie had noticed that Australians started sentences with "Look" a lot. Nothing wrong with it, just interesting. He found it useful to collect signals like that.

Again, Jess's response should have been enough but Ari (Artie later found out that was his name) wasn't going anywhere. He reached out and pushed Jess's book down from her face with his right hand. With surprising speed and strength, Jess dropped the book, grabbed Ari's right wrist with her right hand, and used the back of her left hand to stretch out his fingers painfully, causing him to involuntarily rise up on his toes, then she stood and looked him in the eye and said slowly, deliberately *"I'm reading."* She held on to the Aikido-based wrist grab just long enough to make it 100% clear to Ari that she chose if and when to end it, and then released.

As well as the shock, there was obviously a calculation going on in his head around what he should do next. A calculus of the effort to quell his ego and narcissism, versus the desire to save face in front of his mate and the others in the bar who were watching, the likelihood of him winning if things got more physical, and maybe, just maybe a bit of a voice of decency tell him to stop this stupidity and walk away.

"Fuck you, you crazy bitch." Ari half spoke, half mumbled as he turned on his heels, and ambled away. Jess picked up her book, sat down, and took a sip of her drink. She was pretty sure that was the end of the incident. She didn't reckon the two Israelis would be waiting for when she left. She didn't think people at the bar were that

interested in what was happening. She noticed a chubby, slightly older guy who seemed to notice the whole incident, but that was no big deal.

Artie had let Jess notice him looking a little this time. A little bookmark to refer back to when they talked in the future. He hadn't let her notice him on previous occasions. That was all the interaction he had planned for them tonight. A few minutes later, he paid his bill and left.

71. Jess

Jess Blackman was born in Melbourne. Her family, like many people in Melbourne, liked to think of Melbourne as the cultural capital of Australia. Canberra was the political capital, but like a lot of political capitals, it was hardly a city at all. Just some manufactured neutral territory between other big cities. The same was true of Ottawa in Canada. The Hague in the Netherlands too, compared to the vibrancy of Amsterdam, and the port city of Rotterdam. Brasilia compared to the amazing Rio de Janeiro and São Paulo.

On the other hand, Sydney was the biggest and most famous city in Australia, with Iconic landmarks like the Opera House, Harbour Bridge, and Bondi Beach. But Melburnians thought of their city as more sophisticated, important, and cultural.

Those weren't adjectives that resonated with Jess at all, and she felt pretty uncomfortable and out of place throughout her childhood. She flunked out of school with no qualifications at sixteen, started waitressing, and ended up gravitating to Byron Bay. Byron Bay was a vaguely hippy-ish beach town. Hippy-ish like a tie-dyed t-shirt worn by a rich Californian kid. Not hippy-ish like a couple with no money who lived in a caravan, followed the Grateful Dead around selling veggie curries and wristbands to subsist. (The latter could be found in Nimbin, a town not far geographically from Byron Bay, but a world away culturally.)

Arriving in Byron Bay at seventeen, Jess found herself, at least a little. Found friends. Through a series of part-time classes, found bodywork. She learned Swedish, Thai, and Ayurvedic massage, then Shiatsu, the Alexander Technique, the Feldenkrais method, Rolfing, and a few types of yoga. She slowly transitioned from a waitress with an interest in bodywork, to a physical therapist who still had to waitress a little to balance the books.

Her favorite therapy was probably Rolfing. It was relatively unknown but, in Jess's view, extremely therapeutic for those who were ready for it. Developed by Ida Rolf, Rolfing was a therapeutic discipline that involved manipulating the *fascia*, the soft connective tissue of the body. It was a rather painful technique, and practitioners believed it not only improved the patient's physical condition; it also helped to release emotional traumas and repressed memories, that got 'encoded' in the body. Although it was definitely viewed as unproven and an 'alternative' therapy, Jess's intuition and practical experience suggested it was the real deal.

She liked the Feldenkrais method too. Developed by Moshé Feldenkrais in the first half of the twentieth century, based on his need to recover from a knee injury, Feldenkrais re-taught patients how to move. Dismissed as quackery by many, Jess had had very positive experiences with it.

In the world of yoga, she also particularly enjoyed Kundalini yoga. It was seen as a way to release latent energy trapped in your body, sometimes described as serpent energy or the fiery serpent. It required alignment of the spine and the *chakras*, or energy centers of the body.

Alexander Technique was good too, but she found that practitioners of it relatively arrogant and dogmatic. Not quite Jess's speed.

She couldn't really say that she had definitely found her true vocation in life with bodywork, but it at least felt like meaningful work that made sense to her. And she got quite good at it.

In her first few years in Byron Bay, she had a number of relationships with guys and a few with women. They were more satisfying than her teenage flirtings and fumblings back in Melbourne. She liked the people she slept with on the whole, when she was drunk and when she was sober. Some of the relationships lasted a few months. None of them was terrible. She remained on pretty good terms with almost all of her partners. But nothing felt quite right. Nothing she wanted to commit to.

She also became a bit more experimental with drugs in her newfound hometown. She had tried weed many times while she was in school in Melbourne, and coke a couple of times, but it hadn't been very interesting to her. More just a way of rebelling. In Byron, she took ecstasy many times in clubs, dropped acid a few times, and experimented with magic mushrooms.

Jess agreed that weed was probably a better experience than alcohol, and it didn't make sense that one was legal and the other wasn't. But she couldn't get too worked up about that fact. She was amazed at how passionate some people were about getting weed legalized.

She thought cocaine was a boring party drug. And ecstasy was fun, and maybe a bit risky for those with heart issues, but that was the end of it. Acid was fascinating and terrifying all at the same time. She felt she accessed thoughts and experiences while tripping that she could never get sober. Although some friends told her that skilled practitioners of meditation could get to the same place. And she was slightly scared of the power of acid; she felt like a bad trip could permanently damage her brain.

Mushrooms, on the other hand, felt like 'acid-light' to her, and that became her drug of choice. She took some most weekends. Although she would never presume to recommend them to others, she felt like mushrooms took her on a powerful journey of inner exploration.

In early 2014, Jess finally gave in to that vague, lingering feeling that she hadn't found her permanent place, her permanent purpose in life. Jess remembered reading a quote from Henry David Thoreau saying: *"Most men lead lives of quiet desperation."* Jess forgave him the male gendering, and really related to the sentiment. She thought that most people did lead lives of quiet desperation, but some of them chose to do something about that.

Throughout the first three months of the year, Jess wound down all her commitments and sold or gave away all her stuff. For some reason, the one thing she felt attached to was a bookcase she had bought in a local handicrafts store. She loved the fact that you could fold the shelves up and the sides inwards, then carry it as a flat object. She gave that to Kim, one of her besties, asking permission to have it back if she changed her mind or her circumstances in the future.

On 7 April 2014, with just over thirty-seven thousand dollars in her bank account and a backpack for company, Jess boarded a flight to Kochi in Kerala, India, traveling on a one-way ticket. She was really attracted by Kerala since it was the home of Ayurvedic medicine. She spent a few months receiving treatments and learning to give them. Like anything, some of the places and some of the practitioners were better than others. But overall, it was a very positive experience.

Then in May, Jess traveled overland to Tamil Nadu to an Ashram she had heard great things about. The journey was a bit rough, in terms of the quality of roads, timeliness of transport, and also the attitudes of men towards her. Quite a few tried it on with her. Jess was a confident woman, and if push came to shove, fairly handy physically. But she recognized she was in a strange land where she didn't know the rules or the escape routes. So, she lived on her nerves a bit during the journey.

In contrast, when she got to Anantha Jyoti Ashram, it was like heaven on earth. The name came from Sanskrit. Anantha means infinite or endless. Jyoti means light. The name conjured up the image of endless spiritual pursuit.

It was so, so peaceful. Everyone respecting each other's space. Lots of yoga. Some light work duties. And some fascinating lectures each evening by Swami Prakash. His full name was Prakashananda Saraswati, but he went by Prakash. Jess had never experienced anyone like him. People always talked about an aura, but until then that concept had felt metaphorical to Jess. With Swami Prakash, he seemed to be carrying around an energy that surrounded him and touched everyone he came into contact with.

Somehow when Jess saw him, she always thought of the line from the song by Aussie band Crowded House, *"Everywhere you go, always take the weather with you."* It felt kinda disrespectful, but she couldn't keep it out of her head.

She always felt she was learning so much, both intellectually and through direct energy, every time she was in his presence. And over the days and weeks, it seemed like he had identified her as a worthy student, a vessel for his teaching.

Then it all changed on the night of July 5. Jess was wandering in the woods, and suddenly the Swami was there. She didn't like to remember it in detail, but basically, he made a move on her. She resisted, and then he became more physical. He wasn't taking no for an answer. He was intent on getting into her pants.

Despite all the feelings she had had for him until that point, most notably deep respect, that all changed in an instant. Jess delivered a well-timed and accurate knee into the Swami's solar plexus. He crumpled into a heap that did not speak to the elegance of his normal yogic poses.

Jess didn't wait around to see the ramifications. She packed quickly and left the ashram, never to return. A few days later she boarded a flight from Bangalore to Vientiane in Laos, via Bangkok, to continue her journey.

72. *June 18, 2015. Flores, Indonesia.*

Flores was a relatively remote island, quite far to the East of Indonesia. It was known for Kelimutu, its volcano with multicolored crater lakes, and was also a good jumping-off point for a trip to Komodo island, where Komodo dragons come from. Artie was pleased that Jess had chosen Flores as her next destination. He felt like it was a good place for him to make his direct approach to her.

It was 3am now. They were on their way up the mountain to see sunrise fall on the volcanic pools. Jess had chosen a famous guesthouse where the bus routinely picked people up for this trip. It was challenging enough that the bus was winding its way up the narrow roads with hairpin bends to the top of the volcano at quite a pace. What made it extra challenging was that there was no room inside the bus when it got to the guesthouse, so Jess and Artie were both on top of the bus, with only a very thin rail around the edge of the roof to hold on to. That rail was originally designed to lash down baggage.

And if that wasn't enough, Artie was at the back of the bus, and unbelievably, a giant bat seemed to be chasing the bus up the mountain, frequently getting quite close to Artie. In his previous life, he would have had trouble climbing on top of the bus, and holding on as it swayed around the corners at speed. And he would have been terrified of the bat.

Jess remained unaware of Artie's presence. He had made a bunch of modifications to his appearance since she last saw him in that bar in Siem Reap. He had darkened his skin, gone for brown eyes, and removed the artificial paunch, so he looked pretty lean. This also meant that, although he was obviously significantly older than the backpacker crowd out here, he didn't look too out of place. Too noticeable.

After they got off the bus and were all being given hot coffee from flasks by the tour guides, Artie wandered over to Jess. *"I thought it was supposed to be warm in Indonesia."*

"Yeah, me too. You a Septic?"

"Septic?"

"Septic tank. Yank."

"Oh right, yep. Guilty as charged. Indianapolis. Bob." Indianapolis was far enough from Chicago to be a good cover, but near enough that he knew it well. A thought also went through Artie's head that Indianapolis was less than two hundred miles away from Chicago geographically, but it was about a million miles away culturally. Where Chicago was very ethnically diverse and cosmopolitan, on his occasional trips to Indianapolis, he experienced it as very old school, conservative, white middle America.

"Hey, Bob. I'm Jess. From Australia."

Somehow, Jess was never sure whether to say she was from Melbourne or Byron Bay. Not that it mattered that much. But anyhow, she always just introduced herself as Australian.

Artie didn't talk to her much after that. Just let her wander around enjoying the view. Every now and then they would give each other a glance and a smile.

Even though Artie was strictly on a mission, he could see why Kelimutu was so popular. The volcano has three separate lakes, each having striking and often changing colors. Their names were also intriguing. Tiwu Ata Mbupu, the Lake of Old People, was usually blue. Tiwu Nuwu Muri Koo Fai, the Lake of Young Men and Maidens, was often green. And Tiwu Ata Polo, the Enchanted Lake, was normally red or brown.

As well as its beauty, Kelimutu is considered a sacred site by the local community, the Lio ethnic group based in central Flores. The Lio are a largely agrarian people, who are known for weaving, and their traditional dance and music. The lakes were believed to be the resting place of departed souls.

When they got back down from the volcano a couple of hours later, Artie asked if she fancied lunch. Luckily she agreed.

They went to eat in Moni, the small village that was closest to Kelimutu and hence had a bunch of tourist-friendly places. They had a leisurely chat over a couple of hours in the amusingly named "Good Moni". Every serious backpacker knows that backpacking is not only about going places. It is also about meeting interesting people, both locals and fellow travelers. And also, about serendipity, and trying to avoid rushing anywhere. Almost the opposite of the normal business rat race. The purpose is no purpose. The schedule is no schedule.

In that spirit, Artie and Jess were able to take time to chat, not feel pressured to pack the day with tourism, or even talk about anything related to where they were. Their conversation wandered wildly, between music, movies, food, religion, philosophy, spirituality, and occasionally, tourism. At one point, they got pretty heated about the ingredients of the perfect burger.

Artie argued that a classic burger was a nice juicy beef patty in a bun. It could have cheese on it, certainly onions, a little lettuce, and maybe a slice of tomato. Maybe a pickle. Decorated with ketchup. Nothing more. He genuinely believed this, but also, it also bolstered his persona of Bob from Indianapolis perfectly. Jess was arguing for all kinds of potential additions, from avocado to pineapple.

"*You crazy new world Aussies don't know when to leave a good thing alone.*"

"*You septics are stuck in the past.*"

This conversation was genuinely fun for Artie, but it also served two other purposes. One was him bonding with Jess, to allow the relationship to continue. The other was to continue to feel her out and understand how she ticked. Confirm that she could be the one. She was ticking all the boxes so far.

The final substantive conversation of lunch was about movies. Jess admitted that her favorite movie of all time was *"Good Will Hunting"*. She allowed herself to be vulnerable in admitting that she identified a little with the main character that Matt Damon played.

"Not in terms of being a genius, right? But the not fitting in part. And the not fulfilling potential part. And maybe the dysfunctional and self-destructive behavior's part. At least a little.", Jess admitted.

Artie smiled. He had seen that movie, loved it, and also identified with the Will Hunting character. It also made him wonder about Jess's early life. The movie character had a very troubled childhood which molded a lot of his behaviors in later life. Artie made a mental bookmark but decided not to ask right now.

"Well, it's not that I don't love that movie too, Jess. Incredible that Matt Damon and Ben Affleck wrote and starred in it, and so early in their careers, but I have to step back a couple of decades for my favorite. It's called 'One Flew Over the Cuckoo's Nest'. Have you seen it?"

"No, I don't think so. But I have heard of it. What do you like so much about it?"

"Well, it's quite an offbeat film. It works on a number of levels. On the surface, it is about a criminal who thinks he has found a trick to make life easier. He pretends he is crazy to get moved from prison to a mental asylum, where he believes life will be easier. But he runs into a cruel and uncaring system and a particularly cruel, controlling head nurse."

"Wow. Sounds like a bundle of laughs."

"I know. I know. But in those most bleak and depressing conditions, we seek sparks of beautiful humanity. Finding ways to be authentic, joyful, and naughty. To cheat the system."

"Is that what you love about it, Bob?"

"Well yes. But specifically, I love that it is ultimately about human dignity. Finding our dignity in a cruel, uncaring world. And, if possible, helping others find theirs. There is this one beautiful scene. The main character, Randall Patrick McMurphy, played by Jack Nicholson, breaks a bunch of the patients out of the asylum and takes them fishing. When the harbormaster challenges him as he is stealing a fishing boat, he makes up the story that they are all doctors, on an away day. He introduces them by name. Doctor Cheswick. Doctor Taber. Dr. Fredericksen. Dr. Scanlon, Dr. Bibbett, Dr. Martini, Dr. Seafelt.

You see each of these characters, who have been beaten down by mental health issues and asylum conditions for years, on the yacht, with the wind blowing through their hair, picking their heads up, and feeling a little proud of themselves. Feel a little dignity. Even if just for a moment. What could be a better gift than that?"

Jess smiled. She was silent for a while, just taking in what Artie had said.

At the end of lunch, they agreed to share a boat ride to Komodo the next day. It wasn't that unusual for backpackers to form temporary alliances, do a few things together, and then go their separate ways. Artie felt that Jess could sense pretty clearly that he wasn't interested in her sexually and wasn't dodgy in any other way.

His sense was that he would try to keep things light and easy the next day, then if things worked out, he would start revealing his mission, and his interest for her to be a part of it, over dinner the next night.

73. June 19, 2015. Flores and Komodo Islands, Indonesia.

It was another early start. They left the guest house at 4am, to get to the boat pier for 4:30. The boat left for Komodo at 4:45, with eleven tourists and the pilot on board.

Artie noted that they were both wearing sensible shoes. The guidebooks make it clear that as well as Komodo dragons, Komodo island has a massive snake population, and flip-flops were not a good idea. It seemed that several of the other tourists on the boat with them had failed to get that memo.

When they arrived at Komodo, there were about sixty tourists, and they were separated into six groups, each group assigned to a tour guide. The tour guides were locals. They knew everything there was to know about Komodo Island, Komodo dragons, and the other flora and fauna of the place. They all carried long, forked sticks to manage the wildlife. They didn't speak English though, so the tour guide spoke to the whole group of 60 before they split up into groups.

"Komodo Dragons look slow, but they can be fast over short distances. They kill their prey by biting them and injecting them with toxic bacteria. They then follow their prey around for the next few hours until they die. So, keep your distance from them, and always do what your guide says. There are lots of snakes here on Komodo too, so stay on the path.

"You will walk around for a while, then go to the feeding ground, and watch us feed them goats. Then you will come back here. On the way back, we will stop the boats off the coast, if you would like to snorkel or swim."

In both their heads, Artie and Jess reflected on how they felt about a 'show' where goats were fed to Komodo dragons. But neither of them came to a strong enough conclusion that meant they were going to refuse and go back early.

They didn't stick together the whole time, but they found each other easy company. They were both more interested in seeing the dragons than photographing them. And they had a good chat along the way.

When they got back to Flores early evening, they fell into a nice-looking restaurant and ordered some dishes to share. Nothing fancy. Stuff like *nasi soto*, a very basic rice soup dish. Before the food came, Artie excused himself and went to use the toilet. It always surprised Artie how close the toilets were to the kitchens in these small, local Indonesian restaurants. Seemed unhygienic. Then someone told him that the reason was to make the plumbing easier and cheaper. Made perfect sense. They were optimizing on a different variable.

Artie returned to the table with a smile.

"Good day, no?"

"Absa-fuckin-lutely. The kind of day I hoped for when I left Oz."

"Jess, I'd really love to share a story with you. It's about my life. It's a bit of a long story, but I'd love to share, if you're up for it."

"I've got nothing else to do right now. Go for it. I'm all ears."

He started slowly, telling her about his life as a techie, feeling a bit lost, and then getting his medical diagnosis.

"Shit man. That's not great news. How long ago was that?"

"One thousand, nine hundred and one days ago!"

"You know the number of days exactly?"

"Yep. And now I am going to tell you why. You still up for it?"

Jess felt like the conversation was ever so slightly veering off the path that she was comfortable with. But she replied, *"For sure."* She was in this conversation now.

He took a long, slow breath. This was the first time he was going to tell anyone the whole story. He had already decided that if she wasn't up for joining him, he wouldn't kill her. He would take the risk of her knowing.

"When I was diagnosed, I went into shock for a while. Then an idea came to me. An inspiration, you might say. It blossomed into a clear sense of purpose. I am going to tell you what it is, and it might freak you out a little, but will you give me the benefit of the doubt and at least let me finish telling you?"

Jess appreciated Artie continually signaling that he knew the conversation might be getting a bit weird for her. But she was all in now. The surroundings had faded into soft, blurry focus, and only Artie and their discussion stood out in sharp relief. She nodded her acceptance.

"I had been going on holiday to Southeast Asia a lot in the few years before I got diagnosed. I had crossed my own lines of morality many times. Nothing too scary. No one underage. No one was forced to do it. Nothing violent. But I had paid for sex, many times. I always treated the women I slept with well. Paid them well. Didn't try to force them to do anything. But I knew how bad it was. Even though they weren't technically forced to do it, maybe their economic circumstances forced them to. Maybe even they had abusive partners who forced them to. It was a stain on my soul."

Jess was listening intently. Artie could see she had a fierce intellect. She knew she hated prostitution. And she suspected she would come out of this conversation hating Artie at least a little. But she was still staying present in the conversation. She was listening.

"I began to decide that I was going to use my last few years to right some wrongs. I knew that didn't absolve me of my sins. But still, it felt like a good thing to do. I trained for nearly three years in various physical and mental disciplines and have been moving around Southeast Asia since June 2013. My goal is 100 interventions before I die. My current total is 70."

"What's an Intervention?"

"Changing the life of one person. Saving a person from a terrible life, or stopping a person from making others' lives terrible."

The energy in the room started to change. Even though Jess was a pretty cool customer, this was, of course, way out of her comfort zone. As it should be. The waiting staff in the restaurant seemed to sense it too, kept their distance, and gave the pair their privacy.

It actually reminded Artie of a time when his company had an offsite in Disneyland. He had a terrible relationship with his boss at the time, and they decided to have an early breakfast together to hash things out. The trouble was all the normal breakfast restaurants were booked, so they ended up in a 'character' restaurant called Plaza Inn on Main Street, USA in Disneyland Park. In there the staff, or 'cast members' as Disney referred to them, dressed up as famous Disney characters and came up to your table. Hugged you. Posed for pictures with you. Characters like Mickey and Minnie Mouse. Goofy. And various Disney princesses.

Mostly designed for kids of course. Certainly, for holidaymakers. Not for businesspeople at an offsite. Especially not ones who hated each other, and were having a tense, passive-aggressive meeting. Each of the characters approached Artie's table with a jaunty gait, arms out, ready for a hug and a photo opportunity. They sensed the vibe, then quickly backed off, never to come back. It was like a comedy sketch, although it didn't feel like that to Artie or his boss at the time.

"Does that mean killing people?"

"Sometimes. If I am absolutely sure they deserve it. I have done that to some violent pimps and some traffickers in the human slave trade, for example."

"And for their victims, I try my best to give them a new start in life. Sometimes with money. Or take them back to their families. I have also set up a place in Laos, with someone who will take care of them, and help them heal. Till they are ready to go it alone."

Artie knew that this must be a lot for Jess to process. The one detail he decided not to tell her at the moment was that he tried to make the punishment concomitant with the sin. He tried to make those he stopped suffer as much as they deserved. Ideally in a way related to how they had made their victims suffer. He thought there was no reason to tell her that right now.

"Wow, man. That's a lot. A lot to take in. And you don't look like that kind of guy. Frankly, you don't look capable."

"I am very glad to hear you say that Jess. And that is no accident. A big part of this mission is never getting caught. Never moving too fast. Never moving too visibly. And never looking the part. Just like a spy. I am trying to look 'grey'."

"Bob. I've got to ask you. Why are telling me this?"

"I am so glad I haven't freaked you out so much that you have walked away. Or ran! I would completely understand if you did. I will answer your question now, but first I want you to know one thing. However you react to my story, you are in no danger from me. I am not a violent man or a wild killer. I have made a very solemn commitment to right some wrongs. I have made the decision to open up to you, and I am about to tell you why. But it is important for you to know that you are in no danger from me, and never will be. Okay?"

At that point, Jess got up and headed for either the front door or the bathroom. Artie didn't know which. But he wasn't going to try to stop her or chase after her, either way. This was her decision.

Quite a few minutes went by, and Artie realized that Jess was obviously trying to get her head straight. Trying to work out what to do in this very extreme situation. He knew that she normally lived by her instincts, and her instincts were good. But her instincts were telling her that he was safe, whereas his words were sending a message so far from that.

After maybe fifteen minutes, Jess returned. Artie realized that he had been expecting her to bolt out the door, and make a run for it, not even returning to the guest house to get her bag. But she hadn't.

"Bob. I'm not gonna lie to you. This has really freaked me out."

"I completely get it. It would be almost impossible for it not to. And I am so sorry to have dumped all this stuff on you."

"OK. So why did you?"

He could feel some of her strength, some of her backbone returning. Which was good.

"I told you my hope is that I complete one hundred interventions before I die, right? Well, my second hope is that I find someone to carry on the mission. Someone to do one hundred interventions too."

He paused as she took this in.

"Me? You think I..."

"While I have been going around performing interventions, I have also been observing. Looking for others who I thought would fit. I have followed three other people who I had hopes for, but they disqualified themselves for one reason or another before I approached them directly. Like I am approaching you now."

"But I don't get it. I'm no killer."

"That wasn't what I was looking for. That isn't what's needed. I was looking for someone smart enough to find opportunities and plan them. Courageous and resilient enough to execute them. Principled enough to never do the wrong thing. And patient and determined enough to see it through to the end.

"You won't have noticed me following you. I let you see me that one time in Siem Reap, when those Israeli guys were bothering you. I dressed a bit fatter and lighter-skinned that night. I saw you notice me."

"Fuck yeah. I remember a guy. That was you!"

"So Jess, I know this is a hell of a lot to take on board. I am not expecting you to answer me now. But would you let it marinate for a few days? I will keep my distance. Give you your space. If you have any questions, I am here to answer them. Then when you are ready to give me an answer, I will take whatever you give me."

Jess paused for what seemed forever but was probably only a minute. *"Alright."*

It seemed like a flippant answer, but it wasn't. Jess delivered it deliberately, with full eye contact, authenticity, and vulnerability. She meant it.

"And one final thing for tonight, Jess. You are the first and only person I have told this whole story to. Please take that as a sign of respect. And whatever your answer is, I will retain complete respect for you. And it will have been a privilege to share this with you."

Jess nodded her acknowledgment of what Artie just said.

They sat for a moment, then got up and paid the bill. They walked slowly and wordlessly back to the guest house together.

74. July 7, 2015. Ubud, Indonesia.

Artie and Jess rose at 6 a.m. and bicycled to a remote spot outside the town to exercise. They had only been spending a lot of time together for a few weeks now, but already Artie's daily stretching, exercise, and training had adapted to incorporate a bunch of great ideas Jess had taught him, from her extensive knowledge of bodywork. Sparring with her was really helpful for both of them.

At one point in their sparring today, Artie had to stop for a teaching point. *"Take the fight out of your face, Jess. Focus your energies on overcoming the opponent. Stay as calm as possible. Sometimes it is a good idea to deliberately use facial expressions and noises to scare, unnerve, or confuse the enemy. But that's not what you were doing. You were tensing up, which made you slower and less effective."* Jess listened carefully, then simply nodded, and they returned to their practice. What he said made complete sense to her and was useful. She had no questions and felt no need to argue or challenge Artie, on this occasion. He saw that she got it, so they could simply move on.

Artie was impressed with Jess's martial arts knowledge and skills, but he was aware that Jess hadn't really explored the use of weapons much. Either using actual weapons like swords, knives, and guns, or makeshift weapons, making use of whatever happened to be around when a fight took place. He felt like this could be a good focus in the time they had training together.

They did a little knife training today.

"It's counterintuitive, but a great way to use a knife is to pull away as you are cutting your opponent. So, you swing the knife in an arc, a curved path, back towards you. That way you can inflict damage but reduce the chances of the knife getting stuck in the opponent. You can also hold the knife like this, so you are engaging your powerful forearm muscles. See what I mean? You have a go."

Like everything else they discussed, Jess stayed present and listened carefully. Questioned and challenged when useful. Then experimented and picked up the techniques and lessons Artie shared incredibly quickly.

Artie watched as she moved the knife from side to side, all the time using her forearm muscles to swing the knife in an arc, starting low, cutting the imaginary opponent upwards, then pulling the knife back as it reached the top of its arc.

When they finished, they stretched out, washed, and cooled off in the local stream, then cycled back to their guest house in Ubud for breakfast. They ate similar meals. Jess ate *bubur ayam*, an Indonesian chicken rice porridge with green onions, crispy shallots, and celery, flavored with soy sauce and other condiments. Artie chose *bubur mengguh*, a Balinese porridge made from black rice.

They were the only guests at the guest house today, and the manager had kindly let Artie put a music tape on. He chose a compilation of some of his favorite early David Bowie songs. As they finished their breakfast, "In the Heat of the Morning" lingered in the air. Artie thought it was an incredibly beautiful song.

Bowie had always amazed Artie in terms of his variety of styles and constant evolution of character. Despite being one of the world's most successful musicians, Artie had heard interviews with Bowie where he said that he felt more like an actor. Playing the roles of musicians. Inhabiting their characters for periods of years. Like Ziggy Stardust. Aladdin Sane. The Thin White Duke. He probably could have made an amazing spy, Artie thought.

They found two comfortable chairs by the pool after breakfast to discuss things further. They started off by joking around, before getting serious. A sign they saw yesterday tickled them both, announcing "Antiques made to order." Ubud was famous for cultural activities and handicrafts, compared to many of the coastal resorts in Bali, that were more famous for traditional seaside holidays. Beaches, diving, waterskiing, etc.

One Balinese resort, Kuta, had been a particular disappointment to Artie in his previous life. He was imagining an exotic, tropical paradise, and instead, he was confronted by young Australian power drinkers and party animals. For an American or a European, Bali was an extremely remote, tropical paradise. For Australians, it was one of the closest overseas holiday destinations, particularly for those on the Northern and Western sides of Australia. It provided the same function as Florida did for US university kids on spring break, or the Costa Brava in Spain did for seventeen- and eighteen-year-old Brits and other Europeans on their first, alcohol, drug, and sex-fueled independent holidays.

Darwin was about 1400 kilometers from Bali as the crow flies. A lot of young men involved in the mining industry in Western Australia worked hard and somewhat dangerous work in the mines, then flew to Bali to blow off steam. Completely understandable for them, but not the kind of vibe Artie was looking for.

Artie got a notebook out of his backpack and placed it gently on the table.

"Jess, as part of my preparation, I studied a lot about tactics for success. I read twenty books on the subject. Some come from a military background. Some from game theory. Some from business strategy."

"Like Sun Tzu's 'The Art of War'?"

"Yes, exactly. Although I think that one isn't quite as good as it's cracked up to be. But that's definitely one of them."

"Ok, which others? Machiavelli's 'The Prince'"?

"You really know your stuff, don't you? Actually, not that one. But I did include "The Book of Five Rings" by Musashi. "On War" by Von Clausewitz. "The Unfettered Mind" by Takuan Soho. "Thinking Strategically" by Dixit and Nalebuff. "The 48 Laws of Power" by Robert Greene. And a few others."

"Which one's best?"

"Well, the point is that they all have good bits, and they are all a bit lacking. So, I sewed together my own book of 100 stratagems and when to use them. It's called 'The Essence of Stratagems'."

"Where can I buy a copy?"

"You can't. There are only two copies in existence. Both handwritten. One is back in my room. The other is here on this table. A gift for you."

Jess opened the notebook and gently thumbed through it. She saw that the book's conceit, its organizing principle, was that there were three ways to win. Winning the battle of spirit, the battle of mind, or the battle of body. The book was organized into three sections. Each double-page spread was an expose of one stratagem. What it was. When to use it. How to do it well.

Jess quietly marveled at the fact that Artie had chosen to write this book, after he had got his terminal diagnosis, and as part of his one-thousand-day schedule to prepare for his mission. She quietly wondered if she might do something similarly powerful, that she could pass on to the one who came after her. Maybe something to do with the body, health, and movement?

She closed the book, nodded her thanks at Artie, then placed the book in her backpack.

After that, they both sat in silence for a long time. Jess reflected on everything Artie had shared with her so far, and the implications for her life going forward, at least for the next couple of years. Artie let her do that without bothering her. These were moments of great honesty, integrity, vulnerability, and openness for both of them. A kind of purpose and trust that both of them had found lacking in their previous lives.

Finally, Jess got up, and wordlessly left Artie at the pool, heading to her room. Artie sat for a while longer, listening to the sound of the water gently undulating in the breeze, and the wildlife surrounding them going about its business, at the almost empty resort. Which they had chosen for that reason.

75. *July 8, 2015. Ubud, Indonesia and Oasis.*

"Jess, I am afraid I've got to leave urgently. I will contact you as soon as I am done."

"No worries. Good luck with it."

It was quite consistent with what Artie had learned about Jess that she wouldn't pry or ask unnecessary questions. It wasn't that she didn't care. It was that she was smart and present enough to realize that Artie would have given her more information or asked for her help if he had wanted to. And she knew that Artie knew that, so he wouldn't interpret her brevity negatively. So, they didn't have to go through the tiresome rituals. The façade of caring.

"More evidence that she's a great choice," Artie thought as he checked out of the place they were staying in.

Artie had received alerts at just after six am that something was wrong. Initially, pressure sensors in the land surrounding Oasis, then external cameras. Finally, the silent alarm had been pressed, almost certainly by Ploy.

Artie knew he couldn't get there in time to respond. As the crow flies, it is about 3468 kilometers from Ubud in Indonesia to Luang Prabang in Laos. The journey would involve a motorbike or car to Denpasar airport, a plane to a big hub airport like Bangkok, and then a flight from Bangkok to Luang Prabang. Then finally about an hour's taxi to Oasis. Easily, twelve to fifteen hours with airport waiting time c.

Artie thought briefly that he could try to hire a private plane to take him directly from Denpasar airport to Luang Prabang. He was quite prepared and able to pay whatever that would cost. But the truth was he had no idea how to do that. And he sensed that even if he did, he would have to be incredibly lucky for a plane to be available.

And the final nail in the coffin of that idea was that the time saving probably wouldn't be of value. Even if he cut his travel time down to five hours, any damage being done at Oasis would have already been done.

So, he set off on his journey taking the more conventional route.

Meanwhile, at around 6 in the morning, Ploy heard the same alarm signals Artie did. She also heard Ding and Dong barking. She got up, armed herself with a knife, and went to the door. She looked out through the peephole. There were three poor, ragged-looking teenagers, poorly dressed in ripped t-shirts and cotton trousers, standing at the door in the rain. The dogs stood at Ploy's side. She calmed them down.

"What do you want?" Ploy shouted, in Lao, without opening the door.
"Please miss. We are tired and hungry, and we aren't sure where we are."
"How did you get here?"
"We come from near Savannakhet. We were offered work, so got in a truck. The bosses just dumped us here, a couple of miles down the road. We don't know where to go, or how to get home. We don't have any money. And we haven't eaten for 2 days. Please miss, can you help us?"

Their story sounded believable to Ploy, and if it was true, she would like to help them. But something in her gut told her to beware. In the end, she decided that she was just on high alert, because of this early morning alarm call.

She put the dogs in the living room, then let the three lads in and directed them to the kitchen table. She could hear some of the other residents stirring, wondering what the commotion was.

Teen 1: *"Thank you so much miss."*

Teen 2: *"We didn't want to disturb you miss. But we were so hungry."*

The third visitor remained quiet. She saw his eyes darting about like he was casing the joint. Although Ploy was now 90% treating them as unfortunate guests, 10% of her was still running through risk scenarios. What she would do if various eventualities occurred.

Ploy heated up the *jok*, the Thai congee she had already prepared in a pan on the stove, to give these waifs a meal. Then she poured some into three bowls and brought them to the table. Ploy had tasted Chinese congee once or twice and didn't really like it. It was a bit tasteless. A cruel description might be that it was like wallpaper paste. Thai congee, on the other hand, like most Thai food, was bursting with flavor. She hoped the young lads would enjoy it.

As she put the first bowl down, things suddenly kicked off. The boy she was closest to pulled a tiny knife out of his pocket, and stabbed Ploy in her right shoulder. Ploy screamed out in shock and pain, and the smart, sneaky stab had rendered her arm useless. She screamed out "*Run*" to the other residents.

"*Where's the money, you old bitch*" said number three now, who had suddenly found his voice. He was speaking a very rough, rural dialect of Lao. It was perfectly understandable to Ploy.

Although all the residents of Oasis could be considered victims, they were all much more than that. All humans are. Artie remembered reading an amazing novel by an ethnically Chinese Canadian woman about a young woman backpacking in Ireland who got gang raped. It was loosely based on the author's own experiences. At the beginning of the book was a dedication to '*all victims and all perpetrators*'. The author went on to state that we are all in fact both. Artie wasn't here right now, but this thought was about to become reality.

The three young men sneered as the five temporary residents of Oasis slowly filed into the kitchen. None of them heeded Ploy's command that they should run.

"*Well look what we have here*", said number one. "*Looks like we might get some money and have some fun before we go. What do you say, boys.*" Three of the girls understood the majority of his rural

Lao, but even the other two had a pretty good idea of what he was saying.

"Okay, who's first? Want to get stabbed or fucked?" said number two. Now all three had knives out.

One of the girls darted back out of the room.

"Ha. A bitch and a coward. It's gonna be fun to take her" said number three.

The woman they were referring to, Lek, darted out into the hallway. She had grown up in the slums of Bangkok, and like many slum residents, she had developed an incredible survival instinct out of necessity. Unlucky for the boys. She opened the living room door. The dogs had entered a very primal state. Their hunting state. They could sense what was going on.

As they sprinted into the kitchen, everything went crazy. Like a well-oiled team, Ding and Dong each went for one of the two stronger-looking boys, numbers two and three. Number one, the one who had stabbed Ploy, was the weakest looking. That's why they had used him as the frontman begging to be let inside.

Three of the young women picked up various kitchen implements – a knife, a heavy pestle, and a frying pan. It quickly dawned on the rather stupid young men that they were outgunned, outnumbered, outsmarted, and out-couraged.

To cut a long story short, the three boys suffered significant damage at the hands of the two canine and six human residents of Oasis. None of the other residents suffered any injuries, and Ploy didn't suffer any more injuries.

Ploy directed them to tie the scumbags up and wait for Artie to get back. She would like to consult with him about their fate, although she was pretty sure she knew what the answer would be.

When the boys were secured, the girls took turns watching over them, while the rest of them went about their daily business. One of the girls, who rather handily had been a seamstress in her early life, applied some antiseptic ointment, then sewed Ploy's shoulder up with a needle that they heated to try to make the process a little more sterile and hygienic. The wound would hurt for a while, but at least it wouldn't remain open and become infected.

When Artie arrived twelve hours later, everything had been tidied up, and the three boys were bound in various makeshift but effective ways on the kitchen floor. Two of the residents watched over them with hawk eyes and sharp knives, while Ploy and Artie held a management meeting in the living room with the still enervated dogs.

The decision was made. Artie replaced the two guards in the kitchen and Ploy sat all the other residents down around the living room table and told them the decision. The boys were to be dispatched, and the bodies would be dissolved using chemicals. All video and sensor data would be deleted and replaced with fake data. Should anyone come inquiring, they were to deny ever having seen any boys.

All nodded their agreement. Ploy believed them because of a combination of having been saved by Artie, shared goals, and maybe a healthy dose of fear too. Although Artie and Ploy were on their side, it was very clear what they could do if they ever deemed it necessary.

Ploy went to the kitchen and brought out a bowl of delicious *jok* for everyone. Their talk shifted to general chit-chat, like what they would each do today. Without any explicit decision, they all seemed to understand that it was time to return to ordinary life like the incident never happened.

Meanwhile, Artie returned to the kitchen, and calmly went to work, quietly trying to make it seem like the incident never happened. Destroying all the evidence.

76. July 22, 2015. Soi Cowboy, Bangkok, Thailand.

It was sometimes said that Bangkok's notoriety as a den of prostitution was caused by demand from American military men on their R&R (rest and recuperation) breaks from the Vietnam War. Artie wasn't so sure that that was the whole story, given that there seemed to be plenty of indigenous demand for the services of ladies (and men) of the night, often in places foreigners didn't go.

But Soi Cowboy, a bright, raucous street between Soi 21 and Soi 23 of Sukhumvit Road, was definitely targeted at foreign customers. Getting its name from T.G. "Cowboy" Edwards, a retired US airman, who opened one of its earliest bars in 1977, Soi Cowboy now had around 40 Go Go bars, with a few spilling over to the streets either side of it. They varied a little in theme. Some focused on music and dancing, some had pool tables, and some were more like western strip clubs. A couple were staffed largely by transgender staff. But the function of all was clear: for foreign men to pick up the staff working there and take them home for a good time.

Two other places in central Bangkok were similarly set up, Patpong and Nana Plaza. But Cowboy was the oldest and most notorious.

Artie had learned that these places had some rather unusual rules. For example, when you wanted to take a bar girl home, you had to pay the bar a 'bar fine' of maybe five to seven hundred Baht for the night. Any further payments to your companion were negotiated directly with them.

Although the customers of these bars were overwhelmingly male, it was not unheard of for couples to come in, or on a rare occasion, single females. So, when Artie and Jess entered the Suzie Wong (a bar named after a 1960 movie about a Hong Kong lady of the night), the staff were not surprised.

When they came in, Al-Kuwari (or Joe, as he preferred to be called in Bangkok) was perched on the left of the bar in the front row, gazing intently at the contortions of a couple of girls who were intent on making him select them for his nighttime exertions tonight. Michael Jackson's "Billie Jean" was providing an upbeat backdrop to the show. Artie and Jess sat back in a booth, watching the dancing girls, playing the role of a Western couple who were titillated by the show.

They had a quiet chat with the mama-san, ordered a couple of beers, slipped her a five hundred Baht tip, and told her that they had just arrived in town, and just wanted to watch the show tonight, intimating that they would be back to get more involved tomorrow. She nodded her consent.

They had been watching Al-Kuwari, for a few nights now. Although their research told them that he was a rich man back home in Qatar, he didn't care for the high-end, exclusive clubs that the wealthy preferred. He liked to 'slum it'. That was part of his kick. He wore jeans and a t-shirt, and travelled freely in the red-light areas of Bangkok, with his bodyguard, Khalid, keeping a discrete distance.

Khalid didn't judge Al-Kuwari in any way. Firstly, because he was fully dedicated to his role of protecting him. Any judgments or feelings beyond allowing Joe to go about his chosen activities safely would have clouded the issue. Made him worse at his job. But beneath that was an extreme form of discrimination. A feeling that non-Qataris, non-Arabs, and in particular non-Muslims (*kuffar*) were lesser beings. Objects to be managed, used, and manipulated at will. And that applied even more so to what Khalid thought of as the dirty, broken husks of humanity who inhabited the world Joe was now visiting.

Artie had first heard of him a few months ago from a mama-san in Soi Nana. She told him that Joe was a regular visitor to Bangkok, coming every few months. He had a reputation for choosing the youngest, most innocent-looking girls in the bars, and treating them to a night of violent, cruel sex, involving various instruments of pain that he carried with him. Khalid apparently made sure Joe's companions never left before Joe was fully satisfied. After confirming that the stories were true, Artie and Jess selected him as her first real target.

They had booked a room in the President Solitaire Hotel, the place where Joe was staying. Located in Sukhumvit Soi 11. It was by no means as palatial as Joe preferred, but decent enough, yet cheap enough that anyone who knew him from back home wouldn't dream of staying there. It was also only a relatively short stroll from Soi Cowboy. Joe booked a suite for himself, and a smaller room for Khalid. Khalid would remain in the suite as long as Joe deemed necessary, which was typically until the girl was tied up, and then retire to his room.

They followed Joe out of the bar with his chosen victim for the night, a tiny, relatively light-skinned woman who seemed to be about eighteen or nineteen years old. Artie guessed that she was Lao. In Thailand, as in many developing countries, being dark-skinned was frowned upon, as it signified having to work outside in the sun. Rich Thais pay for whitening lotions and treatments, which cosmetic companies gladly designed and marketed to them. Artie had met Thai women back home in the US who couldn't get their heads around the idea of tanning salons and tanning lotions.

City Thais are also quite snobbish and feel superior to Thais from more rural areas, particularly the Northeast of Thailand, known as *Isaan*, which is a very poor, farming region bordering Laos and Cambodia. The region where most Thai bargirls come from. The city Thais often associate being from more rural areas with being dark-skinned. This was actually inaccurate. Thais from the central region, including Bangkok, were often darker skinned. Those from areas bordering Laos, for example, were usually naturally much lighter skinned but became dark-skinned from the necessity of working in the fields.

Khalid followed Joe and his girl for tonight at a discrete distance, on the other side of the road. Near enough that he could close the distance in a matter of seconds, if necessary, but far enough away that the casual observer would not connect him to Joe.

Artie and Jess had made the decision that the best strategy was to let Joe get safe and feel comfortable in his room, let Khalid retire to his own room, then act. Artie's job was to neutralize Khalid and then join Jess in Joe's room. Khalid was a brute of a man who only knew force, and so Artie would dominate him, make him feel emasculated before sealing his fate. Then they planned to turn the tables on Joe and use his BDSM equipment on him, starting with the ball gag used to keep his victims quiet.

At the end of the evening, with their goals achieved, they sat with the Lao woman, whose nickname was Som. Artie tried to manage the situation so that Jess and Som remained calm. However loathsome Joe had been, neither Som nor Jess were used to seeing such brutality. Artie wanted things to turn out as positively as possible.

Som didn't want to go to Oasis. She wanted to return home to her family, who were in a village just outside Korat, a relatively large city in Isaan. Jess gave her an envelope filled with a substantial amount of money. Som cried and hugged her for a long time.

Both Jess and Artie hoped that Som could use the money to stay away from the sex industry, and any other kind of trouble, forever, but they recognized that that was out of their hands. Possibly, to some extent, it was almost out of Som's hands too. Some families in impoverished regions ended up making, and having to make, tough choices all the time.

Around four in the morning, the three of them left the hotel. Joe and Khalid's bodies had been dissolved in their respective baths using some pretty powerful chemicals that Artie had prepared earlier. Artie and Jess had changed their appearances a little as a part of throwing everyone off their scent, and they had brought a change of clothes that was elastic enough to fit Som. This outfit was much demurer than the outfit Som had arrived in.

77. 1.

77. July 23, 2015. Hua Hin, Thailand

Jess and Artie were having lunch at a simple restaurant in the center of Hua Hin. Known as the resort where the Thai royal family traditionally took their holidays, it was a much more sedate city than the places favored by and famous with foreign visitors, like Bangkok, Pattaya, Phuket, and Koh Samui. In the north Chiang Mai was traditionally calmer and more laid back, but tourism was rapidly changing that. Even its much less visited neighbor Chiang Rai was feeling the same trends.

Hua Hin was still a little touristy, and had a tiny red-light district, but was a perfect place for Artie and Jess to take a short break in the action. They planned to leave tomorrow lunchtime, but they would rest for today.

For lunch today, they were eating simply. As part of remaining grey, they had both chosen what was called an American breakfast. Frankfurter-style sausages out of a can, two fried eggs each, and a plateful of thick, white, soft, buttered toast between them. The only thing that was at all Thai about the food was how the fried eggs were cooked. Thai people tended to cook fried eggs with much more oil, so they became crispy on the outside, maybe 20% of the way towards being deep fried.

"Jess, I just wanted to say something to you."

"Why so tentative, Artie? With what we've discussed and been through so far, not sure anything could shock me."

"Fair point. I am not nervous, just realized I wanted to say it, and hadn't yet."

"Shoot."

"Well. Inevitably things will go wrong on your mission. They have on mine. They couldn't not."

"Yeah, I get it. There are risks."

"Yes, there are, but that's not all I am talking about. Here are a few examples. You could get injured or killed. Even raped or tortured. At the time, or by getting tracked down later. You could get caught by the police or other authorities."

"I know. It's a risky, illegal, violent path."

"Right. But also, there are other ways things could go wrong. You could accidentally let an evil person go free. Either because you didn't realize they are evil, or because they escaped. Even worse, you could fail to save some victims."

"Now that you list it out, there's lots of shit that could go bad."

"And that's still not all. You could unalive someone you thought was evil, but they weren't. Or they were victims too. And some more subtle stuff. Someone you save might not have wanted to be saved."

Jess was thinking about that last one. Not sure how she felt about it.

"My only point is, Jess. You are doing something important. Something meaningful. And something very difficult in many ways. You must accept that things will go wrong from time to time. But you mustn't allow yourself to get dispirited. Or stop."

Jess met his gaze. She didn't say anything, but it was clear she was listening and thinking about everything Artie said.

"You know Jess. In my former life, I watched quite a lot of sports on TV. I tried to understand what differentiated the superstars from the journeymen. One of the things I noticed was what happened when the superstars screwed up. Missed an open goal. Missed a tackle. They expressed their frustration for a second, then immediately got back to it.

"On the other hand, when the mediocre players screwed up, they moped around for ages afterward. Living in the headspace of past failures. Where the stars were living in the present and the expectation of success in the near future.

"We must learn from our errors, but not dwell on them. I hope you can be like that when the time comes. And of course, your errors won't result in a missed touchdown. Yours may result in undeserved pain, torture, or death.

"Last year, I witnessed a Khmer mama-san beat a young boy to death because he had refused some demands of a customer. I didn't act in time. I am not even sure I could have and kept invisible."

Jess looked at him. They both went quiet for a while.

"You know, you may be one of the biggest serial killers in history Artie", Jess said, in a surprisingly chatty and upbeat way, deliberately poking Artie a bit for fun. Although he hated being described with that term, he loved the fact that Jess was open and brave enough to say that kind of thing to him. He also thought that having a conversation like this might help Jess let off a bit of steam, after the earlier part of their conversation, and last night's activities. Jess was still very new to this life. Her comment also gave Artie an in to share with her a bit more of his perspective on things.

"And I will follow in your footsteps. I might even do a hundred and one, just to go past you on the leaderboard."

Artie felt like this kind of dark humor, gallows humor, was no bad thing.

"I get what you mean Jess. But I have to admit I don't love what we do being labeled as serial killing, even if it is technically accurate. That term is culturally loaded. To mean someone who is doing it for pleasure, or at least for some unjustifiable reason.

"You'd never use that term for a soldier, right?"

"We're not quite soldiers."

"No, no. That's not my point. I am just saying that not all situations with multiple killings fit that term. Also, during my training period, I read about the world's most prolific serial killers. Not a fun read, I can tell you. Not recommended."

"Don't worry, it's not on top of my reading list."

"Good. If you did read it, though, you would find that the top of the list is 'La Bestia' Luis Garavito, who is known to have definitely killed 193 people in Latin America in the 1990s, suspected of killing up to 300, mostly street children. Next is Pedro Lopez, also from Latin America. He has similar statistics, but he targeted young girls. The list goes on. We are not like them Jess, even if the law might regard us as similar. The law is a very blunt instrument."

"Struth. I wish I had never brought it up now. Got me feeling all creeped out."

"No, it's important. We are operating outside the norms of acceptable human behavior, and it's no bad thing to question ourselves every now and then. But as well as those sociopathic perverts, there are also killer doctors, nurses, and owners of care homes, who go about their wicked private missions in a calmer, measured, planned way. Sometimes they think they have a valid purpose, like ridding the planet of old, useless people. Sometimes they have a specific motive, like collecting on life insurance. Sometimes they are just fulfilling a deep desire to kill, like the more conventional serial killers.

"This guy called Harold Shipman in the UK killed 218 patients for sure by injecting them with diamorphine, basically heroin. And because he was a doctor, he could write their medical records, disguising their cause of death. He did it for more than twenty years before being caught.

"There are also groups that take out significant numbers of people. Religious cults. Crime syndicates. In the 1920s, 30s, and 40s, a group known as Murder Inc. took out at least four hundred marks, possibly more like a thousand. Helping witnesses to mafia crimes disappear before the trial. And of course, we are only looking at modern records. No one was keeping such good count and records throughout history."

Jess held up her hands. *"OK, OK. You win. We are nothing like them. This whole conversation makes me want to take a shower, eat popcorn, listen to pop music, and watch some comedy. Are you done yet?"*

"Sorry, Jess. Not trying to freak you out. There's no one else I can share with. And I am so hopeful that you continue to develop your own perspectives on things. What I have done. What you are doing. What the perpetrators we are un-aliving are doing. What their victims have to endure.

"One last comment, and then I promise to leave this topic alone forever. I just wanted to make the maybe obvious point that the serial killers we know about are just the ones we know about. There is nothing to say that there are not many more prolific serial killers out there that never get caught. Never get noticed.

"What gets most serial killers caught is the simple fact that they are driven by powerful compulsions that are stronger than logic. Stronger than their desire not to get caught. It is fairly easy to imagine much more 'successful' serial killers operating under the radar their whole lives, patiently waiting, and observing, taking their opportunities when they can, then disappearing back into the shadows.

"Although we are nothing like them either, we should aim to be similar in that one way. Never break cover. Never compromise the mission. Never reveal any clues about us so we can keep doing the work."

Jess didn't say anything in response. Nor did Artie. He knew she heard him. He knew she knew why he was saying this stuff out loud. Sometimes we have to learn from our enemies, from the dark side. And sometimes we have to say things we already know out loud. Articulation has a power and magic all of its own. Like the rituals that all tribes have developed and repeated throughout history.

78. August 4, 2015. Koh Samui, Thailand.

When Artie first came to Koh Samui, there wasn't much of anything. Now parts of it were like a mini Atlantic City or Vegas wanna-be, with bright neon lights puncturing the night sky of this naturally beautiful island.

These days, Koh Samui, like Thailand itself, has naturally created clusters around specific tourists and their types of activity. In the northeast of the island, Chaweng was mainly a drinking venue for the most uncultured, unsophisticated Western power drinkers and partiers. Lamai Beach was a tiny bit more off-the-beaten-track. There were places in the South of the island for fasting, meditation, and detox, some of them painfully expensive with things like infra-red saunas, for celebrities. Then there was Koh Phangan, an island close to Samui famous for raves and druggie full moon parties. Koh Samui did have a modest red-light scene too.

The diner, on the outskirts of Chaweng, was simply called All Night. Artie reflected that non-English-speaking countries often had ways of using English that weren't terribly wrong, but just slightly weird. He remembered visiting the Netherlands many years ago, and a taxi driver who picked him up in torrential rain turned and said to him in Dutch-accented English, "What a fucking weather". Just the tiny mistake of adding the word 'a' threw it off completely. A restaurant simply called "All Night" seemed that way to Artie too.

He chose a seat at the back of the restaurant, close to the kitchen. The whole restaurant was quite empty, but the few customers present all sat by the windows at the front. Partly out of habit, partly to see the view. And partly because the restaurant had a very slightly unpleasant odor, which grew worse the further you sat from the front door.

Artie ordered a cheeseburger, french fries, and a Coke. Not because that was what he wanted to eat. He knew the cheeseburger would be terrible, as it had been the last few nights. He avoided sodas too these days. And conversely, he knew that if he got the chef to cook some local dish it would be delicious. Unsurprisingly, as an island, Koh Samui was known for its seafood. One of his favorite Thai dishes in his previous life was *plah neung manao*, a steamed white fish with lime and chili. But ordering that wouldn't fit as perfectly with his current persona: A tired American executive here in Samui for a couple of weeks of R&R.

Tonight, the boss took his order. She was a pretty robust-looking woman in her late 40s or early 50s who took your order politely, but efficiently. He had a sense that she wouldn't tolerate customers vacillating for too long over their orders. On other nights, a tired, nervous-looking younger woman waited his table.

The kitchen door swung back and forth with the two women going in with orders and coming out carrying plates of food. Artie got fleeting peeks inside the kitchen. A man was doing the cooking who looked to be maybe in his mid-fifties. He was small and quite dark-skinned, maybe from the south of Thailand, near the border with Malaysia, if Artie had to guess. His mouth was twisted in an unusual expression, his left leg seeming a little shorter than the right, and his left arm was not fully developed. It was a small, curled-up vestigial limb that couldn't really be used for anything.

Jo, as Artie had learned his name was, was incredibly quick and skillful at cooking, despite only using one arm. Artie had initially only come in here to refuel and take a break, but after noticing how Jo was treated, Artie began planning an intervention.

The first time he came in, Jo noticed Artie looking at him. He was used to people looking at him, and even making cruel comments to him. He just kind of giggled at Artie, in a submissive, almost apologetic mode. Artie couldn't help being reminded of his well-heeled university friend Charlie's dog, Chief, who had a problem of submissively urinating, whenever another dog approached.

For the moment, it served Artie's purpose for Jo to think of him as a dumb, slightly cruel *Farang* (the Thai word for foreigner). Over the next few days, Artie saw the young girls who worked for Gee, the boss, laugh and shout at Jo the cook. And Gee would routinely scream at him for not being fast enough or getting any order wrong. Occasionally hit him with a backhand slap. She even poured hot water on him a couple of times when she was rushing and angry.

Although part of Artie's thousand-day training was to suppress any emotion, because it wasn't useful for his mission, seeing how Jo was treated tore at his heartstrings. He later learned that Jo slept chained in the kitchen and ate scraps on the floor. His chain was just about long enough for him to use the outdoor bathroom.

The tourist customers eating, laughing, and joking just a few meters away were blissfully unaware of how their chef was being treated. He hoped that they would have been saddened and outraged, refused to have frequented the establishment, and called the police if they had known, but to be honest, Artie wasn't sure that all of them would have. It was a slightly more immediate scenario than, but similar to, how the kids making their clothes in Bangladesh and the workers making their mobile phones in China were treated. Documentaries exposed those facts from time to time, and became a cause célèbre for a while, but soon died down.

Tonight, Artie made a little eye contact with Jo and happened to notice Jo had a shiny brand-new rice cooker to work with. Jo saw Artie notice the rice cooker and his face broke out into the most beautiful smile Artie had ever seen. For the first time in a very, very long time, Artie cried. He tried to hide his tears from Jo. The song "Ripple" by The Grateful Dead began playing in the diner. In a way Artie couldn't articulate, it seemed like the perfect song for the moment.

Artie thought it might be too confusing and upsetting for Jo to see Gee meet her karma, so he followed her home to take care of that. After securing Gee in position and gagging her, he put on some water to boil. Slowly. He made sure she could see the water boiling.

Later that night, he returned to the restaurant and explained to Jo as best he could that Gee was gone, and that Jo should come with him. Jo was confused but quickly acquiesced.

They hopped on the old motorbike Artie had acquired the day before and left the All Night restaurant as a business without an owner, chef, or explanation. No doubt some intrepid entrepreneur would pick up the pieces and re-open it soon.

A few hours later, a ferry ride and a couple of hundred kilometers away, they stopped for breakfast. Artie bought Jo the best breakfast he could find where Jo wouldn't look too much out of place. Jo enjoyed the breakfast thoroughly, cleaning his plate. Artie talked to Jo a little. He used his broken, very limited, very accented Thai, and Jo seemed to use a mixture of southern Thai and Bahasa Malaysia.

They began the long journey for Oasis. A little bit like a pet cat or dog, Jo seemed to be able to accept that he didn't know where he was going, how long the journey would take, or indeed why any of this was happening, but he would just live in the moment and accept it.

79.

79. September 4, 2015. Old Town, Chicago.

She knew it was wrong, but she couldn't resist. Bertha didn't know Artie very well, but she knew what he looked like. It said Arthur Wilson on the envelope. He had introduced himself as Artie. He was always very quiet, but courteous. They had exchanged smiles in the hallway. Said "*Good morning*" to each other a couple of times. In her early seventies, Bertha didn't get out much more. And no one from her family was left in Chicago. Little courtesies and kindnesses were important to her. And Artie was one of the few residents to extend them to her.

Most of the time Bertha felt invisible. And unfortunately, she completely understood why. She could still remember when she was young, avoiding and dreading getting stuck in conversations with the oldies. She didn't feel old inside. In fact, every now and then, Bertha caught sight of her face in the mirror, or looked down at her wrinkled, freckled hands and thought "*Who is this old woman?*" But she knew that all everyone else could see was her current appearance.

Bertha knew that Artie had moved out a couple of years ago. They had shared neighboring apartments for probably six years until he left. This letter was put in her postbox by mistake by the mailman. She had been to ask the current residents of the place Artie used to live whether they had a forwarding address. A very nice, quiet Puerto Rican couple. The woman was visibly pregnant. But they couldn't help.

The letter looked kind of important, so she opened and read it.

"*Dear Mr Wilson.*

We are writing to inform you that an audit revealed that between 2008 and 2011, our computer systems wrongly matched some test results with patients. These were test results generated using MRI (Magnetic Resonance Imaging) scans. You are one of the patients affected by this error.

At the time, we informed you that you had a thalamic tumor that was inoperable and resistant to traditional therapeutic strategies such as chemotherapy and radiation. The good news for you is that we had somehow mixed your test results with those of another patient. We have now resolved the confusion, and your MRI scan results show no such issue. Nor any other health condition. They effectively give you a clean bill of health.

We are glad to bring you this good news, and very sorry for any distress, hardship, or inconvenience caused by our error.

If you would like to contact us to discuss this, please use the details at the bottom of this letter. We understand if you would like to pursue legal proceedings also, and if you do so, please ask your legal representatives to contact us using the same details."

Bertha was sorry to hear of the misdiagnosis, but glad to hear that her former neighbor had a clean bill of health. It was nice to hear such good news for a change. She just wished she had a way to get this letter to him. She would keep it just in case he ever came back or she heard of his new address.

80. *September 6, 2015. Ho Chi Minh City. Vietnam.*

Artie and Jess sat opposite each other, both eating a bowl of *pho*, the famous Vietnamese noodle soup that had meat, herbs, and a delicate broth.

Artie mentioned how he loved reading the idioms used in a country. They were often colorful and funny, sometimes full of folk wisdom, and always great clues into the way people thought and lived in that country. He just shared with Jess the Vietnamese idiom *"chở thấy sói, quên rừng rậm"*, which translates literally as "don't just see the wolf and forget the dense forest".

It was meant to remind people to consider the broader context, in terms of both space and time and not just focus on immediate threats. It reminded Artie that he experienced Vietnamese culture as quite a cautious one. He wasn't sure if that was a modern thing, perhaps caused by the current communist government, or endemic in Vietnamese culture for a long time.

The first Asian food Artie had eaten when he was about 13 years old, was Chinese. He loved it. He felt sophisticated eating it and tried, rather unsuccessfully, to use chopsticks. When he was 18, as an undergrad student, he tried Indian food. He adored that and also participated in the macho, young man tradition of trying to eat the hottest curries. His mouth got accustomed to the spiciness; his digestive system never quite did.

When he first ate Thai food at home in the US, he thought it was heaven on earth. *Tom yam kung* spicy shrimp soup and green curry with chicken were his go-to dishes. He also kind of liked *khanom pang na mu* (Thai pork toast) as a starter.

When he first ate in Thailand, he fell in love with another type of Thai food. In his experience, normal Thai people didn't eat those coconut-based dishes very much. They favored more stir-fried foods, like squid with holy basil (*kaphrao plah muk*), and salads, like *som tam*, the famous spicy papaya salad. Whenever he ended up eating with a bar girl in Bangkok, Pattaya, or Phuket, they seemed to favor Isaan-style *som tam* with whole baby crabs. It was the spiciest thing he had ever tasted. He eventually learned to handle the chili, but the fermented fish paste (*pla ra*) threw his stomach for a loop every time.

Artie tried Vietnamese food much later, in Chicago's Chinatown. He really didn't enjoy it, but later learned that it wasn't really very authentic. A Chinese restaurant owner's take on what Americans might like Vietnamese food to taste like. Less cultural appropriation, more cultural disintegration.

In Vietnam, he quickly came to love a number of dishes, including *pho*, summer rolls, and *banh mi*, Vietnamese filled baguettes. One of the curious and delightful things about Vietnam is, that because of its time as a French colony, it was possible to get great bakery items, like croissants and baguettes, as well as a decent French coffee. (Vietnamese drip coffee with condensed milk was a whole other, equally delicious, story.) The same was true to some extent of Laos and Cambodia, which also formed part of French Indochina in the past.

Anyway, Artie ended up falling in love with Vietnamese food too and appreciated its gentler, subtler tastes compared to Thai food. One of his favorite restaurants was *Quan An Ngon*, which had branches in both Hanoi and Ho Chi Minh City. It was a rather unique concept. You sat inside a covered restaurant, with amazing food stalls all around the outside. You walked around all the food stalls, choosing your dishes, then went back and got served in the restaurant. Not quite the same as a Singaporean hawker center or a Western food court.

In the years after Artie discovered Asia, and before his life changed to focus on this mission, he traveled quite widely in Asia, always eating the local food, and also seeking it out back home in Chicago. He had come to love almost every Asian country's cuisine. His least favorite was Filipino food. He felt guilty admitting it, but he never found anything amazing to eat in the Philippines. The best thing he found was *bilog*, a bun filled with ice cream. And the best drink was *calamansi* juice. Calamansi was a tiny local lime, which was squeezed into a glass with water and sugar and refrigerated overnight.

The worst was *balut*, fertilized duck eggs. And he was rather indifferent to *halo halo*, a famous Filipino dessert served in a tall glass containing shaved ice, condensed milk, and a variety of ingredients such as jello and sweetcorn.

As Artie and Jess both came to the end of their *pho,* Artie couldn't help thinking about the fact that this dish was written as pho in English but pronounced 'fuh'. He understood that transliterating words from languages with other scripts was challenging, but why make everyone pronounce it wrong? He remembered reading years ago that the Japanese Mount Fuji was previously transliterated as Huzi, making everyone pronounce it completely wrongly until the Hepburn system of Romanization came along.

Artie had noticed Jess had been tense all evening. He didn't mind, but he knew why she was tense, and it wasn't good. It wasn't going to help her with her mission. As they were scouting out a bar earlier in the evening, a German tourist had called her an old bitch. He knew she hadn't cared about the tourist's assessment of her, but she was angry that he was getting away with treating women like that.

Jess had laughed, and walked away, as Artie had hoped. Their mission at that time was just to scout out the bar and be as unmemorable as possible. But she was still carrying the anger, a full three hours later, which wasn't useful.

"*You know,*" Artie said to her, "*There is an old Zen story about two monks walking together. They came to a stream, and there was a woman in a kimono unable to cross the stream. One of the monks picked her up, carried her over the stream, then put her down. She thanked him and went on her way. About one hour later, the monks were still walking, and the other monk said 'We are monks. We are not allowed to touch women.' The first monk said to him 'I put her down on the other side of the stream. Why are you still carrying her'."*

Artie didn't need to say any more. Jess got it. And Artie knew that she got it. He may not have needed to say it at all. But somehow, it felt like the right thing to do. To nudge her, just a little in the right direction. If she was going to finish her mission. Hanging on to any feelings of ego or being offended could only distract Jess, worsen her decision-making, or just generally sap her energy.

81. October 4, 2015. 11am. Manila, Philippines.

As Artie walked off the plane, he felt that familiar Southeast Asian wave of heat and humidity hit him. A stark contrast to the air-conditioned plane environment. He had felt it countless times on his trips to the region. In fact, in his previous life, it acted as a kind of Pavlovian aphrodisiac. In the Pavlovian metaphor, he was the dog. The weather was the bell. He didn't like to admit what the salivation or the food was. But having grown up in Chicago, he could never quite get used to these conditions.

In his previous life, he had visited the Philippines a couple of times. But he had never quite fallen for the place the way he had for the rest of Southeast Asia. He wasn't a big fan of Filipino cuisine. He knew it was terribly judgmental, but he didn't feel that the culture here was as rich as other countries in the region either. He felt that the combination of Spanish and American colonizers had done a real number on any culture that might have been before.

But in his current life, on his current mission, the Philippines was an important country. Some of the worst corruption, worst human rights issues, and worst sex tourism happened here. So, he would continue to be a regular visitor for the next couple of years as he pursued his mission. He also had to study more about the Philippines because he knew less already and was at more risk. Also, if he needed to take anyone back to Oasis with him, things were significantly trickier than in countries like Myanmar, Thailand, Cambodia, Vietnam, and Laos, which were all connected by relatively porous, easy-to-cross land borders.

Artie had a pretty similar routine whenever he arrived in a country. First thing, he called the hotel he had booked to satisfy any immigration people, explaining that he had an unfortunate last-minute change of plans, realized it was very late to tell them, and happily accepted the cancellation fee, whatever it was.

Next, he dumped the items that he carried just for show if ever his bag got searched at the airport. A fancy shirt and shoes, for fictional big social nights out. Aftershave. A guidebook. And a bunch of other things that he believed a middle-aged, white tourist might be expected to bring. He would have liked to keep them for his next trip, but he was following a strict set of rules, and traveling as light as possible was one of them. Everything he dumped cost him around $150, and he considered that a necessary mission cost.

Then he went to a variety of stores, around the city to buy what he needed. He had it down to a list of about 20 items, including a tent, a backpack, a beanie-style hat, some basic medical supplies, some construction tools, a box of small ball bearings, some razor blades, and some fertilizer. Total cost around $180.

All of these items seemed innocent, but Artie had specific potential uses for each. For example, a mid-sized ball bearing with razor blades welded to it made an amazing throwing weapon. Like insurance policies, he hoped never to need these things. He hoped to keep things as simple as possible. But like a conservative citizen, he wanted to have his insurance policies in place.

When he was preparing for this mission back in Chicago, he read quite a bit about the ninja. Glamorized by movies and cartoons, the ninjas were in fact a tough, smart, gritty bunch of assassins. They had it down to a fine art. They were particularly good at traveling fast and light. In Draeger's "Comprehensive Asian Fighting Arts", Artie read that the ninja's minimalist traveling kit consisted of six items: a bamboo stick, a rope, a hat, a towel, a stone pencil, and some medicine. They then carried extras that were specific to each of their missions, including different types of weapons, poisons, and disguises. Artie's kit wasn't quite the same as theirs, but this sentiment had inspired him firstly to have a standard travelling kit, and secondly to keep it minimal.

He tried to go to different stores from the ones he'd been to on previous trips. Tried to spread his purchases across multiple stores. Tried to research them online (under a pseudonym, of course) before coming to minimize travel time, but the kind of low-end hardware and convenience stores he required weren't always easy to find on the internet.

All of these details made a difference, Artie believed. His perspective was that everything came down to statistics. For example, in his previous life, he had never been mugged. Never been in any kind of physical altercation. His strategy was never to look worth robbing. To try to avoid dodgy places at dodgy times. To look slightly physically capable of defending himself, but not noticeably macho. To back down early and often when anything looked like it was getting physical, but in a way that sent signals of disinterest, not weakness. None of these things guaranteed Artie would avoid trouble, but together they massively minimized the probabilities.

Same thing now. He tried hard to be invisible. To be the grey man. Not to be a regular customer anywhere. Not to buy things that could be combined to form a weapon from the same place. To stay far from security cameras when he noticed them. All without appearing to do those things. Without appearing surreptitious. Again, none of these behaviors guaranteed he wouldn't get caught before his mission was complete. But they massively stacked the odds in his favor.

After he had bought everything else that he needed, he bought a second-hand bicycle. He put everything he had bought in the backpack, put the backpack on his back, donned the beanie, mounted the bike, and rode off to the place he had scouted out, on the edge of town.

When he arrived at his planned location, he did some general surveillance, scouted out his three exit routes, pitched the tent, and then went to work on assembling the small variety of weapons, poisons, tools, and props he needed for this phase of his mission. He finished around 5:30 p.m. He washed in the local canal, then did some stretching and meditating as sunset arrived. He lay down in the tent at around 6:15. He went through his plans for the next few days in his head, then allowed himself to drift off into a deep, dreamless sleep.

82. December 1, 2015. Bangkok, Thailand.

"I will take a little off the bottom of the trousers. And bring the jacket in just a little. Would you mind coming in for just one more fitting on Friday?"

"Sure. Thanks again for fitting me in."

Artie had had suits tailor-made in Bangkok in his previous life too. It was quite a kick. Back in Chicago, there was no way he could have afforded a well-made, tailored suit. He guessed it might have cost him over a thousand dollars. In a suit shop on Sukhumvit Road, he was getting a jacket, two trousers, and five fine cotton shirts made for $200.

They were also experienced in catering to the more rotund customers here in Bangkok. One of the innovations he had discovered here was a tiny loop on the front of the trousers, designed to put the prong of the belt buckle through, to keep the belt in place relative to the waist of the trousers. Even for those, like Artie, who, arguably, didn't really have a waist.

An Aussie guy he met in a bar one night called that a 'German loop' in reference to some of the more rotund German sex tourists who frequent the bars of Pattaya. Although, in fairness, the Aussie guy saying this was pretty round, and so was Artie. And they were both sex tourists.

Artie also used to get a kick out of having his name sewn into the inside of the jackets of the suits he bought here. Sometimes in English. Sometimes in Thai script. Not anymore. He got the name "Harry Jones" sewn in this time, choosing a very colorful, highly patterned lining for the suit to make the impression he would want to e.

In truth, Artie had never really needed suits for his job back home. But he loved having a well-fitting suit. And he had liked having something to do during the daytime of his visits to Bangkok, so he could convince himself he wasn't only here for the nightlife.

But that was all in his past life. Artie was just getting a suit made so he could look the part for his next role, which would involve a fancy nightclub in Phuket.

"*Sorry, you have had to come in for four fittings. That's very unusual. Can I offer you a couple of free ties?*"

Artie had used seven or eight tailors in Bangkok. All were run by Sikh families. All used the same Thai tailor and his assistants. All could make great suits, but somehow imported the world's ugliest neckties. Artie never liked them. They reminded him, perhaps unfairly, of Bollywood movies. Way too loud and garish.

"*No thanks. But I really appreciate the offer. Look forward to seeing you Friday.*"

83.   December 12, 2015. Phuket, Thailand.

Phuket had become a destination of choice for Russian tourists. Along with the tourists came Russian-owned restaurants, tour agencies, property developers, and other businesses. Similarly, the Russian mafia had taken hold. They had made their accommodations with the local gangs, police, and army, and largely operated with impunity in and around Phuket.

Jess sat in *Zolotoy Bereg*, an opulent, exclusive Russian nightclub in the heart of Phuket. Royal green walls, ruby red leather sofas and armchairs. Well-turned-out waitresses ferrying drinks and snacks from the bar to the mahogany tables. The cool jazz being sung in earthy French-Canadian tones by the chanteuse on stage seemed to hang in the air alongside the Cuban cigar smoke. The pianist and double bass player accompanying her seemed like the coolest cats Jess had ever seen. Playing beautifully but effortlessly.

High-end vodka and whisky on ice seemed to be the drinks of choice of most of the mainly male customers. Their female companions mostly drank colorful cocktails in dramatically shaped glasses. Many of the customers had two or three companions. It wasn't the kind of place where they would grind up against the customers, but they all wore evening wear with plunging necklines and low backs, sat close to their guests, leaned forward a lot, laughed at their jokes, and found reasons to make physical contact with them from time to time. A much more subtle version of what went on in the girlie bars Artie normally frequented.

A few professional dancers slowly gyrated to the music from inside cages. Unlike some of the other humans in cages Artie and Jess had encountered recently, these cages were open at the back, and just for show. Somewhat ironically, given the mafia ownership and overtly misogynist nature of the club, the ethnicities and nationalities of the staff and female customers would have satisfied even the most demanding human resource directors' demands for diversity. There were various African countries, Russia, Vietnam, Thailand, and several other nationalities represented by the sensually and scantily clad women on show.

Jess played the persona of a middle-aged, middle-class Australian bored housewife, having an experimental holiday. Her clothes deliberately suggested someone who was trying to dress up for a nightclub like this but getting it a bit wrong. A bit gauche. One of the things Artie had been reminding Jess time and time again was that attention to detail in the small matters paid off big time. Even though people didn't even consciously realize they were taking in those small details, they served to make her persona credible.

Artie entered separately and observed from a distance. This was Jess's first solo intervention, and he would not participate unless it became necessary.

Viktor Petrov and Sergei Orlov both spoke excellent, if heavily accented, English. They were mid-level Russian gang members, who both had a reputation for cruelty in their dealings. They were particularly notorious for torturing the children of their enemies, in a very public way, to scare them.

Jess had managed to get them both interested in her over the course of the evening, suppressing every ounce of disgust she felt for them, as she flirted subtly and feigned slight drunkenness, appropriate for her persona. She was currently in the process of slowly convincing them that she would like to have sex with both of them – that it was something on her bucket list. Actually, like a great sales executive, she had managed to make them think it was their idea, and she was slowly, reluctantly warming to the idea.

When they planned this intervention, Artie and Jess felt like getting two of them in one go was attractive, and the confidence that would give them would make it even surer that they would come to her hotel room, rather than insist she go to theirs. They had booked a room at the five-star Rosemont Hotel, and carefully set up the room for success.

Just after eleven, the three of them left the club, with Jess linking the arms of the two Russians on either side of her, giggling and stumbling a little. Artie had left twenty minutes before, had changed clothes, wig, and eye color using a bag they had stashed nearby, and was ready to follow and observe from a safe distance.

Although Artie had trained himself not to feel any emotions, he had to admit he felt a little bit of pride for how Jess was handling things. She was laughing, joking, entertaining Viktor and Sergei, as she led them down the beachside road in the direction of her hotel, only ten minutes' walk away.

But then suddenly, seemingly in concert, the Russians decided to change the plan. Sergei, on Jess's left, put his hand over her mouth and grabbed her top half, Viktor holding her legs. They quickly dragged her onto the beach, to a shadowy spot behind a small boat that was resting on the beach. It seemed like they had done this before. They worked perfectly confidently, in concert, and the place they chose was perfect, out of sight and hearing of passersby.

Jess tried to stay calm. *"Why are you doing this? We were going to have fun together in my hotel room."* Viktor laughed, *"But we like it this way darling,"* even more scarily in his heavily Russian-accented English, and used the back of his hand to slap Jess across the face. It didn't quite knock her out, but she was engulfed in dizziness.

Amazingly, Jess had enough composure to think that now wasn't the right time to try to fight back. She needed to wait till they were in a more compromising position, like when they were about to enter her. So, she feigned even more helplessness than she felt, and let them lay her down, and begin taking their clothes off.

As they leaned over her, she saw them both become rigid, temporarily paralyzed, and they fell over to reveal Artie behind them, two tasers in his hands. Right then Artie made the decision that it would be too difficult and risky to try to take them back to the hotel and give them the punishment they deserved, so he used a thin stiletto knife to quickly and efficiently stab each of them through the back of the neck, severing their spinal cords, ensuring there was zero chance of either of them moving from now on, and letting them bleed out.

Jess was clearly shocked, as well as frustrated and disappointed that things had ended this way, but also pretty damn happy and relieved that Artie was so prompt and decisive. Later, they would discuss their tactical mistake in choosing this intervention this way. They both knew that every mistake was a wonderful learning opportunity. But for now, they just dragged the bodies to a clump of trees and left them with the lack of dignity they deserved.

They hastened back to the hotel, pretending as they walked through reception to be a drunk couple who had been frolicking on the beach as a cover for their sandy, disheveled look. They quickly packed, showered, changed appearances, and left quickly through a back door.

They later decided that, despite Artie's role in their demise, these two would still count as Jess's number two and three.

84. 3.

Section 3 – Yose

Yose is the endgame in Go. Here the play is finished up, with players ensuring that they have properly secured their territory, and possibly gaining or losing a point or two, here or there. When both players pass, the game is over, and the counting of territory is done, to determine the winner and loser.

The Japanese and Chinese counting systems are slightly different. In the Japanese counting system, each player gets a point for every point of territory they surround, and a point for every prisoner they have taken during the game. In the Chinese counting system, players also get points for the territory they occupy, as well as those that they surround.

These two different systems do not change playing strategy much. Yet, somehow Artie preferred the Japanese counting system. It seemed more elegant to him that you only counted the area you surrounded with your stones, not the area they occupied. It seemed to emphasize efficiency and effectiveness.

There is one subtlety that amateur players sometimes miss. Although the goal is to surround as much territory as possible, ultimately the results is not based on how many points a player gets, it is simply based on whether they got more or less than their opponent. It doesn't matter if you get fifty more points than your opponent or just one. This fact should change a player's strategy, if they are truly focused on winning.

If they are ahead in terms of territory, they should play more conservatively, to make sure of the win, even if that means reducing the size of the win. Recognizing the 'bounded rationality' of us as humans, we are always prone to making mistakes, so when you are already 30 points ahead, a move that reduces your chances of throwing that lead away is more valuable than a move that promises the potential of another 20 points.

Of course, some players want to show how much better they are than their opponent by trouncing them by a large margin. A true master focuses on ensuring the win, even if only by one point.

Even though every game of Go is a somewhat isolated event, with the goal being to win, there is always the benefit of learning from each game, ready for the next game, whether you win or lose. Just like any other activity, it is valuable for each player to go off and integrate learnings from the game they just played.

Although Artie was only a mid-level player of Go, he had developed some very strong values about playing. He always thought it was important to end a game in a polite, dignified way. Win or lose, he liked to stay at the table for a moment, look his opponent in the eye, thank them for the game, and briefly discuss things to be learned from the game. Not all his opponents shared his sensibilities.

84. January 4, 2016. Oasis.

The three of them sat around the round wooden table in the kitchen. It was made of reclaimed teak. Artie had noted in his previous life that working-class people in developing countries often used furniture that was almost identical to pieces sold in Western countries for thousands of dollars. He remembered visiting a house in rural Bangkok that was inhabited by a very poor family but had a massive, solid teak floor.

"$473,254. That's where we're at right now. If you can, check every month or so, just to keep a handle on things. It takes two to three thousand per month to run this place, including bribes. Mission costs vary wildly, but you might imagine we do three or four interventions per month, each costing two to three thousand. So, we are typically burning fifteen thousand per month."

Artie paused for a second, realizing that he was using vocabulary and speaking at a pace for native speakers. He looked at Ploy. She completely got what he was thinking, and just nodded slightly for him to continue. She kind of knew everything he was saying anyway, and her next-level common sense allowed her to fill in the blanks when she didn't understand a word here and there. Artie was briefly reminded of how redundant natural languages are. For exactly this kind of reason.

"$240,000 is locked into an annuity, guaranteed to return 5%, which translates to $1k per month. I make money every now and then playing pool. A few hundred here and there."

Artie's mind briefly jumped back to the conversation he had with Harjit in the lunchroom more than a decade ago. It was there that the seed of the financial plan for Oasis was born. In Harjit's emphasis on sustainable financing. Artie was pretty sure that Harjit's religious convictions wouldn't have led him to approve of Artie's mission and methods, though.

"*So, the money is running down quite fast.*" Jess had a worried look on her face.

"*Not necessarily. Whenever there is an opportunity to take money from an intervention in a way that doesn't violate our values, we do it. A lot of the bad guys we send on their way have quite big stashes on site. They make a lot of money, or at least a lot of money passes through their hands. And they are not normally in a position to keep their ill-gotten gains in banks. Cash. Gold. Diamonds. That is normally the way it is. Occasionally we hit large amounts. So far, there have been three times when I have liberated more than a hundred thousand in one intervention.*"

"*Okay. That helps.*"

"*It's important to be careful though. Launder it smartly. Liquidate non-cash assets hundreds of kilometers away from where we get them. Don't use the cash we acquire in the same area either. Just to be on the safe side.*

"*We have four bank accounts we keep some money in also. Krungthai Bank in Thailand. BDO Unibank in the Philippines, Bank Mandiri in Indonesia. And Citibank for our dollars. We don't use banks here in Laos for a number of reasons too boring to go into.*

"*We use cash as much as possible. It's less traceable. When we top up those bank accounts, we do it in local currency. We use separate foreign exchange bureaus to change into local currency first. We are OK with crappy exchange rates. We try to top up with relatively small amounts – less than a hundred dollars, and different-sized amounts each time. No round numbers. We try to use different branches each time. We also try to withdraw small amounts when we need to and from different branches or ATMs each time.*"

Artie had asked a couple of days ago if Jess would be up for becoming the accountant for their operation, so Artie could concentrate on other stuff. That wasn't the only or main reason for his request, but that's the one he gave.

Jess had never been very good with money, or even with numbers, in her life to date. But the sense of purpose she had now made that a non-issue. She would get it done.

"There are also a few cash stashes around this place, and even in the garden. Here is a coded map. When you know what it is, you can see where they are right? I don't even need to explain the coding."

"Right."

"I am sure it is obvious, but just to be clear: we keep our money in multiple locations and multiple formats so we can always get what we want, where we want, and when we want, but also so it is hard to track. The other benefit is, if one of our sources of cash dies, we don't lose everything.

"And we have a very specific attitude to our money. It is there to fund our interventions. To fund this place. To help those we want to help, and harm those we need to harm. We don't love having lots of money. And we don't hate spending money or losing money. Even making mistakes with money. These things happen. We accept bad terms when we exchange currencies or sell assets. It is all about money as a lubricant of our activities. Money as a flow, not a stock. Make sense?"

"Kind of."

"And finally: Ploy, me and now you are the only people who know all this. We are the keepers of the mission."

Artie looked over at Ploy. They maintained eye contact for a second.

"Not only in terms of money, but also in terms of money. Let's keep it that way. Until it is time for you to make your handover."

Jess looked at Artie, then briefly at Ploy. It was not necessary for her to respond.

Jess went to the stove and grabbed another cup of hot tea for the three of them. The three of them sat there in an unenforced silence, sipping their tea. There were many unusual things about each of them, their circumstances, this place, some of their activities and their shared mission. But none of that was visible in that moment, at the coffee table in the kitchen at Oasis. The scene was much more redolent of a family, relaxing at home.

A few minutes later they began a similar session about the security features of this house and its grounds. The location of the sensors and alarms. The location of concealed weapons. How the panic room worked. How to monitor the place remotely over the internet.

Artie had been through this with Ploy several times. In fact, she probably remembered everything better than Artie now. It was the first time for Jess, but she was a quick study.

85. February 4, 2016. Oasis.

Jess was normally a pretty good sleeper. Growing up, she had slept through parties where heavy metal was blasting and people were jumping up and down on the bed she was lying on. But somehow her mind couldn't settle tonight. She forced herself to stay in bed till about three in the morning. Then she made her way to the kitchen for a cup of tea. The dogs greeted her in the hallway and nuzzled her legs, but they somehow knew to keep quiet.

She entered the kitchen, walked over to the kettle, filled it with water, and turned it on before she noticed Ploy. Sitting there quietly. Looking out into the backyard. Staring into the distance. Jess knew Ploy must have heard her, but she didn't look round.

"Ploy, would you like a cup of..."

"Today. My son birthday. He twelve."

"I didn't know you had a son, Ploy. Does he live near here?"

"He die. His sister die. They dad. Me husband. All die."

Ploy still didn't turn round to look at Jess.

"I am so sorry Ploy."

"Me husband. He good man. No mia noi. No cheating. Good to kids. But he like drink lao khao and play cards with his friends."

Jess had learned from Artie that a *mia noi* was a mistress. It translated literally as small wife. It wasn't uncommon for Thai men to have one or more.

"Play cards for money. Always lose. But still play. Borrow money. Not tell me."

Jess knew that her role was to sit and listen. Patiently. As long as Ploy wanted to talk. This was the first time she had heard Ploy say anything that wasn't transactional. Anything more than a few words of command or explanation. Jess was in. All the way in. As long as Ploy wanted her. And she wasn't going to do any of that insincere ooh-ing and aah-ing that people do because they are uncomfortable listening to a sad or painful story. She just remained quiet, fully present and attentive.

"Then one day local mafia come our house. I tell him fuck off. He hit me. Then he wait my husband come home. He make us watch."

Jess could hear a change in Ploy's tone. She wasn't exactly crying, but her voice got stiff and stilted, and in the moonlight, Jess could make out a tear in the corner of her eye.

"He make us watch he kill me daughter. Me son. Then he kill me husband. Then he give me this."

Ploy pointed to a scar on the side of her face. Still without turning round to face Jess.

"He tell me. You never forget. You never cross me. Show everyone in village. Artie take me home me village last year. He take care that local mafia. He let me kill him. It feel good. But still me family gone."

Finally, Ploy did break into tears. Jess knew that Ploy would always feel like this. On birthdays, anniversaries, and all kinds of other days. Jess had heard the saying that *"time is a great healer."* She wasn't so sure. Maybe the grief visited us less often, but it wasn't less intense. More intense, even.

She placed her hands on either side of Ploy's face, leaned in, and kissed her gently on the forehead. The two women embraced. Somehow both gently and fiercely. They held each other for a very long time.

Finally, Ploy broke the silence.

"You go now. I stay."

Jess looked Ploy in the eye. She wanted Ploy to know that although she couldn't do much for her, Ploy was definitely not alone. She was there. There for whatever Ploy needed. There for as long as Ploy wanted.

Jess then broke contact with Ploy's body and walked slowly to her room. She couldn't help feeling that it was no accident she couldn't sleep tonight and wandered out for a cup of tea.

She just realized that she never actually had a cup of tea. "*Oh well,*" she thought.

86.   March 17, 2016. Phnom Penh.

It was a rest day for Artie and Jess. Artie had been keen to take Jess to *Tuol Sleng* since he found out she hadn't been there. Jess was already pretty well-traveled in Southeast Asia, but she had so far not visited the gruesome reminders of Cambodia's still relatively recent genocide.

Perhaps the most famous site was the so-called 'Killing Fields'. Artie thought that both the name and the fact that there was a movie named after them, made them popular. But he thought this place was even more poignant. Originally a high school, Tuol Sleng had become an interrogation and torture center operated by the Khmer Rouge in the late 1970s. It was now known as the Tuol Sleng Genocide Museum.

From Artie's reading, he believed that The Khmer Rouge, and their infamous leader Pol Pot, had operated one of the most evil and misguided regimes in history. It was estimated that twenty thousand unfortunate victims were held in Tuol Sleng between 1976 and 1979. They were made to confess to crimes against the regime using electric shocks, burning, and other tortures that Artie still found difficult to think of.

Just like when he came alone years ago, their guide for the tour of this house of evil was a Khmer person whose family had directly suffered here. Bopha told them that both her parents were academics and considered elitist enemies of the Khmer Rouge. Bopha's calm, matter-of-fact retelling of her parents' ordeal at the hands of that stupid, monstrous regime shook even the hard-to-shock Artie and Jess.

They were even more saddened by her stories of Khmer Rouge activists visiting villages around the country, killing children by swinging them by the feet at trees, so their heads smashed against the trunks of the trees. That way the soldiers didn't have to waste expensive bullets.

A couple of hours later, they left Tuol Sleng, made a sizeable donation to the place, and gave Bopha a rather generous tip. They both also made a point of complimenting her excellent English language skills. Bopha smiled a little and nodded politely in thanks. It felt like Bopha's capacity to feel joy had been forever destroyed. This was the most positive emotion she could feel or show.

Having met her and heard her story, Artie suspected that Bopha might have understood and approved of their mission if they had explained it to her. But he had no reason or plan to do that.

There was no need for Artie to explain why he had wanted to bring Jess here. She understood. And he knew she understood. And the transparency of Artie's motives didn't in any way affect the efficacy of the visit. Jess was reminded, in no uncertain terms, of the evil that exists on this earth. And that any avenue to lessen it is worth pursuing.

The pair slipped into a local eatery and enjoyed a simple meal of Amok, a traditional Khmer coconut fish curry. While they were waiting for their food, they were both silent and reflective for a few minutes. Then Jess simply said, *"That was fucked up, man."*

Artie looked at her and replied. *"Yep."*

Then the food came, and they didn't speak anymore of the Khmer Rouge or Tuol Sleng. They discussed how nice the curry was, then spent a while planning their next few moves.

Sometimes we best honor the dead by simply living well. Artie and Jess had some other, more specific plans in mind.

87. May 3, 2016. Oasis.

"*You need at least five chilis to give it some taste,*" Jo said.

"*Ah, you crazy Southerners. You've got no balance in your food,*" retorted Ploy.

They both giggled. Although they were shouting at each other, it was all play, all fun. Ploy was so glad that Jo had found a bit of confidence since he'd been at Oasis. When Artie told her about how he'd found Jo, it shocked and saddened even Ploy's battle-toughened heart.

Thai food was famous the world over for being spicy. Actually, Thai food was more than spicy. The Thai palate demanded a balance between sweet, spicy, salty, and sour. To Thais, many other countries' cuisines tasted out of balance.

The tiny chilis they used to spice things up were renowned the world over. Known as bird's eye chilis in English, they were called *prik ki nu* in Thai. That rather indelicate name meant mouse shit chilis.

Thai cuisine also uses other chilis, including the *prik chi fa* chili. A much larger and milder chili, Thais typically sliced it thinly and used it for decoration on top of dishes. They considered it almost tasteless, almost like Westerners' attitude to, and use of, parsley. To foreigners like Artie, those bigger chilis still tasted quite spicy.

There are a number of ways of breaking Thailand down into regions, but there is a common six-region grouping often used: the north, the northeast, the west, the central plain, the east, and the south. The center is famous for Bangkok, the capital. The north is famous for Chiang Mai and Chiang Rai, popular holiday destinations. The south borders Malaysia and is home to most of Thailand's Muslim population.

The northeast, known as *isaan*, is a famously poor farming area that borders Laos and Cambodia. *Isaan* is also the region where many of the women who work in the bars of Bangkok, Pattaya, and other holiday resorts come from. Many Isaan villages are relatively basic but have the occasional gaudy, palatial home built by ex-bargirls who had married relatively wealthy foreigners.

Foreigners who have spent a bit of time in Thailand come to know that while Thai food is spicy, the food from *isaan* is crazy spicy. Notably the papaya salad, *som tam*. What those foreigners usually don't know is that southern Thai food could be even spicier. There is a famous southern dish called *khua kling*. Unlike the coconut-based curries of the central plain, khua kling was made of chili, lemongrass, pepper, turmeric, salt, shrimp paste, and galangal. The full-strength version of this dish is too spicy even for most Thais.

Jo had grown up eating and cooking, southern Thai food, and for him, the food from the central plain was almost tasteless. At the "All Night" restaurant where he worked, he had learned to make all his food bland for the foreign customers. Sadly, many times he had learned this through punishment meted out by the now-departed Gee.

Levels of spiciness were one of the three or four topics Ploy and Jo enjoyed good-naturedly bickering about almost daily. The others included the temperature to keep the house at, and whether to let Ding and Dong roam freely or confine them to certain rooms at certain times of day. Of course, on that last topic, Ploy was the disciplinarian. Jo wanted to give the dogs complete freedom, and he hoped they would be by his side as much as possible. Even in the kitchen.

Although Ploy hadn't had much formal education, she had a fast, keen brain, and had picked up much along the way. In contrast, Jo's life had been very sheltered. Not in terms of him being protected. Quite the opposite. He had never been to school. No one ever tried to teach him anything, other than how to serve their needs. He had never been anywhere for recreation.

Jo grew up in a rural orphanage near Nakhon Si Tammarat. He knew nothing of his parents. Although its sole purpose was taking care of the orphans and keeping them safe, the orphanage didn't do a good job of either. Both by design and by accident. There weren't any real beds, and the kids had to share the dirty old blankets. Insects were a big part of their everyday lives. There was no education of any kind. The food was very basic – some rice soup with bits of gristle.

Kids disappeared occasionally. Jo saw money change hands with the staff of the orphanage, and visitors who took them. Jo had no idea what for, but as an adult he could now guess it wasn't for their own wellbeing. At five years old, Jo was taken in by a family who used him as a servant. They had their own kids, but Jo wasn't allowed to play with them, or even talk to them.

He cooked, cleaned, fetched, and carried. The family members all shouted at him when he did something wrong, or not to their liking. He remembered considering himself lucky because they almost never hit him.

The family sold Jo to a businessman visiting the area when he was nine. He was then sold on to Gee, the owner of the All Night restaurant, and he had been there for maybe twenty years, until his recent arrival at Oasis.

Jo's life experience made for limited conversation topics between Jo and Ploy, or indeed between Jo and anyone else. Ploy had a specific goal of slowly educating Jo. Introducing him to knowledge about the world, about art, music, and languages. But she would be incredibly careful not to do it condescendingly. Jo had already had enough of that for several lifetimes.

Ploy walked over and put her arm around Jo, then gave him a kiss on top of his head. This was an unusual amount of physical contact for two Thai adults. Most East and Southeast Asians don't normally do much hugging or kissing. And touching someone on top of the head was very unusual, and typically frowned upon in Thai culture. Jo waved Ploy away, but she knew he liked it. He had had so little warmth in his life, she knew he needed it every now and then.

Ploy had considered killing herself many times after her husband and children were taken from her, so brutally, right in front of her. She was very glad she didn't succumb to that feeling now. She felt she was honoring her family well by serving the residents of Oasis. She had felt like a cracked, empty, dead vessel for many years. Not anymore.

Despite growing up surrounded by Buddhism, Ploy wasn't sure what she believed about religion. She wasn't sure if there was just this one life or whether reincarnation was real. If there was any omnipotent, all-seeing power watching over her and judging her. Whether there was any kind of heaven and hell. But she felt sure that using what remained of her life in support of their shared mission, and the people who stayed at this place, was a valuable use of her time on this earth.

Jo got up and took some of the food scraps outside to feed Ding and Dong. He had formed an immediate, unbreakable bond with the pair. A cruel observer might note that all three had been treated very similarly in their previous lives. All three were mongrels. And now all three were reborn to the life they deserved.

Among working-class Thais, the animals were typically fed the same food as the humans. It was the same in most developing nations. And it was no different here at Oasis. Although Jo and Ploy made sure not to feed them spicy food. Today the dogs were enjoying some minced pork and rice. It warmed Jo's heart to see them going at their food enthusiastically.

He crouched down next to them while he watched them devour their meal. Like many Asians, but few Westerners, Jo could sit on his haunches and relax, without his butt ever touching the floor.

Every now and then the dogs would each take a break from wolfing down their food to look at him. *"Look at me daddy, I am a good dog."* Every time that happened, it brought the warmest of smiles to Jo's face, and the warmest of feelings in his heart. He gave each of them a scratch behind the ears from time to time.

In the background, Jo could hear some music that Ploy had put on. It was "Clair de Lune" by Debussy. Ploy was trying to educate herself and Jo with a wider variety of music. They would listen to Thai folk music and pop songs too, from time to time.

88. May 24, 2016. Manila, Philippines

'Uncle Eric' Barza had spent more than thirty years in the Filippino police force. He was seen as a pillar of the community. He did many good deeds. Organized events for charity. Caught the occasional high-profile criminal. And he had an enigmatic smile that put the Mona Lisa to shame.

People were continually encouraging him to run for political office. *"I am dedicated to policing the streets of this city. And I am dedicated to my crew."* Eric always told them. But in truth, he had it so good, he couldn't imagine it any better. Although he heard that once politicians bought their way in, they could write their own tickets. But it might cost one million dollars to get their role. And you were an even more visible target for fellow politicians, kidnappers, and criminals of all flavors.

Meanwhile, the police force was basically acting as a pyramid scheme of corruption, and he was at the top of that pyramid. And just like the pyramid businesses that now preferred to call themselves network-marketing organizations, the people near the top made obscene amounts of money with almost no effort required. All the way up the chain, the person above took a cut of the takings of the person below. So, the people at the top were getting a cut of everybody's actions.

Eric was a particularly difficult guy to get to. He was always with his police force buddies, and his house was highly fortified. Artie had had him in his sights for some time, hearing some of the barbaric things Eric did and had done, both to maintain his position of dominance and because he seemed to enjoy it.

There was the case of the journalist who got too close to the truth and found himself upside down in a butcher's shop slowly bleeding to death. Or the old couple who had foolishly resisted moving out of their house to make way for a new property development. A fire mysteriously erupted in their house while they were sleeping. Then they were an obstacle no more.

Artie had had a breakthrough the last time he was in the Philippines. He chatted at a bar with someone whose brother was a *sabungero*, a man who ran a stable of cocks ready to fight. Cockfighting was still very popular in the Philippines and a big target for gamblers.

Artie had always hated the use of animals for human entertainment. Cockfighting. Dog fighting. Horse racing. Showjumping. All grotesque and indefensible, in his opinion. In his previous life, he occasionally considered going vegetarian, or even vegan, but never quite got there. After his diagnosis, he briefly considered whether part of his mission could be to act against those who were cruel to animals. He decided the answer was yes, if a clear opportunity arose, but it wouldn't be his main priority.

Artie had learned that every three months there was a big cockfighting event, and Uncle Eric was sure to attend. And to bet big. Although people knew who he was, he didn't want to draw a lot of attention to himself. It wasn't so much about whether cockfighting was legal or not. It is just that Uncle Eric knew that it wasn't the kind of publicity he wanted. He knew that managing your own brand was a critical part of getting to, and staying at, the top.

Because of this, Eric's security detail was extremely light. Two guys outside the cockfight in an undercover car, with a couple of guns and a bag full of cash. One guy inside with Eric who doubled as a security guard and gofer, running errands for Eric, ranging from bringing him celebratory and consolatory drinks to refilling Eric's gambling fund from trips to the car. The guy inside with Uncle Eric tonight was known as Rocko. Artie never did find out his real name.

It was when Rocko was on one of his refinancing trips to the car that Artie made his move. Tonight, Artie walked with a cane. It was also easier for Artie to blend in here. There were many people of European, American, and mixed-race backgrounds. Particularly *mestizos*, who were of mixed Spanish and Filipino descent.

As he walked past Eric, the cane lightly touched the back of Eric's leg. Eric felt the light sting, but when he turned around, Artie was already a couple of feet away, with 3 people between him and Eric. He held his cane so that it wasn't visible to Eric either. It was very unlikely that Eric would see his walking stick and put two and two together, but why take that chance?

Eric was responsible for thousands of deaths, rapes, thefts, and many more bad things by leading and getting rich from his empire of criminal activity that was thinly disguised by police cars, uniforms, and badges. It was of some satisfaction to Artie that he would suffer for about three days from the ricin poisoning before dying.

Artie's tactic tonight was very directly inspired by a famous incident in London in 1978. An unfortunate Bulgarian dissident journalist, called Georgi Markov, received this same fate. As he was waiting for a bus on London's Waterloo Bridge, he received a light puncture on the leg from the tip of the umbrella of a passerby. Markov died four days later in hospital, and by all accounts, those last four days were pretty awful. Later analysis suggested that this rather creative assassination was the brainchild of the Bulgarian secret service in cahoots with Russia's KGB.

In Artie's study of stratagems, he realized that one of the keys to success was to be willing to learn from your enemies. People whose motives and methods one didn't like or approve of. He knew that in his chosen field of work in his previous life, computers, a lot of the most powerful innovations came from the industries of sex and death.

Pornographers were always at the cutting edge of technology. Video streaming, online payment systems, and online marketing and search engine optimization (SEO) all have a lot to thank the water trade for, as Japanese people call it. Artie knew that they were investing a lot in researching Virtual Reality (VR) right now too. There were rumors of sex robots on the horizon too, but that was still a way off.

And it was even more common knowledge that the so-called defense industry was responsible for so many innovations, in the technology field and others. Perhaps the most obvious was the internet itself, which had humble beginning as the ARPANET, invented by the USA's Defense Advanced Research Projects Agency (DARPA), to connect universities and government agencies, starting in the late 1960s.

This all reminded Artie of a very funny night during his undergraduate years at DePaul. Artie's roommate Al had a bunch of his friends over to their place to play a game of Dungeons and Dragons. (D&D.) D&D is a tabletop role-playing game, using dice, where players create characters and embark on adventures in a fantasy world. At one point, the players that night sat around in a circle playing the game and got into a heated debate about whether evil characters could heal as well as do damage.

Artie wasn't playing the game. It wasn't for him. So, he left and went to visit with his other good buddy Wayne. Wayne was a really sweet, really smart kid. Very unfortunately, Wayne's father had passed away in a tragic mining accident just before he came to university. This led him to become a born-again Christian. As Artie entered Wayne's pad, he saw that Wayne and his Christian friends were sat around in a circle too. Wayne waved Artie in, and he sat down. *"Can demons heal?"* asked one of the Christians. A friendly debate ensued about angels and demons and their powers.

As an outsider to, and non-believer in both these cults, Artie was amused by the parallel nature of the black hoodie and Motörhead t-shirt-wearing Goth gamers he had left, and the squeaky-clean evangelists he was now with. For Artie, the sensation was less about feeling superior to them, and more about feeling like the eternal outsider.

Anyway, metaphorically speaking, Artie was not only sure that 'demons could heal', but more importantly that there was an imperative for angels to learn from demons. Learn in an amoral sense. In no way approving of what they did, but still learning from their approaches. If one took an amoral view of illicit businesses like drug trafficking, organized crime, terrorism, and sexual slavery, they were industries with no rules, lots of enemies, and no legal protection. Yet, they thrived under such hostile conditions. Necessity was the mother of invention for them.

The angels needed to get ahead of the demons by being open to learning from their methods. Whilst Artie could never label himself, or this current phase of his life, angelic, he certainly embraced this philosophy.

He was sorry in a way that he wouldn't be there to witness Uncle Eric's suffering and demise, especially since this represented Artie's one-hundredth intervention.

Artie boarded a plane the next day, heading back to Laos. At the same time that he was in the cock fighting arena, Jess was flying solo for the first time in Singapore. After almost one year of training and practicing with Artie, and ten months after her first intervention, unaliving Al-Kuwari in Bangkok. Artie would later learn that Jess had just reached seven interventions.

He was able to sleep a little on the flight. A trick he had trained himself to do to help with his mission. Without the aid of melatonin, or any other drugs. All was well in Artie's world.

100. 7.

89.   July 1, 2016. Oasis.

Artie and Jess were back at Oasis, after a particularly strenuous, and ultimately successful, intervention in Jakarta. They arrived around the middle of the day and sat with Ploy drinking *genmaicha*. Artie liked most tea and coffee but had been stricter about drinks since he started his mission. He found *genmaicha* to be healthy and refreshing. It was a combination of green tea and roasted brown rice. The rice gave the drink an unusual nutty flavor, which lingered as a very distinctive aftertaste.

Artie had kitted out Oasis on a utilitarian basis. He only spent money for functional reasons. Not for artistic ones. One of the few exceptions was that he had allowed himself to buy a set of rather expensive Japanese bowls for drinking tea from, known as *chawan*. These bowls were green. They weren't translucent, but somehow, they felt translucent. They had the two aesthetic qualities prized in Japanese culture that Artie most loved. They were minimalist in design and also asymmetric. The latter was known by the term *wabi-sabi*, the Japanese concept of appreciating beauty that is imperfect, impermanent, and incomplete.

Artie also had put a Japanese plate on the wall as a decoration. It was a plate that had previously broken but had been repaired very visibly using lacquer combined with gold. This art was known as *kintsugi* or *kintsukuroi*. The philosophy of this practice was that breaks should not be hidden but should be used to make the object even more beautiful. Artie had thought that this was a wonderful metaphor for integrating our traumas without feeling the need to hide them. And hence a perfect symbol of Oasis. He had told Jess about the plate's significance once, which brought tears to her eyes.

Normally, Artie would not ask Ploy for any particular food. Ploy made simple, healthy food for whoever was at Oasis, normally with the help of Jo these days and Artie would just take a portion of whatever was the dish of the day. But today, he asked Ploy if it might be possible to have *laab neua* for dinner, a spicy minced beef salad that combined the tastes of fish sauce, chili, mint, onion, lime, coriander, and powdered roasted rice. The powdered roasted rice conferred a lovely nutty flavor on the dish. He also asked Ploy if the beef could be minced rather than sliced. In his experience, Thai people preferred the dish with sliced beef. He loved it with minced beef. He felt that the minced meat absorbed the wonderful flavors of the dish more, because of its increased surface area.

Ploy said sure and asked one of the current residents to bicycle over to the local street market for the ingredients she was missing. These days, Ploy and Jo bickered in a good-natured way in the kitchen, each learning from the other and challenging each other. But tonight, Ploy picked up on a particular vibe coming from Artie and made the decision to take care of the cooking herself. Jo was happy to take a rest this time. Ploy made sure he felt OK by asking him to make one of his signature dishes, a banana flower salad, tomorrow.

Artie and Jess went outside to watch the dusk. They ambled along slowly, chatting about this and that. Artie revealed to Jess that he thought the most interesting philosophical question was whether time had a beginning.

"Why is that the thing that gets you, man. There are so many mysterious things."

"I know, Jess. But for me, it is the one thing that proves that a simple, mechanical view of the universe is not enough."

She arched her eyebrows at him quizzically.

"Look. I honestly don't know what to believe about all the religion stuff. I tend to think most of it doesn't exist and is just stories to satisfy our need for meaning and to control us so we behave well. So, the poor can accept the rich and powerful being rich and powerful."

"Yeah, me too. And?"

"Well, that kind of just leaves me with science. A sort of belief that the universe is like a 3D pool table, with atoms and molecules just

bouncing around, hitting each other, based on physical forces like gravity. Newtonian mechanics.

"That raises a few questions. Like whether we each have free will. But I can live with that. But there is one part that just doesn't make sense to me."

"And that is?"

"Everything that happens has a cause, right? We are walking here because we left the house. We were in the house because we came back from Jakarta. And you can keep going back. For example, when we met in Siem Reap. When your parents conceived you. And mine, me. Etcetera. Etcetera.

Jess was beginning to get where he was going. She had never quite articulated it this way.

"So, for me, everything must have a cause. Everything must have a 'before'. Hence, time can never have a beginning. But everything must have a beginning."

"Surely, time can't have an ending either?"

"Yeah, but somehow that doesn't bother me that much. Space being infinite doesn't bother me either, although I suspect that that comes to kind of the same thing as the time thing too.

"Have you ever read much about Einstein or relativity?"

"All that E equals M C squared stuff? No way, dude. Not my scene."

"Well, he came up with the insight that space and time were connected, and space-time is curved, which sort of allows time to loop back on itself. That is science's current answer, but it doesn't really help me.

"I mean I love the math of it, but it doesn't speak to my issue. It would be like me saying to you I am addicted to chocolate, and I can't stop eating it. And you just say back to me 'scientists have proved chocolate isn't tasty'. Doesn't help.

"For me, the real problem is that causality can't be curved. Causality can't loop back on itself. Everything happens because something just before it caused it. Time can never have a beginning. Yet it must."

"I get it now. I get it. I kind of wish you didn't explain it to me. I think I just caught your brain virus!"

They both laughed gently and naturally as they wandered back to the house.

Artie realized that, for the first time in his life, he was really experiencing friendship. *"So, this is what it's like."* he thought. Because of where he was in his life, and his mission, he had no interest in pursuing a romantic or sexual relationship with Jess. And he felt sure that she felt the same, for the same and maybe some other reasons. Although he also felt like Jess might do anything Artie asked her to, if she felt like she could help him. This was a proper friendship, unencumbered by lust or any other desires and fears that fuck up relationships.

Artie couldn't help smiling to himself that he finally found a true friend. Today of all days.

After Jess and Artie had both showered and spent time in their own space, they came down to the main room and enjoyed a bowl of the spicy beef dish with some sticky rice. All the residents really enjoyed it. Artie complimented the chef. Ploy graciously accepted the compliment but looked at Artie just a little bit longer than necessary. He noticed that she did that.

Artie made his apologies and retired to his room. He sat at the desk in his room and took a small notebook out of his pocket. He opened the notebook to the middle page and added two strokes to the last Chinese character on the page. There were now twenty identical characters on the page, each consisting of five strokes. The character was 正, which meant right, proper, or correct, and was commonly used for counting in Japanese. A total of 100 strokes. Artie gazed at the page with soft focus for a while.

He then opened a small drawer in the desk and took out two letters. The first was a letter addressed to himself, in his own hand. He read the letter slowly and carefully. Then he tore it into little pieces, put it into a small dish, and used a liquid he had in a small vial to destroy the paper it was written on.

He slipped the small notebook into the second envelope and then returned it to the drawer.

Artie then did a little stretching, meditated for about fifteen minutes, and lay down to sleep.

90.   July 2, 2016. Artie's 44th Birthday. Oasis.

Artie woke at daybreak and immediately jumped out of bed. He used the bathroom, took a shower, then sat at his desk. There was a piece of paper and a pen he'd been playing with last night. He had worked out, for no particular reason he could fathom, that he had now been alive a total of 16,071 days. It was 2281 days since he got his diagnosis. 2192 days since he began preparing for his mission. 1193 days since he finished preparations. And 827 days since he left Chicago for the last time.

Artie noted, for no good reason, that 827, 1193, and 2281 were prime numbers, not perfectly divisible by any number except themselves, and 1. 2192 wasn't prime, of course, because it was an even number. He laughed that even on a day such as today, his brain would take walks like this in random directions with no practical use.

He was reminded of the story of Ramanujan. Srinivasa Ramanujan Aiyangar was an Indian, self-educated genius of a mathematician who, through a rather tortuous route, found his way to study at Cambridge University. While he was there, he got very sick and was in the hospital. His colleague G.H. Hardy, a very famous mathematician, came to visit him and mentioned that the taxi that brought him to the hospital had a very dull number, 1729. Ramanujan immediately explained that 1729 was very interesting. It was the smallest number that was expressible as the sum of the cubes of two integers in two different ways. 1729 is equal to nine cubed plus ten cubed, and also twelve cubed plus one cubed.

Artie was by no means comparing himself to Ramanujan, but remembering this story made him smile as well. He loved stories of genius and extraordinary feats. He thought it was because it raised humans, at least temporarily, out of the tyranny of transactions, the meat market of daily life, the hamster wheel of survival.

Jess and Artie rode bicycles out to a forest near Oasis just before daybreak. They left the bikes well hidden in a bush just on the edge of the forest. Probably unnecessary, but force of habit. Artie remembered that one of his colleagues back in Chicago was a big fan of skydiving, and had a sign in his cubicle saying, "habit kills", to remind himself to check and check again every single time he did a dive. Never go on autopilot. Like many things, this was true, but so was the opposite. Habits also save us sometimes.

"*Seven. The answer is seven.*" As they walked into a clearing by the stream, they were chatting about a puzzle Artie had told Jess about last night over dinner. It was a puzzle about a king who had to find which one of one hundred bottles of wine had been poisoned, using the minimum number of slaves to taste the wine.

"*I don't get it, Artie. How can only seven people distinguish between one hundred bottles of wine?*"

"*Let's reduce the problem. Imagine it is four bottles of wine, and one is poisoned. You only need 2 slaves to test. Slave number one tries bottles 2 and 4. Slave two tries bottles 3 and 4. If neither slave dies, bottle 1 has the poison. If only slave one dies, bottle 2 has the poison. If only slave two dies, bottle 3 has the poison. And if both slaves die, bottle 4 had the poison.*"

"*Say it again.*" Artie repeated the four-bottle version slowly.

"*It turns out that the slaves are like the digits in a binary number, Jess. Two slaves can represent four different numbers 00,01,10,11. Three slaves 8 numbers. Four slaves 16 numbers. And so on. It is a power of two thing. And it turns out that two to the power seven is equal to 128, which is more than the number of bottles - 100.*"

"*I am not sure I get it, but I am starting to, I think. Bloody fascinating, mate.*"

You can take the woman out of Australia, but you can't take the Australian vernacular out of the woman, Artie thought.

"*Good. Good. If you'd like, we can talk about it more later.*"

Artie decided not to bother her with how the solution to this problem was related to information theory, or how there was a parallel between this problem and computer parity bit theory, specifically a technique known as Hamming Codes. Artie had always been socially awkward, but one skill he did have was knowing when something he was interested in was too geeky for others.

Rather randomly, this thought reminded him of the saying, *"Knowledge is knowing that a tomato is not a vegetable, but a fruit. Wisdom is knowing not to put tomatoes in a fruit salad."* In this case, Hamming codes were the tomatoes, and his conversation with Jess was the fruit salad.

They stopped talking and began exercising.

As had become their habit over the last couple of months, Jess and Artie exercised together every morning. Stretching, some *chi kung*, the eight-section brocade, and also some Pilates. Artie had adapted his routine a little as he learned from Jess, mainly because her suggestions were good adds, and partly because he wanted to show her that he valued, listened to, and learned from her also.

After exercising, they used a local stream to wash and cool down. They then sat down and drank some nice, cool water from the flasks they brought with them. Despite her next-level observational skills, Jess didn't notice Artie palm a tablet and swallow it with his water.

Unusually, Artie reclined fully, lying on the clearing in the forest floor. "*Jess*", Artie said to grab her attention. As Jess turned to look at him, they made eye contact, and he held up a flower. It was a lotus. Artie lay the flower down gently, then closed his eyes. For the last time.

Jess sat with him, or at least his body, for a long time. A very long time.

Then she made her way back to her bicycle and rode back to Oasis. She chose to leave Artie's bicycle where he had left it. Back at Oasis, she noticed that the beautiful instrumental song, "Merry Christmas,

Mr Lawrence" by Ryuichi Sakamoto, was playing gently in the background. She said hi to Ploy, then went up to her room. Ploy looked at her for just a fraction longer than was necessary. A fraction longer than normal.

Unusually, the two dogs followed her upstairs and into her room. She couldn't remember them ever having done that before. They both pushed their snouts gently against her hands, then ambled over to the corner of her room and sat down together quietly.

Jess noticed a brown manila envelope placed centrally on her small wooden desk. It had her name on it. She read the contents end to end several times. It finished with the minimalist poem by Italian war poet Guiseppe Ungeretti, that Artie had written on the back page of the letter he had written to Jess years ago, in Chicago, before he even knew who his successor would be:

Soldati // Soldiers by Giuseppe Ungaretti

Si sta come // d'autunno // sugli alberi // le foglie

We are as // in autumn // on branches // the leaves

91. July 9, 2016. Epilogue – The Next Game

In his most wonderful book, "Finite and Infinite Games," James Carse talks about the need to completely immerse oneself in a finite game, such as a game of Go, as if it was everything, as if success or failure in that game meant life or death. We need to fully immerse ourselves in our role as the player of that particular game, while it is still going. Force ourselves to temporarily forget that there is anything beyond the game. Just like actors fully immerse themselves in the role they are playing while making a movie. Some actors, like Daniel Day-Lewis, are known for staying in character the whole time they were making the movie, even when they were off-screen.

Ironically, that need makes us, in a sense, more serious when we are playing a game. Less serious when we are being our full selves, before, after, and outside of games.

But once that game is done, we remember we are not that player, but instead, a person who temporarily and voluntarily took the role of player in that game. Ideally, we then learn what we can from that game, reset, and move on to the next activity. The next game.

Jess woke at 7 o'clock on the morning of July 9, 2016. She had allowed herself a week to grieve Artie's passing. Growing up, she had a few Jewish friends, and she knew that when someone died, they would bury them as soon as possible, often the next day. Then they would stay at home for a week grieving. This was called *shiva*. The direct relatives of the deceased would do absolutely nothing, and others would bring them food, socialize with them, and pray with them every evening.

Like many religious rituals, this seemed like a pretty good idea to Jess. It allowed her to digest the fact that Artie was gone, reflect on her experiences with him, integrate those learnings, and then move on. She would never forget the man. And she knew that she might feel waves of grief from time to time. She would let them come and go. That was the way with grief, she had learned. Resisting it was futile, and made things worse. Let it flow through you.

But for now, it was time to continue her journey.

Jess heard noises in the kitchen. Ploy and Jo, happily chatting while getting breakfast ready. She slipped quietly out the back door, walked to a clearing in the nearby woods, and did stretching and exercise for about half an hour. At one point, she wanted to turn to Artie and ask him about a particular wrist stretch he had taught her from Aikido and had to remind herself that he wasn't there.

She returned to Oasis at around 7:40 and walked into the kitchen. Ploy and Jo smiled at her. She smiled back. All three smiles were subtle. Authentic. Unforced. Jo set a bowl of *phở* noodle soup down on the kitchen table. Jess thanked him wordlessly with a *wai*, putting the palms of her hands together in front of her chest, and bowing her head.

This particular vegetarian version of the Vietnamese classic noodle soup was one of Artie's favorite breakfast dishes here at Oasis. The three of them never discussed Artie's passing explicitly. It didn't feel to Jess like they were repressing anything in an unhealthy manner. It just wasn't necessary.

Jess left Oasis at 5:40 on the morning of July 10. Unusually, Ploy got up to see her off. Even more unusually, Ploy gave Jess a hug just before she opened the front door to leave. She whispered in Jess's ear. "*Be strong. Continue. Come back soon.*" Jess looked her in the eye for a moment, then nodded.

The next morning, July 11, at 10:30 in the morning, Jess sat in a café in Manila, eating a *pandesal*, a slightly sweet Filipino bread roll, and sipping a glass of *calamansi* juice, planning her day.

She was trying to create a version of events that she expected to unfold tonight in her head, including scenarios where things go wrong, or unexpectedly. She replayed the scenes in her mind over and over again, each time taking the role of a different stakeholder.

The woman. Her pimp. The customer who would be waiting for his turn with her. What would each of their motivations be? How would they react to Jess's intervention? She had practiced this type of thinking with Artie, but now she was on her own.

She remembered Artie's exhortation in the letter he left her. "*It is my fervent hope that you found our time together helpful and that you were able to learn some things from me to augment your already amazing knowledge and capabilities. I certainly learned many things from you during our time together.*

I have an equally strong hope that you don't feel constrained by my way of doing things. Please, please, please express your own authentic self. It is the only way."

So, she did.

Endnote

The game of Go is used both for the title of this book and to structure the book at a very high level. I have been a lifelong Go player and, sometimes, amateur competitor. Whilst I have never reached the highest levels of the game, I deeply love it, and find it a rich source of ideas applicable beyond the world of Go, particularly in matters of strategy and tactics. The elegant and poignant notion of the *Aji of Dead Stones* perfectly captured the essence of the main protagonist's life.

Many years ago, when I read the book "*Shibumi*" by Trevanian, published in 1979, I loved the fact that he had used Go to structure his thrilling novel. (I loved many other aspects of the book too.) I was aware of that influence when I wrote this book, but I wanted to use Go for my structure even so. I don't feel like I have exactly copied Trevanian, but I did want to acknowledge his influence, and the similarity, here.

Printed in Great Britain
by Amazon